LOSS OF DOWN

FALSE START - BOOK THREE

TRAVIS STARNES

The story, all names, characters, and incidents portrayed in this production are fictitious. No identification with actual persons (living or deceased), places, buildings, and products is intended or should be inferred.

Signup to get free previews of upcoming books before they're released at

http://tstarnes.com/preview-notification-newsletter/

Contents

Chapter 1

I shifted my grip on the bottom of the antique dresser thing. Even if I hadn't just finished the weekend at the seven-on-seven tournament, I would have been winded by all the heavy stuff they had me moving.

After having played all weekend, I felt beat to hell.

Not that it wasn't worth it. Li and her mom had saved me from having to drop out of the tournament early when Dad had had to rush home to take care of Mom. Which meant I'd been able to be there and lead my guys to our first-ever seven-on-seven championship. It wasn't exactly at the same level as winning state, but it still felt good and, aside from the fight with Elijah and Jake, it had been fun and a great way to end the school year.

Of course, I hadn't planned on my first summer activity being rearranging the antique store, but you do what you have to do.

"A little to the left," Li said, her hands on her hips, directing traffic. "No, my left."

"Could have specified that about thirty seconds ago," I grunted, shuffling my feet and bumping the corner of the heavy piece against a stack of rolled-up rugs.

"You spend lots of time lifting weights. Moving a little furniture won't kill you."

"You pick this up and see how it goes. This thing weighs more than Andre," I said, referencing Andrew Price, our center on last year's JV team.

I finally nudged it into the spot she'd pointed at, letting it settle with a heavy thud. I straightened up, rolling my shoulders. I reminded myself again that they'd had to close the store for three days and drive all the way to College Station and back. It kept me from complaining.

Barely.

"You complain a lot for a volunteer," Li said, smiling.

"I'm not a volunteer. I'm an indentured servant. Your mom paid me in spring rolls."

"They were very good spring rolls."

"The best," I admitted. I leaned against the armoire, catching my breath. "So, this is the big summer reorganization?"

"Something like that," Li said, her eyes surveying the chaotic maze of furniture, boxes, and weird-looking lamps. "My mother gets an idea in her head and ... well, you've met my mother."

I had. And I was pretty sure her mother could stare down a charging rhino without blinking.

"Speaking of which ... how's your mom?" she asked, her voice softening as she fiddled with the tassel on a lampshade, not quite looking at me.

The easy feeling in the room deflated. I pushed away from the armoire and picked up a dusty box of what looked like old silverware.

"She's home. They let her go while we were still in College Station."

"Is she okay? Do they know what happened?"

I carried the box over to a metal shelf and set it down with a clatter.

"Not really. She wouldn't let them run most of the tests. Said they were trying to poison her with radiation and stick her with dirty needles. She's resting now. Dad's with her."

It was the same story as always. Doctors were quacks, real medicine was a scam, and some new herb or crystal she'd ordered from a magazine was the only thing that would help. So the hospital had stabilized her with IV fluids, treated the symptoms as best they could, and sent her on her way.

"I'm sorry, Blake."

"It's fine," I said.

That was a lie, of course. It wasn't fine. I knew how she'd end up in the future. Not the specifics because we weren't talking by then, but in the dream she'd fallen down the same wellness rabbit hole and had passed away before I was twenty. By then things had gotten so bad between us that I never really found out what she died of, just paid for the burial, showed up for the funeral, and never visited her again.

Trying to shift the mood I clapped my hands together, sending up another small puff of dust. "Anyway. Forget that. It's summer. We should be celebrating, well, once we're not moving possessed furniture."

Li laughed. "This is celebrating. It is a celebration of commerce and filial piety."

"You and I have very different ideas of celebrating," I said, grinning. "Got any big plans? Besides child labor, I mean?"

"Actually, yes."

She picked up a small, ornate wooden bird, turning it over in her hands.

"I'm going to China next week."

That caught me off guard.

"Really? For how long?"

"Until the middle of July. To visit my grandparents and my cousins. It's been a few years."

"Wow. That's ... awesome, Li."

It was. But a selfish part of me felt a bit of disappointment. I'd been looking forward to a summer of hanging out. I was so used to hanging out with her and Eduardo almost every day that it would be weird to go a month without her.

"Guess our plans to dominate the public pool's snack bar are on hold then."

She placed the bird back on a shelf and said, "We can dominate it in August. Before football starts again."

"Two-a-days start the first week of August," I reminded her.

"Still. It is something. Besides, won't you be gone for camps all summer?"

"Only for two weeks. I leave for the All-American one in LA in about a week and then I'm home until late July, when I've got the Nike quarterback camp in Atlanta."

The camps were my future. Moreno had laid out the whole plan. These were the places to get noticed, to get ranked. They had also been crazy expensive, almost three thousand dollars in total.

"Los Angeles and Atlanta. Very glamorous."

"It's just football. More drills. Probably more puking. I expect to only see the field, weight rooms, and the dorms they're putting us up in."

"You will be great."

She said it so simply, like it was a fact. Like two plus two equals four.

"I'll miss hanging out with you this summer," I said, the words coming out before I had a chance to second-guess them.

Her eyes met mine for a second. "Yes. Me too."

An awkward silence stretched for a moment. I cleared my throat, looking around the store.

"So what happens here? Is your mom closing up shop for a month to go with you?"

Li shook her head. "No, it's just me going. She can't close the store again. She says the antiques get lonely."

"The antiques get lonely?"

"And she doesn't trust anyone else to watch them."

"Ah."

That made more sense.

"Blake! Li!"

Her mother said, appearing in the doorway as if summoned by the mention of her. She was a tiny woman, but she took up the whole room with her presence.

"You moved that armoire? Good. Now, this corner. Move all of it over there. I need this whole section empty."

She pointed to a section of the storeroom cluttered with rickety chairs, stacked picture frames, and boxes overflowing with yellowed linens.

I looked at the pile of stuff, then at Li, who just gave me a helpless shrug. If her mother commanded it, we had to do it.

For the next twenty minutes, Li and I worked, hauling chairs, carefully stacking frames, and moving dusty boxes. I worked up a sweat, which didn't help with all the dust, and felt itchy where it clung to me. Finally, we had cleared a space about twenty feet by twenty feet. It was just an empty patch of concrete floor, surrounded on three sides by towering shelves of antiques.

I put my hands on my hips, breathing heavily as her mother reappeared.

"All done. So what are we moving here? For this much space it has to be huge."

"Nothing. This is for you," she said, walking the perimeter, nodding to herself as if measuring it for something.

I blinked. "For me?"

"Yes. For you." She turned to face me, her expression serious. "I told you that you needed to know how to defend yourself and that I knew someone who could teach you. Well, you also need a place to learn this, so I have arranged to keep this area open for you to use for training. Much too hot to train outside."

"That's ... not going to be a problem now," I said. "Elijah's off the team, so we don't have anything to fight about anymore."

She let out a short, sharp laugh that wasn't humorous at all. "Of course it is a problem. You are a teenage boy, and teenage boys are stupid. They fight. That boy might not be on the team, but that means he has all the more reason to be angry with you. Besides, he will not be the last. Teenage boys care too much for pride, and only know how to deal with their feelings with their fists. Besides, you should learn. You are big, but you keep getting beat up. It's not good."

"Mom," Li said, her voice a warning.

Her mother waved her off. "You need to learn how to protect yourself. How to fight properly. So you do not get your face broken before you can use it to make money."

I wasn't sure if that was an insult or a compliment. "I'm not planning on being a model, Mrs. Sun."

"Does not matter," she snapped. "A broken face is a broken face. Bad for business. Any business. Besides, it's done. I have already called my friend and she has agreed to teach you."

A friend? Teach me what? Karate? Boxing? I imagined some old Chinese man with a long white beard, or an old Japanese man, like Mr. Miyagi from *The Karate Kid*. The idea was actually pretty cool. Maybe I could finally learn how to handle guys like Mason and Elijah without getting lucky or needing my friends to bail me out.

"Your friend?" Li asked. "Who?"

"You do not know her," her mother said, waving a hand at her daughter. "She was a friend of your father and me from before you were born. She lives in Lubbock but she has agreed to drive down once a week and train Blake."

"Really?"

"Yes. She will be here after you get back from your camp in Los Angeles. When you get back I will let you know the date, but it will probably be on a weekend."

A dozen questions flooded my mind. How much would this cost? Where would she stay? But one word she'd said stuck out more than the others.

"Wait ... you said ... *she*?"

Li's mom looked at me like I was an idiot.

"Yes. She. Do you have a problem with your ears? My friend is a woman. Do you think a woman cannot teach you to fight?"

A woman. I looked at the empty concrete space. My mental picture of Mr. Miyagi dissolved, replaced with ... well, I didn't know what. I couldn't picture it. A woman was going to teach me how to fight. Li looked just as stunned as I felt, her mouth slightly open. This was clearly news to her, too.

"She will make you strong," Li's mom declared, giving the empty space one last, approving nod. "So no one can break your face again."

She turned and walked out of the storeroom, leaving Li and me standing in silence. The whole thing was completely insane.

And I couldn't wait to get started!

Of course, first, I had work to do. Cleaning and moving things around the store was not the only work her mom had lined up for me to work off the extreme debt I owed her, after all the time she'd given to me.

She didn't put it like that, of course. She just said she needed my help, and it was understood that I'd be there. At least the next time Eduardo joined us and was put to work just as much as I was. Not that it made it easier, but misery loves company.

We finished up pretty late that day, and I made my way home. Dad was at work, and Mom was still dragging after collapsing while I was at the tournament, so it was really up to me to make sure Josh and I ate. I wasn't sure if I cared much if Josh starved or not, but I wanted to eat something and needed to get to it because if I was up late and cooking, Mom would yell about the racket and smell while she was trying to sleep.

Even with that I was in a good mood, still thinking about what it was going to be like learning to fight. I appreciated her clearing out the space for me, although I still wasn't sure twenty by twenty was enough room to learn the kind of stuff people learned in martial arts.

I pushed through the front door and heard the TV playing in the living room. Before going to the fridge and figuring out food, I went in to check on her. She seemed normal, well, normal for her, since I got home from College Station, but I still couldn't help double-checking.

Mom was on the couch in her robe, lying down and staring at the screen but not really watching.

"Hey, Mom, how are you feeling?"

She didn't answer. Didn't even turn her head. The local news anchor droned on about oil prices while Mom's fingers started to twitch. I was just going to turn and walk away, since it wasn't the first time she just ignored me like that, but something about her hand and the way it was twitching caught my attention. Her thumb bent and straightened, bent and straightened.

"Mom?"

I moved closer and saw her face. Her eyes were open but vacant, focused on nothing. Her mouth hung open slightly and a thin line of saliva trailed down her chin. The twitching in her hand spread up her arm, small spasms that made her shoulder jump.

"Mom!" I grabbed her left shoulder and shook it gently. Nothing. Her right hand kept moving in that horrible, inhuman way. "Mom, can you hear me?"

She made a sound then, not quite words, followed by gibberish. "The … the purple … purple … purple …"

She started to twitch even more; now her whole body was involved. I had no idea what to do. In my dream, I'd seen people hit by cars, stuff dropped on them, and burned on construction sites, but nothing like this. No seizures.

I reached for the phone on the side table, but her left hand suddenly shot out and grabbed my wrist. Her grip was weak, trembling, although the seizure itself seemed to have stopped.

“Don’t,” she managed, though the word came out slurred.

“You’re having some kind of seizure. You need help.”

“No.” She blinked hard, several times, and I watched awareness creep back into her eyes. She pulled her hand away from mine and wiped at her mouth with the back of her wrist. “Just a migraine.”

“That wasn’t a migraine.”

“Blake, stop.” She stood up too fast, swayed, and had to grab the arm of the couch for support. “I just zone out sometimes.”

“Zone out? Mom, you were talking nonsense. Something about purple.”

“I don’t know what you’re talking about. I was just thinking about something. You’re making this into something it’s not.”

“You need to see a doctor.”

“I don’t need anything except for you to stop badgering me.”

I pulled the phone off its cradle. “If you won’t call, I will.”

She lunged forward and yanked the phone from my hand, nearly dropping it in the process. “You will not embarrass me like that. I’m fine.”

“You’re not fine! You were completely out of it for almost one minute!”

“I’m just tired.”

“That’s not being tired, that’s ...”

“Enough!” she yelled. “I know my own body better than some teenager who thinks he knows everything.”

“You’re impossible,” I said, stalking away from her and into the kitchen, although my giving up on using the phone was mostly a ruse.

As soon as I got into the kitchen, I picked up the phone in there and dialed the station. Part of me had worried they would have to call him in his patrol car and have him call me back.

That wasn’t what I needed.

Thankfully, after a few minutes, he came on the phone and said, “Officer Sims.”

“Dad, you need to come home.”

“What’s wrong? What happened?”

“Mom had some kind of seizure. She was twitching and she wasn’t responding.”

Mom showed up behind me and grabbed for the phone again, "Give me that."

I twisted away. "Dad, she needs to go to the hospital."

"I'm fine!" Mom shouted loud enough for him to hear. "Blake's overreacting!"

"I'll be there as soon as I can," Dad said and hung up.

Mom glared at me, but the anger didn't hide how pale she'd gotten. A bead of sweat rolled down her temple despite the air conditioning running full blast.

"You had no right."

"You were having a seizure. Stop lying to yourself!"

She slapped me. Not hard, but the shock of it made me step back. Her hand shook as she lowered it, and tears welled in her eyes.

She seemed a little shocked that she'd done it. After staring at me and her hand for a moment, she turned and went back into the living room saying, "Sorry."

I didn't follow her. She wasn't going to be reasoned with, not when she was like this. I'd just leave her be and let Dad deal with her. Instead, I started working on getting dinner ready, some spaghetti which would feed us for a few days, and was one of the things I'd been taught to make for myself in the dream.

I was just about finished when the front door slammed open and Dad rushed in.

"Heather? Blake?"

"Kitchen," I called.

He appeared in the doorway, looking frantic. Mom appeared a moment later, looking annoyed.

"What happened?"

"He's being dramatic," Mom said.

"I'm not. She had a seizure. Her whole body was twitching; she was drooling, mumbling, and unresponsive."

"Heather, honey, we should get you checked out."

"Not you too."

"If Blake says you had a seizure ..."

"What does he know about seizures? He's fifteen."

Dad touched her forehead. "You're burning up."

"It's hot outside."

"Heather, please. Let me take you to the emergency room."

“No. Not again. Why won’t either of you listen to me? I’m fine!”

“You’re not fine,” Dad said. “Blake, tell me exactly what you saw.”

I described it again, the vacant stare, the hand movements, the nonsense words, how long it lasted.

“That sounds like a seizure to me. We need to get you to a neurologist.”

“I don’t need a neurologist. I need my family to stop ganging up on me.”

“We’re trying to help you,” Dad said.

“If you wanted to help, you’d leave me alone.”

“Heather ...”

“No! I’ve had enough of this.” She stormed toward the stairs, using the wall for support. “I’m going to lie down. Don’t follow me.”

Dad started after her. “Heather, wait.”

“Leave me alone, Tom! You’re just being paranoid.”

“It’s not paranoia if you’re having seizures!”

“I’m not having seizures! I had a headache! A bad headache!”

“Headaches don’t cause what Blake described!”

“Then Blake’s wrong!”

“Or you’re in denial!”

“How dare you!” Her voice went shrill. “How dare you take his side over mine?!”

“There are no sides here. There’s just your health.”

“My health is fine!”

“Your health is not fine if you’re having seizures!”

“Stop saying that word!”

They went back and forth, getting louder and louder.

I couldn’t take it anymore. Their fight would go on for hours, the same argument circling round and round. Mom would dig in harder the more Dad pushed. He’d get frustrated and give up eventually, and nothing would change.

I’d done what I could.

I headed upstairs to my room, shut the door, and turned on my stereo. Pearl Jam’s “Ten” was still in the CD player from the night before. I cranked up the volume, letting the guitars drown out everything else.

Chapter 2

I was back at Li's the next day, partly because I still wanted to help them out, but also because I didn't want to be at home. Dad had the day off, and things were still tense between him and Mom. You could practically feel it.

Hell, even Josh gave them a wide berth, and he didn't give a shit about anyone.

I sighed and tried to wipe down the side of the dresser, only for the rag to snag, caught on a carved groove. When I yanked it free, dust floated up, settling right back where I'd been cleaning for the past five minutes.

Damn, I couldn't win for losing.

"You are very far away today," Li said.

I looked up and over at her, where she was wrapping a porcelain doll in tissue paper to put it with the other stuff her mom was pulling off the floor and moving to a back storeroom.

That creepy-ass thing should be hurled in the trash, if anyone asked me, not that I would say that to Li's mom.

"Yeah. Sorry."

"That wasn't a complaint. Just an observation," she said as she nestled the doll into a box of packing peanuts and reached for the next evil little statue, a clown with its smile painted on forever. "Melanie? Your mom?"

"Melanie?"

Had she asked me that a month ago, maybe that would have been a reasonable question, but Melanie and I were done, I hadn't talked to her in weeks, and even then, it hadn't been more than a sentence.

"I just thought … I don't know. I was trying to think of what it could be."

"No, it's my mom. It's getting really bad."

"Is she still refusing to see a doctor? I thought after she went to the hospital last weekend, maybe ..."

"Yeah, I'd kind of hoped the same thing, but maybe she was out of it enough she couldn't fight my dad about it. Or maybe she felt bad enough finally, that she got over her thing. Whatever it was, she's definitely not going back to the doctor, and she needs to. Yesterday, I think she had a seizure. Her whole body was shaking, she was drooling, she couldn't hear me. For like a whole minute she was just ... gone."

"Oh my God!"

"I know. I tried to call nine-one-one, but she came out of it and ripped the phone right out of my hand and then slapped me when I argued with her. Said it was just a migraine and I was overreacting."

"Did your dad see it?"

"No, I called him at work and he came home, so she was done with whatever was happening by the time he got home. I told him everything and he tried to get her to go to the hospital and she just started yelling at him, too. They fought for hours. It's exhausting."

"Maybe she's scared."

"Scared of what? Getting better?" My voice jumped, and I pulled it back down. "The time she was actually scared was when she collapsed, she let him take her to the hospital, so if she was scared, she'd agree to go. 'Cause she's already done that. What if Dad or I aren't around next time she falls, or she's standing and has a seizure? She could fall, hit her head, or worse."

I know Li was trying to be comforting, trying to say it would be alright, but I knew it wouldn't be. I had all this knowledge from the dream, and I couldn't do anything with it. It wasn't like I could just say to Dad, 'Hey, she's really sick and might die if she doesn't get to a doctor.' He already knew that. He'd tried to get her to go.

I felt helpless.

"It's like she's a kid who doesn't listen to anyone. And no matter what I or anyone else says, she just doesn't listen. She does what she's going to do and damn the consequences."

"In her own way, my mother is kind of the same," Li said after a moment.

I looked up from my cleaning.

"I'm not trying to compare our situations. I can't imagine what I'd do or how it would tear me up if she was sick and wouldn't get help. The last thing you said just made me think about it. Once she decides something, that is it. Set in stone. It doesn't matter what I think or say or what is actually happening. Her reality is the only one that counts."

"Yes! Exactly."

"I think that's just how some people are. You can't talk them into changing. You can't reason with them. You can't show them facts or prove they are wrong. Hell, the more you show them they're wrong, the more you reason with them, the more they just dig in their heels. Nothing gets through. Ever."

"Yeah," I said, just staring at the top of the dresser for a minute. "So what's the answer? Just let my mom get sicker until something terrible happens?"

"No. I'm not saying that. Sorry, I'm not trying to give you advice or anything. You should do what you think is best, fight as hard as you must to help her. I just think you have to protect your own heart, you know. I think you have to realize that with some people ... you simply can't change their minds. You can only change their circumstances."

"I don't get it."

"It's like ... some people you can never convince of something, no matter how hard you try. Like, hypothetically, you could try to tell my mom that you knew for a fact that I would be happier going to a state school and working as a waiter or something, but you're never going to convince her. You could show her studies and tell her that I'd live ten years longer 'cause I'd have less stress, and she'd still say it's nonsense. Her opinion on that will never change."

"Do you want to be a waitress?"

"No, that's not the point. The point is, instead of trying to change her mind, if I really wanted to do it, I'd have to change the situation. I'd have to make it so the choice isn't between me becoming a doctor and me becoming a waiter, but instead it's between me becoming a waiter and me dropping out of school and living under a bridge. She'd still be pissed, but if it was between new options, and the new option was worse, then you're kind of picking the answer you want for her."

"So blackmail?"

"I mean, kind of. It's not blackmail, really. It's more like ... new consequences."

"I'm not sure I can do that for my mom. It's her health. I mean, how can I pick something worse if the current option she's apparently okay with is dying?"

"I know. I wasn't trying to say it's what you should do; I was just thinking out loud. I mean, I don't know, is there something that matters to her more than her own life?"

"My brother," I said, making it sound more like a slur.

"Oh."

"I wasn't being serious; there are probably other things. Maybe if Dad threatened to leave her. She always hated being a public spectacle and that would certainly do it. Plus, she loves him, I guess. That might be enough. But I'm never going to get him to make that threat. And if he did, she'd know he was bluffing and call him on it."

"Yeah, that's the problem. If you're going to change the options, you have to make those other options real, 'cause you can't try it again if you didn't follow through the first time."

"Yeah," I said.

We both got quiet after that. Li wasn't wrong. I couldn't change her mind, so I needed to change the options.

But what the hell could the other option be?

By the weekend, I had to start getting ready to leave for camp, but I hadn't figured out what to do about Mom yet. The seizure had really scared me, and I wanted to figure out something to do before I left. Her collapsing while I was at the tournament had really torn me up. I'd gotten distracted by her going to the hospital, thinking she might get help, but that hope had been quickly disabused when she had the seizure and still refused to go to the hospital.

And Dad wasn't having any luck with her either. That much was clear.

I spent all of Saturday packing, trying to get a week's worth of clothes and some entertainment for the plane, plus my football gear, all in a single large duffel bag. I probably could have borrowed a larger suitcase from my parents, but I was stubborn and wanted to have as little to carry in and out of camp as possible.

That worked as a distraction for a bit, but by Sunday, I was packed, ready for my flight early the next morning, and still had my Mom problem to deal with. Dad was at the station and wouldn't be home until later that night, which worked because, for what I had in mind, I didn't want him here.

I found her in the living room, remote in hand, flipping between talk shows without really watching any of them. The curtains were drawn shut despite the afternoon sun outside, and she had that same vacant look she'd been wearing more often lately.

"Mom, we need to talk," I said, stopping just inside the door, leaning on the doorjamb.

She didn't look away from the television. "If this is about the doctor again, I'm not interested. I'm tired of having this conversation."

"Good. Because this isn't a conversation." I pushed off the door frame and walked further into the room, sitting down on the couch opposite her. "This is me telling you what is going to happen. You're going to let Dad take you to a doctor, a real doctor, to get your head looked at and find out why you're having seizures and collapsing. You're going to do it this week while I'm at camp."

She let out a short, sharp laugh that had no humor in it. "Don't be absurd."

"That's option one," I said, ignoring her. I felt a strange calm settle over me, the kind you get when you've already decided to jump. "That's the easy option and the one I'd prefer. You go, you get checked out, you listen to what they say and take the treatments they give to you. And once we know what's wrong, we deal with whatever it is, together."

"And why am I going to suddenly give up everything I believe and agree to go see one of those quacks and become another guinea pig sold to big pharma?"

"Because it is better than option two."

"And what is option two?" she asked, finally looking away from the TV.

I met her gaze. I could still hear Li's suggestions. I'd been hearing them all week, the words rattling around in my head. I could hear my own words, the ones I hadn't bothered to speak out loud but that I'd practiced again and again, in preparation for this moment. You don't change their minds, you change their choices.

"Option two is that I don't get on the plane tomorrow, I don't go to Los Angeles. I don't go to the camp in July. Instead, I call Coach Holloway and let him know I won't be playing any more football, effective immediately. Then I call Coach Moreno and let him know I don't need his services anymore."

I don't know what she thought I was going to say, but it definitely wasn't that. I saw a flicker of genuine shock cross her face.

"Why in the world would you do that, after all the work you put in?"

"Because it's the only option you've left me, because I won't need them, because the next thing I'd have to do is drop out of school and test for my GED. Which will free me up to get a full-time job. Big Sky is always hiring, and I could make okay money working in the oil fields, and it means I'll be here, all the time. I'll be here to keep an eye on you, make sure you're okay when you have another one of your episodes, which we both know will happen. And I'll be here to call the ambulance myself and get you to the hospital once you pass out because you won't be able to stop me."

She stared at me, speechless. Her mouth opened and closed a few times.

"That's not all. I will also walk down to the county building and file a formal complaint with Child Protective Services."

The color drained from her face. "For what?"

I couldn't believe she could even ask that with a straight face.

"About what? You're kidding me. Pick one. I could talk about Joshua's truancy, all the times he's skipped school that they've called you about and I've told you about. All of which you've ignored. Or maybe I could talk to them about your neglecting his other ... behavior." I knew I didn't have to specify what I meant. She knew exactly what I was talking about, even if she didn't want to address it herself. "I'll tell them about your refusal to give him proper medical care. No more annual checkups, no vaccinations, nothing. And I'll tell them about your refusal to seek medical attention for yourself, creating an unstable and unsafe home environment. Trust me; one of those things will be enough to get them to investigate. You know deep down, even if you won't ever, ever say it, how Joshua is. You think he's fooling everyone, but he isn't. People see it. Do you really think the state of Texas will ignore the things he does? Do you think they'll just call him 'troubled' and look the other way like you do?"

"You're threatening to ruin this family. To tear us apart, just because I won't do what you want."

"Ruin it? Have you not been paying attention? It's already ruined! Between not controlling Josh's behavior and not taking care of your health, you're tearing this family apart all by yourself. Don't you see the pressure you've put Dad under?"

"He's just upset because he can't control everything, and you're just like him!"

"I'm not completely like him, because as much as Dad might yell, as much as he might threaten things, you know he'll go right to the edge and back down. You know he loves you too much to actually do what has to be done to get you to come to your senses. And you turn that love back on him, manipulating him. But I'm not him. Or if I am, I'm also fifteen, stupid and impulsive enough that I will do things without thinking about the consequences. Or I'll think about them and come to the conclusion that the consequences are worth it. But most importantly, I love you so much that I will burn this whole house down, this whole life down, just to make sure you don't die in it."

The breath hitched in her throat. Her fury seemed to deflate, replaced by something hollow and afraid.

"Look at me. I want you to see that I'm not joking. I ... will ... do ... it," I said, waiting until she looked me in the face. "I will destroy my own future. I will bring strangers into this house who will pick apart every single thing you've ever done as a mother. They will look at Joshua, they won't see your perfect little boy, and hopefully, they will get him the help he actually needs. I will do all of it. To save you. Don't think I won't. Don't you dare challenge me on this."

I stood then and stared at her. On the TV, some family that had just gotten reunited after meeting their long-lost dad was crying and hugging each other. She just stared at me, her eyes searching mine, looking for the lie, for the bluff. I glared back, making it as clear as I possibly could that I wasn't bluffing.

Finally, she let out a long, shuddering breath and her shoulders slumped. She looked away from me.

"Fine," she said, the word small and brittle. "I'll do it."

Relief washed over me so hard my knees felt weak. I knew this had hurt her, and I felt bad about it, but I also knew this was the only option to save us.

"Good," I managed to say, swallowing hard. "I'm sorry. I know this is … I'm sorry. I love you and I want you to be in my life for a long, long time."

Chapter 3

I walked back to my room after the conversation with my mother, closing the door behind me and dropping onto my bed. I felt terrible for having to give her an ultimatum, but it was the only way I was ever going to get her to see a doctor and actually get help. It also created new problems.

Specifically, money. It always came back to money.

I'd been so focused on getting her to agree to treatment that when I got back in my room and had a moment to think, I realized I hadn't really considered what that treatment would cost. In my first life, Mom had stopped going to doctors entirely at some point, although I don't remember when. I remember her getting sick, her and Dad fighting, but I'd been caught up in my own issues in my dream and hadn't paid much attention to her or Josh. By Christmas, Dad was dead, and I'd been wrapped up in my own grief, on top of dropping out of school because she wasn't working and we were going to lose the house.

We'd lasted one or two years like that, with my working as much overtime as I could get to barely scrape by. During that whole time, she'd never talked to me about what was wrong, or even that it was as serious as I knew it was now.

But I didn't have any memory of her going to doctors often.

I knew enough about the healthcare system to know that whatever was causing her seizures wouldn't be cheap to treat. Brain scans, specialists, medications; the bills would add up fast. And that was on top of everything else we needed money for.

I had chosen her over Coach Moreno, the camps, the other trainers I would eventually need, and everything else that would help me build the future I wanted.

I pulled out my notebook and flipped to the page where I'd been tracking our betting wins. The numbers looked good on paper, and I knew the winning now would be the biggest yet, but Dad had made it clear after our last big score that we couldn't keep this up indefinitely. Too much attention, too much risk.

I'd always known sports betting was a short-term solution. You could only get lucky with "hunches" so many times before people started asking uncomfortable questions, and our bets were getting way too specific to be luck.

It's why I'd done the Amazon investment, but that was a long-term play and wasn't going to pay off for at least several years, and I needed cash now.

I stared at the ceiling, trying to remember what else I knew about the next few years. The problem was, in my first life, I'd been completely tuned out to anything that didn't involve sports or work. I knew some big events, of course. The kind of stuff that registered even when you weren't paying attention, but turning that knowledge into money was a different challenge entirely.

It's why I'd started with sports betting, because I knew how to turn that knowledge into money. But everything else? I knew people could make money knowing this stuff, but I had no idea how to do it.

I knew the Olympics would be in Atlanta next year, and there'd be some kind of bombing with that guy, Richard Jewell. I knew Clinton would survive his impeachment and that W would become president after him. I knew about 9/11, of course, although the thought of making money off that felt wrong in so many ways.

Not that I knew how to make money off of any of that. I did know someone who did, though.

Mr. Henderson was exactly the kind of guy who could figure out how to turn information into money. If I could convince him that my "hunches" were reliable, he might be able to help take all the money I'd made from gambling and build on it. The problem was getting him to believe me.

I walked over to my desk and pulled out the book where I kept important phone numbers, flipping through until I found Henderson's number. As if to reinforce that he'd done well for himself already, one of the numbers he'd given me was a cell number. We weren't in the big brick cell phone era anymore, but phone plans now were to pay by the number of minutes used, so most people had pagers and landlines.

Checking downstairs, I found that Mom had retreated to her bedroom to lie down. I still felt bad about what I'd done, but it was for the best she wasn't there to hear me.

Picking up the phone, I dialed his cell number.

"Henderson."

"Mr. Henderson? This is Blake Sims."

"Blake! Good to hear from you, although a little surprising. You know we aren't expecting any new information about your investment for months, or more likely, a few years."

"I know. I was actually calling because I wanted to talk to you about some other potential investments."

"Other investments? What did you have in mind?"

"Well, I'd rather discuss it in person if that's possible. Do you think you have some time?"

There was a pause. "I could probably squeeze you in near the end of the month, umm, maybe the twenty-first?"

"That would be perfect. As soon as you can manage." I hesitated, then decided to take the plunge. "In the meantime, I want to tell you three things that you should pay attention to so you can ask me how I knew about them when we meet up."

"How you knew what?"

"The Houston Rockets are going to win the NBA championship, Salt Lake City is going to get awarded the 2002 Winter Olympics, and Alanis Morissette is going to release an album that's going to be huge. The big songs on it will be 'You Oughta Know,' 'Hand in My Pocket,' 'Ironic,' and 'You Learn.' "

The silence stretched long enough that I wondered if the connection had dropped.

"What?"

"I know, it's weird and doesn't make any sense. Just pay attention to the news over the next few weeks. When we meet, ask me how I knew."

"You understand how strange this phone call is, right?"

"I know how it sounds. But just ... watch out for those things, okay? I think you'll find it interesting."

Another pause. "All right, Blake. I'll humor you. But when we meet, hopefully, you'll try to explain it better."

"I will. Thanks, Mr. Henderson."

After I hung up, I went back up to my room and sat down at my desk, opening my notebook to a fresh page. If I were going to convince Henderson that my information was valuable, I needed to have some information to give him.

The smart play would be to give him just enough to prove my credibility, but not so much that he could cut me out entirely. Henderson had gone with me on the Amazon deal because Coach Plummer asked him to and it checked out when he looked into it, but he was still a businessman. If I handed him a roadmap to the next decade, what would stop him from taking that information and leaving me behind?

I needed to be smart about this.

Six months of information seemed like the right starting point. Enough for him to work on with a target of making money in a short time. Once we had some money coming in and a better working relationship, I could gradually share more, and we could look at longer-term plans.

Aside from safeguarding the information I had, I also needed money fast enough to start covering Mom's medical bills without eating through all of the gambling money.

I started writing down everything I could remember that would happen between now and the end of the year. There wasn't a lot. Most of the stuff I remembered from the dream was of getting up, working, going to bed, and the occasional drink with buddies.

Aside from the stuff I already gave him, there was ... what? O.J. Simpson's trial was still ongoing, and I knew how that would end. It was huge, so maybe it would be worth something. There was that government shutdown later in the year. That I remembered because we'd been working on a building that was partially federally funded, and when everything stopped, we lost the work until the funding came back.

It had been a massive pain in the ass.

I tried to think about business news, technology developments, anything that might present investment opportunities. Microsoft was coming out with Windows 95. It had already been announced, and I remembered people going absolutely apeshit over it. There'd been midnight sales and everything. The Internet was starting to take off, though most people still didn't understand what it would become, but I guess I'd kind of made that bet already with the Amazon investment.

I didn't have any actual dates for this stuff, but they should be big enough for Mr. Henderson to track down and invest in.

I wrote down what I could remember, trying to organize it chronologically. It wasn't much, but it was a start. The key would be presenting it in a way that demonstrated value, because this wasn't just finding things worth investing in, but also things Henderson would be able to follow up on.

Then there was what in the hell I'd tell Henderson about how I knew this. The truth was obviously off the table. Making up another story about 'researching' this stuff wouldn't work. I'd gotten away with it once, but he would definitely smell bullshit if I tried that again.

In the end, it became an 'I hope I think of something' problem. Mostly, I just hoped he'd help me, because otherwise I had no idea how to keep the money coming in.

I barely got any sleep that night.

Partly because my brain wouldn't let go of Mom's illness and how I was going to pay for all of her medical stuff, but also because of the camp. I was traveling by myself since Dad wanted to stay with Mom. I hadn't told him yet about my ultimatum to her since I knew he'd be equally as pissed as she was, but he was still worried since she'd collapsed last week, and he didn't want to leave her alone while I was halfway across the country.

It was a little weird, traveling as an unaccompanied minor. You get a lot of attention with flight attendants and stewardesses coming to find you to help you along in the process until they realize you're a teenager and not a little kid, at which point they just ignore you and let you do your thing.

The cab dropped me off in front of Pardee Tower on the USC campus, and I paid the driver with cash from the money I'd taken out of the bank that morning. I had the card for my winnings bank account, and from my dream, I remembered that you'd pay everywhere with cards, even in cabs, but like cell phones, it wasn't a thing yet.

The campus was beautiful, with green grass and palm trees. It was basically as different from West Texas as a place could be. The weather was also amazing. When I'd left home, it had been in the mid-nineties and, according to the pilot when we landed, it was seventy-three with perfect blue skies here.

Coach Moreno was standing out front where he'd said he'd be with some other kid, who I guessed was another of his students, standing next to him.

The kid was taller than me by a little bit, broader too, with auburn hair cut short.

"Blake." Moreno didn't waste time on greetings. "This is Raymond Clark from Georgia. Ray, this is Blake Sims from Texas."

"Nice to meet you." Ray extended his hand, and his grip was firm but not aggressive. "You must be the freshman Coach mentioned."

"That's me."

Behind him, a woman with auburn hair similar to Ray's was talking to a man wearing a polo shirt, and a girl about my age stood next to them, looking around the campus with obvious interest.

"My family wanted to drive up to UCLA while we're out here," Ray explained. "They're thinking about coming back for a real campus tour later this year since this is one of the schools recruiting me."

The girl turned when she heard her brother's voice and walked over. She had the same green eyes as Ray, bright and sharp, and when she looked at me, it was like she was sizing me up, trying to figure me out.

"Blake, this is my sister, Charlotte."

"Just Charlie," she corrected, and held out her hand like her brother had. "You're really young for this camp."

"Fifteen."

"Wow." She didn't let go of my hand right away. "That's either really impressive or really stupid."

"Charlie," Ray said.

"What? I'm just saying what everyone's thinking."

"If in doubt, usually it's the second one," I said, which got a laugh out of her.

Her parents came over then, and Ray made introductions. Mr. Clark had the same solid build as his son, and Mrs. Clark had a warm smile that reminded me uncomfortably of what my own mother's smile used to look like before everything started going wrong.

"Where are your parents, Blake?" Mrs. Clark asked, looking around as if they might materialize from behind Moreno.

"Back home. My mom's been sick, so my dad needed to stay with her."

The warmth in Mrs. Clark's expression shifted to concern. "Oh, I'm so sorry to hear that. Is it serious?"

"We're still figuring it out."

There was an awkward pause where nobody quite knew what to say, and then Mr. Clark cleared his throat. "Well, you can't be out here all alone for the whole camp. Why don't you join us for dinner tonight? We found a great Italian place near our hotel."

I looked at Moreno, unsure if that was allowed.

"Camp doesn't lock you in," Moreno said. "You're free to go with family as long as you're back by curfew."

"They're not my family ..."

"Close enough," Mrs. Clark said firmly. "You're both working with Coach Moreno, which makes you practically teammates already."

Charlie was watching me with those bright green eyes, and when I caught her looking, she didn't look away. "You should come. My parents already said they're paying, so you might as well take advantage of free food."

"Charlie makes it sound so appealing," Ray said dryly.

"I'm honest. It's a virtue," she said.

"It's something."

I felt myself relax slightly, watching them bicker. "I'd love to come. Thanks."

"Perfect," Mr. Clark said. "The schedule they sent said you'd be done today around seven, so we'll pick you up around then. Does that work, Coach?"

Moreno nodded. "Should be okay."

"Alright, you boys have fun. Let us know if you need anything, Ray," his mother said, giving him a kiss on the cheek before heading to the parking lot.

Raymond rolled his eyes at me, but I was pretty sure he liked the attention.

After the Clarks left, Moreno turned to both of us and said, "Check-in is on the ground floor. Get your room assignments and drop your stuff. Today is mostly orientation and going through everything. After your dinner, I want both of you in bed, and I want you to get some good rest. You paid a lot to be here, so you need to get the most out of it. Questions?"

"No, Sir," Ray said.

"Good. Most of the guys here are juniors and seniors already being recruited by major programs." Moreno looked at me when he said it. "Ray here has offers from Ohio State and UCLA. You're going to have to prove you belong here, Blake. Every single day."

"I know."

Moreno nodded and looked at Ray. "And you, don't get comfortable. I know you like to think you're hot shit, but these other guys are also nationally ranked, and they're all the big man at their schools. You're not just representing your schools or yourselves here, you're also representing me. If either of you coasts, I'll know, and we'll have words. Understood?"

"Yes, Sir," we both said.

Moreno checked his watch. "I've got a meeting while I'm out here, and you don't need handholding today. I'll see you both tomorrow morning."

That said, he left without looking back, which was very Moreno-like.

The check-in area was set up in what looked like a common room on the first floor, with several folding tables manned by college-age counselors wearing matching All-American Camp staff shirts. A line of players snaked through the room, most of them bigger and older than me, talking and laughing with each other while they waited.

Ray and I joined the line, and I tried not to feel completely out of place. Most of these guys looked like they could start varsity at any school in the country.

"So you're out in West Texas, right?" Ray asked after a minute.

"Yeah, Wheaton. It's a school out in the middle of nowhere."

"You start varsity as a freshman?"

"No, I was on JV. They don't put freshmen on our varsity team ever. Actually, our coach has a thing about not even letting freshmen on JV, saying he wants them to stay on the freshman team to get experience, but our JV quarterback was struggling, so they moved me up halfway through the season. I'll be starting varsity this year, though."

"That's still rare. No other quarterbacks at your school?"

I shrugged. "Our starter graduated, and his backup moved, so it was kind of left open."

"Still." Ray was quiet for a moment. "Coach Moreno doesn't take just anyone. What's your story?"

"No story. I just work hard."

"Everyone here works hard."

"Then I guess I work harder."

Ray laughed, and it sounded genuine. "Fair enough. Charlie was right; you're either really impressive or really stupid."

"Your sister says what she thinks, huh?"

"Always has. Drives our parents crazy sometimes, but ..." He trailed off, then grinned. "Actually, yeah, it just drives them crazy. There's no 'but.'"

"She seems smart."

"Honor roll, debate team, student government, the whole package. She'll probably end up at a better college than me." There was pride in his voice when he said it, no resentment. "She's got her heart set on pre-med, wants to be a doctor."

The line moved forward, and we were maybe five people from the front now. Someone behind us was talking about their recruiting visits.

"What about you?" I asked. "Are you leaning toward Ohio State or UCLA?"

"Still deciding. Ohio State's got the tradition, but UCLA's program has really grown in the last few years. My dad wants Ohio State. Says it's a better football school."

"What do you want?"

"I don't know yet." He looked uncomfortable admitting it. "I've still got a little time to decide, so I'm trying not to think about it too much right now."

"Yeah, I ..."

Before I could finish speaking, someone yelled, "Blake!"

I was a little surprised that someone here would know me, and even more surprised when I saw Max Flores pushing through the crowd toward me.

"Blake! Dude, I didn't know you'd be here!"

I grinned, genuinely happy to see a familiar face. "Hey, man, good to see you. Yeah, we both have a private coach who signed us up."

"This place is crazy, right? I saw the practice field on the way in, and it's huge, and did you see some of these guys, man, they're huge, and ..."

"Max," I interrupted, still grinning. "Breathe."

"Right, sorry." He took a breath, then noticed Ray. "Oh, hey. I'm Max Flores, La Marque High."

"Raymond Clark. Grayson, Georgia."

"Cool, cool." Max turned back to me.

"Max and I played against each other at a seven-on-seven tournament last weekend," I explained.

"Coach let you do seven-on-seven?"

"It was a fight to get him to agree, but yeah. The guys really wanted me to play."

"For good reason," Max said. "They won the whole damn thing. This guy has a hell of an arm and is freaky fast."

I waved him off, but Ray looked at me like he was reevaluating some things.

Max didn't notice it at all and said, "Right, sorry. I get excited."

He wasn't apologetic at all, and I could see Ray trying not to smile at Max's enthusiasm. "But seriously, this camp is going to be amazing. Have you seen the coaching staff list? There are like five former NFL guys."

"I saw it."

"And the competition is supposed to be ..."

"Really good, yeah. So why are you here? They don't let in a lot of sophomores."

"They let you in," Max said, grinning.

"Fair enough. My coach knew some people and got me in. I was wondering who your connection was, in case I didn't have the same connection next year and wanted to ride your coattails."

"Ha, fair enough. My coach, not a fancy private one but our head coach, played ball in college with one of the guys running things this year and put in a word. I guess he thought I deserved it."

"You do. It's crazy how good you are."

Max finally seemed to realize he was monopolizing the conversation and looked at Ray again. "Sorry, I didn't mean to edge you out. Where in Georgia?"

"Loganville. About an hour outside Atlanta."

"That's cool. Are you guys any good?"

"Some. We almost made state last year. Lost in the semis."

"Damn. Tough break."

We reached the front of the line, and one of the counselors looked up from his clipboard. "Names?"

"Raymond Clark."

"Blake Sims."

"Max Flores."

The counselor scanned his list, made some checkmarks, then pulled out three key cards from a box. "Clark, you're in room four eighteen. Sims, four twenty-two. Flores, four thirty-one. Fourth floor, take the elevator or the stairs are around the corner. Curfew's ten-thirty tonight, lights out at eleven. No guests in rooms after curfew, no alcohol, no leaving campus without checking out with your floor counselor first. There's a weight room in the basement you'll have access to. Got it?"

"Yes, Sir," Ray said.

"Yeah," I said.

"Got it," Max added.

The counselor handed us our keys and a packet of information. "Orientation is in an hour in the main auditorium. Don't be late."

"Alright, well, I guess I'll see you guys at orientation," Max said, heading off to find his room.

Ray gave me a slight nod. "Guess so. Let's go find our rooms."

Chapter 4

Leaving Ray, since he wanted to call his parents and let them know the room he was in, I took the elevator up to the fourth floor and looked for room four twenty-two, which wasn't particularly hard to find.

The door was open when I got to it, and I could hear people inside talking. The room was pretty bare bones: two desks, a closet, and two bunk beds.

Two guys were sitting on the bottom two bunks, and the top bunk on the right had a suitcase on it, but the guy, whom I assumed it belonged to, was sitting at a desk.

I thought that one of the guys on the bottom bunks probably needed it. He had thick shoulders and a neck like a tree stump and must have weighed three hundred pounds. The other guy on the bottom bunk was clearly in good shape, but not nearly as huge, with dark hair and blond highlights.

The third guy in the chair was African American and lean. If I had to guess, I'd say lineman, quarterback on the beds, and the third guy was a running back or maybe a receiver.

As I walked in, the guy with highlights looked up and said, "Wrong room, kid. This is for players."

"How'd you even get into this camp? Your daddy know somebody?" he continued.

I didn't let it get to me. I knew his type: another Elijah, thinking he was hot shit and better than everyone, making himself feel good by tearing someone else down.

I threw my bag up on the available top bunk and said, "I earned it."

I also learned enough dealing with Elijah, and a dozen other guys like him in my dream life, to know you also didn't just back down.

He'd smell blood in the water and come at me even harder.

"Definitely somebody's little brother," the big guy said.

"I'm Blake," I said to the guy at the table, who'd kept quiet and hadn't chuckled along with blond highlight's taunts.

"Jarrett. That's Trevor and Derek," he said, nodding first to the blond highlights, then over to the hulk.

"He doesn't need our names. He won't be here long," Trevor said.

I ignored him. "Thanks. I'm headed down to the assembly."

"It doesn't start for another twenty minutes," Jarrett said.

"I want a good seat."

The truth was, I wanted to get away from them before I said something that would make the next three days even more miserable. The camp was really only three full days, plus a little on Friday, and I didn't want to miss any of it dealing with their bullshit.

Thankfully, no one bothered to follow me. I figured I could focus on what I was here to do and only go back to the room to sleep, just try to avoid them entirely.

I made my way downstairs and found the main auditorium already filling up with players. Most were most definitely older, seniors and maybe some juniors. I spotted Max near the front and worked my way over to him.

"Blake!" he waved me over to an empty seat. "How's your room situation?"

"Three seniors who think I'm lost."

"Same here, except mine just ignore me completely. Like I'm invisible."

"Might be better that way."

The auditorium continued filling up, and I started to understand just how out of place we were. Every guy here looked like he could start varsity at any high school in the country.

After about twenty minutes, when most of the room was full, a man in his forties walked onto the stage, wearing khakis and a polo shirt with the camp logo.

"Good evening, gentlemen, and welcome to the All-American Football Camp," he said into the microphone. "I'm Director Bob Carson, and for the next four days, you're going to be pushed harder than you've ever been pushed before. You're going to eat, sleep, and breathe football. You are here because you are among the best high school football players in the country. Make no mistake, no matter how good you are back home, here you are amongst the best of the best high school players in the country. This is where we separate the players who think they're good from the ones who actually are. We have forty of you here from across the country. By Friday afternoon, we'll know which of you have what it takes to play at the next level."

The room went quiet.

He clicked a remote and a schedule appeared on the screen behind him.

"Your days will start at six AM with conditioning. Seven to nine will be position-specific drills. Nine-thirty to eleven-thirty is team practice and scrimmages. Lunch, then afternoon classroom sessions on film study and strategy. Three to five is more scrimmages and situational football. Dinner, then evening meetings with your position coaches. Every step along the way, you will be evaluated. From how you play, to your skills, to how you eat meals. ***Literally everything*** is on the table; you will always be watched."

Max leaned over and whispered, "When do we sleep?"

"It's not all work, however. Thursday night, you'll have a break for the camp barbecue, where we will celebrate the work you've done during the week. Friday morning, we'll have our final competition, a relay-style challenge that tests every skill you've learned this week. Friday afternoon, during the closing lunch, we'll announce our camp MVP, which is based on our relay-style challenge and the evaluations your coaches will be making."

Carlisle clicked to the next slide, showing photos of previous camp attendees.

"Every MVP from this camp has gone on to play in the NFL. In addition, more than seventy percent of our attendees have made it to Division I programs in college. You have a lot to gain from this camp if you take advantage of it, which I recommend. Now, let me introduce your coaching staff." He gestured to a group of men standing off to the side. "We have college coaches from USC, UCLA, Stanford, Texas, and Oklahoma, along with former NFL players serving as position coaches."

He started calling names and having coaches step forward. Most I didn't recognize, but when he got to the quarterbacks coach, I sat up straighter.

"Working with our quarterbacks will be former NFL quarterback Cliff Daniels, who played eight seasons for the Bears."

Cliff Daniels stepped forward, a tall man with graying hair. I remember seeing him play when I was younger and thinking how amazing he'd been.

"All right, we'll have a short break for you to get with your position groups so you can meet everyone, and then we'll feed you and let you get some rest. I know some of you flew a long way to get here, and you all need to get a good night's sleep so you can start tomorrow right."

The auditorium erupted into motion as players started moving toward their assigned areas. There were chairs already set up in a room for the eight quarterbacks, including Trevor, Ray, and me.

Cliff Daniels entered last and closed the door behind him. "Take a seat, gentlemen."

We all found chairs. I ended up between Ray and a quiet kid who looked like he might be a junior. Trevor sat one row ahead of me.

"Let me start by saying this," Daniels began, moving to stand in front of us. "Quarterback is the most competitive position at this camp. Not just because it's the most visible, but because there's only one of you on the field at any given time. Running backs can share carries, receivers can split targets, linemen rotate in and out. But when the ball is snapped, you are the one running the show."

He looked over us, making eye contact with each of us.

"That means the standards are higher and the expectations are higher. You'll also find the pressure is even higher. Some of you are used to being the best quarterback in your conference, maybe even your state. But right now, you're just one of eight guys fighting for playing time in our scrimmages."

"Coach, I have to ask, what's the policy on age requirements? I mean, some of these guys look like they should be in middle school!" Trevor said with conviction.

Coach Daniels turned his *total* attention to Trevor, which suddenly whipped the smile off his smug face.

"The policy is simple. If you earned your way here, you belong here. Age, size, where you're from ... none of that matters once you step on the field. What matters is what you do with the opportunities you get. If you're playing games trying to see who's the biggest or toughest, you are wasting this opportunity."

Trevor almost seemed to shrink in on himself.

"Morning position work will focus on fundamentals. Footwork, throwing mechanics, reading defenses, pocket presence, and afternoons will be for watching film, both from major college and professional games, as well as film from the scrimmage that morning and the day before afternoon scrimmage. Evenings, we'll discuss plays for the scrimmages, teaching you the finer points of running an offense."

"Who gets to take the snap for scrimmages?" asked one of the seniors.

"You will be rotated through so everyone gets a chance, but you will get less time on the field than other positions, and the lion's share of the snaps will be given to those who are making the most of their opportunities."

Coach Daniels stopped and made the room-wide eye contact again.

"Let me be clear about something. This isn't about who's the most physically gifted or who has the strongest arm. Those things matter, but what I'm really looking for is who can think fastest, adapt quickest, and lead when the pressure's on," he said, and checked his watch. "We've got ten minutes before dinner, so let's get started by talking about the basics of the position and find out what exactly each of you knows."

The Italian place the Clarks picked was called Vincenzo's, tucked into a strip mall about fifteen minutes from the campus. The parking lot was packed, which seemed like a good sign.

Inside, red and white checkered tablecloths covered every table, and the smell of garlic and tomato sauce filled the air. A hostess led us to a booth in the back, and I slid in next to Charlie while Ray sat across from me with his parents on the outside.

"This place has the best lasagna," Mrs. Clark said, opening her menu. "We found it the last time we were out here visiting UCLA."

"When was that?" I asked.

"Last summer. Ray had a camp at UCLA, and we made a family trip out of it."

"And Charlie complained the entire time," Ray said.

"I did not complain the entire time."

"You complained about there being too many people, the traffic, the hotel pool being too cold ..."

"The pool was freezing. That's not complaining, that's stating facts."

I couldn't help grinning. Their rhythm made it clear that, in spite of their outward sibling annoyance, they really liked each other.

A waiter appeared and took our drink orders. When he left, Mr. Clark turned his attention to me.

"So, Blake, tell us about Wheaton. What's it like out there?"

"Small West Texas town. Really small. One of those places where everyone knows everyone."

"And how's football there? I assume your family being willing to pay Coach Moreno's fee, that they must have high expectations for your future."

"I guess so," I said, not really wanting to explain I was paying for everything. "Started on JV last year as a freshman, which they don't do at our school, and I'll be starting on varsity this fall."

Mrs. Clark's eyebrows went up. "They don't usually let freshmen play varsity?"

"No, ma'am. Our school has a policy against it, actually. Coach says he wants to give freshmen a chance to get used to playing high-level ball. He doesn't even like putting freshmen on JV, but our quarterback situation got desperate."

"Desperate how?" Charlie asked.

"The guy we had on JV was having trouble, and the losing streak was pretty bad, and Coach didn't want to move our backup on varsity back down, so I got bumped up halfway through the season, and my backup got to start on the freshman team."

"Your backup and your starter on last year's varsity were both seniors?" Ray asked.

"No. Our starter was a senior and graduated. Our backup was a junior, but he had to move away."

"And how'd that go, getting to move up?" Mr. Clark asked.

"Good. JV doesn't have playoffs, so we were done when the season ended, but we turned the record around and won most of our games late in the season, once I convinced the coach there was a better way to play."

"What does that mean?" Charlie asked.

"Um, well ... okay, I don't want to sound cocky, but he was big into running plays, and we were getting jammed up all the time. I convinced him to let me pass more and maybe give me a little more freedom to scramble, and it worked."

"That does sound cocky," Charlie said. "Telling your coach how to run the team."

"Well, what we were doing wasn't working, and my suggestion worked, so ..."

"There's something to be said for results," Mr. Clark said approvingly.

The waiter returned with our drinks and took our food orders. I went with spaghetti and meatballs, figuring I couldn't go wrong with the basics. Charlie ordered chicken parmesan, and Ray got the lasagna his mom had recommended.

After the waiter left, Mrs. Clark leaned forward slightly. "Your coach must think highly of you to bring you all the way out here. This camp isn't cheap."

"Well, it's mostly on my dad and me, but my coach thinks I can make it to the next level if I work hard enough, and he's been really great about giving Coach Moreno access."

"How long have you been working with him?"

"Coach Moreno? Since the middle of the year. My dad and I saved up for it."

"Your dad sounds supportive," Mrs. Clark said.

"He is. He's been great about all of it."

"And your mother?" Mrs. Clark asked gently. "How is she doing?"

"I guess the same. They don't really talk to me about it, but the support is there."

Again, this wasn't the kind of thing I wanted to get into with people I had just met, even though they seemed pretty nice. They were grilling the shit out of me, though. I guess it was more interesting than talking amongst themselves ... and I was getting spaghetti out of it, so it seemed like a fair trade.

"That must be hard on you."

"It's harder on my dad. He's the one dealing with it."

"Do you have any siblings?" Charlie asked.

"A younger brother. Joshua. He's thirteen."

"Is he into football, too?"

"No. Josh is into ... other things."

I left it at that, and thankfully, Charlie didn't push. Ray changed the subject, talking about our practice schedule for the week, and the conversation shifted to camp talk.

The food arrived, and for a few minutes, everyone focused on eating. The spaghetti was legitimately good, way better than anything that I'd had back in Wheaton.

"So, Charlie," I said between bites, "How about you? What's your thing?"

She laughed. "I have a lot of things. I'm on the debate team. Student government. Varsity volleyball."

"That's a lot."

"She has a ten-year plan," Ray said. "Literally written out in a binder."

"Organization is not a character flaw."

"It is when you color-code your class schedule."

"That was one time, and it helped me visualize my course load."

I grinned. "What color was English?"

"Blue. Math was red, science was green ..."

"Oh my God," Ray muttered.

"Don't knock it. I got straight A's."

"You get straight A's anyway."

"Exactly. The system works."

Mrs. Clark shook her head, smiling. "Charlie's always been like this. Even as a little girl, she had to have everything organized."

"It's a good quality," I said. "Better than flying by the seat of your pants."

"Thank you." Charlie pointed her fork at Ray. "See? Blake gets it."

"Blake's just trying to make a good impression."

"Is it working?" I asked, looking at Charlie.

She tilted her head, considering. "I'll let you know."

Ray made a face. "Please don't flirt at the dinner table."

"We're not flirting," Charlie said.

"You're absolutely flirting."

"I'm being friendly. There's a difference."

"There's really not."

Mr. and Mrs. Clark were watching this exchange with obvious amusement, and I felt myself relaxing in a way I hadn't in a while. This was easy. Fun, even.

"What about you, Blake?" Charlie asked. "What do you do besides football?"

"Not much, honestly. Football takes up most of my time, especially with the extra training. I did run track during the spring and did seven-on-seven with some guys from my team. I guess besides that, I like hanging out with my friends, listening to music, that kind of thing."

"What kind of music?" Ray asked.

"Mostly rock. Some hip-hop. Pearl Jam, Soundgarden, Nirvana. Dr. Dre, LL Cool J."

Charlie's eyes lit up. "No way. I love Pearl Jam."

"Yeah?"

"'Ten' is one of my favorite albums. I must have listened to it a hundred times."

"Same. 'Black' is probably my favorite song on that one," I said.

"'Black' is great, but 'Alive' is where it's at."

"'Alive' is good, but 'Black' has more depth to it."

"Depth doesn't matter if the song doesn't make you want to move," Charlie said.

"Well, I'm not much of a dancer."

"Still, it's an emotional journey."

Ray groaned. "Now they're arguing about Pearl Jam."

"I like that they have something in common," Mrs. Clark said.

"You know I have a CD from one of their live shows."

"Really?"

"Yeah." She paused, then added, "When we come back to campus next time, I'll bring it."

"What are y'all doing while we're at camp?"

"We'll be in the area, but we're going to Disneyland tomorrow."

"Disneyland? Really?" I couldn't keep the shocked tone out of my voice.

"Don't start."

"I didn't say anything," I said, holding up my hands.

"You were thinking it."

"I was just surprised. You seem a little old for Disney."

"I'm fifteen. That's not too old for Disney."

"If you say so," I said, purposefully making it sound as doubtful as possible.

"I do say so. And for your information, I'm going because my parents wanted a family trip, not because I'm secretly obsessed with meeting Mickey Mouse."

Ray was shaking his head. "This is painful to watch."

"Then don't watch," Charlie said without looking at him.

I took another bite of spaghetti, trying not to grin too obviously. Charlie was fun to talk to, quick with comebacks and not afraid to give as good as she got.

"So you play volleyball?" I asked.

"I did play. Well, I still play. Club team, and I'll be trying out for varsity this fall."

"Are you any good?"

"I'm very good."

"Confident much?"

"Honest. There's a difference. Life's too short to pretend to be something you're not."

"Nice," I said.

Ray made a noise that might have been agreement or annoyance. Hard to tell. We kept it light from then on, going back and forth for the rest of the meal. Ray and his parents mostly stayed quiet and let us, which I appreciated, although Ray made plenty of remarks at our expense whenever we paused. The waiter came back to clear our plates and ask about dessert. Mr. and Mrs. Clark declined, but Charlie ordered tiramisu. We finished the dessert, and Mr. Clark paid the check despite my half-hearted offer to chip in. I could afford it, of course, but I also didn't want to end up with questions on *why* I could afford it. Mrs. Clark waved me off before I could even finish the sentence.

"Our treat," she said firmly. "You're far from home, and we're happy to have you."

"Thank you. This was really great."

And it was. Better than great, actually.

We headed out to the parking lot, and Mr. Clark drove us back toward campus. Ray sat in front, and I was in the back with Charlie and her mother.

"So you'll bring that CD if you come back to campus?" I asked quietly.

"Yeah. I mean, we gotta pick up Ray, so I'll see you then."

"I don't want to take your CD from you."

"I got it burned from a friend's CD. I'll just have them burn another one."

"Oh! Well, that would be great then."

"I don't have to, though, if you don't really want it."

"No. I do. Besides, it also gives me an excuse to see you again."

Ray turned around in his seat. "I'm right here. I can hear you."

"I know," I said.

"And you're still doing this?"

"Yep."

He shook his head and turned back around, muttering something under his breath that sounded like "unbelievable."

We pulled up to the dorm, and Mr. Clark put the car in park. "You boys have a good night. Get some rest."

"Yes, sir," Ray said, already opening his door.

I climbed out after Charlie did, and she gave me a small wave. "Good luck this week."

"Thanks," I said. "Have fun at Disney."

"I'll try not to have too much fun without you."

"Please don't encourage her," Ray said, already halfway to the door.

Mrs. Clark leaned out her window. "It was lovely meeting you, Blake. Take care of yourself."

"You, too. Thank you again for dinner."

They drove off, and Ray and I headed into the building. The lobby was mostly empty, just a few guys hanging around watching TV.

"Your sister's cool," I said as we waited for the elevator.

Ray gave me a look. "You know if you do anything, I'm going to have to kick your ass, right?"

"Hey, we're just being friendly."

"Uh-huh," he said, but at least he was smiling.

Chapter 5

We'd already been up since five-thirty. Breakfast, an hour of conditioning, and then position drills with Cliff Daniels had come next, where we'd spent another two hours doing drop-back mechanics and release-point adjustments.

That had all been really educational, except for the conditioning part, but now was time for what we all were really looking for.

Team practice and scrimmaging.

The entire offensive side was crammed into a meeting room with our offensive coordinator, a stocky guy named Coach Warren, and our defensive coordinator, Coach Mitchell, who stood in front of a whiteboard covered in diagrams of formations.

"We will only be practicing a pro-style base," he said, tapping the board with his marker. "We are going to do straightforward zone concepts. Nothing fancy, nothing cute. Trick plays are all well and good, but in high-level ball, they will twist you up more than get you yardage. You read the defense, you take what they give you, you move the chains. Rotations for this morning's scrimmaging are: Clark in the first pod, Hutchinson second, Tilson third, Mack fourth, Arnold fifth, Delmar sixth, Hall seventh, Sims eighth if we get that many rotations, otherwise you'll be limited to the fundamentals period."

That was not what I was hoping to hear. Fundamentals period meant I wouldn't touch the team session. I'd be off to the side with a graduate assistant, throwing into a net while the other quarterbacks got real reps.

He then went through pods of offensive linemen, backs, and receivers. I couldn't help but note that we only had enough of all the other positions for three full pods, with the receivers spreading out into a fourth, so after the first run, the groupings would be all changed up.

"You'll rotate through in that order during live periods with each group getting five to ten downs, depending on positioning," Warren continued. "Questions?"

Nobody said anything.

"Good. Offense, stay here. Defense, Coach Mitchell's going to go over your setups in the other room."

The defensive players filed out. Warren spent the next twenty minutes breaking down coverages and formations. I made notes on all of the plays in the playbook they'd given us, but it was a lot and coming fast.

When the meeting finally ended, I followed the other quarterbacks outside to the practice fields.

"Sims, you're with me."

A graduate assistant in a camp polo waved me toward a side field where orange cones marked out a footwork grid. He looked maybe twenty-two, clipboard in hand, whistle around his neck.

"Let's see your drops," he said.

I ran through three-step drops, five-step drops, seven-step drops, the basic routine Coach Moreno had me do. The graduate assistant watched without expression, making notes on his clipboard. After ten minutes, he had me throw into a net set up twenty yards away, working through a progression of routes: slant, out, comeback, post.

Most of this was pretty familiar from my training with Coach Moreno, and I felt good about it. He, apparently, felt something else.

"Your timing's late on the out," he said after my fifth throw. "You're waiting to see the receiver make his break instead of anticipating it."

"I can fix that."

"Do it now. Run it again."

I reset, dropped back, threw. Better. Not perfect.

He made another note on his clipboard. I peeked over and saw a list of names. Next to mine, he wrote "developmental."

The word felt like a punch to the chest.

"Keep working," he said. "Net drills for another twenty minutes, then water break."

He walked off toward the main field where the team sessions were already going strong. I could see the first-string offense running through plays, Raymond taking snaps with the starting receivers. Even from here, everyone already looked like they were at the college level.

I turned back to the net and kept throwing.

The fundamentals period dragged. More footwork drills. More throws into the net. The graduate assistant corrected my release point, my follow-through, the angle of my shoulders. Some of it was good tips, but some of it seemed to go against the stuff Coach Moreno was telling me.

I did what the guy here said, since he was in front of me and there was no use arguing, but I made a mental note to stick with Coach Moreno's way. Something I did remember from my dream life, that dream me took a long time to realize, was that just because someone was in a position of power, or older, doesn't mean they're always right.

We were only about twenty minutes from calling the scrimmage time and heading to lunch when they finally called me.

"Sims, you're up," Warren called.

I strapped on my helmet and took my position behind the center.

The center was a thick kid from somewhere in Arizona, his stance wide and low. My receivers spread out; none of them had the quick feet or route precision of the guys running with Raymond's group.

I'd noticed Max had gone with pod two, even though he was also a sophomore.

"Red right, slot west," I called in the huddle after looking over and seeing the sign. "Z slant on two. On two. Ready?"

A couple of guys nodded. One didn't seem to be listening.

"Break."

We lined up. I surveyed the defense: four down linemen, two linebackers showing blitz, corners playing off coverage. Simple Cover 2 look, safeties splitting the deep field into halves. The free safety was cheating toward the boundary, probably expecting us to attack the numbers advantage on that side.

"Blue forty-two! Blue forty-two!"

The linebacker on my right crept forward another step. Definitely coming.

"Set, hut, hut!"

The snap came clean, hitting my hands with good velocity. I took a quick three-step drop, my eyes locked on the free safety. He backpedaled hard into his deep half, opening up the middle of the field exactly like I'd hoped. The corner on my Z receiver's side opened his hips outside, his feet already turning to run with what he thought would be an out route.

My receiver broke inside at five yards, his head whipping around to find the ball. I threw before he completed his turn, leading him into the open space between the linebacker and the safety. The ball hit him in the chest for maybe eight yards. He caught it and tried to turn upfield, but the linebacker wrapped him up immediately.

"Again!" Warren shouted from the sideline.

I jogged back to the huddle. Same play, different snap count to keep the defense honest.

"Red right, slot west. Z slant on one. On one."

"Break."

We lined up. The defense looked identical, but the corner had crept up a yard, sitting at seven instead of eight. He'd seen the slant. Smart.

"Blue forty-two! Set, hut!"

Quick snap. Three-step drop. The corner jumped the route the instant my receiver made his break, driving hard on the ball. I'd already released it, trusting the timing, but my throw was a half-second late and the corner nearly picked it off. He got both hands on it, bobbled it, and it fell incomplete.

"You're waiting too long!" Warren yelled, his voice cutting across the field. "Trust your reads!"

My face burned inside my helmet. I knew I had thrown late. I'd felt it the moment I released the ball, that fraction of hesitation that turned a completion into a near-interception.

Third snap. Warren called for a different look: trips left formation, three receivers bunched to the boundary with a single receiver split wide to the field. Flood concept to the boundary, trying to create a horizontal stretch on the defense.

"Ace right, trio, flood left on two," I called in the huddle. "Back, you're checking the flat defender. If he sits, you're my outlet. On two."

The running back nodded, his eyes serious now.

We broke and lined up. The defense shifted, bringing an extra defender to the trips side. The linebacker to that side dropped deeper, taking away the intermediate window.

"Green nineteen! Green nineteen! Set, hut, hut!"

Five-step drop this time, deeper pocket. I felt the rush coming from my right, but the tackle picked it up. My eyes went to the trips side: flat route, shallow cross, wheel route up the sideline. The linebacker drifted with the flat like I'd expected, his hips opening to stay with the running back leaking into his zone.

That left the wheel one-on-one with the corner, who was already three yards behind. I threw it deep, putting air under it, trying to drop it over the corner's head and into my receiver's hands. The ball hung up there for what felt like forever, spiraling against the blue California sky.

The receiver had to slow down to make the catch, my ball placement off by a couple of yards, but he adjusted and hauled it in at the sideline for about fifteen yards before stepping out of bounds.

It was a good catch and a subpar throw. The slowdown could have let the coverage pick it off if they'd been paying enough attention, and I prepared for another correction.

Instead, Warren said, "Better. That's anticipation. You saw the linebacker move and you trusted it."

Fourth snap. Coach Warren signaled in a play from the sideline, inside zone run with a play-action boot. I'd sell the fake, roll right, look for the tight end on a corner route or the back leaking out into the flat.

"Ace right, tight, twenty-three boot right on one," I said. "Tight end, sell the block and then get to the corner. Back, after you fake the zone, swing to the flat. On one."

"Break."

We lined up in a balanced formation, tight end on the right, running back offset behind me. The defense loaded the box, eight guys within five yards of the line of scrimmage. They were daring us to throw.

"Blue forty-two! Set, hut!"

The snap came back and I reversed out, faking the handoff to the running back who hit the line hard, selling the run. The linebackers bit, crashing in. I rolled right, my eyes downfield, looking for the tight end.

But the defense brought pressure from my blind side, a blitz I hadn't seen in my pre-snap read. The defensive end who should have been sealed inside had looped around, and now he was closing fast on my outside shoulder.

I felt him before I saw him, felt the pocket collapsing, felt that familiar spike of adrenaline that came with pressure bearing down. My tight end was blanketed, the corner sitting right in his hip pocket. The running back had leaked to the flat like I'd told him, but a linebacker was already breaking on him, ready to jump the route.

The smart play was to throw it away. Step up, throw it into the dirt at my receiver's feet, live to fight another down. That's what Moreno would tell me. That's what Coach Warren wanted to see.

But the defensive end was closing and I saw daylight to my right, a gap between him and the linebacker flowing to the flat. The first-down marker was twelve yards away and there was nothing but grass between me and it.

I tucked the ball and ran.

My legs churned, eating up the yards. Five yards. Six. The linebacker peeled off the running back and drove at me but I had the angle. Seven yards. Nine. I slid just past the marker, maybe thirteen yards total, and the whistle shrieked before I even hit the ground.

"Sims! Get over here!"

Coach Warren was pissed. I pulled myself up and jogged over.

His face was red, a vein visible at his temple. "What the hell was that?"

"Pocket broke down, Coach. I saw the ..."

"I don't care what you saw." He stepped closer, jabbing a finger at my chest. "The pocket broke down because you missed the blitz and didn't call the audible. Worse, you were on first down. You had plenty of time for another snap, but getting pounded into the dirt and injured, or worse, fumble, would have thrown that all away. When you scramble like that, you make everyone else wrong. Your back was leaking for the check-down. You had the option route on the left if you'd climbed the pocket instead of bailing. Instead, you tucked it and ran."

"I got the first down."

The words came out before I could stop them. Defensive. Stupid.

"This game isn't about getting lucky, it's about learning to play smart. Against real speed, that linebacker plants you two yards short and you're face-down on the turf wondering why you didn't throw it away. You want to play hero ball, go back home. This is about making the right decision, not the flashy one."

"Yes, sir."

"Get some water. You're done for now."

I walked off the field, my face burning hot enough that I could feel it through the helmet. I yanked it off as I reached the sideline, my hair plastered to my forehead with sweat.

Ray caught my eye from where he stood with the first-string offense, waiting for his next series. He gave me a small nod, sympathetic, but I looked away before he could say anything or see the tears burning in my eyes. I didn't want sympathy.

I understood Coach Warren's point, but being able to see an opening and take it was what made an offense dangerous. Plus, the linebacker did see it, and he was too slow to stop me. Even if I'd gotten pulled down short, it was still better than throwing to the back. He had his guy right on top of him and he would have been pulled down as soon as he made the catch. We would have still ended up one yard closer than if I'd made the throw.

The graduate assistant with the clipboard was talking to another coach near the equipment table, and I saw him gesture toward me while making more notes.

I grabbed a water bottle from the cooler and sat on the bench, watching the rest of the scrimmage unfold. Ray took his group through a beautiful eight-play drive.

Man, was he good.

Every throw came out on time, hitting receivers in rhythm. When the pocket got messy on one play, he climbed it like Moreno had taught us, buying an extra second before delivering a dart to the tight end for five yards.

Trevor had a stronger arm than Ray but forced throws into tight windows, trying to make something happen when nothing was there. His third pass of the series got picked off by a safety who read his eyes the whole way.

At least he got chewed out as badly as I had.

Tilson was safe to the point of being boring, checking down on every play, never taking a chance. Mack had decent touch but terrible footwork, his drops sloppy enough that he was constantly off-balance.

The scrimmage ended before I got a second chance. Warren blew his whistle three times and players started breaking off toward the water station. I stayed on the bench, turning my helmet over in my hands, staring at the scuff marks on the facemask.

"You good?"

Max dropped down next to me, his own helmet tucked under his arm. Sweat dripped down his face but he was grinning, the kind of expression that said he'd had a good practice.

"Yeah. Fine."

"Warren's hard on everybody. Don't take it personal."

"I made a stupid play."

"You got the first down."

"That's what I said. Didn't help."

Max shrugged. "Coaches got their system. You gotta play their way or they don't trust you. Even if your way works."

I didn't answer. Max clapped me on the shoulder and headed off to join a group of receivers near the water cooler, leaving me alone with my thoughts.

After the scrimmage ended and everyone started to all head to the locker room to get out of their pads and go to the dining hall for lunch, I sat a little longer, mostly 'cause I didn't want to deal with

Trevor who I knew was going to say something. Then I saw Coach Moreno standing near the sideline, talking to Coach Warren. I started to head toward them, then stopped when I caught the edge of their conversation.

"He's got tools," Moreno was saying. "Needs reps, not correction stations."

Warren shook his head. "Kid needs to learn how to play a system. His high school coach might change things up for him, but a college program is going to want him to fit in, not try to make the system fit him."

"He's young. He'll figure that part out. Give him a full run-through look later this week. Let him work with real targets, real timing."

"Reps are limited, Phil. I've got four guys ahead of him who are actually being recruited. He can use this time to improve his fundamentals and get a real shot next year."

"Humor me. One full run-through."

Warren sighed, long and heavy. "Fine. But if he can't stay on program, I'm pulling him."

They shook hands and split off in different directions. I stayed where I was, gripping my helmet.

One full run-through. That was all I'd get. One chance to prove I belonged here, and if I blew it, I'd spend the rest of camp throwing into a net.

Once they were out of sight, I headed to the locker room to get out of my gear and head to lunch.

I'd waited outside, pouting, and if I was being honest with myself, long enough so that the locker room was mostly empty when I walked in. I shed my pads but left everything else on, since I'd just have to get geared up again later that afternoon, scrimmaging.

Although it seemed pretty certain I wasn't going to get a lot of time to actually play then, either.

"Well, look who it is."

I turned to the sound of the voice and found Trevor standing in the doorway with three other seniors, including Derek, one of our roommates, spreading out to block the exit. I was kind of glad Jarrett wasn't there.

He seemed okay. It would suck to find out he was an arsehole too.

"Excuse me," I said, moving to push past him.

"Where you headed, freshman?"

"Lunch."

"That's not how this works." Trevor stepped closer. "See, you're the low man here. That means you carry our gear. Fetch our water. Make yourself useful."

I looked at the other three. They wore the same smug expressions. Apparently, they didn't just pull in the best players from around the country for this camp; they also pulled in some of the biggest jerks.

"I'm good, thanks."

"That wasn't a request." Trevor's hand shot out and grabbed my right hand, the one I threw with. His fingers dug into my knuckles as he squeezed. "Accidents happen during contact drills. Especially to cocky little freshmen who don't know their place."

The pressure increased. Not enough to break anything, but enough to send pain shooting up my forearm. I tried to pry his hand off, but he had a hell of a grip.

I could barely get a finger loose.

"Let go."

"Say 'yes sir' first."

"No," I said, gritting my teeth to ignore the pain.

Trevor's grip tightened. The other guys moved closer, forming a tighter semicircle.

"Blake?" Ray's voice cut in from behind them.

All five of us turned to the sound of his voice and saw him standing in the doorway behind them.

"Everything okay?" he asked, looking past Trevor.

"Just having a conversation with the freshman." Trevor released my hand but didn't step back. "Nothing that concerns you, Clark."

"Looks like more than a conversation."

Ray walked in, and despite being roughly the same size as Trevor, something about his presence made the other seniors step back.

It didn't hurt that, while I was indeed the low man on the totem pole, Ray was at the opposite end. They all knew the coaches were paying special attention to him.

Which made him a much worse target.

"You know who brought Blake here?" he asked.

"Do I care?"

"Phillip Moreno, the best private quarterback coach in the country. Don't you think it's weird that a sophomore could get a place at this camp? It's because Moreno has connections with almost every major college program in the country. Probably wouldn't appreciate hearing about hazing, and there's a good chance word would go out to the colleges you guys are recruiting for."

"We weren't hazing anyone."

"Right, it looked like just a friendly handshake," Ray said, and looked at me. "You okay?"

I flexed my right hand, testing the soreness. "Fine."

Trevor's jaw tightened. He stared at Raymond for a long moment before stepping aside.

"See you tonight, Blake."

They filed out, leaving Ray and me alone in the equipment room.

"You sure you're okay?"

I rotated my wrist, working out the stiffness. "Yeah. Not the first time I've dealt with guys like that."

"Trevor's been pushing people around since he got here yesterday. Thinks he's hot shit. Come on. Let's get lunch before it's all gone."

The cafeteria was jumping when we got there. I followed Raymond through the line, grabbing a burger and fries. Max spotted us from across the room and waved.

"Over here!"

We made our way to a table where Max sat with three other players.

"This is Shane, that's Devon, and Luis."

"Saw you out there this morning. They had you running the same drill for like an hour," Luis said.

"It was more like an hour and a half," I corrected.

"Brutal," Devon said. "But that's how it goes when you're the youngest guy here. Max said you were a sophomore, too. I guess they're not going to baby you."

"I don't expect them to," I said, a little more frosty than I'd meant to be.

I must have still been flexing my hand, trying to work out the pain in it, because Max asked, "What happened to your throwing hand?"

"Trevor happened," Ray said.

The table went quiet.

"He hurt your hand?" Luis asked.

"Yeah. He surprised me, grabbed my hand and squeezed. I was about to beat the shit out of him before Ray showed up."

Shane shook his head. "Trevor's an arsehole. Been pulling that crap with anyone he thinks he can push around since yesterday. Don't let guys like that think they can intimidate you. They only respect you if you stand up to them."

"Or if you can throw better than them," Max added.

Devon laughed. "That too. Though Trevor's pretty solid."

"He's not as good as he thinks he is, and the coaches will notice he's an arsehole. They're always watching, not just on the field, and that shit is going to come back on him," Ray said.

I bit into my burger and let the conversation kind of go on without me. I'd been frustrated all morning, and the run-in with Trevor only made it worse. I had to deal with this stuff back home; I didn't want to have to deal with it here, too. Although, that was far from my biggest problem.

I needed to find a way to get off the sidelines.

"It won't last the whole camp," Ray said as an aside while everyone else was talking amongst themselves. "You just gotta show them you have what it takes."

"And how do I do that?"

"Listen," Raymond said. "Watch the guys getting playtime, pay attention to what the coaches are telling you, and ask all the questions you can."

"And don't waste energy being pissed about playing time," Devon said. "That's ego talking. You want to improve, or you want to look good?"

"Remember you're a sophomore. You're going to get more shots at this, so just get what you can out of it. Or does it matter to you if you're the top dog or not?" Ray asked.

"I guess you're right," I said.

"Bullshit. I mean, yeah, get everything you can out of this, but don't stop wanting to be on the field," Luis said. "Everyone here is the big dog back home, and we wouldn't be here if we weren't competitive. You're asking him to cut out what makes him what he is. Would any of us be okay being on the sidelines in his place?"

The rest of the guys looked at each other.

"Exactly. You wouldn't. Here you're training with National Football League players. You've got college scouts, and even some of the coaches, out here watching what we've got. You're all killers, so stop trying to neuter our friend here."

I laughed. "Thanks, man, but he's also right. I need to stop being a baby and get the most out of this, while I keep trying to get minutes on the field."

"Sounds like a plan," Ray said, slapping me on the shoulder.

Chapter 6

The afternoon scrimmage time went worse than the first. As I feared, I was left in development the whole time. Hopefully Coach Moreno had convinced them, and I'd get more playing time tomorrow, but for today at least, I got none.

Still, I tried to do what we talked about at lunch: focus on the things they were teaching me. The problem was, I was with basically an extra hand who was assigned to run me through drills. He was clearly a college player, although we didn't talk enough for me to find out what college.

The thing was, he might have known when I was doing something wrong, but he wasn't a coach. He couldn't tell me exactly how I was doing it wrong, or how to fix it.

I only got, "Nope, do it again," which wasn't exactly helping me grow. I wasn't the only one facing frustration.

"Well, that sucked," Max said as he came off the field.

I'd watched his last cycle where he was in at the same time as Trevor's pod, and he'd had a tough time of it. Some was on him, some bad timing where he'd put himself in the wrong place and be in poor position to get the ball. But a few were definitely on Trevor, who'd overthrow and make him have to really work for it, and then complain loudly to anyone who would listen how Max was screwing things up.

I don't think the coaches held those against him, but it didn't do great things for a guy's self-confidence.

"Could've been worse."

"How?"

"The coaches could have been the ones to yell at you," I offered.

Raymond stretched his throwing arm. "You planning to just accept fifth pod treatment all week?"

“I guess, but I got one go this scrimmage. Like, I get we have a lot of guys needing field time, but I don’t want to just be off doing drills while other guys are getting two and even three times up.”

I just gave him a look.

“Sorry, I know you have it worse.”

“It’s okay, it’s not a contest of whose getting shafted the most. Actually, I had an idea. We finish off with some film and then go to dinner, and then are on our own for the rest of the night, right? How about I see if we can get our own field time. It might not be the same as a full scrimmage, but doing some reps together is better than running the same drill a hundred times.”

“I like it. There were a few other guys who didn’t get a lot of time either. Should I check with them?”

“Yeah, why not. I’ll talk to one of the coordinators and see if I can get the okay, so make sure they know it’s a big maybe until then. But the more the merrier.”

We got changed and headed for the dining hall where everyone was eating. I didn’t eat with the camp the night before, but it was just about as rowdy as it was during lunch.

You’d think a bunch of guys who just spent the day playing their hearts out would be too tired to cause this kind of a ruckus, but you’d be wrong.

We split up and while I went through the line to get food, Max took off to find some people. After getting as much as they would give me, I was a growing boy after all, I looked around and found Christian, a cornerback and the other sophomore in the camp.

“At least the food’s decent,” Christian said as we sat down.

“They know better than to starve a group like this,” I pointed out, digging in.

Max showed up with Jacob, a junior lineman, and Jarret, my only decent roommate, and took seats across from us.

“So what’s this big plan Max told us you had?” Jarret asked.

“I’ve been thinking, none of us are getting enough reps in the regular sessions.”

Christian looked up from his chicken. “No kidding.”

“What if we ran our own practice? After dinner. Just an hour or so.”

“Like extra work?” Jacob asked.

"Yeah. Position drills, route running, coverage work, line technique, whatever we need. If we're not going to get it during the day, we get it on our own. I mean, we're here to get better, right?"

Jarret set down his fork. "Are they going to let us use the field?"

"I'll ask. But I wanted to see if you guys were interested first."

"I'm in," Max said, although I already knew that.

Christian nodded. "Yeah, why not. Can't get worse than today."

"Same," Jacob said.

Jarret shrugged. "Sure. Not like I've got other plans."

I almost smiled at that. "Good. Let me go ask about the field."

I found Assistant Coach Mitchell near the drink station, refilling his water bottle. He was younger than most of the staff, maybe late twenties, and probably on staff at one of the colleges involved.

He was a little too old to still be playing college ball.

"Coach Mitchell?"

He looked up. "Sims, right?"

"Yes, sir. I wanted to ask about using one of the practice fields after dinner. Me and some of the guys who didn't get much playing time today want to get extra work in."

"How many guys?"

"Five right now. Just an hour. We'll keep it simple, no contact."

He considered it. "What kind of work are you planning?"

"Position drills mostly. Route running, coverage work, line technique. Just fundamentals."

"You'd be out there unsupervised."

"Yes, sir. We can handle it."

He tapped the water bottle against his palm. "Field three. You've got it till eight. Don't run late, don't break anything, and clean up after yourselves."

"Yes, sir. Thank you."

I headed back to the table and gave everyone a thumbs up. Max grinned.

"We're on. Field three. He gave us till eight and curfew still counts."

"Nice," Christian said.

We finished eating and grabbed our gear. The field was empty, as expected.

"Alright," I said once everyone gathered. "What did you struggle with today?"

"Footwork," Max said. "My routes felt off, and I couldn't get separation."

"Release techniques," Christian added. "Kept getting jammed when I tried to mirror receivers in drills."

"Everything," Jacob said flatly. "I spent the whole time running sprints. Didn't get a single rep on actual blocking."

Jarret nodded. "Same. I need work on reading holes and pass protection. Felt like I was guessing out there."

"Okay." I looked around at the group. "We've got a quarterback, a receiver, a running back, a lineman, and a corner. Let's figure out what we can do with that."

I started simple. "Jacob, you work on your stance and hand placement. Max, run some routes so Christian can work on coverage. Jarret, let's get you some reps on pass protection first."

Jacob dropped into his stance, working on his first step. I had him practice his punch over and over, focusing on hand placement and keeping his feet moving.

Meanwhile, Max ran routes against Christian. Max's speed gave him an advantage, but Christian's technique was solid when he didn't overthink it.

"Stay in phase," I called to Christian. "Don't bite on the head fake."

Max ran a double move and Christian bit hard, giving up separation.

"See? You're reacting instead of reading."

"Yeah, I got it."

Next rep, Christian stayed patient and broke on the ball when Max made his cut.

"Better."

I turned to Jarret. "Alright, let's work on pass pro. I'm going to drop back; you pick up Jacob coming through."

Jacob came at Jarret with his hands up. Jarret got his hands inside but didn't reset his feet. Jacob pushed him back easily.

"You're too high," Jacob said. "Get your pad level down and keep your feet moving."

Jarret tried again. This time he stayed lower and absorbed Jacob's rush better.

"Good. Now do it five more times," I said.

Movement caught my eye from the edge of the field. Ray walked toward us, along with Devon and Luis. All three had been in the first and second pods, getting plenty of reps during the regular sessions. Ray carried a football, tossing it from hand to hand.

Ray stopped at the edge of the field. "What're you guys doing?"

"Extra practice," I said. "We weren't getting reps during the day."

Ray looked at the setup, at the five of us spread across the field. "You set this up?"

"Yeah. We've got the field until eight."

"Mind if we join? Help out?"

"Yeah, alright," I said. "That'd actually help a lot."

Ray clapped his hands together. "Alright. We've got two quarterbacks, two receivers, a running back, two linemen, and a corner. Let's run some actual concepts. Half offense, half defense."

We split up. Ray took Devon and Jarret on offense with Luis blocking. I took Max on offense with Jacob blocking and Christian playing defense.

"Let's start simple," Ray said. "Run some basic plays, work on execution. Offense, let's see what you got."

I lined up under center with Jacob in front of me. Max split out wide with Christian across from him. On the other side of the field, Ray had Devon and Jarret in formation.

"Blue eighteen, blue eighteen, set hut!"

I dropped back. Max ran a quick out and I fired it to him. Christian closed fast, but Max had already secured the catch.

Ray ran his play next. A play-action with Jarret faking the handoff and releasing to the flat. Devon ran a deep post. Ray hit Devon over the middle for a big gain.

We rotated. This time I ran play-action, faking to Jarret before finding Max on a comeback route. The timing felt better, the throw arriving right as Max broke.

"Nice," Ray called over.

We kept going, trading offensive and defensive roles. When I played defense, Christian and I worked together to cover Ray's receivers. When I played offense, I worked through my progressions, reading coverage and making throws.

Ray came over during a water break. "Your shoulder's still flying open on some throws. Lock it down until the ball's out."

"Yeah, I felt that on the last one."

"Other than that, you're making good reads. Just clean up the mechanics."

We ran more plays. I worked on keeping my front shoulder closed, feeling the difference in velocity when I got it right. Max and Devon traded off running routes against Christian, each rep getting more competitive. Jacob and Luis rotated between offense and defense, working through different blocking scenarios.

"Alright," Ray said after a while. "Let's run a mini scrimmage. Four plays, see what happens."

We lined up. I had Max and Jarret on offense with Jacob blocking. Ray played linebacker with Christian at corner and Luis on the line.

First play, I handed off to Jarret. He hit the hole and Luis shed Jacob's block to make the stop.

Second play, I threw a quick slant to Max. Christian jumped the route and nearly picked it off.

"Good read," I muttered.

Third play, I ran play-action and found Max on a deep corner route. The ball dropped in perfectly.

"That's what I'm talking about," Max said.

Fourth play, I dropped back and saw Luis coming free. I stepped up in the pocket and threw a strike to Jarret on the flat for a first down.

"Good pocket movement," Ray said.

We switched sides. Ray took over on offense with Devon and Jarret. I played linebacker with Christian at corner and Jacob on the line.

Ray ran four plays, mixing runs and passes. I managed to make one stop on Jarret in the backfield, but Ray picked apart our coverage on the other three plays.

"Holy crap, you sure you shouldn't be a running back? You are fast as hell," he said as he saw me close ground and catch up to Jarret.

"Ha, no. I'm fast, but I don't have the moves. Besides, I like throwing the ball."

We rotated through different scenarios, everyone getting chances to work on what they needed. The competition stayed friendly, with no tackles, just tagging if you got close, but intense. Nobody wanted to lose, even in practice.

I checked my watch. Seven fifty-five.

"Alright, that's time," I called out. "Let's clean up."

Everyone grabbed the cones and equipment. Max jogged over as we walked toward the locker room.

"That was good, man. Thanks for setting it up."

Christian clapped my shoulder. "We doing this again tomorrow?"

"If they let us."

Ray walked on my other side, Devon and Luis just ahead. "You did good work tonight, Blake. Really good."

"Thanks for helping. Made a big difference having you guys there."

"Hey, it helped us too. Just 'cause we get field time doesn't mean we can't work and get better."

We rounded the corner of the building and nearly walked into two men standing near the entrance. They wore polo shirts—one said Alabama across the chest, the other had a little Florida State logo where a pocket would be. Both had lanyards around their necks with laminated badges.

The Alabama guy spoke first. "You guys just coming from the field?"

"Yes, sir," Ray said.

"Saw you out there. Good work." He looked at Ray. "You're Clark, right? The Georgia kid?"

"Yes, sir."

"Saw you throwing during the sessions today. Strong arm, good decision-making." He gestured at the rest of us. "This your idea? The extra practice?"

"No, sir. It was his," Ray said, pointing at me.

"What's your name, son?" The Florida State guy asked.

"Blake Sims from Wheaton in West Texas. Quarterback."

"You a senior?" The Alabama guy asked.

"No, sir, sophomore."

"Really?" He asked, his eyebrows going up. "And you got into this camp?"

"Yep. I'm not the only one. Max and Christian up there are also sophomores," I said, pointing at the guys as they got to the door to lead into the locker room.

"And this was your idea? Getting everyone together for extra work?"

"Yes, sir. We weren't getting reps in the regular sessions. Seemed better than doing nothing."

"Smart." The Florida State guy said. "Shows initiative. Leadership. How old are you?"

"Fifteen."

They exchanged a glance. The Alabama guy nodded. "Well, keep it up. We'll be watching."

"Thank you, sir."

They walked off, heads together, as we caught up with Max and Christian, who'd held at the door to the locker room and turned back to see what we were doing.

"Dude."

"What?"

"Those were scouts. College scouts. And they were talking to you."

"They were talking to Ray."

"They asked about you," Ray pointed out.

I just shrugged. I was trying to be humble, but yeah, that had definitely broken in my favor.

"Come on," Ray said. "Let's get cleaned up."

We headed inside, talking about doing this tomorrow. I made a note to try and find the same assistant coach as before and see what we could do, since everyone was excited. I didn't blame them. Besides getting in extra work, it had been fun.

Which sometimes I think we forgot about in all the work.

I grabbed my stuff from the locker and headed back up to my room, ready to take a shower and call it a night. It was almost eight-thirty, and I'd been up since six and going basically all day.

I got to the room and found Trevor with his hands in my bag and Derek looking at him and laughing it up.

"Close the door," Trevor said.

I didn't move. I stood in the doorway, my body angled toward them. Every instinct told me to turn around and walk out, but I wasn't going to let him just get away.

"What are you doing?" I demanded.

"Just looking?"

"Well, don't. Get your hand out of my fucking bag!"

Derek pushed himself off the post of the bunk bed he'd been leaning on and took a step toward me.

"You owe a tax," he said.

"A tax?"

"Yeah," Trevor said. "You had your boyfriend go tell on us. You think we wouldn't figure it out after you had one of the coordinators talk to us about our 'attitude?'"

"I think they can just watch you and figure it out for themselves."

"We haven't done shit," Trevor said.

"If you call being a major league asshole doing nothing, then sure."

Trevor also took a step toward me. I backed up half a step before I caught myself. The door was still open behind me, and if I was smart, I'd make a run for it. Trevor and I were about the same height, and he had maybe ten pounds on me.

Maybe I could take him, and maybe I couldn't, but there was no way I'd be able to fight off Derek even if he was by himself. The guy had fifty pounds on me, and that was probably underestimating it.

The two together? Not a chance.

I glanced at the door. If I moved fast, I could get through before Trevor closed the distance. But I'd have to turn my back, and Trevor looked like he was waiting for exactly that. The second I turned, he'd grab me.

"You don't want to do this," I said.

"Pretty sure I do."

Well, that decided it. I'd just have to hope I was faster than him. I turned my head, just checking, and I felt my stomach drop. Another senior, one I'd seen hanging around Trevor during meals, had moved in behind me. He was shorter than Derek but wider, with a neck that disappeared into his shoulders.

“You guys starting without me?” he said.

Trevor smiled. “Just getting warmed up.”

I was boxed in now. Trevor in front, Derek to the side, the other senior blocking my exit. Three on one, and at least two of them were bigger than me.

I was screwed.

I shifted my weight to the balls of my feet and loosened my shoulders. If they were going to do this, I'd at least make them work for it. Go for Trevor first. He was the leader, the one driving this. If I could land something solid before Derek grabbed me, maybe it would be enough to make them think twice about round two.

Trevor saw me getting ready, and his smile widened. He liked this. The anticipation. The power dynamic. The chance to put someone in their place.

“Come on, freshman. Show us what you...”

“What the hell is going on?”

Jarett appeared behind the senior in the doorway, with Max right beside him. Jarett's eyes went from me to Trevor to Derek, and his whole face changed. I could see him doing the math on it and realizing what was happening.

“Blake, you good?” Jarett asked.

“Been better.”

“Max, go find a coach. Now.”

Max hesitated for half a second, looking between me and Trevor, then took off down the hallway before anyone could stop him. The senior in the doorway started to turn, like he was thinking about going after Max, but Jarett stepped up close to him.

“You want to move aside?” Jarett said.

The senior crossed his arms. “This doesn't concern you.”

“This is my room too.”

“Don't listen to him,” Trevor said.

The guy looked from

“I'm not going anywhere.”

“Trevor, call off your guard dogs. This is getting out of hand.”

The guy in the doorway balled his hands into fists, and for a second, I thought he was going to swing, consequences be damned.

At least, until we all heard someone else walking up. Multiple someones.

If Trevor was smart, he'd call this all off now. It was drawing attention, and pretty soon this whole floor was going to be gathered outside our door.

Thankfully, the footsteps were apparently Ray's as he appeared first, followed by Devon. Ray did about the same progression as Jarett had done, looking over me, Trevor, and his two guys, and figuring out what was going on.

"You've got to be kidding me," Raymond said.

"Mind your business, Clark," Trevor said.

"This is everyone's business. We all worked our asses off to get here and paid a lot of money for the privilege. I'm not going to let you screw that up for everyone."

"What are you going to do, run back to the coaches and tell them what's going on?"

"Damn straight I will. I told you to stop being an idiot, that you were going to end up getting kicked out of camp. Looks like you didn't listen."

Devon moved to stand beside Jarett, blocking more of the doorway. The senior who'd been guarding the exit looked at Trevor, then at Ray and Devon, and the fight just went out of him. He'd signed up to back Trevor's play, not to fight half the camp.

"Screw this," he said, pushing past Ray and Devon and moving into the open hallway. "I'm not getting kicked out for this."

Derek still hadn't moved, but that was enough to break him too. The fight had gone out of him. He looked like he wanted to be anywhere else, doing anything else. Trevor saw it too, and he was stupid enough to be annoyed, instead of coming to the same conclusion as the two of them.

"Derek," Trevor said.

"Man, I don't know..."

"You backing out on me?"

"Jarett is right. This is stupid. We're going to get sent home."

"Only if you quit."

"It's not quitting. It's not being an idiot."

More footsteps came, these at a run. Max appeared behind Ray with an assistant coach I didn't recognize in tow. I assumed Max had already started explaining, because the coach looked pissed.

"What's going on here?" the coach demanded.

"Nothing, Coach," Trevor said. "Just talking."

"Didn't look like nothing from what this young man described." The coach pointed at Max. "He said three seniors were cornering a freshman."

"That's not what was happening."

"Then what was happening?"

Nobody answered. Trevor's mouth worked like he was trying to find a story that would hold up, but there wasn't one. Derek was looking extremely hard at the ground.

The coach's face got redder. "All of you, out. Now. Except you." He pointed at me. "You stay."

Trevor, Derek, and the others started filing out.

"You hurt?" he asked.

"No, sir."

"They touch you?"

"No, sir."

"What happened?"

"Nothing. We were just talking."

"Look, I get it. No one wants to be a snitch, but it's just you and me. Tell me what happened and I'll take care of it."

"With all due respect, Coach, that will just make it worse. You kept me in here and threw everyone else out. If I confirm something was happening, which I'm not, they'll know it came from me. Hell, if you bust them now, they'll assume it. By tomorrow, no one will want to work with me. I'd rather keep my head down and get the most out of this camp."

He took a second, thinking, and said, "I didn't consider that. But, we can't have people causing disruptions. If I leave you in this room with them, won't they try it again?"

"Probably. Move me out of the room if you have to, but please, just let it drop other than that. Doing anything else makes this situation worse on me and will distract everyone in the camp. Moving me, everyone gets to save face and we get to focus on what matters."

"You sure?"

"Yes, sir, I am."

Max said from the door frame where he'd clearly been listening. "Coach? I talked to Jonathan, one of the guys in our room. He said Blake can take his spot here, and he could move into Blake's room. That way nobody's doubling up or anything."

The coach looked annoyed at Max for ignoring him, but looked to me and asked, "That work for you?"

"Yep."

"All right. Get your stuff together. I'll have someone keep an eye on the hallway while you pack."

He left. I stood there for a second, letting the adrenaline drain out of my system. My hands were shaking slightly, and my heart was still racing. Max stepped into the room with Jarett behind him.

"You okay?" Max asked.

"Yeah."

"That was intense."

"Could've been worse."

Jarett walked over to my side of the room and started pulling some of my stuff out of the closet, tossing it over to my duffel bag.

"Pack fast," Jarett said. "Before Trevor gets any ideas about coming back."

I grabbed clothes, shoved them into the bag.

"Thanks, guys," I said.

Jarett shrugged. "Hey, you helped us, why wouldn't we help you? Besides, Trevor's an asshole."

"I guess," I said.

What I'd said to the coach was true, this was the best way to handle it, out of the available options, but it wasn't going to stop the gossip. By tomorrow morning, everyone at camp would know that Trevor tried to jump me. Some of the guys would agree with Ray and Jarett, but others would see me as a snitch and it would be a problem.

I just hoped it wouldn't distract me too much from what I was trying to do here.

I zipped up my duffel bag and slung it over my shoulder. My notebook and playbook were still on the desk. I grabbed them and tucked them under my arm.

"Ready?" Jarett asked.

"Yeah. Let's go."

In addition to Max, I was now rooming with Christian, the other sophmore, and a running back who wasn't around and I hadn't really met but who Max said was alright. I was halfway through unpacking my duffel when someone knocked on the door.

"Yeah?" Max said from his bed were he was just lounging.

A kid I didn't recognize stuck his head in. "Blake?"

"That's me."

"You've got a visitor downstairs. Lobby."

"Thanks." I dropped the shirt I'd been holding back into my bag and headed for the door, wondering who'd come to see me.

Coach Moreno would have just come up to the rooms. He knew the people at the camp and pretty much had full rein. That was about where my list stopped, since there was no way anyone else I knew would be out here. My parents definitely couldn't have taken off the time.

The lobby was mostly empty except for a few guys sprawled on the couches watching TV. Charlie stood near the front windows, wearing cutoff jean shorts and a Braves T-shirt, her auburn hair pulled back in a ponytail. She waved when she saw me.

"Hey."

"Hey yourself." I walked over, genuinely surprised. "What are you doing here?"

"I brought you something." She held up a CD case. "A promise is a promise, remember?"

I took it from her. Pearl Jam's logo was scrawled across the front in marker, along with a track list in neat handwriting.

"You made this?"

"Don't sound so shocked. I'm capable of basic technology."

"I didn't mean it like that."

"Sure you didn't." She was smiling though. "My parents are waiting outside so I can't stay long. We just got back from Disney and they wanted to grab dinner before we head back to the hotel, but I figured I'd drop this off first since we were driving past anyway."

"You didn't have to do that."

"I know. But a deal's a deal." She shifted her weight from one foot to the other.

"So how was Disney?"

"Oh my God, it was amazing." Her whole face lit up. "I went on Space Mountain like five times in a row, did Indiana Jones a couple of times, Big Thunder Mountain twice, and I talked my dad onto Splash Mountain. I promised he wouldn't get that wet so he's a little pissed at me, but it was worth it to see his face."

I found myself grinning at her enthusiasm. "Sounds like he had a great time."

"He pretended to be annoyed but I caught him smiling."

"Your dad sounds cool."

"He's a total dork but yeah, he's pretty great." She tucked a strand of hair behind her ear. "What about you? How's camp going?"

"It's okay." I hesitated, not sure how much to say. "The coaching is good. I'm learning a lot."

"But?"

"What makes you think there's a but?"

"Because you just got this look on your face like you stepped in something unpleasant. Come on, what's going on?"

I glanced around the lobby, making sure no one was paying attention to us. "Just having some trouble with one of the guys here. He's being a jerk."

"Older kid?"

"Senior. He's decided he needs to show me my place, but I think mostly he just wants to make himself feel big. I've run into his type before."

I was kind of his type in my dream life, at least until everything fell apart, so I couldn't say too much about it.

"I get it," Charlie said. "I did this volleyball camp thing last summer. There was this girl, she was like seventeen, and she made it her personal mission to make all the younger players miserable. Constantly criticizing everything we did, taking our equipment, talking trash during drills."

"What'd you do?"

"Honestly? I just focused on getting better. Eventually the coaches noticed she was being a problem and they talked to her, but until then I just kept my head down and worked." She shrugged. "It sucked but I wasn't going to let her ruin the whole experience, you know? I was there to improve, not to make friends with some insecure senior who felt threatened by freshmen."

"That's pretty much where I'm at."

"It's so stupid," she said. "Like, why do people have to be like that? You're all here to get better. You'd think they'd want to help instead of tearing people down."

"Some people only feel big when they're making someone else feel small."

"Ugh, yes. Exactly." She checked her watch. "I should go. My parents are probably wondering what's taking so long."

"Right. Thanks for this." I held up the CD.

"It's a good mix. There's some Nirvana on there too, and this band called The Cranberries that I think you'll like."

"I'll check it out."

We stood there for a second, neither of us moving. Charlie opened her mouth, closed it, then smiled slightly. "Okay, well..."

"Yeah."

She stepped forward like she might hug me, and I started to lift my arms, but then she stopped and took a half step back and suddenly we were both just standing there awkwardly, too close but not quite touching. Her cheeks were pink.

"Okay, bye." She turned and headed for the door.

"Bye. Have a safe drive home."

She waved without looking back and pushed through the glass doors. I watched her jog across the parking lot to where a silver minivan was waiting, saw her climb into the back seat. The van pulled away.

I looked down at the CD in my hands, at the careful track list written in purple ink. She had put time into this. Everything on here was either a song we'd talked about, or a similar song she'd thought I'd like. She had thought about what I'd like and made this specifically for me.

I turned and headed back toward the stairs, passing the TV area where a few guys were arguing about which channel to watch. My new room was on the second floor, third door on the left. When I got there, Max was stretched out on his bed throwing a football up and catching it.

"Who was it?"

"Just a friend." Not exactly a lie.

It was late and everyone was starting to turn in for the night, since we had another big day tomorrow. I set the CD on the desk, next to the notebook where I kept my plays and notes from Coach Moreno. Through the window I could see the practice fields, empty and dark.

Tomorrow would be another busy day, but for tonight, I had a mix tape from a girl with green eyes and an infectious laugh, and that felt like its own kind of victory.

Chapter 7

The next day was more of the same: up early, conditioning, and then the breakout session. Trevor was giving me glares throughout the session, when he thought no one was looking, but otherwise, he kept his mouth shut and we made good progress.

I hoped that meant he'd back off, and the rest of the week I could just focus on what I needed to focus on, but I had a sneaking suspicion that wasn't going to happen.

At least not with how he was glaring at me.

"Sims, you're up. Five plays," one of the coaches said, snapping me back into focus.

That was the problem, being off on the side in development while four other QBs got fifteen to twenty snaps each. There was just too much downtime which allowed my mind to wander. and the repetitive drills didn't help with that.

I also couldn't help but notice I got only five snaps while Ray got almost twenty-five, and even the guy before me got fifteen. It felt like a deliberate snub. Maybe it was just because the session was almost over.

That was what I was going to tell myself, if for no other reason than it didn't make me feel quite so bad.

Max clapped my shoulder pad as we passed. "Show them."

The offensive line settled into their stances. I recognized a few faces from yesterday's extra practice. Christian was at center, Jacob at left tackle, along with one face I didn't care to see: Derek. He hadn't spoken to me since the episode in the room the night before, but just like Trevor, I didn't think it was over for him.

We actually had fewer defensive linemen at the camp than any other position, so the guys out here were the second team, and they'd been playing for almost thirty minutes now.

I stepped into the huddle.

"Twins right, Z post, H drag, Y corner. On two."

The defense was showing a base 4-3 as I moved behind center.

"Blue forty-two, blue forty-two, set hut, hut!"

The ball hit my hands. I took a three-step drop, the pocket forming around me. The corner route came open faster than expected. The safety bit on the post, leaving a window. I stepped up, planted my back foot, and fired.

My receiver hauled it in at the sideline, twenty-two yards downfield.

"Good read, Sims!" Daniels called out from the sideline.

I jogged back to the huddle. No celebration, no high-fives. Just football.

"Twins left, 22 Power, Y option. On one."

The play was designed to attack the weak side. The middle looked soft.

"Set hut!"

The snap came fast. I faked the handoff, pulling the ball back against my hip. The line surged forward. The tight end released into his route, finding the soft spot between the linebackers. I hit him in stride.

He rumbled forward, breaking one tackle before going down. Fourteen yards. First down.

On the next play, the defense adjusted, showing pressure up the middle. Derek shifted over to the strong side, and the linebacker next to him crowded the line.

This was a blitz read. The flat route would come open when they pushed the pocket.

"Green eighteen, green eighteen!"

I adjusted the protection, sliding the line toward the blitz threat.

"Set hut, hut!"

The ball came up. The blitz came immediately. Two linebackers shot the gaps. I felt the pocket compress, bodies surging toward me from both sides. The flat route broke open just like I'd seen it in my head. My tight end cleared into space, arm up.

I stepped into the throw. The ball left my hand clean, trajectory perfect.

I was watching the ball, following long enough to see the tight end pull it in for a successful play, when Derek's shoulder caught me square in the ribs and drove me straight into the ground.

The impact drove every bit of air from my lungs in a single, violent compression. Sky flashed overhead, then grass, then nothing but the shock of contact. I hit the turf on my back, the world narrowing to a pinpoint of white noise and empty lungs.

I couldn't breathe. Couldn't pull air in. My chest tried to expand and found nothing, just empty burning.

I was dimly aware of all hell breaking loose around me.

"What the hell was that?!"

Voices came through the static. Someone grabbed Derek, pulling him back. A whistle shrieked.

"That's a late hit! Way late! What are you thinking, Crown?"

I rolled onto my side, gasping. My ribs screamed. Still couldn't breathe right, just short, desperate pulls that didn't fill anything.

"You good?" Christian asked, kneeling beside me.

I managed a nod, still fighting for air. Spots danced at the edges of my vision.

"That kind of shit will get you thrown from a game and is bush league. Not only were you late, but the level of contact would have been excessive even if you hadn't been. Put the two together, and your side would be giving up a bunch of yards on penalty, and you might be out of the game!"

"It was a good hit!" Derek's voice, defensive.

"Bullshit. The ball was already caught by the time you hit. That was maybe the latest hit I have ever seen!"

I pushed up onto my hands and knees. The grass felt too close, my head too light. Jacob and Max pulled me to my feet. My legs wobbled.

"I'm fine," I said, not really meaning it but not wanting to seem weak.

Coach Warren approached, face red. "You need a minute?"

"No, sir."

He stared at me for three long seconds. "You sure?"

"Yes, sir." My ribs felt like someone had taken a bat to them, each breath agony.

"Okay. Crown, you're staying in, but one more hit like that, and you'll not just be done for the day, you'll be out of the camp. Understood?"

"Yes, sir."

The coaches backed off. Derek caught my eye for half a second, then walked away, back to the line.

"That was garbage," Max said.

I waved him off, walking back to the huddle. My hands were shaking. I clenched them into fists, released, clenched again. Two more plays. Just had to power through.

The offense gathered around me.

"Ace right, X deep out, Y seam, H check. On one."

I should have called something quicker. A three-step drop, something that got the ball out fast. But I called the play anyway.

Behind the line, I set my feet. The defense showed the same base look. I was very aware of Derek now, still outside.

"Set hut!"

The snap hit my hands wrong. I bobbled it for a fraction of a second, then secured it and took my drop. Three steps, hitch, plant.

But I didn't plant. I pulled up short, weight on my front foot, back foot barely touching grass. The seam route broke open. Wide open. I rushed the throw.

The ball sailed high and outside, wobbling. My receiver had to dive for it, couldn't make the catch. It hit the grass ten yards downfield.

"Sims!" Coach Warren's voice carried disappointment. "What was that footwork?"

"Sorry, coach."

One more play.

I called the formation quickly, barely looking at the huddle. "Twins right, Z corner, H flat, Y drag. On two."

Something safe. Something quick.

"Blue forty-two, blue forty-two!"

The defense shifted. Derek crept closer to the line, showing blitz. My stomach clenched.

"Set hut, hut!"

The ball came up. I took my drop, already tensing for the hit. The corner route needed time to develop. The flat would come open sooner. I focused on the flat, on getting the ball out fast, on not getting hit again.

My back foot hit the ground wrong, skidding on the grass. I threw anyway, off-balance, arm dragging. The ball came out weak, floating.

The cornerback broke on it immediately, nearly intercepting. The pass fell incomplete at his feet.

The whistle blew, long and final.

"Alright, that's enough. Let's break for lunch!"

I jogged off the field, heading for the locker room when Coach Warren waved me over.

"You injured?"

"No, sir."

"Then what happened on those last two?"

I couldn't look at him. "I rushed them."

"You flinched." His voice stayed level, not accusing. Just stating a fact. "Crown got in your head?"

My jaw tightened. I wanted to argue, to say that wasn't it, that I just made mechanical errors, but he was right. I'd felt Derek on every snap, waiting for him to come through again, to put me back on the ground, rules be damned.

"Yes, sir."

"That happens. You took a late hit from a kid who's got fifty pounds on you." He paused. "But you can't let it get in your head. You understand?"

"Yes, sir."

"Go get some water. We'll talk more later."

I grabbed my helmet and walked toward the sideline. Ray fell into step beside me.

"That hit was dirty."

"Doesn't matter."

"It does, actually. Warren should've pulled him."

I didn't respond.

Max appeared on my other side. "You okay?"

"Fine."

"You don't look fine."

I stopped walking, turned to face both of them. "I'm fine. Stop asking."

They exchanged a look but didn't push it. We continued toward the water station. Other players milled around, some watching our group, others talking in small clusters. A few glanced my way, then looked away quickly.

I grabbed a water bottle and drank half of it in one pull. The cold helped. Not much, but enough.

Coach Daniels approached from the equipment area. "Sims."

"Yes, sir?"

"First two plays looked good. Real good," he said, stopping in front of me. "Last two looked like someone who was thinking instead of playing."

"Yes, sir."

"You're going to get hit in games. It happens. Your job is to make the throw on the next play. Put it out of your mind."

"I know."

"Good. Because this afternoon you'll get another shot, and more tomorrow. You're going to take hits at this level. Can't let them make you hesitate."

"No, sir."

He nodded once and walked away. I watched him go, then turned back to the locker room.

My ribs throbbed. I pressed my hand against them carefully, feeling for damage. Nothing broken, probably. Just bruised. Just pain that would fade. But the hesitation, that flinch in my feet, the way I'd rushed those last two throws, that would be harder to shake.

What had Charlie said last night? *Focus on what you can control.*

Of course, not everything worked out how I wanted it to. *Focus on what you can control* sounds good until what you can control didn't include any real playing time. After such a bad showing in the first scrimmage, they'd kept me off the field and in development the entire second scrimmage.

We were now halfway done with the camp, and I felt like I was blowing the opportunity completely, and I didn't know how to turn it around. I did manage to get another extra practice in, and we'd even added some new people to the group, but I couldn't get out of my head.

It wasn't even Derek anymore. I couldn't get it out of my head, stop myself from blowing it. I knew I needed to shake it, but I just couldn't seem to do it.

"Same time tomorrow?" Max asked as we walked off the field.

"I think so. They said the schedule tomorrow night is different. They have that BBQ dinner thing, but if we can, I'd like to."

Ray clapped my shoulder. "You looked better out there tonight. That deep ball to Christian was perfect."

I knew he was trying to be supportive, but for each good pass, I'd screwed up another one. And this wasn't even as competitive as the full scrimmage.

"Thanks," I said, clearly not meaning it.

"Don't let it get to you too much, man. We've all had games like this when stuff doesn't go your way. You'll shake it off."

I nodded. Now if only I could figure out how to shake it off.

We split up at the dorms. Max was meeting one of the other receivers, and I headed back to our room to get a change of clothes and head for the showers, letting hot water beat against my shoulders until the tension started to ease. When I got back to my new room, Christian was already stretched out on his bed reading a playbook.

I changed into sweats and a T-shirt, then grabbed my notebook to review the plays we'd run. I was getting tired, but I wanted to put in a little more work before I called it a night.

I was just starting to make progress when suddenly Coach Moreno pushed through the door and said, "Blake, with me. Now!"

Christian just looked at me like *what the hell*, but I shook him off, dropped my book, and hopped off the top bunk.

"Yes, sir."

Moreno turned without another word. I followed him down the hall to a common room where three guys were watching MTV. He jerked his thumb at the door.

"Out."

They might not know who he was, but every kid, especially one in sports, knew the tone and had been well trained to jump when they heard it. They scrambled out of the room so fast one of them left their Coke behind on the table.

Moreno shut the door behind them and moved to the TV they'd been watching. He pulled a tape from his jacket pocket and shoved it into the VCR that sat on the bottom shelf of the cart.

"Sit."

I dropped onto the couch.

The screen flickered to life showing practice footage from the first scrimmage. The camera angle showed the full field from an elevated position, probably up in the box. I watched myself take the snap, drop back, scan right, see the blitz, and step into the pocket like they'd pushed me to do. I made my read, trusting my line, and shot a pass that connected. Then Derek came through untouched and drove me into the turf a full second after I'd released the ball.

Moreno rewound it. Played it again.

"What do you see?"

"Late hit."

"I don't give a damn about the hit. What else?"

I watched myself get up slowly, favoring my ribs. Shaking out my throwing hand.

"I got hit."

"And?"

The tape kept playing. My next snap I bobbled the ball, stepped back, and off balance threw the ball. It sailed high and wide. The receiver made a dive for it, but couldn't get his hands on it.

Moreno froze the frame. "There. Right there. You're already beat. In your head, you're done. One hit and you folded."

I didn't say anything, because what could I say? He was right.

He advanced the tape to my final throw, another incompletion that had almost been picked off completely. "Two plays. Two awful throws. Not because your mechanics broke down, although they did, but because some linebacker got in your kitchen and you let him live there rent-free."

"He came in late. Coach Warren barely ..."

"I don't care what Warren did or didn't do. Football's violent. People are going to hit you. Sometimes it'll be a clean hit and sometimes it'll be dirty. The great ones don't give a damn either way. They get up and make the next throw." He ejected the tape and grabbed another one. "You know what separates championship quarterbacks from the guys who wash out?"

"Talent."

"Wrong. Sure, it's important, but a lot of talented people never make it out of college." He tapped his temple. "It's right here. The physical part's easy. Anyone can do it with enough training and work. Arm strength, footwork, mechanics, I can teach all that, but I can't teach you not to flinch. That's on you."

The new tape started, and footage from an NFL game came on. It must have been from years ago, because I recognized the logos and even some of the players, but none of the people on the field were guys who were playing now. I watched as a quarterback in a white jersey got absolutely destroyed by a blitzing linebacker. The hit looked worse than Derek's by a mile. The QB stayed down for a moment, then pushed to his feet. Next play, he threw a thirty-yard completion down the seam.

"Leo Price, 1989 playoffs. Took that shot in the third quarter that hit so hard it cracked two of his ribs. Even with that injury, he came back and threw three touchdowns in the fourth." Moreno fast-forwarded. "And this."

Another hit. Another QB getting plastered. Then getting up and leading a scoring drive.

"Franklin Reed, Super Bowl XXV. He got his bell rung so hard he doesn't remember playing the second half of that game to this day, but do you know what he does remember? Getting that Super Bowl ring and the MVP after he led his team from behind to win."

The tape rolled through clip after clip. Quarterbacks absorbing punishment and bouncing back. Making plays. Winning games.

Moreno stopped the tape and turned to face me. "Football's a game of physical dominance, but it's won and lost between the ears. The defense doesn't just want to knock you to the ground, they want to knock your confidence into the ground, because if they can get you off your game, then the game's over. You'll hesitate. You'll second-guess. And you'll lose."

"I know that."

"Do you? Because what I saw today tells me you don't. You let one bad sack get inside your head and ruin your whole day. That's not quarterback play. That's weakness."

The word stung.

"I'm not weak."

"Then prove it. Tomorrow, when you get your reps, I don't want to see any of that gun-shy garbage. You drop back, you go through your progressions, and you deliver the ball. I don't care if Conrad Russell slips his block and is coming for you, you make the throw first, take the hit second. That's the job."

"What if I don't get reps tomorrow?"

Moreno's expression didn't change. "Then you work harder in the extra sessions you set up. You'll work in development and take everything they can give you. You study more film. You show these coaches you're serious. But you damn sure don't let some punk lineman dictate how you play."

I looked at the blank TV screen. Saw my own reflection staring back.

"There will always be people trying to tear you down. Teammates who resent you. Coaches who don't believe in you. Defenders who want to separate your head from your body. You think any of that stops when you leave here?"

"No."

"Then deal with it. You want to play, then you handle the adversity, handle the pressure, and handle guys coming after you on and off the field because it never gets easier. The competition gets better, the stakes get higher, but the bullshit never goes away. If you can't handle some summer camp drama, you've got no business dreaming about making it to the next level."

"I can handle it."

He opened the door. The hallway noise spilled in.

"Good! Show me tomorrow that you can."

"Yes, sir."

He left without waiting for a response. The door clicked shut behind him.

I sat alone in the common room and thought about my previous life. All those wasted years. Things had gone bad, and it had taken my life down with it. I had this chance to turn things around, and

I'd fixed some things, the most important thing, but that didn't mean I wanted to screw up the dream.

I didn't want to go through all this again just to be back on the job, working construction, dreaming about what might have been.

I couldn't be that person again. I wouldn't be.

Chapter 8

Thursday morning, our last full day, we got up early and went to conditioning just like normal, after that, things started to change.

I had already known the end of the day was going to be different with the big dinner they had planned, and that meant our extra practice time was done, but I didn't know the morning would be messed up too.

After conditioning, we found out that we were skipping our breakout session entirely. Instead, we were led into the film room, which was one of the few rooms that had seats for all of us, and were told to sit and wait.

That part I didn't mind so much. Getting to sit down after conditioning instead of immediately running drills was a nice change.

A few minutes later, the camp director showed up, along with most of the coaches.

"Okay, we have a lot to cover and not a lot of time to do it," he said as he took his place at the front of the room. "I want to introduce you all to Shaun Bailey, the USC media director, who has kindly volunteered his services today. He's going to give you guys a crash course in media training, something more and more guys going into major college programs should get, but don't. After that, we will be shuffling you through the media room here, where we have some press, including ESPN and USA Today, who are interested to hear about the next big names coming into college ball. So without further ado, here's Mr. Bailey."

With that, he stepped aside, and probably the most nondescript man I had ever seen took his place. Average build, average height, slightly tanned with brown hair.

Truly the everyman.

"Hi. I hope everyone's ready to listen, because like he said, this is something I find a lot of our new kids coming into the program are sorely lacking. You're very lucky to get a leg up and those of you headed to D1 programs will have a chance to put these skills to use right away. I know some of you have dealt with local sports reporters, from your hometown paper, maybe a TV station if you're lucky. That's good experience, but it's nothing compared to what you'll face at the collegiate level, especially if you're at a competitive program. You'll be facing national press, beat writers, broadcasters who know the game better than your position coaches. They'll ask tough questions. They'll try to get quotes they can spin into headlines. And if you say something stupid, it'll follow you."

He pulled up a remote and a projector screen descended behind him. A series of headlines appeared, all quotes from college football players who'd said the wrong thing to reporters.

"These are cautionary tales. Player trash-talks opponent, gets destroyed on game day. Quarterback complains about playing time, creates locker room drama. Running back brags about draft stock, tears ACL two weeks later." He clicked through each one. "What do these have in common?"

No one answered.

"They're all preventable. You control what comes out of your mouth! So let me give you the basics." He clicked to a new slide with bullet points. "First rule: never guarantee a win. You can be confident, you can talk about preparation, but the second you promise victory, you've given the other team bulletin board material. Second, don't talk about your individual stats or accolades. It's always about the team. No one likes a braggart or a showboat. They want you to thank your guys, your coach, and God. And that's it. Third, if you don't know something, say so. Don't guess, don't speculate. Fourth, controversial topics stay off limits. Politics, religion, anything that's going to alienate half your fanbase. Fifth, and this is the big one, *assume* ***everything*** is 'on the record.' Even if a reporter says it's off the record, even if they're your buddy from high school, what you say can and will be printed. Remember these rules and live by them, because they will save you when the tape is recording and you are in front of a microphone."

He paused and looked out over us.

"The good news is that today's not going to be that serious. Think of it like practice. Real journalists, real questions, but the stakes are going to be a hell of a lot lower. You're all still in high school so there won't be a lot of column inches devoted to you. You mess up here, it might make a small story in a camp recap. You mess up when you get to college or God forbid in the NFL, it can lead the sports page. So use this as a learning opportunity. Be professional, be respectful, and remember you're representing not just yourselves but this camp. And you're going to be sitting in front of a USC logo, so don't make my life any harder either."

That's the one thing I'd never done. I think Kenneth had been interviewed by the local paper a few times, but no one wanted to talk to a kid playing on JV.

He went through more scenarios, showing video clips of college players handling interviews well and others sticking their foot in their mouths. He demonstrated how to present yourself, how to answer in as even and level a way as possible, how to bridge from a question you didn't want to answer to a topic you did.

"One more thing," he said as the session wrapped up. "Some of you are going to get more attention than others. That's just how it is. If you're a highly ranked recruit, if you've got an interesting story, the reporters will gravitate toward you. Don't take it personally if you only get a few questions. And for those who do get attention, don't let it go to your head. How much attention you get doesn't always follow how well you play on the field. These guys chase interesting stories that'll hold eyeballs. That's what's important to them, not how well someone plays."

Mr. Bailey checked his clipboard. "Alright, first up, Trevor Hutchinson."

Trevor stood and walked down the aisle, giving everyone a cocky grin.

"That's right, starting off with the best," he said as he passed Ray.

Mr. Bailey watched him go, clearly not amused, and said, "While we wait, let's talk about body language."

The next twenty minutes dragged as Mr. Bailey walked through examples of players fidgeting, avoiding eye contact, giving one-word answers that made them look unprepared or hostile. He showed clips of players who handled pressure well, staying calm and personable even when reporters asked difficult questions.

Trevor returned after about eight minutes, looking pleased with himself. He said something to Derek that made his friend laugh.

"Raymond Clark, your turn."

Richardson continued his presentation, cycling through more dos and don'ts. Don't cross your arms. Don't look at your phone. Don't rush your answers, but don't ramble either. Answer the question asked, not the question you wish they'd asked.

Raymond was gone longer than Trevor had been, maybe fifteen minutes in total.

"How was it?" I leaned over and whispered when he got back.

"It was okay."

"What'd they ask?"

"Just stuff. My offers, my stats, why I chose this camp over others, what my family thinks about my recruitment, where I think I'll be going."

"What'd you say?"

"Just that we are looking at all the schools on my list, and that they all have things that make them good choices."

Seemed like a good enough answer. They kept cycling through people, with the average guy only gone like five minutes. Max was only there for like four and said they hardly asked him anything.

"Blake Sims."

I'll admit, I was a little nervous. The side door opened into a hallway, and a staff person waited there, gesturing toward another door.

"Right through here."

I nodded and stepped inside.

The room was smaller than I expected. A rectangular table sat in the center with two microphones positioned in front of a single chair. Four journalists stood around the edges, notepads ready, and a photographer adjusted his camera near the back. Everyone looked up when I entered.

A woman with blonde hair cut in a sleek bob stood near the table, dressed in tailored trousers and a crisp blouse.

"Blake Sims?" she asked.

"Yes, ma'am."

"Jennifer Kowalski, USA Today. Have a seat."

She sat down across from me and started asking questions almost as soon as we were seated. "So you're the youngest player at this camp. How's that working out for you?"

At least I'd expected this question. "It's been an adjustment. Everyone here is more experienced than me, bigger too, in a lot of cases. But that's exactly why I wanted to come. I needed to see where I really stack up, what I actually need to work on."

"Are you finding it intimidating?" A younger male reporter with wireframed glasses asked from the side.

"Sometimes, yeah. But being intimidated doesn't make you better at football. You just have to push through it and focus on learning."

Jennifer jotted notes, her pen moving quickly. "You're here training under Phillip Moreno. That's quite a connection for a freshman. How did that happen?"

I was surprised she knew that.

"A lot of begging, mostly," I said, which got a chuckle out of the wire-framed glasses guy. "But really, I have goals I've set for myself, and to reach those, I knew I needed some kind of private coaching, and the coaches at my school did some checking, and his name came up as the best. I had to try out and prove to him that I was worth his time, and I guess I passed because he agreed to take me on and give me this opportunity, which is something I'll always be grateful for."

"So most of the participants here are hoping to get scouted before their final season starts. That would be pretty early for you. Are schools already looking at you? Have any programs reached out?"

I shook my head. "No, ma'am, not really. I'll be a sophomore next season, and this will be the first time I've had a chance to play on varsity, let alone start. So, I'm pretty sure I'm not on anyone's radar yet, which is fine. I have time. This year it's all about getting my game to the level where next year they will take a look at me, which is what this camp is really about for me."

"But you are wanting to be recruited?" An older male reporter with gray hair asked from the side.

“Eventually, yes, sir, I do. My goal is to get into a D1 school, take us to the national championships, and then get recruited into the NFL. I know that’s probably what every other guy who came in here said, but it’s still the truth.”

“How would you evaluate your performance so far this week?” Jennifer asked, not looking up from her notepad as she wrote.

“Honestly? It’s not what I expected of myself. This is the first time I’ve competed at this level, and it’s taken some getting used to. The speed of the game is different, the complexity of the schemes are different, even just the physicality is on another level. I’ve had some good moments and some rough ones.”

“Specifically, what’s been the biggest challenge?” she pressed.

“Probably the mental side. Reading defenses faster, processing information when everything’s happening at full speed. Back home, I’ve only played in junior varsity so far, where I’ve had a little more time to think through everything. Here, if you hesitate for even half a second, the play’s already broken down.”

“Are you satisfied with your playing time?” the older reporter asked.

“I’d always like more reps, but I understand I’m here to learn first. The coaches have been fair about giving everyone opportunities based on what they show.”

Jennifer looked up from her notes. “There was an incident earlier this week involving conflict with some older players. Can you talk about that?”

Knowing about Coach Moreno was one thing, but how she heard about that, I had no idea.

“There wasn’t much to it. Everyone here is incredibly competitive, and sometimes things can get tense in an environment like this. But that’s all it was.”

“The scrimmage today is extended with more opportunities for everyone,” Jennifer said, shifting gears. “What are you hoping to show the coaches?”

“That I can execute under pressure. That I’ve learned from my mistakes this week. That I belong on the field with everyone else here, regardless of my age.”

“And if it doesn’t go well?” the older reporter asked.

I met his eyes. "Then I'll learn from that too, and hopefully take these new skills back home and put them into practice, and bring my team to state."

"That's confident," the younger male reporter said.

"I'm a high school quarterback. Confidence is practically a requirement."

That got another little laugh from them.

"I think we're about done here. Thanks for your time and answering all of our questions," she said.

"Thank you," I said, standing.

The photographer stepped forward. "Can I get a few shots?"

I put my hand on the chair and tried to look confident, while he clicked through several angles. I had no idea if I was successful or not.

After we finished the media session, we only had about thirty minutes of breakout work, which meant I got maybe ten throws total before they called us all back for the extended scrimmage period.

The bleachers had more people in them than usual: parents who'd shown up early for tonight's dinner, plus the media people and what looked like a handful of scouts.

Coach Warren gathered us near the sideline while the assistant coaches organized us into groups. I waited, watching names get called, watching pods form. Ray went first, obviously, followed by Trevor, just as they had the other days.

"Sims, you're up," he called when it was finally my turn to cycle in.

I jogged over to where the assistant was pointing and found myself standing next to Max.

"Finally," I said.

Max looked at me, broke into that goofy grin of his and said, "Yeah?"

"Be ready. I'm feeling myself today."

"Hell yeah."

We lined up with our group against most of the second-string defense and a couple of guys from the first string, based on how many were in each position group. The offensive coordinator called out the formation and coverage we'd be running against. I took my position behind the center, checking the defense. Seven in the box, two high safeties.

I took my three-step drop, eyes tracking the free safety as he broke toward the flat. Max ran a dig route across the middle, breaking at twelve yards. The linebacker bit on the play-action fake, and I delivered the ball right as Max came open, leading him just enough that he caught it in stride and picked up another eight yards after the catch before the safety wrapped him up.

First down.

We reset. Same formation, although the defense had adjusted, showing man coverage this time. I checked the protection, made sure everyone understood their assignments. The snap came, and I took a five-step drop. Max, who was still my first read, ran a comeback at fifteen yards, using his speed to create separation from the corner. I put the ball on his outside shoulder where only he could get it. He hauled it in and stepped out of bounds.

The next play, the defense brought pressure. Five-man rush with man coverage behind it. I slid the protection right, got the ball out quickly on a slant to our slot receiver. Six yards.

Derek got up from where he'd been blocked and glared at me.

He'd been hoping to put me in the dirt again.

We moved down the field in chunks. Max caught three more passes, including a twenty-yard seam route where he beat his man on pure speed, and I dropped the ball over the linebacker's head into his hands. He took it to the five-yard line before getting dragged down.

On the next play, I play-actioned to the fullback, rolled right, and found Max in the corner of the end zone. Touchdown, if we were tracking that kind of thing.

"That's what I'm talking about!" Max said as we jogged back to the sideline.

A few spots on both sides of the field subbed out, and I couldn't help but notice Derek stayed in. I saw him talking to the defensive coordinator, pointing at me. When we took the field again, Derek had moved to a different position, one that would let him rush from the edge.

The snap came, and Derek shot the gap, but I'd seen it coming. I stepped up in the pocket, eyes downfield. Max ran a post route.

I waited an extra beat, feeling Derek closing from my right, then released the ball. Max caught it in stride, thirty-five yards downfield, and took it the rest of the way to the end zone untouched.

Derek slammed his hand against his helmet as he walked back to the defensive huddle.

A waste of attitude. I released the ball way before he got to me, so if he'd hit me, it would have been late again.

We ran it again. They came with a zone blitz, dropping a defensive end into coverage and bringing a safety from depth. I read it, checked down to the running back in the flat. Four yards.

Next play, they brought pressure again. Derek, this time, straight up the middle. I saw him coming, felt the pocket collapsing, but I also saw Max breaking free on a deep post. I stepped up, planted my back foot, and threw. The ball sailed forty yards through the air and dropped into Max's hands at the goal line.

Derek didn't even wait for the play to end. He was already turning away, heading back to the sideline.

"You're making me look good out here," Max said as we reset.

"You're making yourself look good. Once you kick on the jets, no one can stop you."

We subbed out, and a new group came in. I watched from the sideline as they ran their series. Ray was up again, and he looked sharp, hitting several big plays.

When our turn came again, the defense had changed their approach. The first few plays ran well, although I was starting to miss more, with the defense getting a hand in here or there, deflecting throws where I tried a bit too much.

I brushed it off. I wasn't going to hit every shot I took.

It was nearing the end of my time, with players cycling through every few plays, and Derek came back on the field.

The next play started at the fifteen-yard line. They shifted again and showed blitz once more. I get they wanted to put pressure on me, but they should have pulled back from the line and run more coverage, because so far, they were making it much easier for me to get a completion.

I checked the protection, made sure the guard knew Derek was his responsibility. The ball snapped, and Derek came hard. The guard engaged him, but Derek wasn't a pushover and fought through, reaching for me just as I released the ball, but the receiver misread the cue and slowed down, which put it just out of his reach.

Can't win them all.

I guess Derek got tired of not getting the hit, because he kept coming even after I got the ball off. I saw him this time and, instead of letting him hit me, I twisted and jumped to the side, causing him to miss me completely and hit the dirt face-first. He got up slowly, grass stuck to his facemask.

I was surprised to see that Derek was already gone, when the subs came in again, even though he'd had only the one play.

At least until I saw him with the defensive coordinator getting chewed out for trying for the late hit again.

The defense huddled up with the replaced linebacker but looked to have called the same blitz package.

The ball snapped. The new linebacker came up the middle, and then, for some reason, turned in the wrong direction, following the guard instead of shooting through clean. The hole opened up to my right, big as day.

I saw it. Saw the linebacker realize his mistake and start to correct, which I took to mean that this wasn't a trap. He'd screwed up, and I could see him trying to save it. I saw the secondary backpedaling, trying to get coverage, but he was now out of position and got picked up. Their entire defensive package got screwed up by that one mistake and then everyone trying to correct to fix it. I clocked all that in my head, but what I really saw was open grass.

I know they'd talked to me about scrambling, about needing to stay in the pocket, but the opportunity was right there.

Screw it. I ran.

The linebacker, reaching for me as I passed, was still trying to get back into his spot, but I was already gone. The cornerback came up fast, trying to cut off the angle. I stuttered, gave him a half-step, then accelerated past him, putting every ounce of speed I'd learned in track into it. The end zone was fifteen yards away. Then ten. Then five.

The safety came from my left, launching himself at me. I tried to cut back, but his shoulder caught my hip and we both went down at the two-yard line. My knee hit first, then my elbow, then my shoulder. The ball stayed tucked against my ribs.

The whistle blew.

I got up, breathing hard, and jogged back toward the sideline. The assistant coach who'd been working with our group met me before I reached the bench.

"What was that?" he demanded.

"I saw the opening and ..."

"You're supposed to be working on pocket presence, not trying to run through the defense. We've got running backs for that."

"But the linebacker went the wrong way and ..."

"I don't care what the linebacker did. You stay in the pocket and make your reads. That's what we're teaching here."

"Leave it," Coach Cliff appeared beside us.

The assistant coach turned. "He just ..."

"I know what he did," the former NFL star said. "It was a good read. He saw the gap and made a hell of a play."

"Coach Warren wants us working on ..."

"I know what he wants, but leave it." Cliff's voice didn't rise, but something in his tone made the assistant coach stop talking. "Go check on the next group."

The assistant coach walked away, shaking his head.

Cliff gestured for me to follow him a few steps down the sideline, away from the other players.

"That was a good move, and I'm not going to tell you that you did the wrong thing," he said. "But I want to make sure you understand how rare situations like that are. Don't think you can get away with it all the time. It's a sometimes thing. You understand?"

"Yes, sir."

"Good. If you see a chance like that, take it, but you better be damn sure, because a lot of quarterbacks have gotten suckered thinking they had the shot and got dropped for their trouble."

"I know. I stayed in the pocket every other time, but I saw him go the wrong way, saw him misread the play, and saw him trying to correct for it. I knew it was open."

Cliff nodded. "You'll hear no complaint from me. You're probably going to get ridden hard by coaches who like a more structured offense, and there's nothing wrong with that. Structure wins games. But if you can scramble like that and make it work, and more importantly, know when *not* to do it, that's going to set you apart."

"Yes, sir."

"Mobile offenses have been really becoming a thing over the last ten years, and it's just starting to be taken seriously in college. By the time you graduate, you're going to find more coaches looking for something like that. Just be smart about it. Keep it in your back pocket until it's needed."

"I will. Thank you."

He clapped me on the shoulder once, then walked back toward the defensive coordinator.

I found Max near the bench, drinking water.

"That was insane," he said. "You just broke like four tackles."

"Two."

"Looked like more from where I was standing."

I just shrugged.

Coach Warren blew the whistle three times. "That's time! Everyone bring it in!"

We gathered at midfield. The coaches stood in a semicircle around us.

"Good work today," Warren said. "You've all shown improvement this week. That's what this camp is about. Some of you will go on to play Division One football, some of you won't, but everyone here has gotten better, and that's what matters. We've still got more breakout sessions this afternoon, but no second scrimmage today. Tonight we'll have our dinner and you'll have time to spend with your parents. Tomorrow we have the relay, we'll hand out awards, including camp MVP, and you'll be headed home. Before that, I want you to take a minute and think about what you've learned here. Not just the plays or the techniques, but the work ethic, the competition, the mindset it takes to succeed at the next level. Take that with you, apply it wherever you end up, and it'll make you better at everything you do."

He dismissed us, and everyone started heading toward the locker room.

If I said I wasn't riding high, I'd be lying.

Chapter 9

That night was the barbecue dinner, where families were invited to eat with their kids, and basically, the camp was starting to wind down. It was scheduled at our normal dinner time, so except for the media day that morning, the rest of the day was about the same.

I didn't do quite as well in the second scrimmage, mostly because they were playing heavier coverage on me and not pressing the pocket as much as they had that morning.

I guess the defensive coordinator realized I wasn't going to fold, as I had the day before. On the flip side, most of the spectators and the media people didn't stick around after lunch, so I guess if there was a time to really be on, I'd picked the right time to do it.

It was crazy, for as big as this camp was, we'd only gotten really three serious days of workouts in. Admittedly, even with the crazy schedule I was used to, the last few days had been some of the most grueling of my life.

Well, this life. It wasn't close to my memories of how I felt after a day working construction in the dream.

The cafeteria smelled pretty good when we got there. Actually, even better when you consider that on the other days, we came straight from practice, and today they sent us to get showers and change clothes.

The camp brought in a local company to cater dinner for everyone, and I was starved. I grabbed a plate and loaded it with brisket, ribs, and coleslaw, then spotted Ray waving me over to where his family had claimed a table near the edge of the gathering.

"Blake!" Charlie called out before I'd taken three steps in their direction. "Over here!"

Mrs. Clark smiled as I approached. "We saved you a spot."

"Thanks." I slid onto the bench next to Ray, who immediately elbowed me in the ribs.

"You looked good out there today," Mr. Clark said.

"Oh, you guys saw that?" I set my plate down and reached for the lemonade pitcher. "Some of the coaches weren't thrilled about my scrambling at the end. They prefer if I just keep to the pocket."

"They need to lighten up," Charlie said. "It's a game. It's supposed to be fun."

Raymond snorted. "Tell that to Blake's roommate."

"Former roommate," I corrected.

"What happened with your roommate?" Mrs. Clark asked.

I waved it off. "Just typical camp stuff. Got switched to a better situation."

"Define typical," Charlie asked.

"Nothing worth talking about."

"Which means it's definitely worth talking about," she said.

Raymond cut in before I could respond. "Trevor's an asshole who thought Blake needed to be hazed."

"Raymond," Mrs. Clark said sharply.

"Sorry, Mom. Trevor's a jerk who thought Blake needed to be hazed."

I just shrugged and dug into my food. Maybe it was the Texan in me, but Californians did not know how to do barbecue. It wasn't terrible, and I was definitely going for seconds, but it was a far cry from even mediocre brisket back home.

"So what are you doing the rest of the summer?" Charlie asked me.

"Training, mostly. Got another camp at the end of July, then school starts back up."

"That's it? No vacation?"

"This *is* the vacation."

She rolled her eyes. "That's the saddest thing I've ever heard."

"What about you?" I asked.

"Volleyball camp in early July. Then we're going to the beach for a week in August before school."

"Charlie's ranked in the state," Mrs. Clark said proudly.

"What? You are?"

"Top twenty in Georgia for her age group," Raymond added. "She doesn't like to brag."

"I can brag for myself when I want to brag," Charlie said. "I just don't think it's that interesting."

"I think it's interesting," I said.

"See? Even Blake thinks so."

Max Flores appeared at the end of our table, plate piled high with food. "Room here?"

"Always." I shifted over slightly to make space. "Guys, this is Max, one of my new roommates. He goes to school in Texas, too, although a different part of the state. He's a receiver."

Max half-waved and dropped onto the bench and immediately started attacking his food. "Man, I'm starving."

"How's camp been for you, Max?" Mr. Clark asked him.

Max swallowed before answering. "Better than I expected. Blake helped a lot with the extra practices."

"Yeah, Blake set up extra practices Tuesday and Wednesday nights for some of the guys."

"Really?" Mr. Clark asked.

"Just wanted more reps."

"He's being modest. He organized like ten guys," Max said. "I think the group of us improved more than anyone else at camp because of it."

"That's impressive," Mr. Clark said.

I shrugged. "We all needed the work."

Charlie was watching me again, that expression on her face like she was figuring something out. I focused on my coleslaw and tried to ignore her.

The conversation shifted to camp logistics, then to Georgia football, then to some story about Ray's freshman year that had everyone laughing except Ray himself. About halfway through dinner, just as I got my second plate, Mrs. Clark ran to the restroom, and Mr. Clark and Charlie both went to get more food. Max had already disappeared about five minutes before to go check in with one of the other guys.

That must have been a moment Ray was waiting for, because as soon as they were away from the table, he said, "So."

"So?"

"Charlie likes you."

I kept my expression neutral. "We get along."

"That's one way to put it."

"What's another way?"

"I'm just saying, I know when she's into someone. And she's into you."

"Good to know," I said, giving him a look.

The last time he'd brought this up, he'd warned me off of her, so I was confused by the way he changed things up.

Charlie and Mr. Clark returned, Charlie carrying a plate with a massive slice of chocolate cake. She sat down across from me and set it between us.

"Thought we could share."

"We?" I asked.

"Unless you're too full."

"I didn't say that."

Mrs. Clark returned and we spent another thirty minutes just chatting, too full to eat anything else.

"Oh," Charlie said, as it became clear that things were winding down. "Wait, I almost forgot."

She reached into her bag and pulled out another CD case. "Made you this one, too. Different songs from the other one."

I took it from her and flipped it over to read the track listing written in neat handwriting on the back.

"This is awesome," I said. "Thanks."

"No problem. I had fun making it."

"I'm going to run it up to my room so I don't forget it."

"I'll come with you," Charlie said immediately.

Mrs. Clark frowned slightly. "Charlie ..."

"We'll only be a few minutes," I said. "I'm just dropping it off, then we'll be right back."

Mrs. Clark looked at Mr. Clark, who shrugged. "Five minutes," she said finally.

"Ten," Charlie countered.

"Seven."

"Deal."

We left the table and headed across the field toward the dorms. The hallways were mostly empty; everyone still at the barbecue.

Technically, she wasn't supposed to be up in the player rooms, but I figured it was near the end of camp, so I probably wouldn't get in much trouble.

Besides, all the staff were at the dinner, so it wasn't like there was anyone to catch me. My new room was on the second floor, and I unlocked the door to find it blessedly empty.

"Nice setup," Charlie said, stepping inside and looking around. "Better than sharing with that Trevor guy?"

"Infinitely better," I said, setting the CD on my desk next to the other one she'd made me.

"Good."

I turned around and almost walked into her. She was standing close now, closer than necessary in the small room.

"We should probably head back," I said, but I didn't move toward the door.

"Probably."

She didn't move either.

"Your mom's going to time us."

"So we should make good use of the time we have."

My heart kicked up a notch. "What did you have in mind?"

Charlie stepped closer, close enough that I could smell whatever perfume or shampoo she used, something light and clean.

"What do you think we should do?" she asked.

"I think you're trying to get me in trouble with your parents."

"Maybe."

She tilted her head slightly, looking up at me.

Screw it.

I reached out and wrapped my hand around her waist, pulling her closer as I pushed her back against the post of the bunk bed. Her eyes widened slightly, surprised but not unhappy, and then I kissed her.

She responded immediately, her hands coming up to my shoulders, then one sliding into my hair. The kiss was hungry and urgent, nothing tentative about it, and I pressed closer until there was no space left between us. Her lips were soft, and she tasted like the chocolate cake from earlier, and when she made a small sound in the back of her throat, I felt it all the way through my chest.

I pulled back slightly, just enough to breathe, and she chased my mouth with hers. We kissed again, slower this time but no less intense, and I felt her fingers tighten in my hair. My hands stayed at her waist, thumbs brushing the strip of skin where her shirt had ridden up slightly.

Time stopped meaning anything. It could've been seconds, or minutes, or hours. All I knew was the feeling of her against me, the way she kissed me back like she'd been thinking about it for days, and the small sounds she made when I changed the angle.

Finally, reluctantly, I pulled back. We were both breathing hard and Charlie's face was flushed, her eyes bright.

"We should ..." I started, then stopped because I had no idea how to finish that sentence.

"Yeah," she said, although she sounded as sad about that as I felt.

I stepped back, giving her space, and she pushed off the bedpost. Her hair was slightly messed up where my fingers had been, and she tried to smooth it down.

"Do I look okay?" she asked.

"You look great."

"That's not what I meant."

"I know what you meant." I reached out and fixed a particularly wild section of hair. "You look fine. Normal."

We left the room, and I locked the door behind us. The walk back to the barbecue felt both too long and too short. I reached down and took her hand in mine.

It felt nice. Way different from how things had felt with Melanie. I had vague memories of a couple of serious relationships from the dream. I knew this wasn't going to be a thing; we lived too far apart, but right now I felt as comfortable as I ever had.

"For the record," she said as we approached the tables, "I'm glad I came to California."

"Yeah?"

"Yeah."

We found her family exactly where we'd left them. Mrs. Clark checked her watch and smiled. "Six minutes. Good timing."

"Told you we'd be quick," Charlie said, sliding onto the bench.

I sat next to Ray, trying to look casual and normal and like I hadn't just spent the last several minutes kissing his sister. Ray was watching Charlie, though, and I saw the exact moment he figured it out. Her face was still flushed, and she kept smiling for no apparent reason, glancing at me.

Raymond's eyes cut to me, narrow and suspicious.

I shrugged, going for innocent. I didn't think I pulled it off.

"Everything okay?" Mrs. Clark asked, looking between the three of us.

"Fine," Charlie said quickly. "Blake showed me his room. It's nice."

"Very nice," I agreed.

Ray made a noise that might've been a laugh or might've been a curse. Hard to tell.

Mr. Clark stood up, oblivious to the tension. "Well, we should really get going. Long drive back to the hotel."

Goodbyes were exchanged. Mrs. Clark shook my hand and told me again how good I looked out on the field.

They really were good people.

They started walking away, and Charlie followed, looking back over her shoulder once to wave. I waved back, ignoring the look Ray was giving me.

The next morning, we were back on the field. Thankfully, Ray didn't ask questions about the night before, although he had given me some looks as we headed back up to the dorms that night.

The next morning, we still had conditioning, and then they moved us all back out to the field. Today was for the relays before we had the awards and the end of camp.

The field became organized chaos as players milled about, trying to figure out what was going on. The field looked like it had been divided in half, with fifty yards given to a section. Those who weren't part of the two groups currently on the field would wait in the stands, watching, while the people currently competing were on the field.

Once those groups were done, they'd switch out, and the people on the field would go up in the stands while two more position groups came out and the coaches reset the field.

Thankfully, quarterbacks were one of the first groups up, along with receivers who were on the other side of the field.

"Okay, guys, here's how this is going to work," Daniels said. "There are five stations and you will rotate through them in order. Everyone competes at each one, we track scores, and the top scorer from each group gets recognized this afternoon." He pointed across the field where graduate assistants and volunteers were setting up equipment at marked intervals. "Station one is accuracy. You'll hit the targets. The more you hit, the more points you get. Station two is the speed and mobility course. Fastest time wins, but you get penalties for missed throws or mistakes. Station three is pure distance. Whoever throws the longest gets the most points. Station four tests your reads and reactions. Station five is a two-minute drill simulation. We'll weigh each station based on importance, but cumulative performance determines placement."

"Easy," Trevor said.

Jackass.

We all found our names on the list and headed to our starting positions. I was starting at station three, where two college players had marked off a corridor between the thirty and forty-yard lines with cones. Downfield, past the opposite goal line, they'd set up distance markers every five yards.

A graduate assistant with a stopwatch approached. "You're Blake? Okay, you get three throws. Each throw has to stay inside the corridor to count, and we measure where it lands. Your longest accurate throw is your score. Simple enough?"

"Got it."

"You'll go when the whistle blows. Get warmed up."

I grabbed a ball from the equipment bag and made a few loose tosses to one of the volunteers, working feeling back into my shoulder.

I nodded at him that I was ready and took my position at the thirty-yard line, gripped the ball, and dropped back three steps. I planted and threw, putting everything into it but trying to be mindful of the mechanics. The ball sailed downfield, clearing the goal line easily before dropping at the fifteen-yard marker on the far end.

"Forty-five yards," the assistant called out, marking it on his clipboard.

I reset for my second throw. This one had better trajectory, arcing higher before descending at the twenty.

"Forty-nine yards."

One throw left. I rolled my shoulder, trying to loosen the tightness creeping into the joint, then took my stance again. The wind had picked up slightly, coming from my left. I adjusted my aim and threw.

"Fifty-five yards. Nice work."

I nodded and moved to the next station while another guy took my place. Station four was the read and react challenge. Four sets of volunteers stood at different distances and spread apart, although they were all still pretty close together, with the furthest only about twenty yards away.

"I want you going through your reads. Eventually, one of the guys will flash his light for three seconds. You have to hit his partner before he switches off his flashlight, which represents how long that opportunity is available. Miss the read or miss the throw, no points for that sequence. Okay?"

"Yep."

"Good, here we go."

I went through my reads, one at a time. They knew how long, based on the book, I was to stop at each read, what order I was going in, so theoretically, if I timed it just right, I should look at the guy right as he turned on his light, giving me three seconds to set, throw, and hit my target.

An eternity. Assuming I saw the light right when it flashed on.

The first light was on when I got to my read. I'd gone too slowly, but I still managed to hit his partner before he turned off the light.

On the second one, I saw the light out of my peripheral vision and did get the throw off, but didn't connect in time. I'd overcompensated and rushed through my reads and was looking at the wrong part of the field when he'd turned on his light.

The third one, I slowed down too much again, and didn't connect.

The coach called out a new defensive coverage, which changed my reads.

I ended up hitting five and missing three, which wasn't as good as I would have hoped, but I wasn't sure how accurately this test really matched what a real game would look like. In a real game, I would adjust my reads based on the coverage and if it looked like a receiver might break free.

There were thousands of little tells.

Here, it was just a flashlight and a stopwatch.

I rotated to station five, the two-minute drill simulation. This station had multiple volunteers positioned as receivers running actual routes. The coach would call plays, and I had to execute the full sequence against a running clock.

"You've got two minutes to complete five passes," the coach said. "Short, intermediate, comeback, deep out, and red zone. We're tracking completion percentage and time remaining. Faster and cleaner is better."

The whistle blew.

"Slant route, left side!"

I took the snap from the center volunteer, dropped back three steps, and fired to the slant. Complete. The clock kept running.

"Out route, right side, fifteen yards!"

I found the receiver breaking to the sideline and threw. A little high, but he adjusted and caught it.

"Comeback, left side, twelve yards!"

The receiver ran upfield and broke back toward me. I threw before he turned. He should have still been able to get it, but he didn't even try. Part of me wanted to complain that he could have still gotten it, but I guess they were being sticklers.

Either I threw it textbook, hitting right where I should, or they'd just let it sail on by.

"Deep out, right side, twenty yards!"

I dropped back five steps this time, buying time for the route to develop. The receiver broke hard to the sideline. I threw across my body, leading him outside. He caught it at the sideline and dragged his feet. Complete.

"Red zone, corner of the end zone, back left!"

This was the hardest throw. I had to drop it over the linebacker's head but keep it away from the safety. I lofted the ball high and toward the back corner. The receiver jumped and came down with it.

The coach hit his stopwatch. "One minute, twelve seconds. Four for five. That's a solid score."

I moved to station one, the accuracy challenge. They'd set up garbage cans at three different distances, ten yards, twenty yards, and thirty yards. The ten-yard target was worth five points, twenty yards was ten points, and thirty yards was fifteen points. You had ninety seconds to throw as many times as you wanted, accumulating points for each successful hit.

Trevor was just finishing his turn when I arrived. He'd hit the close target four times but missed a bunch of his attempts at the deeper ones.

"Fifty-five points," the assistant called out.

Trevor saw me and grinned. "Let's see you beat that."

The whistle blew for the third rotation.

I grabbed a ball and threw it at the ten-yard target. Hit. Five points. I grabbed another ball and went for the twenty-yard target. Hit. Fifteen total. The close target again. Hit. Twenty points. I aimed for the thirty-yard target. The ball clanged off the edge of the can and bounced up and in. A lucky thirty-five points.

Time was running. I hit the ten-yard target twice more, then attempted the thirty-yard target again. Miss. I tried the twenty-yard target. Hit. My total climbed to sixty points with fifteen seconds left. I grabbed two more balls and fired both at the ten-yard target. Both hit.

"Time! Seventy points. Strong performance."

Trevor was at station three now, attempting his distance throws. His first attempt wobbled and curved outside the corridor. Penalty. His second throw was better, landing around the forty-five-yard mark. His third attempt had good distance but drifted right at the end, landing just outside the corridor. Another penalty.

"Forty-five yards is your score," the assistant told him.

I tried not to smile, knowing I was wiping the floor with him.

I headed to station two, the speed and mobility course. The setup looked brutal. Ten cones arranged in a zigzag pattern, three tackling dummies positioned to force lateral movement, and a final throw through a hanging tire at the end. Time penalties for missed obstacles or a missed throw.

"You've got one shot," the coach said. "Go on the whistle."

The whistle blew.

I sprinted forward, weaving through the first set of cones. At the first dummy, I dodged left, then right around the second one. The third dummy required a full stop and lateral shuffle. I executed it and burst forward again through the final cones. The tire hung twenty yards ahead. I planted, set my feet, and threw. The ball sailed through the center.

This kind of thing was exactly in my wheelhouse.

The coach checked his stopwatch. "Twenty-one seconds, no penalties. That's the top score so far."

And with that, I was done. I went and looked over Coach Daniel's shoulder to see the scores, and he was nice enough to dip the clipboard so I could see what he was writing.

Ray, of course, was killing it, way ahead of everyone else. Another guy was also ahead of me, but just barely. I was third, and Trevor was fourth.

I was satisfied with the results. I'd watched Ray play. He had a stronger arm than me and, while I could move faster, he could do reads and work out the plays much faster than I could.

Whether that was just experience, because he'd played so many more real games than me, or because he was just better than I was, was hard to tell.

I went with it being the first one, if for no other reason than to save my ego.

We then went up and into the stands to watch the rest of the groups perform. None of the guys from my extra practices, aside from Ray, was number one in their group, but none of them was at the bottom either.

I had to remind myself that these guys were all elite, so I shouldn't take it too hard, but it also gave me some stuff I needed to pay attention to this year.

Both for myself and for the other guys on the team. This was going to be my first year with a chance to go into the playoffs, and I really wanted to take us to state for the first time in more than two decades.

After that, we hit the showers and packed. Once we had the final ceremony and they gave out the awards, we'd get our stuff and it would be time to head to the airport.

While I wouldn't say this had been the perfect weekend, I was sad it was going to be over soon and a little shocked at how fast it had gone.

Chapter 10

We had a few hours for everyone to get ready for that afternoon's closing ceremony. I mostly spent the time hanging out with the guys I'd gotten to know over the week. I might see Max at playoffs this year, but other than that, I wasn't going to see anyone else. So, I wanted the chance to hang out one last time before we had to go.

Finally, they gathered us all up into a lecture hall that would seat all of us, the staff, and those parents who could attend.

Ray went to sit with his family, and I decided to sit with Max. I did that mostly because I thought I had kind of been attaching myself to Ray and his family a little too much, and I didn't want to overstay my welcome. Trevor was three rows ahead of us, surrounded by the other seniors from his group, where he was holding court.

I'm sure he didn't mention he ate it today on the relay.

Director Bob Carson, whom we honestly had not seen much of during the actual camp, took the podium once everyone had arrived.

"Good evening. I hope you all had a good week and learned a lot. I know this was probably a challenge for most of you, but this week was intense by design. We bring together the best young talent from across the country to compete at the highest level, and you've all risen to that challenge."

The prepared speech itself was maybe fifteen minutes with remarks about the camp's history, the importance of team sports for students, and the value of competing against elite peers. The speech was professional and rehearsed, hitting all the expected notes about dedication and potential.

Finally, he got to the part I was interested in.

"Tonight we recognize the outstanding performers in each position group," Carson said. "These awards aren't just about talent. They reflect work ethic, leadership, and the ability to elevate those around you. Let's start with our defensive backs."

The ceremony proceeded through each position. Then they announced the winner of the relay and the winner of the overall best player for each position. The relay played a part in that, but it was a judgment made based on their performance for the whole week, and not just the relay.

Although it was probably not a coincidence that, in most cases, they were still the same person.

It was not a shock that Ray was the leader in our quarterback group. It was also not a shock that he got announced as the overall camp MVP. Ray really was an amazing quarterback and all-around great guy. He absolutely deserved it, although Trevor made a 'what the hell' kind of gesture, looking around at his buddies when Ray got announced as the leader for the quarterbacks.

It honestly made me wonder if Trevor had paid attention at all this week.

Carson wrapped up with final remarks. "Take what you've learned here back to your schools and your communities. The techniques, the competitive edge, the friendships you've made. This camp is a starting point, not a destination. Your future success depends on what you do with this foundation. Thank you, and we look forward to seeing those of you off to the collegiate level next year and hope that those of you who still have a year or two of high school left will join us again next year."

People started standing as the ceremony concluded. Parents moved forward to find their kids, and the organized rows dissolved into clusters of conversation. I remained in my seat, watching Ray get congratulations from his family.

"Blake."

I turned to find Coach Daniels standing in the aisle. "Yes, sir?"

"Walk with me for a minute."

I followed him away from the main crowd to a quieter corner of the arena.

"I wanted to catch you before you left," he said. "I wanted you to know that you did very well this year at camp and, awards aside,

I was very impressed with what I saw. We've never had someone organize students needing additional work into their own extra practices before, and it honestly impressed most of us. That is the kind of leadership that will take you very far."

"I hope so."

"I just wanted to make it clear to you that that was considered in our ranking, and I didn't want you to think just because you didn't place in the top of the quarterbacks that it went unnoticed."

"I honestly wasn't expecting to get placed, but I appreciate you letting me know."

"Good. You've got some real God-given talent, but your work ethic and leadership are what're going to set you apart in the coming years. The only thing you were missing here this year was size and experience, both things you can get over the next two years. We haven't had very many sophomores here, but you should know you placed higher than any of the guys would have if they were just a year behind. Ray did not do as well at camp last year as you did this year. You are leaps and bounds ahead of the competition, comparatively."

"Thanks, Coach."

"Keep working, Blake. I expect to see big things from you in the next few years."

"I understand."

He nodded and walked back toward the main group, leaving me standing alone near the exit.

After a moment, I turned and headed the other way, back to the dorms where most of the guys were going. At this point, the camp was basically over, and everyone was headed to get the stuff they packed up before the closing ceremony and head home.

I didn't see anyone I was particularly friendly with upstairs, so I grabbed my bag and headed down to the lobby, where I asked the person manning the front desk to call me a cab.

It did earn me a look, but I ignored it. I was well aware it was unusual for me not to have someone here to pick me up, but what was I supposed to do?

I went outside where guys were saying goodbye, meeting up with their parents and loading bags, and just kind of milling around. I dropped my bag near the curb and waited.

"Blake," Max called out behind me, weaving through the crowd of people. "Waiting on a ride?"

"Yeah, I had them call me a cab so I can get to the airport."

"Oh, that makes sense. Didn't think ... anyway, it was great seeing you this week. Hopefully, we'll see each other in playoffs this year."

I laughed, although I didn't miss the fact that he didn't want to point out that I had no one here with me. "You really think you'll make it that far?"

"Better chance than you," he said, smiling.

"I'll remember that when I'm looking at my seven-on-seven trophy."

Talking shit was the basic form of communication in any sport.

"Ouch."

"If you get a free week before school starts back, you should come up to Wheaton sometime and visit."

"That would be cool, but we're heading to Vietnam in two weeks so we can spend a month there with my dad's family before school starts."

"Really? Damn, that's cool. I never get to go anywhere."

"You know, if you really wanted to do something, you could move to Wheaton and transfer. Just imagine how we'd crush it on the same team."

"Damn, I wish, but no way. My parents would never move."

"Never move where?" a Hispanic woman said, coming up to us, followed by an Asian man.

"Mom, Dad, this is Blake. Blake, these are my parents."

His dad extended his hand. "I'm Emilio, and this is Luisa."

He must have seen my confusion since, of all the names he could have had, Emilio was not what I was expecting.

"Dad was born in Mexico. His dad was from Vietnam. My grandmother's family is still there. That's who we're visiting."

"Oh, I'm sorry, I didn't ..."

"It's okay," his dad said. "You're not the first to give me that look. Don't worry about it."

"Still. Sorry. It's good to meet you, sir," I said, shaking his hand. "Ma'am."

"Good to meet you," his mother said with a very thick accent.

I switched to Spanish, hoping I didn't butcher it too badly. "Mucho gusto, Señora Flores. Su hijo es muy talentoso."

Her eyes widened, and then her whole face lit up. She responded in rapid Spanish that I only caught half of, something about Max and football and being proud.

"You speak Spanish?" Max's eyebrows shot up.

"Barely. One of my best friends, Eduardo ... his family's from Mexico. They've been teaching me, but I'm terrible at it."

"That was pretty good," Mr. Flores said. "Where'd you say you're from?"

"Wheaton. It's a small town ... middle of nowhere, basically."

She said something else in Spanish to her husband, too fast for me to follow. He nodded, then looked at me with new respect.

"She says you're very polite. That your parents raised you right."

Heat crept up my neck. "Gracias. That means a lot."

"Blake!" Ray called out, heading to join us, with his family trailing behind.

"Go. We need to get headed to the airport. It was good meeting you," Mr. Flores said.

"Of course. I'll see you around, Max?"

"Definitely. Thanks for everything, man. Those extra practices made a huge difference."

The Flores family moved off toward their car, as Ray stopped in front of me.

"So, we'll see you in a few weeks?" he asked.

"That's the plan. I'm just glad I'll know someone there."

"Yeah, I know what you mean. My first year, I didn't meet people until like the last day. It's better your second year because some of the juniors come back for their senior year. They don't say it, but the scouts pay attention to who's here. Of course, you and Max got a jump on that since you'll have three years most likely, which is rare."

"Yeah, I lucked out for sure."

"I mean it. The way you organized those practices, how you helped the other guys? That's leadership. Coaches notice that stuff."

Charlie appeared at Ray's elbow, and my stomach did a little flip. She'd pulled her auburn hair back in a ponytail, and it looked damn good.

"Hey."

"Hey, yourself." I tried to keep my voice normal, aware of Ray standing right there.

"So it's going to be your turn when you come to camp," Charlie said. "I showed you my music, so I expect you to make me a CD to show me yours."

"I guess that's only fair. You showed me yours, so I've got to show you mine," I said, not able to stop the joke before I realized what I was saying.

"For the love of God," Ray said.

"We're just talking about music, Ray," Charlie said like he was crazy for thinking anything else. "Get your mind out of the gutter."

"You two are killing me."

Mr. and Mrs. Clark joined us then.

"We're so glad we got to meet you," Mrs. Clark reached out and squeezed my arm. "You take care getting home, and we'll see you in Georgia."

"Yes, ma'am."

Mr. Clark said, shaking my hand, "Safe travels, Blake. And keep up the good work."

"I will. Thank you, sir."

They started to walk off, but Charlie said something to them that I couldn't hear and hurried back. They slowed, but at least they didn't turn to look at us. Charlie stepped up close, into my personal space, and I could smell that shampoo of hers again.

"So I guess this is goodbye for now."

"I guess so."

She opened her arms, and I stepped into the hug, hyperaware of her parents a few feet away. It lasted maybe three seconds, appropriate and friendly, but my heart hammered anyway. When she pulled back, her cheeks were slightly pink.

"I'll see you soon."

"Looking forward to it."

"Stop groping her, we've got to go," Ray called, having stopped to look back at us.

"Ray!" Charlie's face went redder.

Mrs. Clark sighed. "Raymond Thomas Clark, leave your sister alone."

Ray held up his hands in surrender, still grinning, "Fine, fine."

Charlie caught my eye one more time, her smile soft, before Ray herded his family toward their car. I watched them go, feeling both lighter and heavier somehow.

The cab picked that moment to pull up. The driver popped the trunk and I grabbed my duffel, hoisting it into the back. Through the parking lot, I could see Max's family getting into their SUV and Ray's family climbing into their minivan. The camp was emptying out, everyone heading back to their regular lives.

I stopped for a moment, watching them. I'd been excited about this camp since Coach Moreno had mentioned it, and on the football side, it was everything I'd thought it would be and more.

What I hadn't considered was the personal side. Getting to know Max better, meeting Ray, and, more importantly, meeting Charlie. I thought about that kiss in my room last night. She wasn't the first girl I'd kissed, but compared to Brandy and Melanie, she was completely different.

I don't think I'd ever clicked with anyone as fast as I'd clicked with her.

And now we were just going back to our lives, which still seemed a million miles away. Going back to Mom's sickness and our deal, to figuring out how to pay for her treatment, to dealing with Josh.

It was like I'd gotten to live a different life for the last five days. And honestly, I didn't want it to end.

The cab driver leaned out the window. "You getting in or what, kid?"

"Yeah, sorry."

I slid into the backseat, and the driver pulled away from the curb. I watched USC's campus recede through the rear window and felt a little sad.

Chapter 11

Between the plane not leaving until six California time, a layover, and the time change, it was crazy late when I got home the night before. I'd gone straight to my room, dropped my bag, and passed out hard.

By the time I got up, the sun was well up and my clock told me it was after noon. I still felt like crap and wanted to roll back over and go to sleep, but the last thing I needed to do was sleep all day and stay up all night.

I shuffled down the stairs, half asleep, and saw Dad sitting at the kitchen table, eating a sandwich. I didn't see Mom or Josh, and didn't know if they were at some activity, but him eating lunch by himself suggested they were out together.

"Morning," I mumbled.

"Look who finally dragged himself out of bed."

"Sorry I slept so late."

"I know, it's okay. I was just messing with you."

I stopped and looked at him for a second, hearing something in his voice. "You sound awful chipper."

"Can't I be in a good mood on a Saturday?"

"It's suspicious," I said, grabbing a bowl, milk, and cereal and taking them to the table, fixing myself a bowl.

He chuckled and folded the paper. "Ha, well, I guess I've had a good week."

"Damn, celebrating that I'm not here. I see how it is."

"Come on, Blake," he said.

"Sorry. What happened then?" I said, heading back to the fridge to put the milk away.

"For starters, your mother went to the doctor. Got some tests done, bloodwork and all that. First real checkup she's had since last fall."

I paused, my hand in the fridge, putting the milk back. I kept my back to him for a moment, letting the wave of relief wash over me. It worked. Yes, she'd agreed, but agreeing wasn't going, so hearing she'd actually gone was a massive relief.

"That's great," I said, turning around and trying to sound casual. "Hope it went okay."

"It's a start," he said, and the optimism in his voice was so strong it almost hurt to hear. He'd been carrying so much stress, and for the first time in what felt like forever, a little of it had lifted. "The doctor said that the seizure and headaches could have been caused by a lot of things, so they did some blood work as a first step, and we've got a referral to see a neurologist."

I sat down at the table, taking a bite of cereal. I still felt a little guilty about how this had gone down, what I'd had to do, but hearing Dad talk, hearing that small bit of hope, I knew I'd do it again.

"Okay. So, that has me thinking. I know that stuff can get expensive, all the tests and specialists and everything. I also know insurance doesn't always cover everything. I just want you to know that anything you need, any of the money I've been making, I know we've talked about how to set some of it aside for this or that, but none of that matters if it's needed for her treatment. I want you guys to use the money for whatever we need for her treatment. Her health comes first."

He put his sandwich down and looked at me hard, the joking smile from a few minutes before gone, replaced by something more serious. More thoughtful.

"I appreciate that, Blake, more than you know, but that actually touches on something I wanted to talk to you about."

"Okay?"

"We got the payout from the recent bets, including your hunch about the Rockets in the playoffs. And it paid off big."

I relaxed. As surprises go, that wasn't really one. I always knew how it was going to end, but I guess it was a lot of money. Dad might have been supportive, but we were betting more money than ever before, which would make anyone second-guess.

"Good. What's the final total?"

"A lot. Betting on their run to the finals from where they started brought in one hundred and eighty thousand alone, but that's the small stuff. The bet on it being a four-game sweep against Orlando came back at just over five hundred thousand. This is more money than any of us have ever seen at one time, Blake. We thought things were big when you were at two hundred thousand total, but with your other winnings, minus what we put into these bets, you are sitting at just over nine hundred thousand dollars. This is ... this is a life-changing amount of money, Blake. And that doesn't even count the hundred thousand you have sitting in the Amazon investment."

More than a million dollars, all in. I know this had been my idea, and I'd even sketched out how much I stood to win once the bets were all done and paid out, but seeing the amount on a scratch pad was still theoretical.

Having it in an account and accessible was something else altogether.

"That's ..." I started, but my voice trailed off as I tried to process what we were talking about. "That's amazing. That will set us up. We can afford anything Mom needs now. Anything."

"I know, and trust me, I am very happy that you've managed this because our deductible for the neurologist is already very high and your mom isn't working anymore but ... It also created a few problems."

"What do you mean?"

"The kind we've already talked about. You can't win this kind of money, especially in sports betting, have the streak you've been on, and not have it become obvious. Winning fifty thousand is one thing. Winning five hundred thousand puts you on people's radar, and the casinos aren't stupid. Even with our throwaway bets, we're so far ahead they are starting to lose real money on us, and they are businesses. When someone wins like this on long-shot prop bets, they notice. We played our hand too big with this one and we've apparently tripped every security flag imaginable. We split the bets out across multiple casinos, but they apparently talk enough to share security concerns, and I have had calls from higher-ups at several of the casinos."

Part of me thought, so what. We'd won fair and square. Of course, the rest of me knew Vegas had once been owned by mobsters and, at least according to the movies, had never fully left that history behind.

"What did they say?"

"They congratulated me on my winnings and suggested that I shouldn't continue betting at their establishments. A few didn't straight out suggest I wasn't welcome anymore, but they put limits on how much I could bet and suggested I should not be as successful with my win streak as I had been. All together it means except for some small-time stuff that isn't really worth the flights to Vegas and the time it takes, we're basically done with the sports betting."

"We knew that was coming, though, right? Could we go back to your friend, not for large bets, but for bets the size of what we were doing at the beginning?"

"No. They're paying attention now and they are very good at seeing patterns. I guess if you were just doing up and down bets to win, but even then I'd worry they might figure it out, and I don't want to get my friend in trouble."

"Yeah, okay," I said.

We'd talked about this. I'd even made the call to Mr. Henderson because of it. But seeing the amount of money we'd made when we went from betting a few hundred or thousand to betting twenty or thirty thousand on prop bets, made part of me wished we could keep going.

Unlike the setup with Mr. Henderson, which I wasn't a hundred percent sure could actually be turned into money, this was something I understood. The established betting market on sports games, that made sense to me. I didn't even know if it was possible to make money knowing who would president or big stuff like that.

Yeah, okay, I knew the Amazon thing, but that and Google were basically the only businesses I knew were going to make it big, and Google wasn't even a thing yet.

Or at least, I didn't think it was.

But what happened was what happened. Wishing it was something else didn't do me any good.

"We knew this would happen eventually," I admitted. "I'd always said the betting was a short-term thing. As long as we keep winning more than we lose, the odds against us get shorter until the whole thing falls apart."

"Well, it's fallen apart."

"That's okay. I'm already working on a plan. A way to keep rolling that money into something bigger."

Dad went from looking apologetic to suspicious, giving me that cop look he had. "What plan?"

This was the conversation that I had known I would have to have eventually.

"So my hunches. They aren't just about sports."

"You're going to have to explain more about that."

"Here's the problem, and why I haven't really said anything. I don't really know how to explain it," I said, which was mostly true. "And I definitely don't know how to turn what I have knowledge about into actual investments. Sports betting, yes, but everything else, not a clue. So I set up a meeting with Mr. Henderson."

"I'm not sure that's a good idea, Blake. The Amazon thing was a huge ask, and we had Mr. Plummer backing us up. I'm not sure you want to keep pushing your luck."

"I know. This is different."

"I don't understand any of this. First sports betting, and now this. Blake, you have to tell me what's going on. You have to tell me how you know these things."

That was something I still wanted to avoid. Yes, I had proof that what I said was true, at least in as much as I was right when I said something was going to happen, but explaining it was a dream I had a year ago made no sense, even to me.

It bordered on the supernatural, and telling your parent you were unusual could only end badly. The odds of an overreaction were too high. Telling someone who told someone else, until I ended up in a lab somewhere being experimented on.

If I didn't say anything, people would come to their own conclusions. Besides, he had Mom to worry about, and I still needed him to trust me enough that I could get him to act on Josh. The last thing I wanted was another family member to be a problem for him.

"I can, and I will, if you really want me to. But I'm telling you right now, it's not going to make things easier. It's going to make them harder, because none of it is going to make any sense to you, and it will just bring up more questions, which I won't have answers for. Not for any of it. I don't even have them for myself. I know you say it will be okay and you're here for me, but you're going to get concerned, and it's going to change our relationship. With everything that's going on with Mom, I don't think you need that and I definitely don't need that. Between Mom and Josh, our family isn't doing great, and our relationship, yours and mine, is the one area where there isn't a huge problem. I'd prefer if we kept it like that. We can talk about the stuff I'm doing, and I'll explain it, but I'm telling you now the how will be a problem, and I wish you'd just accept it for what it is."

He studied my face, searching for something. "Are you doing anything illegal? Is someone giving you inside information? Are you in some kind of trouble?"

"No. Nothing like that. Nothing illegal, I swear. I just know things. I have hunches that come true. Always, although not necessarily exactly how I see them."

I added in that last part because some of the memories from the dream were sketchy at best. Dream me didn't always pay enough attention, and I only knew what I knew in the dream, so sometimes I was half-guessing.

"What are you going to tell Mr. Henderson to get him to listen to you?" he asked after a minute. "How are you going to get his help? You can't just tell him you get hunches. Like I said, the Amazon investment was a one-time thing. Managing money based on hunches is another."

"I'm working on that. I already talked to him before I left for camp. I knew he wouldn't just take my word for it, so I gave him things to get proof that my hunches are right."

"Proof? What kind of proof?"

"I made some predictions, things that it would be impossible to guess, and spread them across different areas so the information couldn't all come from one place. When those all come true, he will, I hope, have enough proof to believe me."

He leaned back in his chair, a slow, weary motion. He looked at me for what felt like an eternity, his gaze filled with fear, pride, and profound confusion. He looked at me like he was seeing a stranger sitting at his kitchen table.

"I trust you, Blake. You're a good kid, and I'll back your play. I just hope you know what you're doing, son," he finally said, his voice quiet.

"Me too, Dad," I said. "Me too."

After talking to Dad, I basically did nothing the rest of the day. After how go, go, go I'd been for the last six months, it was nice to just lie around and do nothing. I went to bed early and slept in again on Sunday.

I knew it wouldn't last, and my practices with Coach Moreno would be starting back up after the second camp, so I wanted to take advantage of the time I had.

Unfortunately, it didn't last as long as I wanted. When I came down for a very late lunch on Sunday, I found a list of chores from Dad on the kitchen counter. It wasn't a lot, but it was a lot for how lazy I was feeling.

What I'd rather be doing was going to hang out with my friends, but Eduardo wouldn't be back from visiting family in Mexico until sometime in July. Li would be in China for another two weeks at least. I'd called the house yesterday after talking with Dad about the gambling money, hoping maybe she'd come back early, but her mom said she was having a good time and would probably stay the full month.

Not that anyone wanted to know how I felt about it. Her mom did confirm that I had my first lesson coming up with her friend, so at least there was that to look forward to.

I decided that taking care of the anthill by the back fence was first on my agenda. The thing had tripled in size since I left for camp into a sprawling mound of dirt that stretched nearly a foot across.

The garage was cluttered with the usual mess, my dad's tools scattered across the workbench, boxes of Christmas decorations stacked against one wall, and my old bike that I'd outgrown two years ago, but nobody had bothered to get rid of.

The ant poison was on the shelf near the back, behind the paint cans. My dad kept all the yard chemicals together, organized in a way that made sense only to him. I picked my way through the boxes and around the lawnmower, trying not to knock anything over, wondering why we had to jam everything into a wobbly stack that I had to fight with anytime I needed something.

When I got over there, the first thing I noticed was that something smelled wrong. Not the usual smell this end of the garage had, a mixture of paint and chemicals from all the stuff stacked over here, but something else. Something sweet and rotten at the same time, the kind of smell that made my stomach turn over.

I stopped, trying to figure out where the smell was coming from. I moved closer to the back wall where the shelves were, and the smell got stronger. Worse.

There were boxes stacked near the opposite corner from the chemicals, where my mom had put a bunch of stuff years ago and never moved them since. That's when I noticed the flies. There were always flies, but this was a lot more than normal. Weirder still, they were all bunched up in this one corner. I leaned over them, looking for the source of the smell, and saw something dark tucked behind the bottom box.

Pulling the box forward, the smell hit me full force. I jerked back, my hand coming up to cover my nose and mouth.

A cat. A very dead cat.

It was gray and white, or had been before whatever happened to it. Now it was just a mess with its fur matted and its body stiff and bloated. As soon as I uncovered it, the swarm of flies became a small cloud, scattering as I exposed the body. The smell was so thick I could taste it in the back of my throat.

I backed up fast, my stomach heaving. I made it to the garage door before I had to stop and breathe, gulping down fresh air that didn't smell like death.

Jesus.

I stood there for a minute, hands on my knees, waiting for my stomach to settle. The cat must have crawled in somehow. There was probably a gap under the wall or near the door, some opening big enough for an animal to squeeze through. Maybe it had been hurt, hit by a car or something, or maybe it had just been sick. Either way, it got in, couldn't get back out and it died there behind the boxes where nobody would see it until the smell got bad enough to notice.

What was clear was that I couldn't just leave it there. The smell would only get worse, and it would attract God knows what else.

I needed a shovel. And a garbage bag. The heavy-duty kind, the black ones my dad used for yard waste.

I grabbed the shovel Dad kept leaning against the wall near the door and garbage bags from a shelf above the workbench. I actually stopped and went back for a second garbage bag, just in case one wasn't enough. I pulled my shirt up over my nose and mouth, even though I knew it wouldn't help much, and headed back to the corner.

The cat was small, probably not full-grown, and it wasn't a stray. I didn't recognize it as one of my neighbors' cats, but it had a little collar on it, although no tag that I could see. It had been someone's pet.

I shook out one of the garbage bags and laid it on the ground near the body. Then I slid the shovel under the cat, trying not to look at it or breathe too deeply. The body was stiff enough that it came up in one piece, and I transferred it quickly into the bag. I then, as carefully as I could, tied the bag shut so as not to touch it and then put that bag inside the second one and tied that shut too.

The smell was still there, but at least now it was contained. I carried the bags outside, holding them away from my body as far as possible, and set them by the side of the house where the trash cans were.

I was heading back to the garage to clean up the spot where the cat had been when my mom's voice stopped me.

"Blake?"

I turned. She was standing in the doorway from the house to the garage, wearing the same clothes she'd had on yesterday. Her hair was messy, and she had one hand pressed to her temple like she was trying to hold her head together. But her eyes were clearer than they'd been in weeks. She'd gotten some pain meds from the doctor, and clearly, they were working better than that herbal shit she'd been taking.

"What's all the banging? What are you doing?"

I gestured to the garbage bags. "I was going to start doing chores, and I found a dead cat in the garage. I think maybe it got hit by a car or something and crawled in here and died behind some boxes."

"Oh." She moved closer, one hand still on her temple. "That's awful. Poor thing."

"Yeah. I already bagged it up, although I think it will take a while for the smell to go away. Don't worry, I took care of it."

She gave me a look, reaching out and putting a hand on my shoulder.

"You're a good boy," she said.

"Thanks," I said.

She squeezed my shoulder once and then let go, turning back toward the house.

"Don't forget to wash your hands when you come in."

"I won't."

I could see why Dad looked so much lighter, less weighed down, yesterday. While the headaches weren't gone, she was starting to act like her old self again.

I'd honestly forgotten how much I missed her.

Chapter 12

I got back on the field on Monday, did the practices that Coach Moreno had laid out. I didn't have sessions with him this month, since I had another camp before long. But I knew he wouldn't take that as a reason I could slack off on practicing what I was supposed to learn.

Besides, I had new stuff to work on from the last camp. I might have hated how much time I'd spent in development, but they knew what they were doing when it came to drilling and teaching skills, and I'd learned things there that I could completely apply to my game.

Although I did miss someone helping me set up cones and targets after every play.

I was sweating bullets when I finally dragged myself back home. But I felt good having gotten some work in.

The phone was ringing when I opened the door. Mom must be lying down, Dad was at work, and I guess Josh didn't feel like he needed to answer anything.

I grabbed it and said, a little out of breath, "Hello?"

"Blake, this is Corey Henderson. I'm in town and thought we might meet this afternoon if you're available."

I glanced at the clock on the microwave: two fifteen.

"Yeah, that works. Where were you thinking?"

"The feed store, if that suits you. I have some business with Darren, so I'm here already. Say, three o'clock?"

"Perfect. I'll see you then."

I hung up and headed upstairs to take a quick shower and change out of my sweat-soaked shirt, although I'm not sure how much good it would do, since I had to make the fifteen-minute walk to the feed store after, and would work up another good sweat getting there.

As usual, Coach Plummer was behind the counter, talking to some customers. He saw me and pointed back to the office. Mr. Henderson was already there, sitting behind Coach's desk, doing some work when I knocked and opened the door.

"Blake," he said, half-standing and extending his hand. "Thanks for meeting me on such short notice."

"No problem."

Henderson sat back down and folded his hands on the desk. "Your father won't be joining us?"

"No, just me for now."

His eyebrows rose slightly. "I see. And he's comfortable with that?"

"He knows I'm meeting you," I said, which wasn't true, but I had mentioned I was working on something with Mr. Henderson and he'd only told me to be careful. "But I'd prefer that the specifics be kept between you and me ... unless there's paperwork involved."

"That's a big ask. You're a minor, so there is a limit to the kinds of things you can agree to without a parent or guardian present."

"I know. When we get to that, I will get him involved. Once I explain everything, I hope you'll see that we are on some unusual ground and I worry about how everything will worry him. Plus, he's got enough to deal with, what with my mom being sick and all."

"Oh, I'm sorry to hear that," he said, and then studied me for a long moment, the kind of look that probably worked well in business negotiations. "Talking about unusual grounds, I have to know, how did you predict those three things? The popularity of the Canadian girl's record, I guess you could have just flipped a coin on, but the other two. I'm not much of a sports guy, but I looked it up and no one thought the Rockets were going to sweep like that, and I'm not sure, short of you having a source inside the Olympic committee, how you could have known about Salt Lake City. How could you possibly have known those things were going to happen?"

I'd practiced this part in my head ever since I made the call to him a week and a half ago, knowing this exact question was coming. "This is the part that gets hard to explain. I get these hunches. I can't explain how they work or where they come from, but they are always right. It's how I made the money I'm investing with you, through sports betting. But that's coming to an end because the casinos don't like how much I'm winning."

"I can imagine not. These hunches, do they come frequently?"

"Often enough. Not every day, and they're kind of random, but most of the things I know turn out to be big. Big enough that most people would know about them after the fact. Here's the thing. Like I said, my mother's been sick and had to stop working, and the police department can only pay so much. We've got medical bills coming up and I'm paying for private coaching for football. What I need to do is find a way to turn these hunches of mine into money without ending up in jail or with the feds investigating me. I knew how to make money off of sports, but, like I said, that's coming to an end."

"So what kind of things do you get hunches about, besides sports?"

"Major events mostly. Stuff that everyone, or at least a lot of people, would be aware of. It's hit or miss, like I said, so some things I might think are big I have no idea about, while other things some people might miss I do know about."

"Can you give me examples?"

I'd prepared for this too. "O.J. Simpson is going to be acquitted when the verdict comes down in ... sometime late this year. I'm not sure if it's late summer or fall, but I think it's in the fall. There's going to be a major Amtrak derailment that's going to hurt a lot of people, but I don't know specifically when or which train, just that it's going to happen in the next like four or five months and will be big news."

"If a lot of people are going to get hurt, shouldn't we tell someone? Warn them?"

"Who? If I go to Amtrak or the government and say, 'Hey, I have a hunch that there's going to be a derailment,' do they believe me? I can't tell them what train, I can't tell them when exactly, and I can't tell them where. How do they act on that? And more importantly, once it does happen, do they come back after and assume I knew something specific about it, that maybe I was involved somehow?"

"That's a very good point, I hadn't considered that."

"It's why I don't tell my dad specifics about my hunches. He's a cop and he's going to do what a cop does when he hears that people are going to get hurt, and in turn, he's going to get himself and me hurt because no one will believe that I just somehow know this stuff. Best case, I get put in some kind of facility and jacked up on Thorazine or whatever. Worst case, I end up in a prison cell."

"Then why are you telling me?"

"Because I also have my mother to think about, and you don't know me outside of investments. You're less likely to try to 'save' me if you think this was some kind of psychosis. Also, because you are a businessman, and you want to make money. I hope that since our only connection is financial, you won't want to kill the goose that lays the golden egg."

Henderson's mouth quirked slightly, not quite a smile. "You're remarkably pragmatic for a fifteen-year-old."

"I'm motivated. My mom needs treatments that are expensive, my training is important for me to reach my goal, which is also expensive, and my family is struggling with bills as it is, since my mom isn't able to work. So I have to do what I have to do."

"When you came to me with the Amazon idea, that wasn't from reading articles, was it?"

"No."

"What do you actually know?"

I'd debated how much to reveal, how much would convince him without making him think I was completely insane or worse, take the idea and run with it.

"The investments we've made mean we'll both be private plane rich in the next fifteen years. Generational wealth rich in thirty. But I don't have time to wait on that. It's the long play, and I need money *now*. So I need to make us both serious money in the short term."

Henderson's face stayed carefully neutral, but by the way he went stock still, I knew that what I had said had an effect that nothing else I'd said had.

"I see. So what do you need me to do?"

"I need you to figure out how to profit from the things I know. I need you to turn what I know into financial bets and do it in a way that doesn't get us in trouble. I'm not sure exactly how 'insider trading' works, but I know that if we make a constant run of perfect bets, someone's going to call us on it, eventually."

"That's a legitimate concern. The SEC doesn't look kindly on patterns of unusual trading success, especially when it involves advance knowledge of events."

"Right. So we need to be smart about it, spread things out, make it look like we're just really good at analysis or lucky or whatever. The other thing is that I'll only give you information for roughly six months ahead at a time."

"Why?"

"Let's call it my safety net. Like I said, we don't know each other very well. While I do generally trust you and think you're a good guy – and Coach Plummer vouches for you, I don't actually know you. If I told you everything I know right now, there's an outside chance you might decide you don't need me anymore and shut me out."

"A little insulting, but also pragmatic."

"I wasn't saying it to accuse you of anything. I actually don't think you'd be like that, but this is my one bet to save my family, so I have to be careful. On that front, here's the actual deal I'm wanting to make. I want you to form an investment company. I want to be the majority owner, sixty percent, and you get forty. You're going to do all the work, handle the day-to-day operations, make the actual trades and deals. At the beginning, it will be something you can do on the side. But it will become a full-time thing at some point, and I want you to be prepared for that. In return, I will seed us with half a million dollars and hand you information that's literally impossible to have. Information that will make you obscenely wealthy."

The office fell quiet except for the sound of the store outside the office door and the hum of the air conditioning unit in the window. Henderson stared at me for a long time. This was my big play. I knew that this was a big ask that came with huge risk, but I hoped he'd see what I was offering, how utterly unique it was, and take the chance.

"If we structure it that way, we're going to want to make it a real investment company. Diversify, throw money into legitimate investments that might lose, build a track record that looks organic rather than impossibly successful."

"That's what I was trying to do with the gambling, vary my bets so that I didn't win every time. I still went too big, though. I got greedy."

"We have time to think carefully through the structure." Henderson pulled a notepad from his briefcase and uncapped a pen. "What information do you have for me now?"

I'd looked at my list before coming over here, memorized the things I was willing to tell him. "This will get us through Christmas. Microsoft is going to have a huge launch with Windows ninety-five. I know there is already a lot of talk about it and people think it's going to be a big deal, but they are underestimating it. It's going to be huge, like change the computer industry huge. There will be midnight sales and lines out the door, and it's going to result in major profits for them this year. Also, Disney is going to have an amazing year because of an animated movie they're making called *Toy Story.* It's going to come out, and it will become one of the biggest animated movies ever. Cable news is going to go into overdrive once the O.J. trial reaches closing arguments, and like I said, he gets acquitted this fall, I think."

"Are you certain about that?"

"I am. Everyone's going to remember that 'if it doesn't fit, you must acquit.'"

He gave me a look of confusion at that and said, "The evidence seemed fairly conclusive from what I've read."

"Doesn't matter. Jury's going to acquit. The Bosnian war is going to reach a peace agreement, umm, I don't know when, but soonish. The PlayStation is going to be released in the U.S. and it's going to be a massive hit for Sony. It's going to change the video game industry. And the Israeli Prime Minister is going to be assassinated sometime near the end of the year. I think it's the end of this year. That one could be next year. I'm a little fuzzy on the timeline."

"That's quite a wide range."

"I know. If I get any more hunches between now and when we talk next, I'll let you know. A lot of what I know is sports-related, though, and I'm not sure I'll be able to gamble much anymore. On that note, I'm going to need to pull out some income each time we have a success to cover my mom's medical expenses and my training costs. The rest, however, I am okay rolling over into more investments."

"That should be doable."

"So, are you on board?" I asked.

I'd already given him six months of tips, but I hoped it was enough to whet his appetite and get him on board.

Henderson set down his pen and met my eyes.

"Yes. To be honest, I was already suspicious after the Amazon proposal. You knew too much for having just read about it in magazines, and this conversation confirms that you seem to genuinely know things you shouldn't be able to know. So here's what I propose ... I'll go ahead and set up the investment company as you outlined, sixty-forty split with you as majority owner. We'll structure it properly and create the paper trail we need to make it legitimate. We'll sit down once a month to discuss new information and adjust our positions."

I hadn't expected him to move that fast. "Just like that?"

"Just like that." A small smile crossed his face. "I've spent thirty years working in this business, Blake. I know an opportunity when I see one, even when I don't fully understand the mechanism behind it. If you can deliver even *half* of what you're suggesting, we'll both do very well. It's a gamble, but with me only investing time, and you putting up the cash, I have very little to lose and a whole lot to gain. There's another consideration, which is what to do about your father. He's going to need to know something, since you're fifteen and can't sign contracts on your own."

"That's a valid concern. I told him that you and I were talking and that I had a way to do the same thing I was doing with gambling in other areas. He has been helping me with the gambling already, but I want to be careful."

"Here's what we can do. I'll present it as an investment vehicle for managing the sports betting winnings you have already won, which is essentially true." Henderson picked up his pen again. "But I won't offer additional details unless he asks directly."

"Don't tell him specifics about my hunches. Keep it vague, let him think it's just me being smart about sports, and betting or lucky with guesses."

"I can agree to that with one condition. If things start getting out of control, if I think this is going somewhere dangerous, or if I believe you're in over your head in a way that could hurt you ... I will bring your father into the conversation fully. I won't deceive him about his family like that."

Honestly, it was a fair condition. Better to have him willing to break confidence if things went bad than to have him keep quiet and let me crash and burn.

"Okay. That's fair."

"Good." Henderson made a note on his pad. "I'll start the paperwork for the company formation tomorrow. We should have everything ready to file within two weeks. In the meantime, I'll begin researching Microsoft and Disney, and figure out the best entry points and position sizes. The O.J. trial information is valuable but hard to monetize directly, though there may be some media company plays we can make."

"What about the other stuff? The PlayStation launch, the peace agreement?"

"Sony's stock could be interesting, and defense contractors often shift when peace agreements materialize. I'll need to think through the best approaches. The Israeli Prime Minister's assassination is troubling from a moral standpoint, but if you don't know the specific timing, it's difficult to act on in any event."

"I don't like knowing things like that either," I admitted. "But I can't stop them, and sitting on information that could make us money doesn't help anyone."

"That is a little cold."

"It's practical." I stood up, feeling like the hard part was over. "I should let you get back to whatever you were doing."

Henderson rose as well, extending his hand again. "I'll call you once I have the corporate documents drafted. We can meet with your father at that point and get everything signed and official. After that, we'll establish our monthly meeting schedule."

I shook his hand, surprised at how normal it felt to be making business deals worth hundreds of thousands of dollars while wearing a T-shirt that said "Just Do It."

The walk home was just as hot as the walk there, but at least I didn't have the meeting to worry about, as I did on the way there.

Dad's cruiser was in the driveway when I got home, which meant he'd worked the early shift and maybe stayed a bit late. Honestly, it was hard to keep up with his schedule sometimes. They were a small department, so guys were always having to swap with each other to maintain coverage when someone needed off, so they might work different shifts almost every week.

I could hear him talking in the kitchen as I went in the front door.

"Blake, that you?" he called out when he heard the door close.

"Yeah, it's me."

I found him sitting at the kitchen table with a stack of paperwork spread in front of him, the phone tucked between his shoulder and ear while he scribbled notes on a yellow legal pad. He held up one finger, indicating he'd be done in a minute, and I grabbed a Dr. Pepper from the fridge while I waited.

"Alright, I'll see you tomorrow morning," he said, finally hanging up the phone. He looked me over, taking in my khakis and polo shirt. "I thought you were working out down by the school. What's with the fancy clothes?"

"I called it off today at two. It was just too hot. Mr. Henderson called right when I got home and said he was in town and wanted to meet."

"How'd that go?"

"Better than I expected, actually. He agreed to help me set up the investment company we talked about."

"Just like that?"

"Well, not exactly 'just like that.' Remember I told you I gave him some predictions to verify my knowledge before I went to camp? Well, all three came true, so he's kind of convinced now that my hunches are legitimate. I mean, he's skeptical, but since I'm going to put up the money and he just has to do the work, it's enough upside for him to agree to it."

"You're putting up the money?"

"Yes. Mr. Henderson's going to handle all the legal paperwork and the actual investing. He'll do all the day-to-day stuff, and I'll provide the information about what to invest in and when, and we'll split the profits sixty-forty with me holding the majority stake. We'll start with five hundred thousand from my sports betting money and keep four hundred thousand in reserve for Mom's medical bills and whatever else comes up."

"Five hundred thousand." Dad repeated the number slowly, like he was testing how it sounded. "That's a lot of money to trust to someone, even someone Mr. Plummer vouches for."

"I know it is, but he's been good to us so far, and I'm going to trust he has enough greed not to screw me. I'm not giving him all the information at once, so if he thinks this will make us serious money long-term, he has way more incentive *not* to screw us. And I trust Coach Plummer's opinion. He's known Mr. Henderson for years, and you said yourself that he's a good judge of character."

Dad picked up his pen and started tapping it against the legal pad, a nervous habit that usually meant he was wrestling with a decision.

"What kind of paperwork are we talking about? What would I need to sign?"

"Like I said, he's going to handle setting up the LLC and all the investment accounts, but since I'm only fifteen, I need an adult to co-sign everything. Technically, you'd be listed as the primary account holder or held in trust or something; we'll figure that part out, but we'll have an agreement that gives me control over the investment decisions. I know it sounds complicated, and I know you're probably wondering if I really understand what I'm getting us into."

"Are you asking me if I think you know what you're doing?"

"I guess I am, yeah."

"Do you think you know what you're doing?" He switched back to cop mode, all questions, no answers.

I considered the question seriously before answering. In my dream life, I'd been financially irresponsible and made terrible decisions with money, but that Blake hadn't known what was coming. This Blake had advantages the other one never had.

"I think so, but I'm not going to pretend it's not risky. Any investment is risky, even when you know what's supposed to happen. But I also know that doing nothing is risky too, especially with Mom's medical situation. Those brain scans and specialist appointments aren't going to be cheap, and if she needs surgery or long-term medication, we're looking at expenses that could wipe out our savings."

"You've thought about this a lot."

"I've had to. Mom's condition isn't going to improve on its own, and football training with Coach Moreno costs money, too, and that's just a start. If I want to have any shot at getting to the kind of level needed to guarantee a good spot at a nationally ranked program, I need to keep pushing. And that's going to cost money."

Dad stood up and walked to the window, looking out at the backyard.

"That's true. What happens if your predictions stop being accurate? What if whatever's giving you these hunches suddenly stops working?"

It was a fair question, but only because he didn't know what I knew. These weren't actually predictions. They were stuff I knew for sure was going to happen. But how can you say, 'I had a dream about the future and now I know everything'?

"Then we lose money, possibly a lot of money. But Dad, the alternative is that we try to live off our savings while Mom gets sicker and I miss out on the training I need to succeed in football. I know this is weird and hard to understand, but I really believe this is our best option for long-term financial security."

Dad was silent for a long time, thinking. Finally, he sighed and came back to the table, sitting down again.

"I'm getting nervous about all of this, Blake. Not just the money, but the whole situation. A year and a half ago, you were getting D's and you were in trouble all the time. The way you've changed literally everything about yourself ... and now with these hunches. It's worrying."

"I know."

"Do you? Because I'm not sure you understand how this looks from the outside. I keep telling myself that you're still the same kid, but every conversation we have makes me feel like I'm talking to a stranger."

His words hit harder than I expected them to. I'd been so focused on changing my future that I hadn't really considered how my transformation was affecting the people around me, especially Dad.

"I'm still me, Dad. I'm still the kid who used to build model airplanes with you in the garage. I'm just ... more focused now, I guess. More motivated. Maybe it's because of the stuff with Mom or just the pressure from high school, I don't know, but last year something clicked for me. I realized I couldn't just drift through life anymore."

"And the predictions? The hunches?"

I shrugged. "I told you, I have no way of explaining those. All I can tell you is that they've been right so far, and I think we'd be stupid not to use them while we can."

Dad studied my face for a long moment, like he was looking for signs of mental instability. Finally, he nodded slowly.

"Okay. I'll get in touch with Henderson tomorrow and arrange to transfer the money. I'll sign whatever paperwork needs to be signed."

"Thanks, Dad. I know this isn't easy for you."

"You're right about that. I'm starting to really worry about you."

"I know," I said.

I was hoping he could just hang on and take things on faith until I could prove that all these things were true.

Chapter 13

I was kind of excited as I got to Li's mother's shop on Saturday afternoon. I'd been looking forward to it for days, just imagining the kind of stuff I was going to learn.

And maybe imagining using them on Elijah and Trevor in my less charitable moments.

It was weird going to the shop when Li wasn't there, but Li's mother had been insistent that even though Li was in China, this was still on. She decided I needed to learn to defend myself, and a little thing like my friend not being there wasn't going to stop her mission to have me learn.

I found her inside the shop talking animatedly to a woman I'd never seen before. I assumed this was the person who was going to teach me, except she wasn't at all what I expected.

The stranger was somewhere in her thirties, I would guess, with dark brown hair pulled back in a ponytail, dressed in practical workout clothes with an athletic build that was wiry but still had clear definition to it. She wasn't bulky strong like you sometimes see. I could tell just by looking at her that she was strong, strong.

"Blake!" Li's mom called out when she spotted me. "Come, come. I want you to meet Yesica."

The woman turned and flashed me a huge smile that immediately put me at ease, despite my confusion about who she was supposed to be. She was confident and at ease, a quality I wished I had. Like she knew exactly who she was, and she knew that whatever might happen, she could handle herself.

"So this is the famous Blake I've been hearing about," Yesica said, extending her hand for a firm handshake. "Yeng's told me all about you and how good you are at sports, says you need to learn to defend yourself."

I shook her hand, noting the strength in her grip, and glanced between her and Li's mom. "Nice to meet you."

"Why are you so surprised?" Li's mom asked, seeing my expression. "I told you this was happening today."

"I know. I guess I just expected ... I don't know, something different. Like a martial arts person or something."

Yesica laughed. "You're learning something better. All that Eastern martial arts stuff looks really cool in the movies, and some people can pull it off for real, but trust me when I say that boxing will teach you everything you need to know about protecting yourself. The fundamentals of boxing are the fundamentals of fighting, period."

"Yesica knows more about toughness than anyone I know. She boxed professionally for years, even fought against men for a while and did very well. She will make you stronger, both up here," Li's mom said, tapping her temple, "and everywhere else."

"You fought men?" I asked, my curiosity getting the better of me.

"Exhibition matches mostly, but yeah," Yesica said with a shrug. "When you're trying to make a name for yourself as a female boxer, sometimes you take whatever fights you can get. But that's not what we're here to talk about today. I understand you cleared out a space back here for us to work."

Li's mom gestured toward the storeroom that Li, Eduardo, and I had cleared out for the training.

"Now, before we start anything," Yesica said, her jovial demeanor dropping and becoming serious, "I need you to understand that this isn't just playing around. I can already see by the way you walk, you've got the physical ability, the strength and speed to be good at this, but it takes serious work. Real commitment."

The change in her tone caught my attention. Gone was the laughing, easy-going woman from a moment before, replaced by someone who clearly took her craft seriously.

"I understand. I'm willing to do the work."

"Good, because if I'm going to drive down from Lubbock every week, you better be serious about it. I don't waste my time on half-hearted students."

"I promise I'll take it seriously. Football has taught me about commitment and hard work."

Her smile returned almost immediately. "Alright then. Let's start with the absolute basics. First thing you need to understand about boxing is that it's not about throwing wild punches and hoping something lands. Everything starts with your stance."

She moved into the cleared area and positioned herself with her feet shoulder-width apart, her left foot slightly forward. "This is called an orthodox stance, which is what most right-handed fighters use. Your left foot goes forward, weight distributed evenly between both feet, knees slightly bent."

I copied her position, trying to mirror what she was doing.

"Good, but bring your right foot back just a little more," she said, adjusting my stance with gentle pushes. "You want to be balanced but ready to move in any direction. I'm sure you have something similar in football. Now, hands up. Left hand out in front, right hand by your chin. Your left is your jab hand, your right is your power hand. Keep your elbows close to your body to protect your ribs."

I raised my hands, feeling awkward and unnatural in the position.

"Relax," Yesica said. "You're not trying to pose for a statue. This has to be comfortable because you'll be holding this position for extended periods. Drop your shoulders, loosen up your arms, but keep those hands where they need to be."

She demonstrated the stance again. "Boxing is all about economy of movement. Every motion serves a purpose, whether it's attacking, defending, or setting up your next move."

"It feels weird," I admitted. "Like I'm off balance."

"That's normal. It takes time for it to feel natural. But once you get it, it becomes second nature. Now, let's talk about the most important punch in boxing, the jab."

She threw a quick left hand into the air, her fist snapping out and back in one smooth motion. "The jab is your measuring stick, your range finder, your setup punch. It's not meant to knock someone out, though it can hurt plenty if you do it right. It's meant to keep distance, set up combinations, and control the pace of a fight."

She had me throw some shadow jabs, correcting my form each time. "Don't reach for it, don't lean forward. The power comes from rotating your shoulder and snapping your wrist at the end. Your foot position stays the same, your balance stays centered."

"Like this?" I threw another jab, trying to incorporate her corrections.

"Better. Now let's add the straight right hand, which is your power punch. This one does come from your whole body." She demonstrated, pivoting on her back foot and rotating her hips as she threw the punch. "See how my whole right side turns into it? That's where the power comes from, not just your arm."

We spent the next twenty minutes working on basic punches. Jab, straight right, left hook, right cross. Each one had its own mechanics, its own purpose, and Yesica was patient but demanding in her instruction.

"The left hook is probably the hardest punch for beginners to get right," she explained, showing me the technique again. "You're not swinging your arm like a baseball bat. Your elbow stays bent, your fist stays vertical, and the power comes from your legs and core rotating."

I tried the punch again, feeling clumsy.

"Don't worry, it takes time. Even professional boxers spend years perfecting their hook. The important thing is that you understand the concept."

"How long did it take you to learn all this?" I asked during a brief water break.

"Years," she said. "I started when I was nine, after my father died. My mother thought it would be good for me to have something to focus on, some way to channel my energy. I fell in love with it immediately, but it took me years to really understand what I was doing."

Li's mom brought us each a glass of water. "Yesica was champion in her weight class in Colombia before she came to America."

"Regional champion," Yesica corrected with a modest smile. "But yeah, I had some success. The thing is, boxing teaches you so much more than just how to fight. It teaches you discipline, respect, and how to stay calm under pressure. Those are the things that will really help you, whether you're dealing with bullies or just navigating life in general."

"Can you show me some defensive stuff?" I asked. "I mean, knowing how to punch is great, but what if someone's trying to hit me?"

"Now you're thinking like a real boxer," Yesica said approvingly. "Defense is actually more important than offense. You can't hurt your opponent if you're getting knocked out yourself."

She showed me basic defensive movements, slipping punches by moving my head slightly to one side or the other, blocking with my gloves, and using footwork to stay out of range.

"The best defense is not being there when the punch arrives," she explained. "But when you can't avoid it, you want to make sure it hits the strongest part of your defense, which is usually your gloves or your arms."

We practiced combinations of offense and defense, with Yesica calling out punches for me to throw and then showing me how to defend against similar attacks.

"Remember, in a real fight, you're not just throwing one punch and standing there," she said. "Everything flows together. Jab, move, defend, counter-punch, move again. It's like a conversation, except with fists."

"This is a lot more complicated than I thought it would be," I admitted.

"That's because you're actually learning the right way," Yesica said. "Most people think boxing is just about being tough and swinging hard, but it's really a science. Every movement has a purpose, every punch sets up the next one. Something important to remember is that the mental aspect is just as important as the physical. Boxing teaches you to stay calm when someone's trying to hurt you, to think clearly under pressure, to read your opponent and react accordingly. Those are skills that transfer to every area of life."

We worked on defense against common attacks, with Yesica throwing slow, controlled punches that I had to slip or block. It was more difficult than it looked, requiring split-second decisions about which way to move or how to position my hands.

Everything still felt off, unnatural, but I'd felt the same way about some of the stuff Coach Moreno had taught me and only got comfortable with it after repetition and practice.

"Much better," she said approvingly. "You're getting the hang of this."

Li's mom came back down and asked, "How long have you two been working?"

"About an hour," Yesica replied, checking her own watch. "Good first session, Blake. You picked up the basics faster than most people do."

"Really?" I asked, pleased with the compliment.

"Really. You've got good natural athleticism, and you listen to instruction well."

"So what happens next?" I asked. "I mean, assuming you're willing to keep teaching me."

"I can do every Sunday morning. I'll drive down from Lubbock, we'll work for about an hour and a half, and then I'll head back for my afternoon classes at the gym."

"That's a lot of driving for you," I said. "Are you sure you don't mind?"

"Are you kidding? Yeng's been my friend since I moved to America, and I owe her more than I can ever pay back. When she asks for a favor, I don't say no. Besides," she laughed, "she promised me food every time I come down here."

Li's mom smiled at that. "Speaking of food, I made lunch for all of us. Nothing fancy, just some stir-fry and rice, but there's plenty."

"Now you're talking!" Yesica said, almost skipping. "All this training has made me hungry, and I've been thinking about your cooking since you mentioned it on the phone."

"You're always hungry," Li's mom said, laughing. "Come on; let's go upstairs before it gets cold."

The waiting room at the Midland Memorial Hospital was packed with people. I'd been sitting in the same uncomfortable chair for forty-five minutes, thumbing through a Sports Illustrated from three months ago and wondering how things were going through the closed door that led back into the patient area.

Mom had insisted I didn't need to come, that she could handle this appointment on her own, but it was a long drive to Midland, and even though I didn't have my license, we didn't know how she'd be doing after. I kind of wished Dad had been able to come with her, but his schedule wasn't very flexible some days, and it had been hard enough to get this appointment since this was the major hospital for the whole region, and the tests her doctor had ordered could only be done here.

I didn't want to act like I was uncomfortable, so I pretended to focus on the magazine I didn't care about; but a couple sat across from me, the woman clutching her husband's hand while he stared at a medical pamphlet about Parkinson's disease, and someone behind me couldn't stop coughing.

I felt wildly uncomfortable in my own skin.

The door finally opened, and Mom emerged looking smaller than when she'd gone in, her purse clutched against her chest. Her face was pale but composed, which I didn't know if that was a good sign or not.

"Ready to go, sweetheart?" she asked.

I stood up, shoving the magazine back onto the table, and followed her toward the exit.

We walked to her station wagon in silence. Mom fumbled with her keys for a moment before handing them to me, a gesture that spoke volumes about how the appointment had gone. I had my learner's permit, so it was at least legal for me to drive, and I'd actually made this trip once before, although she didn't know that since it had been with Eduardo to trap his cousin.

But I was still uncomfortable driving her.

Once we were both settled inside with the engine running, I broke the silence. "How did it go?"

"It went okay, I suppose. Dr. Richardson says the medication is helping with the headaches and should keep me from having any more seizures. I have to admit I do feel more present than I have in a while."

"That's good news, right?"

"Yes, it is." She turned to look at me then, and I could see the effort it took for her to focus. "I want you to know I'm trying, Blake."

"I know."

"I just … I know I've been fighting you and your father on this, and I can see how hard it's been for both of you. If I'm being honest, now that I've started this medication, it's like a fog has pulled away that I didn't even realize was there, and I can see clearly again. Enough to see how I'd been acting, that time I slapped you. I just wanted to apologize for that. I know how scared you must have been."

"None of that matters now. What matters now is that you're getting help."

She nodded, but I could see the doubt creeping back into her eyes, the way it always did when she had too much time to think. "They want to do something called an angiography on August eighteenth. Dr. Richardson explained that it's a more detailed scan of the blood vessels in my brain, to get a better picture of what's causing the headaches and seizures."

"That sounds like a good thing. More information means they can help you better, right?"

"I suppose." She pulled one hand free to rub at her temple, a gesture I'd noticed her making more frequently. "It's just, all these tests and procedures, Blake. Sometimes I wonder if they're really necessary, or if the doctors are just adding tests to make more money."

She might be feeling better and be seeing things a little clearer, but clearly the distrust she'd built up about the medical industry wasn't totally gone.

I changed the subject.

"What does Dr. Richardson think is causing the seizures?"

"He's still not sure. The initial scans showed some irregularities, but nothing definitive. He keeps using words like 'atypical' and 'concerning,' which doesn't exactly fill me with confidence."

"Mom, Dr. Richardson has been practicing medicine for a long time, and you said he was recommended as a good neurologist. If he thinks these tests are necessary, then we just need to see this through."

"I know, I know. I'm not saying he's wrong, just that sometimes I feel like I'm caught in a machine I don't understand, being pushed from test to test without anyone really knowing what they're looking for."

The irony wasn't lost on me that she was probably right about them not understanding what they were looking for. Medicine would advance a lot in the next thirty years, even when I died in my dream life, and even then, a lot of stuff with the brain was still unknown. But I don't think that was what she was getting at.

All I could do was reassure her and try to make sure she kept at it.

"Mom, I need you to know how much it means to me that you're doing this." I turned in my seat to face her fully, wanting her to see how serious I was. "I know you have concerns about the medical system, and I know some of those concerns are probably valid, but the fact that you're pushing through that for our family, it means everything."

Her eyes filled with tears, and for a moment, she looked like the mother I remembered from when I was younger, before things had started to turn. "You're my son, Blake. I would do anything for you, even if it scares me."

"I know you would. And I'm so proud of you for being brave enough to get help, even when everything in you is telling you not to trust it."

She reached over and squeezed my hand, her grip stronger than it had been in weeks.

"I won't pretend this is easy for me. Every time I walk into the clinic, part of me wants to turn around and walk out, to go home and pretend none of this is happening."

"It's okay to be scared, Mom. Anyone would be scared in your situation."

"I just hope we find some answers soon."

I could hear the exhaustion in her voice. It made me want to wrap her in a hug and tell her everything would be okay.

"What can I do to help you between now and your next appointment?"

"Just, keep being patient with me if I have bad days. The medication helps, but it doesn't fix everything, and sometimes I still feel foggy or confused or angry, for no reason I can identify."

"I can do that."

"And don't feel like you have to take care of me, Blake. You're fifteen years old, and you should be focused on football and your friends and all the normal things teenagers worry about. I don't want my illness to steal your childhood."

Again, the irony hit me. In the dream life, Dad would be dead now, and I'd be quitting football and getting a job to help support our family. I'd truly given away my childhood in the dream. This was a pittance in comparison.

"You're not stealing anything from me, Mom. Taking care of family isn't a burden, it's just what we do."

She smiled then, the first genuine smile I'd seen from her in weeks. "When did you get so wise?"

"Probably inherited it from my mother."

That made her laugh, a sound I'd missed more than I'd realized. "Flatterer. Though I have to say, you've been remarkably mature about all of this. Most teenagers would be angry or resentful about having to deal with a sick parent."

I thought about the teenager I'd been in my original timeline, how I had been angry and resentful, how I'd pulled away from the family when they needed me most.

"I love you, Mom. That's what matters."

"I love you too, sweetheart. More than you know."

We sat in comfortable silence for a moment, watching other patients and families coming and going from the hospital.

"Are you ready to head home?"

She nodded, settling back into her seat as I put the station wagon in reverse. "I should probably call your father and let him know how the appointment went. He's been worried sick, though he's trying not to show it."

"He'll be relieved to hear you're responding well to the medication."

"Yes, I think he will be."

As I pulled out of the parking lot and onto the main road leading home, I found myself making silent promises to a God I wasn't sure I believed in anymore, bargaining for more time and better outcomes than I'd been shown in the dream.

Chapter 14

The community pool was on the other side of the park from the school, and I could hear the music and voices before I even rounded the corner. Someone had strung red, white, and blue streamers across the chain-link fence, and the pool was absolutely packed.

Mickey spotted me first. "Blake! Get over here, man."

He stood near the deep end with Brian, Austin, and Noah, all of them already in the water. I dropped my towel on a chair and pulled off my shirt before heading their way.

"About time," Miguel said. "We've been here for like an hour."

"Had to help my dad with some stuff."

I sat on the edge and dangled my legs in the water.

Mickey dove under and came up shaking water from his hair. "You ready for next month?"

"Bring it on." I slid into the pool, the cold water closing over my shoulders. "I've already been training, and I'm ready for state."

"How was that camp?" Noah asked. "The one in LA?"

"Intense. Really intense."

Brian swam closer. "Did you meet any college coaches?"

"Better than that. Cliff Daniels was one of the coaches."

"You got to meet Cliff Daniels?" Hunter asked, joining us. "That's badass. How was he?"

That led to a thousand questions about meeting an NFL player and recounting every moment I could remember about it. Of course, I should have expected that. My dad might not have been as interested in it, but these were my people, and hearing that someone met an NFL player, even a former one, was big news.

From there, we started talking about other players we'd love to meet, then games we remembered. Just the kind of stuff guys over-invested in a sport would talk about.

I was halfway through a sentence when Melanie, in a bikini and sunglasses, came walking through the gate with a couple of the other cheerleaders, heading for some lounge chairs.

She must have repaired some of the friendships she'd tanked at the end of last year in her play for Kenneth. I'd also noticed that Tammy wasn't around, so maybe they'd broken up for good.

I honestly wouldn't have been able to live with myself if I'd tanked *the* high school couple just before they graduated, but Melanie had made it pretty clear that she didn't have much of a conscience.

I felt a little knot in my stomach still, seeing her, but I ignored it.

"Don't look now," Tyrell said quietly beside me, "but your ex just noticed you."

"Yeah, I saw her."

"You good?"

"I'm fine."

And I was.

Mostly.

The whole thing with Melanie felt like it had happened in another lifetime, even though it had only been a few months ago. Maybe the thing with Charlie had helped put it out of my mind.

More guys arrived over the next half hour. Andre brought a football, and soon we had a game going in the shallow end. Not a game, really, just tossing it around, trying to make catches while staying balanced in the water. The cheerleaders watched from their chairs, occasionally calling out encouragement or making fun of dropped passes.

I tried not to look at Melanie, but I felt her attention on me. Every time I glanced in that direction, she was staring.

"Ignore her," Mickey said during a break in the game. "She's just trying to get in your head."

"I know."

"Good. Because we need you focused this season. We're going to win state."

The gate opened again, and Kenneth walked in with three other guys who'd graduated with him in the spring. I know we'd only seen them a month ago, but somehow they all looked a little different. Older, maybe.

"Ward!" Brian, who'd been on varsity with him last year, shouted. "Get in here!"

Kenneth grinned and headed our way, dropping his stuff near the deep end. The other graduates followed, and soon we had a crowd gathered around the former team captain.

"How's summer treating you?" I asked.

"Not bad. Working construction with my old man, saving money for school." Kenneth had filled out even more since I'd last seen him, his shoulders broader, his arms more defined. "You guys ready for the season?"

"We're getting there," Mickey said.

"Better be more than getting there," Kenneth said, but he was smiling. "I want to hear about you guys making a run this year. Do what we didn't manage."

"Where'd you end up?" Noah asked. "I heard you were looking at a few colleges."

"Texas Tech. Got a preferred walk-on spot." Kenneth shrugged. "Not a scholarship, but it's a chance to compete and prove myself."

It seemed wild to me that he didn't get recruited. Although quarterback was a hard spot to get picked up, since each team only needed a handful of us, not like they needed a lot of linebackers and receivers.

"That's awesome, man," Brian said.

"Thanks. It's not what I wanted, but it's something." Kenneth looked at me. "Heard you went to some fancy camp in LA. How'd that go?"

"It was good. Learned a lot."

"He met Cliff Daniels," Andre added.

And so it started again, with which players we'd like to meet, who'd be the best coach, and on and on. I floated on my back and just listened, chiming in a time or two when a thought popped into my head.

The guys who graduated were more wistful than the rest of us, I guess, realizing this time of their life was over, talking about memories from their senior season. In a way, I could relate, since I remembered the stuff I went through as I aged in the dream, but it was also different. Those were just memories of things that happened, not the feelings behind them.

They didn't have the emotional weight that I was sure these guys were feeling.

"Cherish this," Kenneth said, floating over to me in a brief moment where I was kind of away from the main pack. "I know everyone says it, but it's true. These next few years go by faster than you think. One day you're a freshman worrying about making the team, and the next you've graduated and wonder where it all went."

"Thanks, Dad," I said, which got a laugh.

"Sure, but I'm serious. Make the most of it. And don't let stupid stuff get in the way. Drama, girls, whatever. With everything that happened, letting it get to my head, I screwed some big stuff up and forgot what was important and who I was."

I didn't point out the thing he let go to his head also broke up my girlfriend and me. While he wasn't innocent in all of that, it had been Melanie's plan, and if he'd turned her down, she would have made a play for someone else.

Still, I hoped he learned that lesson, because he wouldn't be the big dog when he was in college, and it could really come back at him.

"You're going to be good. Better than me, probably. But don't let it go to your head. Just keep doing what you were doing last year, and the team is going to kill. Hell, you're way better than I was when I was a sophomore, and better than a lot of the quarterbacks I went up against last year. Just don't let it go to your head."

"Sure," I said, although after just admitting he let it go to his head, and after what he did, it did come off a little patronizing.

"Let's eat," Hunter announced, heading for the snack table where one of their dads had set out burgers and hot dogs.

I wasn't far behind him. I was starving.

Melanie appeared beside me as I waited for my turn to get some food. "Hey."

I kept my eyes on the food. "Hey."

"How've you been?"

"Fine."

"Me too," she said when I didn't ask.

An awkward silence stretched between us.

"Blake, I ..." She trailed off, then tried again. "I wanted to apologize. For how things ended. I wasn't ... I made some mistakes."

"It's fine, Melanie. We were never going to work out anyway."

"Maybe not, but I could have handled it better. I would handle it better if we tried again."

Did she think I was an idiot? She was just starting to get some of her circle back, and I know that I was just a way to accelerate that. I was under no delusion she actually wanted me for me at all.

I wasn't even sure she was capable of that.

"I don't think that's a good idea." I grabbed a plate and started loading it with food. "We're done. We've both moved on."

"Have we?" She pulled off her sunglasses and tried to give me that 'I'm really just hurt and struggling' look she gave when she wanted someone to take pity on her. "We had some good times, and I miss who I was when I was with you. I was a better person."

"That's not my problem."

Her hurt expression disappeared right away, replaced by annoyance. "Wow. Okay."

I couldn't help but wonder if she realized that each time she dropped the act like this as soon as things didn't go her way, it just made it more impossible to trust her the next time.

"What do you want me to say? You went after Kenneth while we were still together. Hell, you made a play for him twice, and I gave you a pass on the first time. Why would I ever trust you again?"

"That's not fair."

"Isn't it?" I grabbed a soda from the cooler. "Look, I'm sorry you don't get to chalk up 'dating the quarterback' on your resume, but we're done, Melanie."

I walked away before she could respond, heading back to where Miguel and the others had claimed a spot near the diving board. When I glanced back, Melanie stood alone near the snack table, glaring at me like she wanted me dead.

Just like her to see herself as the victim, even now.

"That looked fun," Connor said dryly.

"It was a blast."

"What'd she want?"

"To see if I'd take her back."

Miguel shook his head. "After what she did? That takes some nerve."

"Yeah, well. It doesn't matter."

"Damn straight it doesn't," Hunter said. "We've got bigger things to worry about. Like playoffs."

"Not just playoffs," Hunter corrected. "State. We're going all the way this year."

That got everyone going again. The guys were all positive we were going to win this year. While their confidence was infectious, I would be lying if I said it didn't also make me a little nervous.

There was definitely more pressure this time around. Partly because I wanted it as badly as they did, but also because I really didn't want to let them down.

After the Fourth of July, I finally got a break.

The next twenty days passed without incident, which felt like a gift after the chaos of the previous several months. Joshua kept his head down and didn't do anything creepy, Mom drove herself to appointments without complaint, and I actually saw her taking her medicine. I fell into a routine of throwing drills, weight training, and even cracking open some textbooks to prep for sophomore year. Coach Moreno came by once in the middle of the month and worked with me for a week, getting me prepped for camp, and left me with workout plans that left me incredibly sore ... which didn't help on top of Yesica's boxing sessions. By the time Sunday morning of camp rolled around and Dad drove me to the airport, I'd almost forgotten what drama felt like.

Almost.

The flight to Atlanta took forever. I watched Texas shrink beneath the clouds, then spent three hours wedged between a businessman who snored and a woman with a crying baby. I tried reading the magazine I'd bought at the Hudson News stand, but my legs didn't fit in the space well, and the guy next to me was taking up both his armrests and spilling into my seat a bit.

Even with that, I was excited. A week of high-level competition with some of the best high school quarterbacks in the country.

At least this time I didn't have to take a taxi from the airport. I'd called ahead and arranged for a ride.

When I finally walked through the terminal at Hartsfield, I spotted Charlie before I saw her parents. She stood outside the gate, wearing denim shorts and a white tank top, her auburn hair pulled back in a ponytail. The second she saw me, her face lit up.

"There he is!"

I barely had time to drop my bag before she closed the distance and wrapped me in a hug that almost knocked me over.

"Hey," I said into her hair.

"Hey, yourself." She pulled back, grinning, "You look taller. Did you grow?"

"Pretty sure I'm the same height I was a month ago."

"Hmm. Maybe I just forgot how tall you are."

Mr. Clark appeared behind her, Ray at his side. "Blake! Good to see you, son."

I shook his hand. "Thanks for picking me up, Mr. Clark."

"Wouldn't have it any other way." He clapped me on the shoulder. "How was the flight?"

"Long."

Mrs. Clark came up last, carrying a purse the size of a small suitcase. She gave me a quick hug. "Blake, sweetheart, you must be exhausted. We'll get you to the dorm so you can rest before orientation tomorrow."

"I appreciate it."

We headed toward baggage claim, Charlie falling into step beside me while Ray walked ahead with his parents.

"So," she said quietly, "how've you been?"

"Busy. Training, mostly. Some family stuff, but it's going better now."

"Your mom?"

"She's doing okay. She's going to the doctor and has an appointment coming up when I get back from camp that should tell us more."

Charlie nodded. "That's good. I've been thinking about you."

"Yeah?"

"Don't let it go to your head."

"Too late."

She bumped my shoulder with hers. "I'm serious. I'm glad you're here."

"Me, too."

We reached the baggage carousel and waited for my duffel to appear. Ray wandered over, hands in his pockets.

"Y'all planning to flirt the whole way to the dorm?" he asked.

Charlie shot him a look. "We're catching up."

"Uh-huh."

"Don't be jealous," I said.

Ray snorted. "Trust me, I'm not."

My bag finally came around, and I hauled it off the belt. Mr. Clark led us out to the parking lot where their Suburban waited, and we piled in. I ended up in the back seat between Ray and Charlie, which felt like the universe testing my self-control. She smelled as good as ever, and every time the car turned a corner, her knee bumped against mine.

"So what've you been up to?" I asked, keeping my voice casual.

"Tennis camp for two weeks. Volleyball conditioning. Some SAT prep because Mom's convinced I need to start early."

"You're a sophomore."

"Tell her that."

Ray leaned forward. "She got ranked number twelve in the state for her age group. In tennis."

"That's incredible."

Charlie shrugged. "It's something."

"It's more than something," I said.

"What about you? Besides training, I mean. Did you do anything fun?"

"Define fun."

"Anything that didn't involve a football?"

"I'm learning how to box."

She blinked. "Seriously?"

"A friend of a friend is a trainer and a boxer. My friend's mom set it up. Once a week, fundamentals and conditioning."

Ray twisted around. "Wait, you're learning to fight now?"

"Self-defense," I corrected. "But yeah."

"Why?"

"Because sometimes knowing how to throw a punch comes in handy."

Ray exchanged a glance with Charlie, and I could tell they were both thinking about Trevor and what happened at the USC camp.

"Smart," Ray said finally.

We drove through Atlanta's outskirts, past shopping centers and subdivisions that looked identical to the ones back home. Mrs. Clark kept up a steady stream of questions about my flight, my family, and whether I'd eaten dinner. I answered as best I could, but mostly I was just happy to be here.

The Nike camp was being held at Georgia Tech's campus, and when we pulled up to the athletic dorms, I started to get excited.

"Looks nice," I said, grabbing my bag from the back.

Mr. Clark walked us to the check-in desk, where a college-aged kid with a clipboard and a Nike polo took our names and handed us room keys.

"You're in room 314," the kid said to me.

"Thanks."

I stepped back and was surprised when Ray was assigned the same room. Well, surprised but happy. I was glad I'd get to avoid the drama of the last camp. We headed toward the elevators, Mr. and Mrs. Clark trailing behind. Charlie stayed close, her hand brushing mine once as we walked.

The elevator ride felt longer than it should have. When the doors opened on the third floor, we found room 314 was halfway down on the left. I slid the key card into the lock, and the door clicked open.

Inside, the room was small but functional. Two beds, two desks, two dressers. A window overlooked the parking lot. Ray tossed his bag onto the bed on the right, and I claimed the one by the window.

"Not bad," Ray said.

"Could be worse. Two instead of four is an upgrade."

Mrs. Clark poked her head in. "Do you boys need anything? We can stop at a store if you forgot something."

"I think we're good," Ray said.

"Blake?"

"I'm all set. Thank you, though."

She smiled. "All right. We'll let you two get settled. Blake, you're welcome to join us for dinner Wednesday at the house."

"I'd love that."

"Perfect. We'll pick you up around six."

Mr. Clark shook my hand again. "Good luck tomorrow, Blake. Work hard."

"Yes, sir."

They left, but Charlie lingered in the doorway.

"You coming?" Ray asked her.

"In a second."

Ray rolled his eyes but stepped out into the hall, giving us space.

Charlie moved closer. "I'm really glad you're here."

"Me too."

She reached up and adjusted the collar of my shirt, her fingers grazing my neck.

"Charlie ..."

"What?"

"Your brother's right outside."

"So?"

"So I'm trying to behave."

She smiled. "Since when?"

I laughed. "Fair point."

She stepped back, still grinning. "See you around, Blake."

"Yeah. See you."

She slipped out of the room, and I heard her and Ray talking in low voices as they headed back toward the elevator. I dropped onto my bed and stared at the ceiling, letting my mind go blank.

Ray came back a few minutes later, shaking his head.

"What?" I asked.

"Nothing. Just my sister being ... my sister."

"She's being nice."

"Uh-huh."

"What's that supposed to mean?"

Ray sat on his bed and started unpacking his duffel. "It means I know my sister, and I know when she likes somebody."

"We're friends."

"Right. Friends who can't stop looking at each other."

I rolled my eyes, and we unpacked in silence for a while, hanging clothes in the narrow closet and stashing gear under the beds. I was folding my last shirt when Ray spoke again.

"So, Moreno set this up."

I looked up. "What?"

"Us rooming together. He called my dad last week and asked if we'd be cool with it. Said he didn't want a repeat of what happened at USC."

"Moreno did that?"

"Yeah. Guess he figured you'd have a better time if you weren't stuck with some random guy."

"That's actually pretty thoughtful."

"He's a good coach. He cares. I just don't think he wants you to know he cares."

The orientation meeting started at seven. We filed into a conference room on the first floor, where rows of folding chairs faced a projector screen. The place filled up fast, quarterbacks from all over the country finding seats and sizing each other up. I was surprised when I spotted Trevor near the front. He saw me too, and his mouth twisted into something that might've been a smirk.

"Great," I muttered.

Ray followed my eyes. "Ignore him."

"Plan to."

We found seats in the middle of the room, close enough to see but far enough back to avoid attention.

The lights dimmed, and a man in his fifties stepped to the front. He wore Nike gear from head to toe and carried a clipboard like it was a weapon.

"Good evening, gentlemen. I'm Coach Phil Drummond, and I'll be your head coach for the next two weeks. Welcome to Nike's Elite Quarterback Academy."

Applause scattered through the room.

"You're here because you're the best of the best," Drummond continued. "But being the best at your high school doesn't mean squat here. Everyone in this room has an arm. Everyone's got footwork. Everyone thinks they're going pro. So what's going to separate you from the pack?"

He paused, letting the question hang.

"Work ethic. Football IQ. Leadership. Composure under pressure. Those are the qualities we'll be evaluating. You'll have position coaches from some of the top college programs in the country. You'll run drills designed by NFL coordinators. And at the end of two weeks, the coaches will rank every single one of you based on performance. Rankings matter. Scouts will see them. Recruiters will see them. You want to move up? Earn it."

The program was a lot like the All-American camp, just without the scrimmaging. A mix of drills and film, film and drills. The staff was a mixture of college coaches from around the country, along with a few college players working as assistants. Then he covered the rules: curfew at ten, lights out at eleven, no leaving campus without permission, no alcohol, no drama.

Afterward, when we got to our room, Ray pulled out his playbook and started flipping through the pages.

"You study your stuff?" he asked.

"Some. Moreno's got me running his system."

"How's that going?"

"Hard. But good."

Ray nodded. "Yeah, I figured. He doesn't mess around."

"What about you? How's your season looking?"

"Tough. We lost a couple of seniors, so the line's rebuilding. But we've got talent. If we can gel early, we'll make a run."

"State championship run?"

"That's the goal."

I leaned back against the headboard. "Same here. My team's got the pieces. I just have to put it together."

"You starting varsity this year?"

"Yeah."

We talked for a while longer, swapping stories about our teams and the coaches we loved or hated. Eventually, the conversation drifted to other things. Ray asked about my family, and I gave him the edited version: Mom's doing better, Dad's supportive, and no mentions of my brother.

"What about you?" I asked. "What's Charlie up to when she isn't doing camps and studying?"

Ray groaned. "Please. Not this again."

"What?"

"You know what."

"I'm just asking how your sister's doing."

"Uh-huh. And tomorrow you'll be asking if she's seeing anyone, and the day after that you'll be asking for her number."

"I already have her number."

Ray threw a pillow at me. "You're the worst."

I caught it and laughed. "She gave it to me at USC. Not my fault."

"Yeah, well, try not to break her heart or whatever. She actually likes you, which is weird because you're kind of a pain."

"Wow. High praise."

"I'm serious, man. She doesn't usually get like this about guys. So if you're going to do something, do it right."

I was a little surprised by him. He wasn't just being a protective older brother. He was giving me permission, in his own way, to pursue something with Charlie.

"I'm not sure anything can happen. It's not like we live close enough to date, and you guys aren't moving to Texas any time soon."

"Yeah. It's too bad, though. You're a step up from the losers she normally dates."

"Really?" I asked, puffing up.

"Shut up."

We fell quiet after that, the kind of comfortable silence that comes when you don't need to fill every gap with words. Ray eventually grabbed his Discman and put on headphones, and I pulled out the notebook where I'd been tracking drills and game notes, but I couldn't focus on them.

While I was right that it was kind of impossible for anything to happen between us, it really was nice to think about.

Chapter 15

Wednesday after our last practice, instead of heading to the dining hall for dinner, Ray's dad picked us up and drove us about forty-five minutes to their house, which sat in a quiet neighborhood.

Thankfully, they had the A/C blasting, because the system at the campus was being worked on while school was out, and it had been barely cooling us at all, which in the south was a tough way to spend a week.

Especially when you're out on the field during the day running your ass off.

Mrs. Clark had made fried chicken, mashed potatoes, green beans, and biscuits that were still warm when we sat down. The food alone made the trip worth it.

"So, guys, how's the camp been?" Mr. Clark asked, passing me the bowl of potatoes.

He'd asked some questions on the drive over, but had saved most of them until we got to dinner so we didn't have to repeat the same thing to Ray's mom.

"Better than USC," I said, which was true enough, as I started to tell them about everything we were doing in the week.

Truth be told, the week had gone amazingly well. Sure, Trevor still shot me dirty looks during drills, and he'd made a few comments when he thought no one was listening, but we didn't have any more attempts at cornering me in a room. And since we weren't doing full scrimmaging and the times we did simulations they had coaches in the role of lineman, there were no more late hits either.

I don't know if it was that or just that the last camp had helped me progress, but my performance on the field was much better. I really felt I was picking things up faster and had more confidence. Even with that, Ray was kicking my ass every day. If I were being honest, I think I might have a little edge physically on him, and I definitely would once I got to my senior year if I kept up the level of work I was doing, but there was something to be said for experience, and Ray was at another level.

"That's good to hear." Mrs. Clark smiled. "Raymond mentioned you've been doing extra work in the evenings."

"Just trying to keep up."

"He got known for it at the last camp and when we showed up for the first practice the coach said, 'Sims, we know you like extra practices, so we made sure you have the field till nine each night.' "

"I kind of played myself on that one," I said, which got a laugh out of Charlie.

"How's your mother doing?" Mrs. Clark asked.

"She's better. The medication's helping a lot, and she's scheduled for some tests in a few weeks, so we should know more then."

"That must be a relief for your whole family."

"Yeah, it is."

Charlie had been quiet through most of the meal, letting her parents grill the two of us, but I caught her watching me a few times. When our eyes met, she'd smile and look away, like we were sharing a secret no one else could hear.

After dinner, Ray checked his watch and said, "I'm gonna head out, meet up with some guys from school. Do you want to come, Blake?"

Before I could answer, Charlie jumped in and said, "No, we're going to watch a movie."

I glanced at her, then back at Ray, giving him a shrug as if to say, 'What can I do?'

"Yeah, I bet you are," he said, rolling his eyes.

"Raymond," Mrs. Clark said, but she was smiling.

"We'll be back in two hours to get you boys to the dorm before curfew," Mr. Clark said, grabbing his keys from the counter. "Charlie, you good?"

"I'm good."

"They'll behave themselves," Mrs. Clark said, which suggested she was staying behind with us.

While I got it, I would definitely prefer not to have a chaperone.

Raymond grabbed a jacket even though it was probably still ninety degrees outside. "Try not to miss me too much."

"I'll do my best," I said.

He left with his dad, and suddenly the house felt bigger, quieter. Charlie stood in the kitchen doorway, barefoot in shorts and a T-shirt, her hair pulled back in a ponytail.

"So, movie?" she asked.

"What did you have in mind?"

"*The Lion King*," she said. "It's my favorite movie. Unless you've already seen it?"

Of course, it was her favorite. I had actually seen it, but in the dream life. I hadn't had much time to watch movies this last year, with everything going on.

"I haven't."

"Perfect," she said, beaming as she led me toward the family room.

The family room had a big sectional couch facing a TV that was nicer than anything we had back home. Charlie grabbed the remote and started messing with the VCR while I sat down on one end of the couch, leaving space between us.

"I've gotta make some calls," her mom said, heading back toward the kitchen.

"Sure thing, Mom. We'll keep it down," Charlie said, and then looked at where I was sitting. "You're going to sit all the way over there?"

"Well, your mom was right there," I pointed out.

"Blake." She rolled her eyes and patted the cushion next to her. "Sit here."

I got up and sat right next to her. The movie started, and for the first few minutes, I watched in silence while she very quietly sang along with the opening number. Charlie might have been a great student and a star athlete, but she wasn't going to end up on Broadway any time soon.

And yet I found her completely adorable, until the end of the first number when she was watching the movie and I was watching her.

"What?" she said.

"Nothing."

I couldn't keep the smile off my face, though, and she just shook her head and put her index finger against my jaw, pushing my head until I was facing the TV.

We watched for a little bit in silence, right up until the dad died, when she slid over closer to me, closing the little gap that was left until our legs were pressed right up against each other.

Ten minutes in, she moved again, closing more of the gap between us. Our torsos were almost touching now.

"Cold?" I asked, keeping my voice low.

"Little bit."

The house was perfectly comfortable, but I didn't call her on it. Instead, I stretched my arm along the back of the couch behind her shoulders. She leaned into me immediately, her head resting against my shoulder.

I tried to force my heart not to beat so fast, just in case she could hear it. Another song came on and she started mumbling her way through it, which was cute.

And at least now she couldn't call me on smiling so much at her.

Charlie's hand found mine, her fingers threading through mine where they rested on her shoulder as she snuggled in closer to me.

"Enjoying it?" she asked, looking up at me.

"Yeah, it's really good, although I don't think I'll be joining you in any sing-along."

"You're no fun," she said, smiling.

She stared into my eyes for a moment, before dropping her gaze to my lips, then back up. The movie played on in front of us, but I couldn't have told you what was happening on the screen. Everything narrowed to the space between us.

I turned more fully toward her, my hand coming up to cup her cheek. Her skin was soft and warm under my palm.

"Blake," she whispered.

I kissed her.

She made a small sound in the back of her throat and kissed me back, her hand sliding up to my neck. Her lips parted, and I forgot about the movie, about the camp, about everything except the taste of her mouth and the way she pressed closer.

We broke apart after a moment, both breathing harder. She looked dazed.

"Wow," she said.

"Yeah."

She kissed me again, harder this time, more insistent. I responded in kind, my other hand finding her waist, pulling her closer. She shifted, turning more fully toward me, her hands tangling in my hair.

The movie was completely forgotten, just background noise, something that existed on the periphery.

Charlie pulled back eventually, just far enough to catch her breath. "We should probably watch the movie."

"Probably."

But neither of us moved to put space between us. Instead, she leaned in again, her mouth finding mine. This kiss was slower, more deliberate, and I savored every second of it.

When we broke apart, she smiled against my lips. "Or maybe not."

"The movie can wait."

She laughed, the sound breathy and quiet, before kissing me again.

Some time later we stopped and she looked at the clock.

"Ray will be back soon. It's almost time for you to go."

"I know."

"We should ..."

I kissed her before she could finish, and she melted into me, any thought of stopping abandoned. My hand slipped under the hem of her shirt, my fingers brushing across her smooth, warm skin.

She froze as I made contact, and I moved my hand back. I hadn't intended to cop a feel, not with her mom somewhere nearby, but she didn't know that and probably expected me to push it.

I pulled back and stroked her hair, fixing where I'd mussed it as I'd run my hand through it, tucking a stray strand behind her ear.

Ray came home a few minutes later and gave us a look, seeing how flushed we both were, but her parents were kind enough to ignore it.

I swear, nothing I'd experienced so far had compared to how tonight felt.

Friday afternoon arrived too fast. I folded my last clean shirt and stuffed it into my duffel bag, then surveyed the room one final time to make sure I hadn't forgotten anything. The week had passed in a rush of drills, mock scrimmages, and late-night conversations with Ray and a few of the other guys I got to know at the camp.

Although a lot was the same at this camp and the All-American camp, this one had definitely gone better for me. I'd gotten as much time on the field as everyone else instead of being shunted off to development, and there'd been no repeat of the hazing, or at least attempted hazing, from the last camp.

Ray had won the MVP award a few hours before, which surprised exactly nobody. He'd been the best quarterback there from day one, consistently doing everything a high-level quarterback needed to do. I was happy for him, proud of my friend, if a tad bit jealous. I knew I had no chance for it. I just didn't have the experience yet to do things as fast or as smoothly as Ray did, but I'd be lying if I said I didn't want to come out on top.

All of us were competitive, or we wouldn't be here.

Trevor had taken it less graciously, storming out as Ray accepted his award, missing the last little bit of the closing ceremony. I couldn't help but wonder if he realized these coaches talked to each other and, after being at two major camps where he showed this kind of attitude, that it could definitely affect his recruiting.

I doubted he gave it a moment's thought. He had talent but no introspection and a chip on his shoulder that was going to cost him eventually.

My own performance had been solid. I didn't have a moment that got close to when Cliff Daniels had pulled me aside at the end of the All-American camp, but my overall results had been a lot more consistent. Hopefully, enough for the coaches to remember me when I came back next year.

Right now, I knew I wasn't the best quarterback at this camp. Ray had that locked down, and a couple of the other seniors performed close to him. But I also had something they didn't have: time. When I was a senior, when I had three more years of Moreno's training and actual game experience under my belt, I'd be able to compete with anyone. Hell, if you compared me now to where Ray had been at fifteen, I was pretty sure I was already ahead.

The thought made me smile as I grabbed my bag and headed downstairs. Ray was waiting in the lobby, talking with a couple of guys from camp. He saw me and waved me over.

"Ready to head out?"

"Yep."

"Great. I think I just saw them pull up," he said, nodding toward the front windows where I could see their Suburban.

We said goodbye to the other guys and headed out to join them. Charlie climbed out of the passenger seat when I got there.

"Hey," she said, coming around the car.

"Hey, yourself."

Mrs. Clark rolled down her window. "Morning, Blake. You all packed?"

"Yes, ma'am. Thanks again for the ride and for inviting me over for dinner the other day."

"Oh, honey, it was our pleasure. You're welcome anytime."

Ray scoffed as he put our bags in the back.

I ignored him and climbed into the back seat, and Charlie slid in next to me instead of getting in front with her mom. Ray sat up front with her.

The drive to the airport took about forty minutes through Atlanta traffic. The whole way, Mrs. Clark asked about the rest of camp, and Ray and I took turns filling her in on the week's highlights.

Charlie was quiet next to me, her knee occasionally bumping mine when the car hit a pothole or changed lanes. Every time it happened, I was hyperaware of the contact, of how close she was, of how soon I'd be on a plane back to Texas.

We pulled up to the departures terminal, and Mrs. Clark put the car in park. Ray hopped out and opened the trunk, grabbing my bag while I climbed out my side.

"Well," Ray said. "This was good."

"Yeah, it was. Thanks for everything, man."

"Sure, and hey, maybe we'll end up at the same school someday. I'd love to have you as my backup in college."

"Who's to say you wouldn't be my backup?"

"As if," he said, laughing. "Stay in touch, yeah?"

"I will. Promise."

Mrs. Clark came around the car and gave me a hug, maternal and warm. "You take care of yourself, Blake. And tell your mother we're praying for her."

"I will. Thank you, Mrs. Clark."

She smiled and patted my cheek, then got back in the driver's seat. Ray followed, but not before giving Charlie, who had also gotten out of the car and was standing, waiting to say goodbye, and me a pointed look that said *behave yourselves.*

Charlie and I stepped away from the car, moving a few feet down the sidewalk where we had something resembling privacy.

"So," she said.

"So."

"This sucks."

"Yeah. I wish we lived closer so we could try and make this a thing."

She was quiet for a moment, looking down at her feet. Then she looked back up at me. "We can still write and call. I'd like to at least stay friends. Who knows, right? We might end up at the same college. Life's weird like that."

"I hope so. I'd like that. The writing and calling part, I mean, but also the other thing."

"Good." She dug in her pocket and pulled out a small piece of paper. "Here. This is the number to the phone in my room and my address."

I took the paper, then pulled out my wallet and found an old receipt, and I wrote my home number and address on the back and handed it to her.

"There. Now you have no excuse not to bug me."

"Oh, I'll bug you." She tucked the paper in her pocket, then looked back at the car where her mom and Ray were trying very hard to pretend they weren't watching us. "Your plane leaves in like an hour."

"I know."

"So you should probably ..."

"Yeah, I should."

Neither of us moved. A taxi honked somewhere behind us, and I knew this was the last chance for anything before we went our separate ways, to our separate lives.

I stepped closer to Charlie, and she looked up at me, her eyes almost pleading. I put my hand on her waist, pulled her up against me, and kissed her.

Her hands came up to my shoulders, fingers gripping the fabric of my shirt, and she kissed me back just as hard. Everything else faded away: the noise, the heat and the ticking clock counting down to my departure. There was just the two of us.

I don't know how long we stayed like that, but long enough that Ray had to yell out the car window, "Alright, Romeo, get out of here before you miss your damn plane!"

Charlie and I broke apart, both of us breathing hard, both of us grinning like idiots. Her cheeks were flushed pink.

"Call me," she said.

"I will."

"Promise?"

"Promise."

I picked up my duffel bag, shouldered it, and gave Charlie one last look before turning toward the terminal entrance. At the door, I looked back. Charlie was standing right where I'd left her, one hand raised in a wave.

I waved back, then turned and walked through the sliding glass doors into the airport's cool interior, a little sad at the thoughts of what couldn't be.

Chapter 16

As much as I didn't want camp to end, partly because it closed the door on me and Charlie, I was excited because both Eduardo and Li were back. Li had just gotten back the day before I did, and her mom had a lot of things for her to do, so we all agreed to meet Saturday night for dinner at Jimmy's and to get some burgers. I spotted them through the window before I even got in the door, sitting at a booth in the back.

"You're back," Li said as I made it inside and joined them.

"I'm back." I caught her in a quick hug, surprised by how tight she squeezed me. "How was your flight?"

"So long. I still haven't been to sleep, actually, and will probably crash the second I get back home. Jet lag is no joke."

"How was China? How's your family?" I asked.

"Crowded. You wouldn't believe how many people were there, and this wasn't even a holiday. My grandmother said that in October, it would be almost three times as many people."

"Which is a lot for a poor country girl," Eduardo said, smiling.

"Ye-haw," Li replied in her most deadpan voice. "But it was good to see everyone, though. My cousins are all playing basketball now, and they all had a million questions about playing on the school team."

A waitress came by, and I ordered a burger and fries. We came here enough that we didn't need to look at the menu anymore.

"So how was camp? Both of them?"

"Good. Really good, actually. The USC one was rough at first, and I had some problems with a guy there, but it got better. The Georgia one was solid the whole way through. I was middle of the pack or maybe toward the bottom at both camps, but I'm also two years younger than most of the guys ahead of me, and experience counts for a lot, so I just used it as training to get better and tried not to focus on the competition aspect too much."

"Like you could ever not be competitive," Eduardo said.

"I said 'too much,'" I pointed out. "I made a friend at the first one, a guy named Ray from Georgia who's also training with Coach Moreno. His family was really great and took me in, especially when I went to Georgia. He was amazing, though. Took MVP at both camps."

"Damn, he must be good," Li said.

"He is. It's why I kind of backed off my normal competitiveness. He's also a good guy, which helped. Still, I think once I have his experience, I'll be even better."

"There he is."

"I said backed off, I never said it disappeared completely. Anyway, his whole family was pretty nice. They were really great."

"Why'd you say it like that?" Li asked, her eyes narrowing at me.

"What do you mean?"

"When you said 'they,' there was a thing in your voice," she said, and then it was like a light bulb went off. "Who was she?"

"What?"

"Come on, admit it. There was someone else, right? You said you spent time with his family. Unless his dad is someone famous, I'll bet he has a sister."

"Fine. Yes. He has a sister."

"I knew it," she said triumphantly. "Spill it."

"Her name's Charlie. Charlotte, but she goes by Charlie. She's ... she's cool."

Eduardo had started smiling now, too, and Li looked like Christmas had come early.

"Cool how?"

"Just cool. We talked some at USC and hung out a few times in Georgia. She's smart, really smart. She wants to be a doctor and is apparently really good at volleyball. She made me some mix CDs."

"Pretty?"

Our food got dropped off at the point, and I grabbed a fry. "Yeah."

"How pretty?"

"Li."

"Answer the question."

"Very pretty, alright? Auburn hair, green eyes, about Eduardo's height."

"So what happened?"

"Nothing happened."

"Blake."

"Maybe we kissed. That's it."

"You like her," Li said in a sing-song voice.

I ignored them and ate my burger.

"Yep. He likes her," Eduardo said.

"So, what's the deal? You two going to date?"

"No. I live in Texas, and she lives in Georgia, and there's no guarantee we'll ever be in the same place again. We exchanged numbers, and we'll probably talk sometimes, but that's it."

"Because of the distance."

"Because of the distance."

Li shrugged. "Makes sense. Long distance is stupid."

"Thank you."

"But you still like her."

"Can we talk about something else?"

Eduardo was still grinning. "How's your mom doing?"

Better topic. "Good, actually. Really good. I managed to strong-arm her into going to a real doctor, and the medication is helping a lot. She's getting tests done, following up with doctors. We're making progress."

"That's good."

"What about you? Meet any boys in China?"

"Hardly. I spent all my time with family, and besides, they see me almost as much a foreigner as if you'd gone there. They all say my Chinese is bad, I act too American, and on and on."

"Your Chinese is good," I said, my mouth half full. "I've heard you speak it."

"Not to a native speaker, it's not. Trust me; my mom points it out all the time."

"But you had fun?"

"Sure. I mean, it wasn't fun like you had fun," she said with a twinkle in her eye. "But it was nice seeing family. Not exactly Disney World, but I'm glad I went."

"Good. What about you?" I asked Eduardo. "We both spilled. How was Mexico?"

"Okay. Worked some at my uncle's shop, hung out with my cousins, the younger ones, I mean."

"Speaking of cousins?" I said, half as a question and half as a statement.

"Court date's coming up in September, and my mom talked to the prosecutor last week. They said they're going to make an example of him to try to get control of some of the gang problem in the city. Armed robbery, kidnapping, because they tied up the guard, possession with intent to distribute, and the capper, attempted murder of a police officer. He's not getting out anytime soon."

"Good," I said.

"Yeah. His gang came apart after everything went down. Arrests, guys fleeing to other cities, the whole thing collapsed."

"I know he had some of your other cousins in the gang. Are they okay with everything that happened?"

"My aunt's a little upset, but she's not surprised. He's been going this way for a while. Everyone else is basically out of the gang. Our whole family's blackballed because of all the attention it brought down on them, and how he made it all his idea. Any kind of connection to Raf means they're out. Most of my cousins are having to find other things to do, legitimate jobs and stuff. It's weird."

"Weird how?"

"Weird like they're actually showing up for family dinners now. Weird like they're not constantly looking over their shoulders. My uncle Carlos got a job at a warehouse, and Mateo is talking about community college when he finishes school."

"That's good, though," Li said.

"Yeah. I'm just glad all this mess is behind us."

"So did you start training with my mom's friend?" Li asked me.

"Yes. Did you know she was a boxer?"

"Yeah," she said, like I was an idiot.

"Well, I didn't. Here I was expecting to learn martial arts, and this Colombian boxer shows up."

"Because she's Mom's friend, you thought she'd teach martial arts?" Li asked, smiling. "Real racist of you there, Blake."

"Shut up. It was an easy mistake to make," I said, throwing a napkin at her and smiling too.

"She's something, though, isn't she?"

"Yeah, the lessons are good. She's less intense than I'd thought she'd be. I was expecting this serious fighting instructor, but she's funny and not at all the hard ass. Don't get me wrong, she works the hell out of me, but she's pretty great. And man, does she love food."

"Don't we all?" Eduardo said.

"Oh, no," Li added. "Not like Yesica. No one likes food like she does."

Eduardo smiled. "Sounds like someone I know."

Li kicked him under the table. "I don't talk about food that much."

"You mentioned dumplings three times since you got home."

"Because I forgot what the real thing tasted like. Chinese food in Wheaton is terrible."

"There's that place in Midland," I offered.

"Terrible. Everything tastes like it came from a can. My grandmother would cry."

I finished my burger. This was good, just sitting here with them, talking about nothing important. I'd missed my friends more than I'd realized.

"This was fun," Li said.

"Definitely. I'm coming by tomorrow for boxing lessons," I said. "We do it every Sunday."

"Great. I'll be unconscious, though. I can already feel the exhaustion starting to hit."

We all left money for the bill and headed out onto the street.

"Well, say hi if you get up."

"I will, and you should call Charlie."

"I will. See you tomorrow."

I headed home, shaking my head as I heard them laughing behind me.

Sunday, I made it to Li's mother's shop just before eleven to meet Yesica for our boxing lesson. I was surprised to find the front door locked and no sign of anyone. I went around back and found the back door propped open, which was also unusual. I stood there for a moment and could hear some kind of rhythmic thumping from what sounded like the basement.

Assuming the door was propped open for me, since I was supposed to be here now, I went inside, pulling the door shut behind me, and headed to the storage area.

The thumping got louder the closer I got, all but confirming Yesica was already here and doing some kind of workout. Sure enough, as I rounded the corner, I could see her at the heavy bag, already sweating.

"You're late," she said without turning around, throwing three quick punches that made the bag swing hard on its chain. "I've been here since ten-thirty."

"Sorry. My dad needed help moving some furniture this morning."

"I guess I can give that a pass, but remember, training is about being regimented. Today we're only going to work jab-cross. I know it's tempting to want to get to the fancier stuff, but this is your base. It's your foundation, so it's just jab-cross until your form stops making me want to cry."

I dropped my gym bag near the wall and started wrapping my hands the way she'd shown me last week. "Sounds boring."

"Boxing is boring. It's the same movements ten thousand times until your body remembers them when your brain is too tired or too scared to think."

Which, honestly, wasn't all that different than throwing a football. The wraps felt tighter this time, more secure. I'd practiced at home a few times, wrapping and unwrapping to try to get it right.

If all went to plan, my hands would be my moneymaker, so I didn't want to put them in jeopardy.

Yesica circled me, checking my work.

"Better. Still loose here ..." She tugged at my right hand. "But better. Now, stance."

I settled into position, left foot forward, right foot back, knees slightly bent.

"Chin."

I tucked it down.

"Good. Now shoulders."

I rolled them forward.

"Stay loose, though. You're too stiff." She pushed my shoulder and I rocked back slightly. "See? If you're tight like that, every punch moves your whole body. You need to be loose but controlled. Like ..." She demonstrated, her shoulders relaxed but ready. "Your turn."

I tried to match her position, forcing myself to relax muscles I hadn't realized I'd tensed.

"Better. Now, jab. And keep that chin tucked. The second it comes up, I'm stopping you."

I threw a jab. It felt decent.

"Again."

Another jab.

"Your shoulder rolled up before you threw. Do it again."

I threw three more jabs, focusing on keeping my shoulder in position until the punch extended.

"Now add the cross. Jab-cross. But slow. I want to see every part of the movement."

I threw the combination in slow motion, watching my own form.

"Good. Now, thirty jab-cross combinations. I'll count. If your form breaks, we start over."

The first ten felt awkward but manageable. By fifteen, my shoulders burned. At twenty-three, my left jab drifted wide.

"Stop. That jab went sideways. When you're tired, everything falls apart. This is why we drill. Start over."

"From zero?"

She laughed, but not meanly. "You think your opponent cares that you're tired? From zero."

I started over. This time, I made it to eighteen before my right cross dropped low.

"Again."

The third attempt got me to twenty-five before I shifted wrong and lost my balance.

"Again."

"Are you serious?"

"Very serious. Do you want to learn to defend yourself, or do you want to look cool throwing sloppy punches that won't help you in a real fight?"

I took a breath and started again. My arms felt like lead, but I focused on each movement individually. Jab. Cross. Reset. Jab. Cross. Reset.

"Twenty-eight, twenty-nine, thirty. Good." She clapped once. "Now you see the difference between movement and technique. Your body wants to cheat when it's tired. Wants to take shortcuts. But shortcuts get you hurt."

I leaned against the wall, breathing hard.

"Water. Then we do it again on the double-end bag."

"We're doing that thirty more times?"

"Yes. But first, water." She handed me a bottle from my bag. "And while you drink, watch."

She faced the heavy bag, settled into her stance, and threw thirty jab-cross combinations so fast I almost couldn't count them. Each punch landed with a sharp crack. Her chin never rose, her shoulders never tensed, her footwork never faltered.

When she finished, she wasn't even breathing hard.

"That's what ten thousand repetitions looks like," she said. "You see how boring it is, but boring works."

I drank more water and tried not to think about how far I had to go.

"Now, double-end bag." She pointed at the smaller bag suspended between two elastic cords. "This one moves. Teaches you timing and accuracy. If you go too fast, the bag will be in the wrong position and you won't connect right. Same drill. Thirty jab-cross combinations."

She demonstrated, throwing a jab that made the bag snap backward, then timing her cross perfectly as it rebounded forward. The bag bounced and swayed, but every punch landed clean.

"Your turn."

I threw a jab. The bag flew backward, and when I tried to throw the cross, it was still too far away. I missed completely.

"See? You have to time it. Feel the rhythm. Try again."

I threw another jab, waited for the bag to swing back, then threw my cross. It connected, but barely.

"Better. Keep going."

The double-end bag was infinitely more frustrating than the heavy bag. It moved unpredictably, and my timing stayed a half-second off no matter how hard I concentrated. By the time I'd completed thirty combinations, my wraps were soaked with sweat.

"Good. Now we do it again."

"Again?"

"Did I stutter?" She grinned. "Again. And this time, I want you to think about something. Every time you throw a combination in a real fight, you're giving someone a chance to hit you back. So you can't just stand there after you throw. You have to move. Understand?"

"I think so."

"You think so or you know so?"

"I know so."

"Good. Watch." She threw a jab-cross at the heavy bag, then immediately pivoted to her left, her hands still up, her chin still tucked. "In a real fight, you throw and move. Throw and move. Never stay in the same place. Show me."

I mimicked her movement, throwing a combination at the heavy bag and pivoting left. It felt clumsy, and I nearly lost my balance.

She laughed, not unkindly. "Okay, so we have work to do on that, but first, let's get your combinations solid. Heavy bag again. Thirty more."

By the time I finished the next round, my arms shook and my T-shirt clung to my back.

"Better. Your form held longer this time. You made it through all thirty without major mistakes. Now we add footwork drills. But first, you get two minutes of rest for doing it right."

I sat on the floor and tried to remember why I'd thought that learning boxing was a good idea.

"You're doing good, you know," Yesica said, dropping down beside me. "Most people get frustrated or bored and quit after the first thirty. You kept going, and that's the most important thing."

"Feels like I'm not getting anywhere."

"That's normal. Doesn't football feel the same? You practice and practice, but it's still slow building skills? Trust me, over time you'll look back and see you're making progress."

"How long does that take?"

She shrugged. "Depends. For me, maybe three months before I stopped thinking about every punch. For some people, longer; for others, never. But you have good instincts and you're young. Your body learns fast at your age."

"When did you start?"

"Nine years old. My father took me to a gym in the village where I grew up. Well, it wasn't even a gym, just a small building where a friend of his put up a bag. After he died and my mother moved us to the city, there was this gym an old friend of his had, and he promised my mother he'd look after me. Turned out looking after me meant teaching me to fight."

"I'm sorry. About your dad."

"It was a long time ago." She stood and offered me her hand. "Come on. Time for footwork."

She pulled me to my feet and pulled out a footwork ladder, laying it out on the floor. This I was familiar with since we used it in football for agility drills.

"You know how to do ladder work?"

"Yeah. We do it at football practice."

"Good. So you do two feet in each box, quick as you can, down and back. Then we add punches. You throw a jab-cross at the end of every pass. Understand?"

"Got it."

The ladder work itself felt familiar, which was something, but adding punches at the end made everything harder. I had to transition from the quick footwork to a stable stance fast enough to throw clean combinations, and the shift kept throwing off my timing.

"Faster on the feet, slower on the punch," Yesica called. "Don't rush the combination just because you finished the ladder fast. Take the extra half-second to set your stance."

I nodded and ran through again. This time, I planted my feet properly before throwing, and the jab-cross landed solidly.

"There. See? Better." She demonstrated, her feet flying through the ladder so fast I could barely track them, then settling into a perfect stance to throw a combination that would have knocked someone cold. "Fast to slow to fast again. That's the rhythm."

We ran through the drill a dozen more times. On the eighth pass, I accelerated too much coming out of the ladder and my front foot caught my back foot. I stumbled forward, arms windmilling, and barely caught myself before face-planting into the wall.

Yesica burst out laughing. "Oh my God, you almost ate that wall."

"It's not funny."

"It's a little funny." She was still laughing. "Sorry, sorry. But you looked like ..."

She mimicked my stumble, exaggerating the windmilling of my arms, and I couldn't help grinning despite myself.

"Okay, maybe a little funny."

"See? You can laugh at yourself. That's important. Nobody gets better without making mistakes." She patted my shoulder. "Again. And this time, don't try to kill yourself."

The next attempts went smoother. My feet found the rhythm, and the transitions from footwork to striking started to feel less jarring.

"Good. Now we change it." She moved one of the heavy bags to the side of the ladder. "Run the ladder, throw your combination at the bag, then pivot off-line and exit. Like you're escaping after you throw. Make sense?"

"I think so."

I ran through the ladder, threw a jab-cross at the bag, then pivoted left and took two quick steps away.

"Better. But you dropped your hands when you pivoted. That's when someone catches you. Again, hands up the whole time."

We drilled the sequence over and over. Footwork, combination, pivot, exit. Footwork, combination, pivot, exit. Every time I made a mistake, she called it out. Every time I did it right, she nodded and said "again" like getting it right once didn't mean anything.

After the twentieth rep, she finally called a halt.

"Okay. That's good for today. You're learning. Your form is getting better, your footwork is improving. You still have a lot of work to do, but you're not hopeless."

"Thanks. I think."

"You're welcome." She grabbed her water bottle and drained half of it.

I was starting to get my wraps off when a thought occurred to me, "Mrs. Sun isn't here?"

"She was when I got here, but she said she had to run to check on a piece of furniture somewhere. I don't know the place, but she said she wouldn't be back before two."

"Oh," I said, and had another thought. "Do you want to go get some lunch? The diner is just down the street. I know getting fed is part of your deal with her for teaching me."

She didn't even hesitate. "Absolutely."

We cleaned up the training area, folding the ladder and making sure the bags were secure. I changed into a clean T-shirt from my gym bag while Yesica ducked into the bathroom.

Five minutes later, we walked to the Silver Spoon. The lunch rush had started, but we found a booth near the back.

"Order whatever you want, I'm buying," I said. "Seriously."

"I won't say no to free food," she said, picking up the menu and studying it with the focus most people reserved for important documents. "Okay, so I'm thinking the double cheeseburger, chili fries, cheese sticks, and a chocolate shake. Is that too much?"

"Are you actually going to eat all that?"

"Don't worry about me. Nothing goes to waste."

We ordered, Yesica getting everything she'd listed while I ordered just a burger and fries.

"Can I ask you something?"

"Sure."

"You said you used to fight professionally. Like, real fights. Not just training."

"I did. Amateur mostly, but I had a few professional bouts. Even fought an exhibition in Vegas once, before a middleweight men's fight, although it was treated more as a novelty than a real fight. It's getting better, but female boxing just isn't taken seriously on the big stage yet."

"So why'd you stop? You were good enough to fight in Vegas."

"My mother got sick. She was still in Colombia, and I was traveling for fights, so I didn't get to see her much. I was making decent money, not rich, but decent, but she was all by herself and after the cancer diagnosis, she really needed someone there with her, so I temporarily retired. And after, I just never went back."

"I'm so sorry. That's how you met Mrs. Sun?"

"Yes. The doctors in Colombia, they tried, but the treatment wasn't good enough. So I brought her to Houston, used every dollar I'd saved from boxing to pay for better doctors, better treatment, experimental therapies. Everything."

Our food arrived, and Yesica immediately grabbed a cheese stick, digging in while she talked.

"Yeng's husband was one of her oncologists. He was very kind and tried everything he could, but some cancers, you know, they don't care how good the doctor is or how much money you spend."

"Yeah," I said, not sure what to say to that.

"And suddenly I had nothing. No money left, no immediate family in America, no boxing career to go back to because I'd been away too long, my visa was expiring, I had no job, and nowhere to live."

"What did you do?"

"I was ready to go back to Colombia and try staying with my mother's cousin, but then Yeng heard what was happening from her husband. She showed up at the hospital the day after my mother died and said I was coming to live with her. I tried to say no, that I couldn't impose, that I'd be fine. She said, 'You have no money, no papers, no place to go. You're coming with me. End of discussion.'"

"That sounds like her."

"She gave me a room, helped me get my papers sorted out, and loaned me money to open the gym in Lubbock. She saved my life. I owe her everything."

"That's really something," I said.

"It is. But enough sad stories, let's talk about boxing. You asked why I stopped fighting, but you should really be asking what fighting taught me that I can teach you."

"Okay. What did it teach you?"

"Most people, they think boxing is about throwing punches, about being tough or aggressive or powerful. Sure, those things matter, but the real secret of boxing, the thing that separates good fighters from great fighters, it's focus."

"Focus?"

"Boxing is about form. It's about protecting yourself and being ready for the opponent to give you an opening. Those guys who just throw haymaker after haymaker, they don't have the control, and they leave themselves open. Boxing is a mental game, as much as it is physical."

"That makes sense," I said. "Football is kind of the same way."

"Most sports, at a high enough level, are."

The rest of the lunch went like that, her demolishing a huge plate of food while we talked about the importance of conditioning and footwork.

Honestly, the more we talked about it, the more excited I was to learn more, even if it was going to be hard work.

Chapter 17

Mom gripped the door handle as I pulled into the hospital parking lot. She was scheduled to have her MRI today, which had been on the calendar for over a month. The doctor said it would tell us more about what was causing her headaches. She'd been going to her appointments on her own, but just before breakfast, she had a headache that made it almost impossible for her to stand.

Dad was at work, and her appointment was in Midland, which meant I was going to have to drive her. I'd had my learner's permit for a few months, so it was legal, but I don't think the adult in the car having her eyes closed the whole time was what they had in mind.

"Park close," she said as we pulled into the hospital parking lot.

I found a spot near the entrance and killed the engine.

Inside, Mom checked in at the desk and started to fill out the paperwork, but she was so shaky, I had to take the pen and do the writing for her.

A nurse called her name after ten minutes, and we followed her down a hallway lined with closed doors, each one identical except for the numbers. She opened the door to exam room four and gestured us inside.

"Go ahead and have a seat, Mrs. Sims. I need to get your vitals."

The room was small, barely big enough for the exam table, two chairs, and a rolling stool. Mom sat on the exam table while the nurse wrapped a blood pressure cuff around her arm. I took one of the plastic chairs against the wall, watching the numbers climb on the monitor.

"Blood pressure's a little elevated. Are you feeling anxious?"

"Just a headache."

The nurse made notes on her clipboard, then checked Mom's temperature and pulse. "Someone from transport will be here in a few minutes to take you back for your scan. You'll need to remove any jewelry or metal objects."

Mom pulled off her earrings, watch, and wedding ring, holding them out to me. Her hands were shaking.

"I'll keep them safe," I said.

After the nurse left, we sat in silence. The room felt too quiet, too still. A clock on the wall ticked away the seconds. Neither of us said anything the whole time, just sat there. I wanted to break the silence, but I didn't know exactly what to say.

Finally, a young guy in scrubs opened the door. "Mrs. Sims? I'm here to take you to MRI."

He helped Mom into a wheelchair even though she insisted she could walk. Hospital policy, he said cheerfully. Mom looked small in the chair, diminished.

"I'll bring her right back," he told me. "Probably about an hour total."

I watched them disappear down the hallway, and I was left alone in the exam room with nothing to do but wait.

I tried sitting. Stood up. Sat down again. The clock on the wall moved too slowly, each minute stretching out for what seemed like forever. I counted the perforations in the ceiling tiles. Studied the anatomy poster on the wall showing the human brain. Picked up a pamphlet about MRI safety and read it three times, just trying not to go crazy.

After what seemed like forty-five minutes of trying to do something, I checked my watch. Only fifteen minutes had passed.

This was like being in limbo, where time didn't exist.

I tried to remember what had been wrong with Mom in my dream life, but it was always vague and fuzzy. We'd gone no contact before she ever got a diagnosis, and I wasn't even sure she was interacting with the medical establishment at all then.

At her funeral, all anyone would say was that her 'illness' took so much from her. Of course, I remember the people who were her friends. All whack jobs who'd rather wave crystals over themselves than take a pill.

Footsteps in the hallway made me sit up straight, but they passed by our door. More waiting. More silence broken only by muffled voices from other rooms and the constant ticking of that clock.

When the wheelchair finally squeaked outside the door, I was on my feet before the door opened. When the transport guy wheeled Mom in, I was shocked at how gray her face looked.

"Little dizzy," she said before I could ask. "They said that's normal."

"You want to lie down?"

"I'm fine."

She wasn't fine. Her hands shook as she transferred from the wheelchair back to the exam table. The transport guy left, closing the door behind him, and we were alone again.

"How long until the doctor comes?" I asked.

"They said he needs to review the scans first. Could be a while."

It was a while. Another forty minutes of waiting, clock time not real time, listening to footsteps pass by in the hallway, watching Mom hold her head in her hands. She refused the water I offered. Refused to lie down. Just sat there on the edge of the exam table, shrinking into herself.

When someone finally knocked on the door, I could tell from the doctor's face that it wasn't good. He carried a tablet and a manila folder, closing the door quietly behind him.

"Mrs. Sims." He pulled the rolling stool over and sat down, facing us. "I've reviewed your MRI results. There's a mass in your skull base, anterior region. Based on the imaging, it appears to be a meningioma, which is a tumor that develops in the meninges, the protective layers surrounding your brain."

The words seemed to come from very far away, like I was hearing them underwater.

"Cancer?" Mom's voice cracked.

"Meningiomas are typically benign, which means non-cancerous. However, this one is quite large, approximately five centimeters, and its location is causing the symptoms you've been experiencing." Dr. Mitchell stood and flipped on the lightbox mounted on the wall, pulling several large films from the manila envelope and clipping them up one by one. "Let me show you."

The images showed cross-sections of Mom's skull. The doctor pointed to one area with his pen.

"You can see it here. This lighter area shouldn't be there. That's the tumor."

I stared at the films, trying to make sense of what I was seeing. There it was, a mass that didn't belong, taking up space.

"Is that what's causing the headaches?" I asked.

"Yes. The tumor is also responsible for your loss of smell, Mrs. Sims, which you mentioned started several years ago. As it's grown, it's begun to compress other structures, leading to the seizures and other neurological symptoms."

Mom made a small sound, almost like a whimper. I'd never heard her make a sound like that before.

"There could have also been other effects that you didn't notice right away. Changes in personality, mood instability, difficulty with emotional regulation. All of these can result from a tumor in this location affecting the frontal lobe."

I thought about the last three years. Mom's increasing irritability, her inability to handle stress, the way she'd become someone different, angry all the time. I knew it had something to do with her illness, but seeing this, it became all the more clear.

"You said typically benign," Mom said. "What does that mean?"

"It means we need to do a biopsy to determine definitively whether the tumor is benign or malignant. The imaging characteristics suggest benign, but we can't be certain without tissue samples. However, even if the tumor is benign, its size and location make it dangerous. Left untreated, it will continue growing. It could become malignant over time, and regardless, the pressure on your brain will cause increasing neurological damage."

"What do you recommend?" I asked after she didn't say anything.

"Surgical removal is the only viable treatment option. Given the size and location, this will be a complex procedure requiring a specialized neurosurgeon. I can give you some suggestions."

"Surgery?" Mom asked, as if that was the only thing she'd heard.

"I understand this is overwhelming. This tumor has likely been growing for years. The fact that you're still functioning as well as you are is remarkable. But that won't last. The seizures will become more frequent and severe. There could be vision problems, cognitive decline, more personality changes." He paused. "Without treatment, this tumor will kill you."

The small room seemed to shrink even further. I felt like I was going to be sick.

"There's chemotherapy too, right?" I asked, remembering treatments I'd heard about in my old life. "You can shrink it before surgery?"

The doctor turned to me. "Unfortunately, meningiomas don't typically respond well to chemotherapy, although it is sometimes used in conjunction with surgery. Radiation is a lot more risky and, while possible, has a much lower chance of success. Surgery is really the primary treatment. However, I do want to start you on a course of chemotherapy to see if we can slow the growth and reduce some of the swelling around the tumor before we operate. It's not standard protocol, but given the size and your symptoms, I think it's worth trying."

"When?" Mom asked.

"I'd like to schedule your first treatment within the week, and you'll need to contact the neurologist you settle on and get an initial appointment with them. They'll need to review your scans and determine the surgical approach, but it also depends on how the chemo affects the tumor size."

"What are the risks," I asked, "of the surgery?"

The doctor looked at me for a long moment before answering. "There are always risks with any surgery, especially one this complex. Potential complications include infection, bleeding, damage to surrounding brain tissue, vision problems, and changes in cognitive function. There's also a risk that we won't be able to remove the entire tumor if it's too deeply embedded in critical structures."

"And if we don't do the surgery?" Mom asked.

"Mom ..." I started.

"No, it's a fair question," the doctor said. "Without surgery, the tumor will continue growing. You'll have more seizures, potentially fatal ones. Your cognitive function will decline. Eventually, the pressure on your brain will cause severe neurological damage and death."

"I need to think about this."

"Of course. Take some time to process everything and talk to your family. I need you to understand, though, that time is *not* on our side here. Every day that tumor continues growing is another day of damage to your brain."

He pulled out a prescription pad and started writing. "I'm going to increase your anti-seizure medication and add a steroid to help with the swelling. That should help with the headaches. Stop at the desk to schedule the chemotherapy."

He shook both our hands and left. Mom and I sat in silence.

"Mom ..."

"Don't." She stood up, swaying slightly before catching herself on the exam table's edge. "Let's just go."

I followed her out of the exam room, down the hallway past all those identical doors. At the front desk, she scheduled the chemotherapy appointment. The receptionist smiled and said something cheerful about seeing us then, like we were coming back for a spa day instead of to have poison pumped through Mom's veins.

The walk to the car felt endless. Mom moved slowly, one hand pressed to her temple, the other clutching her handbag. When we reached the station wagon, she handed me the keys again without being asked.

I drove more carefully on the way home, hyperaware of every other car, every stop sign. Mom leaned against the passenger door window, eyes closed. I didn't know if she was sleeping or just trying to escape.

Halfway home, she spoke without opening her eyes.

"You can't tell Joshua."

"Mom ..."

"I mean it, Blake. He doesn't need to know yet. Not until we know more."

"Dad needs to know. You heard what the doctor said."

"I'll tell your father," she said, opening her eyes and turning to look at me, "but Joshua is too young. He wouldn't understand."

I honestly didn't care if we told Josh one way or another. That little psychopath would undoubtedly not care. He'd already shown how little sympathy he had for her or anyone else.

Of course, I'd have to be a monster to say that out loud, especially on a day like this, so I kept my opinion to myself.

"Okay."

"And I don't want people at church knowing. Or your school. Or anyone. This is private, family business."

"People are going to notice when you're going to chemotherapy appointments and having brain surgery."

"We'll deal with that when we have to."

I pulled into our driveway and killed the engine.

Mom got out of the car before I could come around to help her. She walked to the front door, fumbling with her keys. I didn't follow immediately, just stood next to the car, watching her struggle with the lock for a few seconds before she got it open and disappeared inside.

In the sudden quiet, I leaned against the station wagon's sun-warmed hood and stared up at the cloudless sky.

I thought about all the times I'd been angry at her over the past few years, all the fights, the frustration and the moments when I'd wished she was different. I'd felt justified to be angry at the time, but now it felt wrong.

The front door opened again. Mom stood in the doorway.

"Are you coming in?"

"Yeah." I pushed off the car. "Just needed a minute."

Inside, Mom went straight to her room without another word. I heard her bedroom door close, then silence.

Some time later, I had no idea how long, the phone rang, making me jump. I grabbed it before it could wake Mom.

"Blake? It's Dad. How did the appointment go?" my father asked on the other end of the line.

I opened my mouth, but for a second, nothing came out. Then I told him everything.

I was late getting out onto the field. Today was the first day of tryouts for the new season, and I was the last one to get there. I wasn't really late, just a few minutes, but everyone still looked at me as I jogged up.

I'd wanted to be early today, to show Coach I was ready for this season, but I hadn't been sleeping, and the stress at home had gotten bad. Mom completely withdrew into herself after the diagnosis. She hadn't gone back to the 'woo-woo' stuff, but it was definitely bugging her.

I knew she hadn't made her appointment with the specialist the doctor had recommended yet. I was trying to be patient and give her time, because it was a lot to deal with, but I also didn't want her to wait too long. The doctor had made it clear that the longer she let the tumor grow, the worse it was going to get.

Dad was trying his best to keep the house together, work his normal hours, comfort her, and do everything there was to do, but he'd suddenly become a single parent, for all intents and purposes, and it was a lot for one guy.

Especially a guy who was told the woman he loved might die.

Still, I should have gotten here sooner. As soon as I was back on the field, the world seemed to right itself a little bit. This was my happy place.

Of course, it was soured a bit by the fact that every eye turned to look at me as I ran up. Word had gotten out, clearly, and everyone was giving me a look of sympathy as I joined them.

Honestly, I kind of wished no one knew. I didn't need this kind of focus.

"Glad you could join us," Mickey said, giving me one of his grins.

"I wanted you to see what the field looked like before I took it over," I said, which got a bigger grin.

Trust Mickey not to take anything too seriously. God love him.

"Bring it up!" Coach Holloway said, blowing a whistle.

The freshmen had already broken off with Coach Heidemann, which left the guys who'd either be on JV or Varsity to gather up around him.

"We lost a lot of guys from last year, most of the team in fact, so this is going to be almost an entirely new squad. We had a good group last year, but we only made it to region. I do not think that is our ceiling. We look to be mostly juniors and sophomores here, which means we have two good years before there's another major shift in players, but that doesn't mean I want us to just plan to win next year. I think we have a real shot at our first state championship *this* year. But, we only have so many spots, and I want to make sure we have the best team we can field." He paused, letting that line hang. "You want one of those spots? *Earn it!* You've got this week to show me and my staff who belongs out here on Friday night."

A few heads turned my way, including Gabriel's and Jorden's. I knew what they must be thinking. They'd left Gabriel on the freshman team and put Jorden as my backup on JV last year, and then I'd beaten both of them out for seven-on-seven.

We all knew the score, not that I was going to throw it in their faces. They both knew they wouldn't be starting, and there was only room for one of them as my backup, meaning the other would be stuck on JV.

I couldn't imagine what it must be like, to know you're trying out for second place. I felt a little bad for them, actually.

Although not bad enough to give up my spot.

"Quarterbacks, receivers, backs, you're with Coach Easley after flex. Linemen, go with Coach Kerr. Defense with Coach Mayfield. Hydrate, helmets on, and do your best. Let's get to work."

We broke and spread out to do warm-ups. Although I'd still been doing my workouts every day, I knew I'd been phoning it in the last week, so it felt good to really get moving, stretching my muscles and falling into those familiar patterns.

Finally, warm-ups were done, and it was time to get down to it. Mickey fell in step next to me as we followed Coach Easley to the half of the field we had to work with.

"You back in one piece?" he asked.

"Mostly," I said.

"Good. I need you to make me look good."

"Don't ask the impossible," I said, which earned me a shove.

"Alright, skill positions!" Coach Easley clapped his hands together. "We're starting with route fundamentals."

Jorden stepped up first, which hopefully would be less for him to complain about. He'd spent a good amount of time last semester talking about the favoritism I got after I beat him out for seven-on-seven. And honestly, he wasn't bad. Coach called out routes, slants, outs, posts, and Jorden did a good job getting the ball where it needed to go, although it didn't quite have the zip on it that you'd want it to have. On a fifteen-yard out to Joe, the throw arrived late, forcing Joe to slow his route.

"Timing, Kinsell!" Coach shouted. "That ball's got to be there before he breaks!"

Jorden then overcorrected and fired the next throw harder, a post which overshot his receiver. Jerry had to leap, barely getting fingertips on it.

That was his last go, and he was pissed as he came off the field, glaring at me as if I had something to do with how he threw.

Gabriel went next. He had a quicker release than Jorden, more compact, but his deep ball lacked touch. When Coach called for a corner route to Miles, Gabriel's throw hung too long, giving an imaginary safety time to close. Miles caught it, but Coach Easley was already shaking his head.

"Neiva, you're muscling it. Let the ball work for you."

After a few more turns, Coach rotated us again, giving me a shot at it.

I stepped into the imaginary pocket. Easley called a dig route for Mickey, fifteen yards downfield, break inside. I took a three-step drop, eyes tracking Mickey's release. He exploded off the line, sold the corner with an outside fake, then planted hard and drove inside. I released the ball the moment his foot hit the ground, leading him just enough that he caught it in stride without breaking pace.

"That's timing!" Easley jabbed a finger at me. "That's what I want to see!"

We cycled through routes, and I was honestly on my game, landing the ball where it needed to be each time. I'd had a lot of time to throw in the net at the All-American camp, and most of the solo work I'd been doing in between was for accuracy, since throwing at different targets was about all I could do when I was by myself practicing.

While there was a lot more I needed to work on, that part of the practice was starting to really show.

Of course, it was different with real receivers, where timing mattered as much, if not more, than accuracy, but I'd had time at the camps to work on that, and it was one of the major things Coach Moreno worked on with me when he was in town.

That and reads.

"Good," Coach said after I hit Austin on a quick slant. "Real good."

We moved into accuracy drills, letting the receivers go do their thing. Coach set up targets at different depths: ten yards, fifteen yards, twenty-five yards, and had us hit specific spots.

This was exactly what I had been doing for the last several weeks, and I was ready for it. Jorden went first, hitting two out of five targets. His deep ball fell three yards short. He'd been overthrowing a bit during the receivers' work, including that deep, so I knew he had the arm to make the throw.

He was probably just overthinking it.

Gabriel did a little better with three out of five, with one rimming out of the trash can, which showed he wasn't exactly on target.

On my turn, I was ready. The ten-yard target was a simple out, and I put the ball right into the trash can. The fifteen-yard one required more touch, and I dropped the ball directly on top of it. The deep ball needed more arc and distance, and I let it fly, watching as it landed right where it needed to be.

"Five out of five," Easley called out. "Good consistency, Sims."

We did a few more run-throughs of this before we got the receivers back for timed routes. Easley had the receivers line up and run specific patterns on a snap count. He told the guys separately what to run so we couldn't overhear it and had to watch them to see what they were going to do. We had to deliver the ball at the exact moment the receiver made his break, no hesitation.

This was where Moreno's training really showed. I'd spent months working on anticipation, on releasing the ball before the receiver came open, trusting that he'd be there when it arrived. Jorden and Gabriel both waited to see the receiver break before throwing, which meant the ball was always a step late.

I hit six straight timing routes, putting the ball exactly where it needed to be when it needed to be there.

"That's how you do it! See how the ball's already there? That's trusting your receiver!"

During a water break, Miguel came over and said, "Those camps really helped, huh?"

"More, all the training I was doing in between and all spring. The camps were great, but you can only do so much in four days."

"Well, whatever it was, keep doing it. You're killing it."

I just nodded and watched the defense guys working on blocking drills with Coach Kerr. He was really putting them through it.

"Y'all see Hunter?" Miguel asked. "Dude's been running hard all practice."

I glanced over. The receivers were out doing pass-catching drills, and he was right, Hunter really was hustling. I was glad he'd managed to straighten up after breaking off from Elijah. We wouldn't ever be close friends, but he had potential and didn't need to be throwing it away backing Elijah's petty little games.

"He wants varsity," I said. "Can't blame him."

The whistle blew. Back to work.

Now we were doing drop-back mechanics and footwork. Coach set up cones for a three-step timing drill, making us hit each depth in turn. Three steps for quick game, five for intermediate, seven for deep drops.

I went through the progressions, taking the imaginary snap, three-step drop, hitch, and throw. Five-step drop, plant, and drive. Seven-step drop, set, and deliver. My feet hit the marks every time, weight balanced, throwing shoulder back.

"Good rhythm, Sims."

Jorden struggled with the seven-step drop. His footwork got choppy, throwing off his timing. The longer we went, the more he was getting in his own head. He had a bad habit of trying to "make up" for mistakes and overdoing it, and then doing that again the next time, compounding the problem.

After that, we moved to red zone drills, situational work inside the twenty-yard line where the field compressed and windows tightened. Holloway set up goal-line scenarios, making us put the ball in tight spaces with Coach Wilson sending over a couple of running backs to give us more targets.

"First and goal from the five," Holloway called out. "Sims, you're up. Quick slant to the front pylon."

I took my drop, eyes on Mickey as he released from the line. He broke inside at three yards, and I fired the ball low and away from where the defender would be. Mickey caught it at the goal line. Touchdown.

"Corner route, back of the end zone," Holloway said. "Miguel."

Miguel lined up outside, sold an inside move, then broke hard to the corner. I waited an extra beat, then dropped the ball over his outside shoulder just before he ran out of bounds. He caught it, dragging his feet.

Jorden took his reps and threw three passes. One was incomplete high. One was caught but would've been knocked down by any decent defender. The third was decent, a quick out that hit Joe in the hands.

Gabriel managed two completions out of three, but both were safe throws, and a good defense would have predicted them and had a chance to knock them down.

The drills continued. Situational work, two-minute offense without a defense, just making sure we could hit our drops and deliver accurate throws without being under pressure. I threw eighteen passes in that segment and completed sixteen. The two incompletions were my fault, one overthrow on a deep post, one that I didn't lead the receiver enough.

By the time Coach Holloway blew the final whistle, I was really starting to feel like I was in the zone after a week of not-great practices.

Nothing clears your head like a little focus and exercise.

"Good work today," Holloway said as we all gathered up. "Hit the showers. We go again tomorrow, same time."

The team started breaking up, heading toward the locker rooms. I grabbed my water bottle and was halfway to the building when I heard Coach Holloway's voice behind me.

"Sims, hold up a second."

I turned. Holloway was walking toward me, Coach Easley a few steps behind.

"Yes, Coach?"

Holloway stopped a few feet away, his expression serious. "You got a minute?"

"Sure."

He glanced around, making sure no one was close enough to hear. "You really have been putting in the work this summer and last semester, and it shows. We wanted to talk to you about our plans for this season. It goes without saying you're going to get the starting varsity spot, although I'd appreciate it if you didn't talk to anyone about that."

I'd be lying if I said I wasn't expecting it, although I was a little confused about why he was telling me. If he wanted me to keep it to myself, the easiest way would be to just not say anything.

"I'm telling you this because we need to start thinking seriously about our plans for this season. I've spoken with the other coaches, and we've decided to build the team around you, but you need to be ready for that because it means a lot of time on the field. I've spoken with Coach Moreno and had a call from Cliff Daniels of all people, who said he worked with you at one of your camps. They both believe, and we agree, that we could set ourselves apart by making a mobile offense, taking advantage of your speed and versatility to keep our opponents on their toes. I need you to understand what it means to have so much of our game plan resting on you."

I wasn't surprised that Coach Moreno had talked to him. He and Coach Holloway had spent time together last semester working with me collectively, but I was surprised at the call from Daniels. There was no reason for him to call my high school coach, and the fact that he did said a lot for the kind of guy he was.

And I was excited for the opportunity. An offense that let me run when I needed to and wasn't focused on working our backs as much was my dream.

"I understand, Coach."

"Do you? Because this will be a lot of pressure. You're going to be playing against some serious teams, and the pressure is going to be high. And everyone will know we are putting that weight on you. If we lose, you're going to get the blame no matter what we do to soften it."

I was pretty sure I'd get the blame even if the offense wasn't built around me, but either way, I wanted this.

"I'm ready, Coach."

"I think you are," Holloway said. "It's not just about on-field work. You've been putting in more time practicing than any player I've ever coached, and I know that's why you've come so far, but at the end of the day, this is a team game, and one man alone can't decide it. When I say you need to step up, it's not just in your playmaking. *It's in your leadership.* I need you to work with your guys, *communicate*, and lead them to victory."

"The other boys look to you on the field. Both Coach Holloway and I've seen it," Coach Easley added. "You've gotta stay on your game and don't let any stupid shit get in your way. Be there for them, help them when they struggle, and show them what a Mustang really is!"

"I will."

"Good," Holloway said. "Because this is your chance. We lost some great players last year, and we've got holes to fill. But we've also got potential, guys like Hernandez, Evans, your buddy Roach. They're hungry. Pull them together, get them believing in the system, and we can make a real run at this thing. All the way to state. I'm not gonna lie to you. It's gonna be hard. Most of these guys are older than you. They're gonna test you, push back, question whether you've earned it. You gotta prove it every day. Every practice. Every game."

"Yes, sir. I can handle it."

Holloway studied me for a long moment, then nodded. "Good! Show us. Now go shower. You smell like a locker that ate a dumpster!"

Chapter 18

The second day of tryouts went as well as the first. The camps had been really challenging and, in spite of being proud of Ray, I'd been a little bummed to be in the middle of the pack and not at the top.

It honestly had me second-guessing if I was as good as I'd thought I was.

It was clear now that a big part of that was just the level of competition. Not that my guys weren't good, because they were, but the All-American camp had some of the best players in the *country*, and it showed with the level of skill everyone had.

Seeing how things felt when I was back home, how much easier it seemed, it actually made me want to do more camps next year. If I had it like this all the time, where I was a step ahead of everyone around me, I wouldn't push myself to the edge. And I wanted that extra push.

Again, not that I would ever say any of that in public. Just thinking it, I realized how conceited it made me sound, even to myself. But I needed to be honest with myself if I was going to get to that next level. And to be truly competitive, I needed to be seriously challenged.

Not that it wasn't nice to feel like the top dog again.

I got home and was about to head upstairs to take a shower when I saw Mom on the couch, same spot as yesterday, and the TV was on some talk show I didn't care about.

I hadn't pushed her since the diagnosis, but we were now a full week out and I had a sneaking suspicion she hadn't made any calls about the next step in her treatment. While I hated to push her, considering how she was feeling and the news she'd got, I wasn't willing to lose her either.

I veered away from the stairs into the living room, which is about when she noticed me, which showed just how zonked out she was. I knew she was hitting the pain meds the doctor had given her, and was glad that it helped with her pain, but just medicating herself until she withered away wasn't the answer.

"How was practice?" she asked weakly, looking up at me.

"Good. Did you make that appointment yet?"

"Not yet, honey. I've been meaning to, but ..."

"Mom. It's been almost a week since the doctor told you about the tumor."

"I know." She looked back at the TV. "I'll do it tomorrow."

"What about the chemo? The doctor said you need to start that to shrink the tumor before surgery."

"I've scheduled it."

"But are you going to go?"

She didn't say anything.

The frustration that had been building all week finally boiled over. "Mom, we talked about this. I don't want to nag you, but the doctor was really clear that if you don't do anything, this thing is just going to keep growing until it kills you."

"Don't be so dramatic."

"I'm not being dramatic, I'm being realistic. This isn't going away on its own. Tumors don't magically get better."

She turned to face me, and I could see the exhaustion in her features. Her skin looked pale, and there were dark circles under her eyes. The biggest tell of how she was feeling was that she hadn't even bothered to put on makeup, something my mother did religiously every day of my life.

"I know it's serious, Blake, but brain surgery isn't exactly something you rush into. I need time to think about my options."

"What options? The doctor said this is the only option."

"He's not the only doctor in the world."

I closed my eyes and took a breath, trying to remember what Li had said about changing circumstances instead of minds.

"Fine, but you at least need to see the neurosurgeon and start the chemo. That's what you agreed to do."

"I said I would take care of it."

"When?"

"When I'm ready."

"That's not good enough," I said, sitting down in Dad's chair, across from her. "You heard about how bad it can get."

She bristled at that. "What do you know about it? You're fifteen years old."

"I know someone whose parents had to get surgery like this. They waited to get treatment and it took months to even get an appointment with the specialist. By then, the damage was worse than it needed to be."

That wasn't actually true. What I remembered was how hard it was to get in for treatment in my dream life, not that I could explain that.

"That's different."

"How?"

"It just is."

"Mom, please. I've been giving you space because I know this is a lot to process, but you can't keep putting this off. The doctor said ..."

"I know what the doctor said, but I'm also talking to Yogi Theodor about some alternative therapies that might help shrink the tumor without having to do surgery."

And there it was. The exact thing I'd been dreading.

"No."

"Excuse me?"

"No," I said again. "We had a deal. You agreed to see a real doctor and get real treatment."

"Yogi Theodor is a real healer. He's helped countless people with ..."

"He's a quack. Mom, we've been through this. His 'treatments' don't work. They're just going to waste time you don't have."

Her face flushed. "You don't know what you're talking about."

"I know that conventional medicine is the only thing that's going to save your life."

"You're a child ..."

"One of us is acting like a child, and it's not me." I stood up.

She stood too, and I could see her hands shaking. "Don't you dare ..."

"Don't I dare what? Tell you the truth? You have a five-centimeter tumor pressing on your brain. It's causing seizures. It's causing personality changes. And if you don't get it removed, it's going to cause permanent brain damage and then it's going to kill you."

"Stop it."

"No." I moved closer. "Do you understand what's going to happen if you keep ignoring this? The neurological damage is going to become irreversible. You're going to lose your vision. You're going to have trouble walking, trouble talking. You're going to lose control of yourself completely."

"You're trying to scare me."

"I'm trying to save your life. I've done research on this, Mom. I've read about what happens in the later stages. It's not pretty. It's not something you can wish your way out of."

She was quiet for a moment. I hoped that meant she was breaking down, realizing she was making a mistake again.

After a moment, she weakly argued, "But the cost ..."

"Dad said he'd talked to you about that."

"He did, but I think he's just saying it to make me feel better. There's no way we can actually afford all this."

"Yes, we can. I know for a fact we can afford it. Dad wasn't lying to you."

"How would you know?"

Because I'd spent the summer betting on sports outcomes I already knew would happen and making investments in companies I knew would succeed, but I couldn't exactly tell her that.

"Because we went over all of our finances to see if I could afford Coach Moreno. And our insurance will cover a lot of it. The department has good coverage."

I don't think she believed me, but she couldn't argue the insurance part, at least.

"Even if we could afford it, I'm not ready to ..."

"Ready for what? To stay alive? To be here for your kids?"

"Don't you put that on me. You think I want this? You think I'm choosing to have a tumor in my head?"

"No, but you are choosing not to treat it."

"I'm scared, Blake," she finally admitted. "I'm scared of brain surgery. I'm scared of what they're going to have to do to me. I'm scared of what happens if something goes wrong."

"I know you're scared. But I'm scared too. I'm scared of losing you."

"You're not going to lose me."

"I will if you don't get treatment." I moved closer to her. "Mom, please. I know this is terrifying, but the alternative is so much worse. And I meant what I said before. If you don't follow through with our agreement, I'm going to quit football. I'm going to drop out of school. I'm going to get a job and stay home to make sure you do what you need to do."

"You wouldn't."

"Try me." I held her gaze. "I will not give up on you. I don't care if you're angry with me. I don't care if you hate me for pushing this. I'm not watching you die because you're too stubborn to get help."

Her face crumpled, and for a moment I thought she was going to cry. But then she just looked tired, more tired than I'd ever seen her.

"Fine."

"Fine, what?"

"Fine, I'll call." She sat back down. "I'll make the appointment with the neurosurgeon."

"And the chemo?"

"And the chemo."

I checked my watch. It was only four-thirty. "It's early enough. You can call right now."

"Blake ..."

"I'll sit with you while you do it."

She looked at me with something between frustration and resignation. "You're not going to let this go, are you?"

"No."

She closed her eyes for a long moment. "Okay. Hand me the phone."

Thursday's scrimmage started the same way Wednesday's had ended. We'd started scrimmaging late the day before and would do mostly that today and tomorrow until we got down to team selection.

Which worked for me. I loved getting to play.

The offense lined up in a spread formation, four receivers wide with Noah in the backfield. I took the snap from Andre, three-step drop, and found Brian cutting across the middle. The ball left my hand before the linebacker could react. Brian caught it in stride, turned upfield for eight yards before safety Justin Sharp brought him down.

"Again. Same play," Coach Easley yelled from the sideline.

On the next go-round, the defense adjusted this time, the linebacker shading inside to take away the crossing route. I saw Austin breaking his route short on the outside and hit him for six yards. Third and four. Henry ran the corner route from the slot on the next play, finding the soft spot between the corner and safety at twelve yards. I led him toward the sideline and he hauled it in for seventeen yards, first down.

I was feeling good. Comfortable, and all of the conditioning here and at the camps had really helped improve my stamina over the summer. Austin and Brian had both been on varsity last year, and except for at the disastrous party last year, and the Fourth of July thing this summer, I didn't know them well.

Next, they called for both of them ran deep routes on the left side, trying to pull the safeties over while Henry ran a fifteen-yard dig from tight end. The ball snapped and I dropped back five steps. The dig route came open right on time. After we switched some of the offensive players out, I fired it in there and Henry caught it for thirteen more. Noah took the handoff on the following play, following Joe's block through the right side for seven yards. The defense rotated, bringing an extra man into the box. I checked to the quick slant without waiting for a call, hitting Mickey for five and another first down.

I was really feeling myself today, one of those days where I felt I could do no wrong, getting the ball where I needed to, keeping my footwork on point, and just killing it.

The next play was a zone read. I faked the handoff to Noah and kept it myself, finding the cutback lane for eight yards before Don Manoux wrapped me up. The contact jarred my shoulder but nothing hurt. Just football. Goal line situation now, red zone. I took the snap from under center and hit Henry on the quick out for six yards and the touchdown. The defense hadn't adjusted fast enough to the formation change.

Coach Easley blew his whistle. "Next group. Sims, Richman, Slagle, Lillard, take a break. Defense Nielsen, Kroli, Dean, you're up."

I jogged to the sideline where water waited while Jorden pulled on his helmet and ran out onto the field.

"Making it look easy out there," Gabriel said.

"Thanks."

The whistle blew and Jorden took the snap. He dropped back but held the ball too long, checking through his progressions twice, missing an open throw to Mickey that was tight but doable, before throwing it away. Next play, Jorden handed off to Jamal. Connor pulled from his guard spot but got caught inside, and Jamal got stuffed for a loss of two.

The same corner route concept I'd run earlier came next. Jorden took the snap and dropped back. The pocket collapsed faster this time, Connor getting beaten inside by Jesse Kroli. Jorden scrambled right and threw the ball at his tight end's feet. Incomplete. Four more plays and Jorden threw two passes, an interception, and got sacked once. When the whistle blew for rotation, he yanked his helmet off, face red.

Coach Easley waved for the groups to switch. I pulled my helmet back on and headed out. I know we hadn't exactly gotten along in the past, but I tried to give Jorden some encouragement as he walked past me toward the sideline.

"Tight coverage out there."

He didn't respond.

Back on the field, the defense had rotated in fresh players. Kevin stood at defensive tackle now. I took the snap and dropped back on the post route. The offensive line held up but Kevin gave pressure up the middle. I stepped up in the pocket and found Miguel breaking open, threw it for eighteen yards before Kevin got close enough to hit me.

The next series kept moving. Quick slant to Miguel for nine. Austin beat his corner on a comeback for twelve. Noah broke a run for fifteen after I faked the play-action pass. We just walked the ball down the field. Not every pass hit or every run made it through, but we were getting the completions we needed to move the ball, which is what Coach Holloway preferred over big, high-risk, high-reward strategies. Two plays later, I threw a touchdown pass to Austin on a fade route. He went up high over the cornerback and brought it down just over the line.

The whistle blew again. "Offense rotate. Blake's group to the bench."

Connor and Jamal were near the water cooler and both looked tired and a little dejected. Connor's face was flushed, freckles standing out against the red.

"You guys doing all right?" I asked.

Connor nodded. "Just trying to keep up."

"That last play where you pulled, you got caught inside because the defensive end slanted in. You have to read that and adjust your angle. If he goes inside, you go around him to the outside."

"Yeah, I saw that after. Just couldn't react fast enough."

"It'll come. You're strong enough; just need more reps reading the defense."

"I keep getting hit in the backfield before I can make a cut," Jamal said.

"The line's still learning, but you can help them by being more patient. Let the play develop before you commit to a hole. You're fast enough that you don't need to press."

"Feels like if I wait, the defense is already there."

"Sometimes they are. But if you hit the wrong hole early, you'll definitely go nowhere. Trust your blockers."

Gabriel walked over, helmet under his arm. "Your guys did better that last series."

"Still got beat a few times," Connor said.

"Everyone gets beat. You kept playing through it."

Out on the field, Gabriel took the snap and handed off to Jerry Roach. The play gained four yards, better blocking this time.

Gabriel ran through his series, completing short passes and moving the chains in small chunks. Pass to Miles Clement for seven. Handoff to Jerry for five. Quick out to Miguel for eight. The offense moved in short chunks, nothing explosive. After six plays, they'd driven forty yards, all underneath stuff.

Coach Easley blew his whistle. "Jorden's group, you're up."

Jorden jogged back out. Jamal went with him at halfback. First play was a run up the middle that gained three. Four vertical routes came next, forcing the defense to cover deep. Jorden took the snap in shotgun and dropped back. The pocket held this time and all four receivers ran straight vertical stems. The defense played two-high safety, splitting the field in half. Jorden stared at his primary read on the left side, pump-faked, then threw it anyway into double coverage. Incomplete.

Connor looked over at me from the sideline. "Why didn't he check to the other side?"

"He locked onto one receiver."

"But the right side was wide open."

"Yeah."

Jorden tried another deep shot next and completed this one, getting another first down. I thought maybe he'd turned the corner and things were going to start looking better, but on the next snap, he immediately scrambled right, even though his blocking held up. He ran for six yards, short of the first down.

"What was that?" Gabriel said from beside me.

"He was frustrated and trying to make something happen."

He'd started the day out okay, but as small misses added up, he started to crumble under the pressure. The next series went even worse. Three incompletions and a sack across four plays. When he came off the field, Jorden threw his helmet at the bench. It bounced and rolled, drawing looks from everyone.

Coach Easley walked over. "Kinsell, go cool off."

Jorden's face went red but he nodded and walked toward the equipment shed.

"Sims, you're back in. Let's see if you can score from the forty."

I grabbed my helmet and jogged back out. The defense had rotated again. I was getting more field time than Jorden or Gabriel and I was starting to get a little winded.

Option route for Henry based on coverage. I took the snap and dropped back three steps. He read the zone and sat down in the window. I hit him for nine yards. Joe followed Albert's block through the left side on the next play for six yards and a first down. Miguel ran a twelve-yard comeback on the outside after that. I took my five-step drop, made his break right on time, and I threw it before he even turned around. The timing had to be perfect or the corner could jump it. He caught it for eleven yards.

The next three plays moved the ball in chunks. Quick pass to Austin that the defender got a hand on, knocking it to the ground. Handoff to Joe for eight and then a screen to him for thirteen. We got down to the fifteen-yard line. Miguel ran the corner route from the left slot. I took the snap, three-step drop, and threw it before he made his final break. The ball led him toward the pylon. He caught it in stride and dragged his feet inbounds for the touchdown.

The whistle blew. "Rotate. Let's go."

Gabriel ran his series through, mixing runs and short passes. He completed six of eight passes, moved the offense down the field, and threw a touchdown to Mickey on a quick slant. Solid work.

When Jorden's turn came up again, Coach Easley called him over first. They talked for thirty seconds, Coach Easley pointing at the field and making throwing motions. Jorden nodded. I could see he was still in his own head, pushing himself too hard.

He took the field for another series. First play was a completion to his tight end for eight yards. Better. Second play was a run that lost two yards when Connor got beaten inside again. Jorden took the next snap and dropped back on a post route. The pocket collapsed faster this time, and he scrambled right, looking for someone to get open. No one did. He threw the ball away.

That was actually the right call for once. Sometimes the defense just gets through and you're not going to make your play.

It happens.

Third and four now. Three receivers to the left on the next play, all running short slants. Quick read, quick throw. Jorden took the snap but hesitated instead of making the pass, checking through all three receivers before throwing to the middle one. The ball came out late and got batted down by the linebacker who had time to read it. Incomplete.

Jorden walked off the field, not looking at anyone. Coach Easley didn't say anything this time.

The scrimmage continued with rotations. I ran two more series. First one, I hit Mickey deep for thirty-two yards, then Austin on a crossing route for nineteen, then Mickey again, who ran it in from the eight-yard line for the score. Second series, I completed five straight passes, working down the field in rhythm until I hit Henry in the back of the end zone for six. Gabriel ran one series that stalled at midfield after three incomplete passes. Jorden didn't get called back in.

By the time Coach Easley blew the final whistle, I was feeling tired, but it was a good tired. The kind that meant I'd actually done something.

"Bring it in," Coach Holloway called from the far sideline.

Everyone jogged over, forming a loose circle around the coaches.

Coach Holloway waited for everyone to settle. "Better intensity today. Defense, you gave up too many big plays. We'll work on gap discipline tomorrow. Offense, some of you looked sharp. Some of you need to work on reading the defense faster and trusting your mechanics."

His eyes went to where Jorden stood at the back of the group.

"Tomorrow's the last day of tryouts. We'll finalize the rosters by the afternoon. If you want to make varsity, you've got one more day to prove it. Show up ready to work."

He looked around the circle. "Questions?"

No one spoke.

"All right. Hit the showers. See you tomorrow morning, seven AM."

Chapter 19

Friday was the last day of tryouts, and even though I knew I already had my spot, I was still a little nervous. The best thing that had happened the year before was getting off the team with Elijah, and while he wasn't a problem anymore, it showed how much it mattered who I had around me.

And I really wanted my friends on varsity with me.

So I got an early start and was at the field house well before time to start, the first one there, in fact. As I got myself mentally ready, guys started trickling in, but nobody said much. Everyone knew what today meant and was in their own head.

Finally, Coach Holloway called everyone out to the field. We all jogged to midfield where he stood with the other coaches, clipboard in hand.

"Final day, gentlemen. We've seen what you can do, so now's the time to put it all together and make it count. Today's about consistency. Questions?"

Nobody spoke.

"All right. Warm up. We start in ten."

The stretching line formed up and I fell in beside Mickey. Miguel joined us a moment later, rolling his shoulders.

"You ready?"

"As I'll ever be."

We ran through the warm-up drills, my arm feeling loose and strong. Two camps this summer had done exactly what Coach Moreno promised. I felt like a better version of myself.

I took the first snap of the day and everything went textbook. We ran the same play again, and the defense adjusted, with a linebacker shading inside to take away the crossing route.

A good adjustment.

I wasn't going to let that stop me and checked to Austin on the outside, hitting him for six and giving us third and two. We managed another fifteen yards after that, but Connor got beat inside on the next play when Jesse slanted hard and got into the backfield before Connor could adjust his angle, forcing me to throw it away, since I couldn't see a route to scramble.

"Nielsen, read the defensive end. If he goes inside, you go around him."

"Yes, sir."

We ran it again. This time, Connor saw the slant coming and adjusted, sealing Jesse outside. But then, it was a lot easier to adjust when the play is telegraphed.

We did another series before Coach rotated me out and Gabriel in.

"I should have had him," Connor said as we walked off the field. "I keep screwing it up."

"Everyone gets beat. You adjusted."

I was trying to lift his spirits, but it wasn't good. Yes, everyone got beat, but when you're on the bubble and it's the last day of tryouts, it's a bad time to have it happen.

Gabriel took the field and ran his series. He was showing he was best at short passes and moving the ball in small chunks. It wasn't spectacular, but it would do the job and he wasn't missing reads or trying for anything too big.

I wasn't sure he'd be able to handle those big moments when the defense slipped up and let one of your receivers get some distance, which would hurt him in the long run. Coach was also using him to open up the running game, which I guess gave us some versatility when the passing game wasn't working, although his more narrow range of plays would also make it easier for the other teams to scout.

When my turn came back around, the defense had rotated in fresh players. Kevin was at defensive tackle now, and he was good with quick hands and solid instincts.

My series went well. The key was that the defense was respecting the run game that Coach was still putting in when they went too hard at my receivers, which meant the play-action was working. When they had to honor the fake, it opened up everything else. That's what made a pro-style offense click; you had to keep them honest on both sides.

"Offense rotate."

I joined Tyrell, who was at the water station. He wasn't getting as many reps as Andre, but he was looking good out there and had made some really solid blocks.

"Looking good out there."

He nodded but didn't say anything. I think he was in his head.

Jorden took the field for his series, and right away I could see the problem. Coach had clearly called for shorter passes, only having a guy or two deep to try and draw off defenders, but Jorden was doing his reads wrong, looking to the deep guys first, even though they took more time to develop, and he would burn his close-in guys if he held the ball too long. I think I knew what he was doing. He was hoping to get a big play, something he could point at to justify that he was supposed to be here.

But that wasn't the way to do it, and he was ending up with all of his receivers jammed up every time and having to throw the ball away.

"The right side was wide open," Miguel said.

"Yeah." He was taking enough of a beating. The last thing I needed to do was pile on.

This was Jorden's issue. He had really good arm strength. It had been better than mine last year, before I started putting the work in, but he was getting ahead of himself and couldn't process the field fast enough. He'd pick his target and commit to it, even when the defense took it away.

The next few plays showed the same pattern. He'd complete one pass when the defense happened to line up wrong, then immediately miss his reads on the next rep. He was trying to make something happen instead of taking what was there.

Not that he was terrible. It worked sometimes in JV where you could just out-athlete everyone, but varsity defenses were faster and more disciplined. They'd read that tendency and jump his routes.

His next series was worse. He couldn't complete anything and took a sack when he held the ball too long. When he came off the field, he yanked his helmet off and walked straight past everyone toward the equipment shed.

That was his bigger problem. He didn't control his frustration. It made him snap at his teammates and make bad decisions on the field.

Just not good all around.

We rotated through a few more times. My drives kept moving thanks to Coach mixing things up, giving me options for longer balls but keeping the defense guessing. I wasn't trying to be a hero, and liked that he was leaving me options in case someone made a mistake.

The only thing I didn't do a lot was scramble. Admittedly, camp and Coach Moreno had been beating that into me, while it was something that was great to be in my bag, I needed to save it as a last resort and only if I was sure of the opening.

It hadn't made me cautious, exactly, but I was becoming more selective about when to do it. Which is probably why the one time the pocket cracked and I did see a path, I punched right through and made it to their safety before they stopped me.

Gabriel was still playing it safe on his drives, which was smart. He might not have Jorden's natural talent, but he could see the senior coming apart and just got out of his way, letting Jorden lose the backup spot instead of trying to win it.

Like I said. Smart.

He also wasn't going to be bad as a backup. He was showing he could hold the offense together when I came off the field. He may not make any big gains, but it meant we had a fallback option, especially if I could get us ahead, Gabriel could keep it together and finish off the game, keeping me from burning out.

Jorden wasn't the only one having it rough, though.

Jamal was going through it. The line blocking for him wasn't the starters, so he couldn't get any push, but he was also hitting the wrong holes and pressing instead of being patient like the coaches kept telling him. Playing at running back was hard when your line wasn't winning, but he needed to show better vision if he wanted to make it.

Connor also made a couple more bad reads and let the line slip each time. Those were starting to add up and were going to haunt him.

By the time Coach Holloway blew the final whistle, I was happy with my performance, but worried about my friends. Everything that could be done had been, and the chance to change things was over. And for some of them, that was a problem.

Now it was up to the coaches.

"Good work today. We need a little time to discuss the roster. Be back here at five."

He left, and we all started to make for the parking lot, since that was a good two hours from now.

"You guys want to get food?" Miguel asked.

"Yeah. Diner?"

"Andre, Mickey, are you driving?" I yelled out as we made it to the parking lot.

A lot of us were three to six months away from getting our driver's licenses, and with the seniors from last year graduating, we were running short on drivers.

They were down for it, though, and between all of us, we squeezed Joe, Jamal, and Tyrell in with Mickey, and me, Connor, and Gabriel in with Andre.

I was glad to see Gabriel starting to come back around. Last year, he'd had Elijah and Jorden in his ear, and he'd started to act like I was the reason he wasn't in a better spot on the team, in spite of the fact that the coaches had already said they weren't going to let freshmen on JV, and I was an exception.

My leaving the freshman team opened it up for Gabriel to start, which had done him a world of good.

But people can be talked into anything.

It was between the lunch and the dinner rushes, so the Silver Spoon was mostly empty. We waved to the waitress and squeezed into a corner booth and then dragged another table up to it, kind of making our own thing.

They were used to our antics, though, so they rolled with it, and the waitress brought over our menus and water without any comment.

We'd eaten here enough times that I already knew what I wanted.

"Cheeseburger and fries," I said when she came back.

Everyone else was ready to, and we basically ordered as soon as the menus were dropped off, with everyone mostly getting burgers, except Tyrell, who got a chicken sandwich, and Mickey, who ordered some kind of wrap.

"So," Joe said once the waitress left. "Sam Houston still calling?"

Mickey grinned. "Yeah, I did a visit last month, and it was cool, but the coach wants me to come back in October."

"Are you going?"

"Probably. It's double-A and not single-A, but it's not like anyone else is climbing."

"It's still D1, so you'll be in the big games, even if you don't make it to a bowl," Joe said.

"I know, but it's why I really want us to do well this year. If we take state, especially with how good Midland is going to be this year, we're going to get some looks, and maybe I could get a look from Tech, at least. Maybe even A&M."

Andre nodded. "Trust me, I'm in the same boat, and I'm not even doing as well as you. UoH said maybe I could get a walk-on spot, but no one's recruiting me."

"Don't worry," Miguel said, smiling. "Blake's going to take care of it. We win state, you guys will all get picked up, and we're all playing against each other in three years."

"No pressure," I said.

"Hey, I'm holding onto your coattails so hard I'm like a weighted vest," Miguel leaned back. "You gotta carry my ass the whole way."

I laughed and threw an ice cube at him, getting a glare from the waitress.

"If we make the team," Jamal said quietly.

That kind of hit everyone. Not so much because they thought they weren't going to. Mickey and Andre were both pretty much a lock, but although Jamal and Connor were good guys, I think everyone realized they weren't going to make it.

"Don't think that way," I said.

"Come on, Blake. The rah-rah thing is great, but you were at the same practice we were," Connor said. "I got beat out so many times, Coach basically benched me the last third of tryouts."

"You can't change what is done," I said. "If you only get JV, yeah, it sucks. Sucks hard. But you're sophomores. You kick ass on JV and next year move to varsity, and we'll all be together."

"Yeah," Jamal said, but I knew that wasn't what he wanted to hear.

They could have probably lived if it was just me, but Miguel and Tyrell both looked good and would at least make it to varsity, even if they didn't start.

It was hard for guys who were this competitive to turn it off.

"Well, I've given up trying to be a starter," Gabriel said. "I'm just hoping I get to be your backup."

"You're definitely getting it," Andre said. "I mean, we all know it's not going to be Jorden."

"Jorden's trying, he just puts too much pressure on himself," I said, hoping we could avoid talking about him behind his back. That kind of thing always got back to the person and would blow up in our faces. "He keeps seeing that one next big play he can make to fix it all. It's like a gambler with too much sunk in."

"Whatever it is, he's not doing himself any favors," Joe said.

The waitress brought our food, and the conversation kind of slowed down as we all focused on eating. After a full morning of play, we were starving.

Not that we stopped talking altogether. Andre started to brag about some girl he'd met at a party last weekend. Miguel gave him shit about it, since he'd just crashed and burned the month before.

I just ate my burger and listened to everyone talk. I liked these guys and was looking forward to a full year with them. Doing track in the spring was great, but nothing beat football season.

"What time is it?" Connor asked.

Andre checked his watch. "Four."

"We should head back soon," I said.

"Yeah." Jamal pushed his plate away, most of his burger still on it.

"Are you going to eat that?" Joe asked.

"Not hungry."

I felt bad for him.

"I'll take it," Joe said, pulling it off his plate.

They did love to eat.

We finished up, and Andre and Mickey drove us back to the school. We walked into the field house together, the locker room already filling up with players talking in small groups.

Four-thirty came and went, then four forty-five. At five minutes to five, Coach Holloway walked in carrying a sheet of paper, Coach Easley, Coach Mayfield, and Coach Wilson following behind him.

Everyone went quiet.

"All right, listen up." Coach Holloway held up the paper. "We've made our decisions. I'm going to read the varsity roster first, then JV. If your name gets called for varsity, stay here. JV guys, Coach Wilson will take you to the gym."

He looked down at the sheet.

"Varsity offense. Quarterback, Blake Sims."

I got a couple of pats on the back, but that was the most expected announcement of the day.

"Backup quarterback, Gabriel Neiva."

Gabriel almost sagged with relief, even though we all told him he was a shoo-in. With how Jorden had played this week, it was all but guaranteed.

Jorden had already struggled last year on JV, so the guys who were going over there were going to have a rough year.

Unless he fixed some things.

The list went on. Noah at halfback, Joe at fullback, which basically meant no spot for Jamal. Brian, Mickey, Miguel, and Austin at wide receiver. Andre at center.

He went through all the offensive line guys, and Connor's name didn't come up, which sucked, but was again not that big of a surprise. The big surprise was when he finished naming everyone, and Tyrell's name never came. It meant we had no backup for Andre, although the only other guy we had who could play center was a transfer who really did badly enough at tryouts that I wasn't sure he'd make any team.

It also made me think that Tyrell was guaranteed a varsity spot, but maybe they decided to keep him on JV so the team didn't have a weak center *and* a weak QB.

Which sucked for Tyrell.

Coach Holloway looked up. "That's varsity. Everyone else, you're on JV. Follow Coach Wilson to the gym, and he'll go over your schedule."

When the last of the JV guys left, Coach Holloway addressed those of us remaining.

"Congratulations, you've earned your spots on this varsity team. Practice starts Monday at three-thirty, and we go every day after school. We've got three weeks until our first game against Irvin, and I expect every single one of you to show up ready to work. This team has the talent to go all the way, but talent doesn't mean anything without discipline and commitment. Understood?"

"Yes, sir," we answered together.

"Good. Get out of here. Enjoy your weekend. Monday, we get to work."

I arrived at Li's mom's shop a little early so I could hang out with Li before we started, but I found Yesica already there, listening to some Latin pop station and working on the heavy bag when I came in.

"Good, you're on time. Today, we start defense."

I dropped my bag and walked over. "I thought we were still working on punches."

"You know the basics already, and just need to spend time on the bag getting comfortable with them. That's a repetition thing you can do it on your own time," she said. "You are practicing when I'm not here, right?"

I didn't want to tell her most of my focus had been on the football field or doing straight conditioning. I actually should have been practicing this, too. It was good conditioning, and there would be some carryover with upper weight work, and the speed training would help.

But I knew that in most sports, it was all about getting reps to get to that ten-thousand-hour mark. That it took time to get whatever I was training at to feel like second nature.

Instead, I said, "Sure."

She gave me a look and I think she knew I was full of shit, but let it slide. "Just as important as knowing how to hit people is knowing how not to get hit. Actually, it's more important, I think.

Any idiot can throw a punch, but smart fighters don't get hit in the first place. Defense isn't about being tough; it's about being smart. You see the punch coming, you move. You make them miss, you make them tired, you make them frustrated. Then when they're off balance, that's when you counter."

"So how do I see it coming?"

"Watch my shoulders." She settled into her stance. "Eyes lie, people look one way and go another, but shoulders never do. Shoulders tell you where the power comes from, where the punch is going. You watch my shoulders, you'll know what's coming before it gets there."

She threw a slow jab, and I watched her right shoulder dip forward just before the punch came. Then she threw a cross and her left shoulder rotated back to generate the power.

"You see it?"

"Yeah."

"Good. It's harder when they get really moving and you're trying to throw punches and block. There's a lot going on, so you have to get used to it. A lot of that comes from sparring. The first defense we're going to work on is slipping. When I throw the jab, you're going to move your head just enough so it misses. Not a big movement, just small. Big movements mess you up. With small movements, you stay in range and stay balanced. The goal is to make me miss by an inch, that's all you need."

She threw the jab again, slowly, and I moved my head to the left. The glove passed by my ear.

"Good, but you leaned back. Don't lean, just move your head. Your feet stay planted, your base stays strong. If you lean, you're off balance and you can't counter. Again."

We went through it maybe twenty times until I got the idea of what she wanted. I could see she was right, that it would take a while before I really got the feel of it, but I understood what she wanted me to do. The hardest thing was how small the movement was. I kept wanting to really get out of the way, but she was right; it threw me off balance.

"Better. Now we add the cross. Jab comes, you slip left. Cross comes, you slip right. Read my shoulders, see which one is coming, and move before it gets there."

She started throwing combinations, still slow but faster than before, and I worked on reading her shoulders and moving my head. Sometimes I got it right and felt the glove pass by harmlessly. Sometimes I was too slow and caught it on the side of my head.

"You're thinking too much. Stop thinking, just react." She laughed, mid-sentence, like she'd just remembered something funny. "Your body knows what to do, let it do it."

That was easier said than done. Every time I tried to just react, I ended up moving the wrong way or not moving at all.

We kept going and she gradually increased the speed, although it would be a while until I was going to be able to dodge an actual punch thrown at any kind of speed. My neck was starting to hurt from all the movement, and I could feel sweat running down my back.

"All right, that's enough slipping for today. You've got the idea, now you just need to practice it on your own. Now we're going to work on blocking. This is probably the most important thing I'll teach you because when you can't slip, when you can't move, you still need to protect yourself." She raised her gloves again and moved into her stance. "There are two main blocks we're going to focus on. First is the high block, protects your head. Watch."

She held her gloves up near her temples, elbows in tight. "When I throw at your head, you bring your gloves up and use your forearms to deflect the punch. Don't just hold them there like a statue; you have to angle them so the punch slides off. Like this."

She demonstrated slowly, angling her left glove so an imaginary punch would deflect away from her face.

"Now the low block, for body shots. Elbows come down tight to your ribs, gloves cover your stomach. Same thing, you angle so the punch doesn't land clean. Try it."

I raised my gloves and she threw a slow jab at my head. I brought my left glove up but she still caught me on the side.

"You're too slow. The block has to be there before the punch arrives, not after. And angle it; don't just put your glove in front of your face. Again."

We went through it over and over. She'd throw at my head, I'd try to block. She'd throw at my body, I'd try to get my elbows down in time. Most of the time I was late or my angle was wrong and the punch still got through.

"This is harder than slipping," I said after taking another one to the ribs.

"Not harder, just different. Slipping is about reading and reacting. Blocking is about speed and positioning. But blocking is what saves you when everything else fails. You can't always move, you can't always see it coming, but you can always block if you're fast enough. Now we add combinations. I'm going to throw high-low, high-high, low-high. You have to read where it's going and get the right block up. Ready?"

I wasn't, but I raised my gloves anyway.

She came at me with a jab to the head and a cross to the body. I blocked the jab but was too slow getting my elbows down and took the cross on my ribs.

"See? That's what happens. They set you up high, then go low. Again."

We kept working through different combinations. Sometimes I'd get the first block but miss the second. Sometimes I'd get both but the angle was wrong and the punches still landed. My forearms were starting to ache from the impact, even through the gloves.

"You're getting tense," she said after another series. "Relax. Tight muscles are slow muscles. You need to be loose until the punch is coming, then snap the block into place. Like ..." She thought for a second. "Like you're throwing a football. You're loose until you release, then everything tightens. Same thing."

That actually helped. When I tried to stay relaxed until the last second, my blocks came faster and I caught more of her punches.

"Better. Now we're going to add parrying. That's when you use your glove to redirect the punch instead of just blocking it." She demonstrated, using her right glove to push my jab to the outside. "You're not stopping the punch, you're making it miss. Takes less energy than blocking, and it sets you up to counter."

She showed me how to parry with both hands, how to read which side the punch was coming from and to use the corresponding glove to redirect it. It felt even more awkward than blocking because the timing had to be perfect.

"This is going to take a while to get good at," she said, almost reading my mind. "But it's worth learning now. When you spar for real, you'll need all of these moves. Slip what you can, block what you can't slip, parry what you can't block, and cover up if nothing else works."

We spent another twenty minutes working on parrying. Most of my attempts were too early or too late, and the few times I got the timing right, my angle was wrong and the punch still came through.

"All right, enough of that. Let's work on the high-low game." She reset her stance. "I'm going to throw at your head and your body, at random. You have to recognize where it's going and put up the right defense. Block, parry, slip if you can. Just react. And I'm going to speed it up, so you won't have time to think."

She came at me and I tried to keep up, but it was too much. Punches came from different angles and different heights, and I couldn't process it fast enough. I'd block high when she went low, slip left when she came straight, parry too early or too late. My arms were burning, and my head was getting fuzzy from trying to track everything at once.

"Stop." She lowered her gloves. "You're overthinking again. Your brain is trying to solve a puzzle, but there is no puzzle. It's just reaction. See the punch, react to the punch. That's it."

"How do I just react when there's so much to remember?"

"By doing it a thousand times until your body remembers instead of your brain." She grabbed her water bottle. "That's what training is. You do it slow until you understand it, then you do it fast until you don't have to think about it anymore. You're still in the understanding phase, so don't beat yourself up."

I grabbed my own water and drank. My forearms were sore and my shoulders were tight from holding my guard up.

"How long did you train before you fought men?" I asked as we took a little break.

"A long time. I started when I was nine, but when I got to fight, it was always against girls. I don't think they let me fight a man outside of training until I was seventeen. Why?"

"Just curious. I mean, you said you fought in exhibition matches before the men's fights. That had to be intimidating."

"Well, most of those exhibition matches were against other female boxers. I guess the people liked watching two girls wailing on each other, but it was a great opportunity. Fighting against guys, though, was terrifying. The first time, they put me up against this big guy. Low in the men's weight class, but he would be a heavyweight for women. I thought I was going to throw up before I even got in the ring, but my coach, he told me something that helped. He said the size difference doesn't matter as much as people think. Big guys, they get used to using their size. They lean on it. But if you don't give them your base, if you make them work for every inch, they get tired faster than you do."

"How do you not give them your base?"

"You always keep moving. You circle, you pivot, you make them chase you. And when they commit too hard, that's when you counter. Big guys, they throw their weight around, and when they miss, they're off balance. That's your opening. You won't have that problem much. You're tall and you've been putting on muscle even since we started training, but that's something you need to remember. There's always a bigger guy. Always. It's important you learn to use that so you can be ready when that happens. You've got to be smarter, faster, more disciplined, and make them respect you not because you're bigger, but because you don't give them anything easy."

"Did you ever lose?"

"So many times, but I never lost because I gave up. I lost because the other person was better that day, or I made a mistake, or I got caught, but I never just let them have it. Come on, back to work, and this time, don't drop your guard when you're tired. Boxing is a game of stamina, and they want you to throw a lot of shots to wear you out, just like you're doing to them. When someone's tired, that's when they leave openings."

We went through another series of exchanges, and I tried to hold my form even though my arms felt like they were going to fall off. She kept shortening the rest periods, kept making me work through the cover-step-counter sequence, kept pushing me through the fatigue until I wanted to just sit down and stop.

"That's it," she finally said. "You're done for today."

I pulled off my gloves and leaned against the wall. I felt like a wet noodle.

"You did good. Better than last week." She pulled off her own gloves, then stretched her arms overhead. "Next week, we do more of the same. The longer we keep at it, the more it'll all come together, but you've got to spend time on the bag working on your punches and shadowboxing, working on your dodges and blocks."

"I can't wait."

"You say that now, but I'm going to work you harder. Much harder."

Li's mother appeared at the top of the stairs, calling down in Mandarin. Yesica's face lit up immediately, all the intensity from training vanishing.

"Food's ready. Come on, she made dumplings."

"I can't today. First day of school tomorrow and I've got stuff I need to get ready."

"Your loss," she said, laughing.

Chapter 20

Monday morning, and it was time to head back to school. The first day of my sophomore year.

The parking lot was packed with cars and trucks, with everyone arriving early. That wouldn't last. In a month, a lot of these kids would barely make it before the bell. I got to sleep in, at least. I knew we'd be starting morning practices again, but for a few days, while everyone got settled, it was nice not to get up at five. I made it through the parking lot and headed toward the main doors, where groups of students clustered on the concrete steps, catching up after the summer.

I stopped here or there, talked to Eduardo, and then found Miguel, Mickey, and Tyrell all grouped together on the front steps. We'd picked up our schedules on Friday, but hadn't had a chance to really compare schedules before now.

I was in classes with Eduardo now, and a few of the guys, but a lot of the team was still back in the remedial classes while I'd made the jump to on-level after all of the work I put in last year.

The warning bell rang, and it was time to actually start the school day. Inside, the hallways were chaos, people greeting each other, comparing locker locations, and complaining about how much they didn't want to be back. I navigated through the crowd toward my first period, which was English with Ms. Lawson.

I made it to the classroom and found a seat near the middle. A few other students filed in, none of them people I knew well, and then Ms. Lawson started taking attendance. She was probably in her early forties, dressed in a conservative blouse and slacks, and when she finished calling names, she launched straight into the syllabus without any first-day pleasantries.

Two essays, weekly reading responses, vocabulary quizzes every Friday, and a final project in December. The reading list she handed out was longer than anything I'd seen last year, not counting the extra work I had done, and when someone asked if we'd really have to read all of it, she looked at him and said yes.

When the bell rang, I grabbed my bag and headed to second period, which was Algebra II with Mr. Mossley, who was equally aggressive with the assignments. By third period, which was Biology with Mrs. Gordon, I was starting to feel like they'd gotten together to make this year much harder. Every teacher emphasized how much work we'd have, how much they expected from us, how this year would separate the students who were serious from the ones who weren't.

I was taking notes on the lab setup procedures when an office runner showed up with a small slip of paper. Mrs. Gordon opened it and read it over for a second before folding it and slipping it into her pocket.

"Blake Sims?"

I looked up.

"You need to report to the guidance office."

A few students turned to look at me as I packed up my notebook and pen, slung my bag over my shoulder, and walked out of the classroom. The hallways were empty except for a freshman who looked lost, clutching a map of the school and staring at room numbers.

The guidance office was on the first floor, near the main entrance. When I walked in, a secretary looked up from her desk.

"Blake Sims?"

"Yes, ma'am."

"Have a seat. Mr. Brennan will call you in a moment."

I sat in one of those plastic chairs that lined the wall outside the counselors' offices. Through the glass window, I could see a thin man with wire-rimmed glasses sitting at Mrs. Patterson's old desk, reading through a file folder. I didn't know who he was, but he definitely wasn't Mrs. Patterson.

After a moment, he looked up, made eye contact with me through the window, and got up, coming over and opening the door.

"Blake Sims?"

"Yes, sir?"

He turned and headed back to the desk. I assumed that was my invitation to join him, so I followed him in.

"I'm Mr. Brennan, the new guidance counselor." He sat back down and opened the folder on his desk. "I was going through some of the students' records, familiarizing myself with everyone, and yours stood out. I wanted to meet you and talk over some concerns I have."

"Okay?" I said, again as a question, since I had no idea what was going on.

"The first thing I noticed was that you made some significant changes to your schedule from how it was last year. You were in remedial classes fall semester." He flipped a page. "Then standard classes spring semester, and now you're registered for all regular-level courses."

"I worked hard to catch up over freshman year."

"And you're the starting varsity quarterback."

"Yes, sir."

He set the file down and folded his hands on the desk. His expression wasn't hostile, just evaluating, like he was working through a complicated math problem.

"Help me understand the timeline here. You went from remedial reading and math last year to on-level classes this year. That's not typical."

"I studied a lot. My teachers approved the move, as did the vice-principal."

"I'm sure they did." He leaned back in his chair. "But the jump from remedial to regular-level coursework is substantial. Most students need several years of work before they're ready for that transition. You did it while playing JV football, running track, and playing in another football league."

"I worked for it."

"I'm not questioning your work ethic, I'm questioning whether adequate safeguards were in place to ensure you were actually prepared for this jump, or whether accommodations were made."

"What kind of accommodations?"

"The kind that allow promising athletes to move through the academic system faster than their non-athlete peers," he said matter-of-factly, as if this was a thing that was happening all the time. "I've seen it before. A talented player gets fast-tracked because the school wants them on the field, and then when they hit junior or senior year and the coursework becomes genuinely difficult, they struggle, or worse, they don't graduate."

"That's not what happened."

"Then walk me through it. How exactly did you go from remedial to regular level in one year?"

I forced myself to stay calm. Getting angry wouldn't help.

"I attended every teacher's classroom hours, and I had help from a tutor outside of school. I did every assignment that was given and was graded the same as the other students were. I will admit, I was in remedial classes because I didn't take school seriously in middle school, which is before there really are student-athletes. The start of my freshman year, though, looking at what was required and what I might have to do if I didn't get a scholarship, I realized I needed to make a change. Plus, I grew up some. My teachers saw all of that and told me to show them that I could do the work. I did, and I also did the additional work the teachers started giving me to get on level after I proved I could do it. It didn't just happen all at once, and it didn't happen like someone waving a magic wand. I did the work to get where I am."

"What were your grades last semester?"

"Mostly A's and B's."

"In standard-level classes."

"Yes, sir. It was all A's for the work in remedial classes, which I also did."

"And you think you're prepared for the increased workload of regular-level courses while also being the starting quarterback on a varsity team that practices two hours a day?"

"I know I am. I think this year will be easier, since last year I did every assignment, took every quiz and every test for each of the on-level classes while still doing all of the required work in the classes I was in at the time. Basically, I have half the classes I did last year because of that."

He must have picked up how frustrated I was, being called out after working my ass off last year, because he said, "Blake, I'm not trying to attack you. I'm trying to make sure you're set up for success. In my experience, students who try to do too much too fast often hit a wall, and when they do, it's painful for everyone involved: the student, the family, and the teachers who have to watch them struggle."

"I'm not going to struggle."

"You say that now, but varsity football is a significant time commitment. Add in regular-level coursework, which requires substantial independent study time, and you're looking at a very full schedule. Most students struggle to balance just one of those things."

"There are other athletes in regular-level classes," I pointed out.

"Yes, and I'll be monitoring their progress as well, but most of them didn't make the jump you did. Tell me about your study habits. How many hours a night do you spend on homework?"

"Two or three, usually."

"And you think that's enough?"

"Sometimes it's more. It depends on which classes I need to work on. Are you saying that isn't enough?"

"I'm not; I'm just concerned with how confident you sound about your ability to handle this."

"That's because I am."

He studied me for a long moment.

"All right. I'm going to allow you to continue with your current schedule. However, I'm implementing a few conditions." He opened a desk drawer and pulled out a form. "First, you'll report to a mandatory study hall every Wednesday afternoon. I'll be supervising it myself. This gives you structured time to work on assignments and allows me to assess how you're managing the workload."

"I have practice after school on Wednesdays."

"I know, and I will discuss this with the coaches. In this school, academics come first and athletics second. Next, I'll be communicating with your teachers every two weeks to get progress reports. If any of them express concerns about your performance or preparation, we'll schedule an immediate meeting to discuss adjustments."

"What kind of adjustments?"

"That depends on the concern. It might be additional tutoring and study hall time, modified assignment deadlines, or in more serious cases, a schedule change. If you're truly prepared for regular-level coursework, you'll have no problem demonstrating that in study hall and maintaining strong grades. But if it becomes clear that you're struggling, I'm not going to let you continue to struggle because you're determined to prove something."

"I'm not trying to prove anything. I'm trying to get a good education."

"Then we want the same thing." He signed the form and pushed it across the desk. "Sign this acknowledging that you understand the conditions."

I picked up the pen and stared at the form. Everything in me wanted to argue, to tell him he was wrong about me, that I had managed my own schedule last year and I could do the same this year, but I knew his type.

He might complain about me being overconfident, but he was the kind of guy who always thought he was right and knew better than everyone else, and the type who wouldn't take students "talking back" to him.

I signed the form and pushed it back.

"Good." He filed it away in my folder. "One more thing. I want you to understand my perspective here: I don't have anything against athletes. What I have is a lot of experience watching students, athletes and non-athletes alike, make choices that seem reasonable in the moment but create serious problems down the line. My job is to help you avoid those problems."

"By assuming I'll fail?"

"By making sure you have support if you do struggle. There's a difference." He closed the folder.

"Is that all?"

"For now. I'll see you Wednesday afternoon for study hall." He stood up. "I hope I'm wrong, Blake. I hope you excel in all your classes and prove that you were absolutely ready for this transition, but I've been doing this job long enough to know that hope isn't a strategy."

He might say he didn't have anything against athletes and he hoped I excelled, but everything I could see suggested the exact opposite.

Wednesday, when practice wrapped, I jogged over to where Coach Holloway was talking with Coach Easley near the equipment shed. Most of the guys were already heading for the locker room or their cars.

There was something I wanted to do, but I hadn't wanted to hit everyone with it on the first day of school, so I waited a few days to give everyone a chance to acclimate first.

"Coach, mind if I grab everyone for a second before they leave?"

Holloway glanced at me, then at the dispersing team. "What for?"

"I want to do a film session to get into the swing of doing them and go over some stuff I learned at camp, and I thought I'd see who wants to come."

He studied me for a moment, then nodded. "Make it quick. You and I still have practice in an hour."

"I will," I said, turning and whistling, waving my arms. "Hey! Everyone, hold up a second!"

The team slowed, some guys stopping mid-stride, others turning back from the parking lot. There were maybe thirty of them scattered across the practice field and the edge of the lot.

"I'm heading to the media center to watch some film of last year's games, break down some things we did right and things we did wrong. Anyone who wants to come is welcome. We'll probably go for an hour, maybe a little more."

A few guys exchanged glances. Hunter shook his head and kept walking toward his car. That was disappointing. I'd thought I was making progress with him.

"When?" Andre asked.

"Right now. The media center's open for a little bit longer."

Mickey grinned. "You gonna provide snacks?"

"No."

"I guess I can come anyway."

A few guys laughed. I waited another moment, letting the offer settle, then headed for the school building.

The media center sat off the main hall on the second floor, near the library. This late in the day, the place was mostly empty, with just Mrs. Palmer at the front desk stamping something and giving me a look when I came in with my duffel over my shoulder.

"You the one Coach Wilson called about?" she asked.

"Yes, ma'am. For the film."

She slid a key and a small plastic case across the counter. "The cart's already in the back room. When you're done, lock up and bring this back."

"Yes, ma'am."

The back room had the shades pulled half down. A TV on a rolling cart sat against the wall, with a VCR on the little shelf and a stack of tapes on top, labeled in block letters: IRVIN DEFENSE 94. COOPER SECOND HALF. SCRIMMAGE 94.

I set my duffel near the wall, pushed a couple of tables back to give us space, and started pulling chairs into loose rows.

Austin walked in first, with Mickey and Jerry behind him and Miguel trailing.

"Look at this," Mickey said. "Fancy."

"This is where they hide the good chairs," Jerry said, dropping into one and leaning back until it squeaked.

"Don't break school property before we even start," I said.

"Relax. I'll be gentle."

From the doorway, Andre snorted. He came in with Albert, Elton, Keith, and Paul. The room shrank a little with that much of the line walking in. I expected a lot of my offensive side guys, but I was happy when, a minute later, several of the defensive guys started to filter in.

I did a quick count. Twenty-three. Not everyone, but a good chunk of the team. Enough to matter.

"Y'all can spread out," I said. "We're not in church."

Jerry scooted his chair until his knee bumped Austin's. "Confession time, brother. Forgive me, for I have sinned ... and I can't wait to tell you about it."

"Jesus Christ," Austin said.

"He ain't here," Jon Duncan, one of the defensive linebackers, said from behind him.

Andre stayed near the middle, halfway between me and the TV. He didn't sit until the rest of the line found spots. That was who he was, even when he wasn't trying.

I picked up the tape labeled IRVIN DEFENSE 94 and slid it into the VCR. I pressed play and hit pause when the static flipped over to the first shot of a game from last season.

"All right, settle down," I said. "Before we start, this isn't a coach thing. Nobody made you come, so I appreciate everyone who showed up. Now I guess I'm going to talk a lot, but I also want to hear from you. Especially the guys on the line. I know a whole lot about moving the ball, but the only thing I know about your job is when you let someone through and I get smashed, so if you see something, say something. This doesn't work if it's just me yapping."

"Too late to back out?" Jerry asked.

"You can still leave," I said. "But we will laugh about you when you do."

He stayed where he was.

I hit play. The tape rolled into the opening kickoff, then cut ahead to a series where Irvin was on defense. Their front in the shot had two down linemen and two stand-up ends, with linebackers lined up just off their hips.

I hit pause and the picture froze on a slightly blurry image of their weak-side end in a two-point stance, toes almost touching the line of scrimmage. The linebacker inside him leaned his weight toward the line.

"All right," I said. "First thing. Who sees what?"

Andre sat with his forearms on his knees. "That end's cheating. He's too close."

"Good. What else?"

"The backer's rolled down inside," Albert said. "Looks like he wants to hit the B-gap."

"Yeah," Andre said.

"What do you safeties see?" I asked.

Luke squinted at the screen. "The strong safety's flat-footed. He's not bailing. Means they trust the corner and he's thinking run or short stuff."

"Exactly," I said.

"So they're bringing heat," Julius said. "Edge and backer. They want to blow up anything to the right."

"Right," I said. "Irvin likes to bring pressure to the field side on early downs. They don't always, but more than most. This is first and ten. So, line ... what does that mean for you guys?"

Andre answered, but his eyes went to the other linemen. "We call the slide to the tight end side. If we run zone, we have to move our feet fast or that end crashes the play. If it's pass, we kick to the blitz and Joe has to get across."

"So if you call forty-one, I'm checking backside end?" Joe asked.

"If we're in six-man protection, yeah," I said. "But here's what one of my coaches this summer kept drilling into me: it's not just the play call. We have to recognize the front and have built-in answers. If we don't like the look, I need to be able to get us out of the bad play. That only works if all of us know what 'bad' looks like."

"Then don't call bad plays," Jerry said.

"That's the goal," I said. "Help me out."

There were a few laughs. It loosened up the room a little.

"Run it," Andre said.

I hit play. The offense on the tape ran outside zone to the right. The end came screaming downhill, the linebacker shot the gap, and the back got smothered in the backfield.

"The back was dead before he got the handoff," Tyler said. "They never had the block for him."

"This is what I mean," I said. "We can't walk up, see that, and still run straight into it like we didn't see anything; we have to have a check. Maybe we flip the play, maybe we hit a quick slant behind the blitz, maybe we go to a draw. But that starts with all of us seeing the same thing."

Gabriel lifted his hand. "How much of that do you want us to decide at the line? Coaches get salty when we start freelancing."

“I’m not talking about freelancing,” I said. “I’m talking about having built-in stuff. If Coach calls strong zone, but they bring the safety down and roll the corner, we call an audible that takes us to weak zone or to a quick game. It’s still his structure, just us using it right.”

“And you’re going to tell Holloway he needs more audibles. Right now we have, what … ten, and they are pretty broad. You’re talking about specific audibles for specific matchups.” Mickey said.

“I know, and I’ve already talked to him about this,” I said. “We’re going to try a few for our first few games on the most likely scenarios and see how it works. But it’s not just about that. There are things each of you would adjust if you saw the play coming, even if it wasn’t called. We need everyone to pay attention so we can trust each other to make the right reads and make the adjustments that need to be made.”

We started the tape again and broke down most of the game, going through what we’d done right and what we’d done wrong. Irvin was our first game in two weeks and the one we had the most time to prepare for.

It would also set the tone for the season, so I wanted us to do well.

At some point during the next set of clips, movement near the door caught my eye. Coach Holloway and Coach Easley stepped inside and leaned against the back wall. They didn’t say anything, though, just stood there watching.

I popped out the tape and put in one from JV, since more than half the guys in the room had been on JV last year, and I wanted them to analyze their own performance. The next play showed our offense in trips right, with Austin isolated backside. The defense rolled coverage to the trips side and left the corner on Austin with no safety help.

“Stop,” I said. “Okay, this is one I want us to remember. Look at Austin’s side.”

“One on one,” Mickey said.

“Right,” I said. “If we get this, I don’t care what the play call is, I’m giving him a shot, but that means the line has to buy me time, and Joe has to handle any extra. Joe, where are your eyes here?”

"Inside backer," he said. "If he comes, I step up."

"Exactly," I said. "Austin, what are you running?"

"Fade," he said.

"What if the corner plays outside like he did here?"

Austin thought for a second. "Then I stem him inside, stack him, and give you my hands late."

"Good."

Jerry raised a hand. "What if you still throw me the ball instead?"

"Then Coach Easley benches me," I said.

"And we give him a beatdown in the parking lot later for making such a bad call," Andre said with a laugh.

"Traitor," Jerry said.

The tape rolled again. We watched as we actually ran the play. I hadn't made the right read and thought the coverage was too tight to get it to Austin, so I'd ended up throwing a hitch for four yards. Watching it now made me want to kick myself.

"And that's on me," I said. "Austin had the edge and he could have gotten free, but I waffled and went to my throw away instead. We got the completion, but not the yards."

That got them started discussing other possibilities, what we could have done here or there. Not all the suggestions were good, but they were thinking and getting focused, which was part of the point.

I think it helped to call myself out on my own mistakes. We did a few more plays and then I hit stop, causing the screen to switch to blue.

"This is good practice for everyone, and I think we should do it more often, but it's important that we all buy in. Not everyone came today. I know it's late notice and it's fine; nobody was forced to come. If this is going to work, though, we need as many of us as we can get. It doesn't help if just us sit in here and the rest of the starters show up Friday and have no idea what we're talking about."

"Some of those guys might not like being told to come by a sophomore," Keith said.

He wasn't saying it to be nasty, just honest.

"I get that, and I'm not trying to pull rank. I just know where we want to go this year and I know how hard that is going to be. I'm not even saying I need to lead this. In a perfect world, a lot of you seniors would be up here going through the plays. So, talk to your position groups. If you see somebody dragging, tell them you're coming and you want them here, not because it's my thing, but because it's our season and we want to win."

Andre sat back and looked from the screen to the guys around him.

"They'll listen more if they hear it from us," he said. "From the guys they line up beside."

"Can we vote to kick Jerry out?" Mickey asked.

Jerry pointed at him. "Jealousy is an ugly thing, Evans."

"You'd know what's ugly," Julius said.

Even Coach Holloway huffed a laugh from the back.

We watched a few more plays, this time with Julius and Don calling out defensive calls, pointing out where they had failed to communicate. Luke showed us how he and Calvin read route combinations. The room turned into a back-and-forth between sides of the ball that, during practice, usually spent more time trying to outdo each other than help.

"Alright," I said finally. "This is the last thing and then we're done. Last year, as the season ended, I started working out with some of the track guys, with all of us helping each other work on problem areas. It's something I plan on doing this year, but with a focus on football until the spring. Starting tomorrow, I'll be at the field at six in the morning to practice. Anyone who wants to join, we can add in stuff that could help you. I'm not running the practice; we're all in it together, so you can decide what we work on. We can run routes, we can condition, we can work on protections, and if the weather's bad, we can come in here and look at a little film. Whatever builds us up. I know it's early and I know it sucks. Trust me, I'd rather be at home sleeping too, but state doesn't care that we're tired."

Half the guys started grumbling.

"If you don't want to come, you don't have to. I'm not forcing anybody and nobody's taking attendance. You're not in trouble if you don't come. I'm just telling you where I'll be. If you want an extra chance to fix something, to work on something, or just to get a little more field time, this is your chance to make it happen. I'm going to be there either way."

There were a few more mutters and jokes, but under it I could see wheels turning. From the back, the coaches slipped out without a word.

"I'll be there," Andre said.

He said it to me, but loud enough for everyone in the room to hear.

"I don't know if I can hit six every day," Austin said. "But I'll be there most of the time."

Mickey wiped an imaginary tear from his eye. "So brave."

"Shut up," Austin said.

More of the offensive guys said they'd be there. Some conditionally, some not. I was more surprised when the defensive guys started to say they'd be there too.

"I guess we have to show up too, but don't expect us to be friendly," Julius said.

"I never do," I said. "In all seriousness, I think it'd be great if you came. It's going to make us all better. Alright, I know we all have homework, and I can hear Jerry's stomach growling from here, so let's call it. See you guys tomorrow."

Voices started to overlap again as everyone grabbed bags and drifted toward the door. I ejected the tape, slid it into the plastic case, and set it on the cart. I slung my bag over my shoulder and headed out to return the key to the front desk before I went back down to the field house for the one-on-one work Moreno had arranged for Coach Holloway to work on with me.

Chapter 21

Saturday, after my workout, I was back home around mid-morning. The first week of school was done and in the books, and so far, things were going well with the team. I'd had nine guys show up for my first morning practice, although only eight showed up Friday, but Jerry had mentioned he'd be busy that morning.

From their reaction during the film session on Wednesday, I'd actually hoped for more, but it was a start. I was halfway through a bowl of cereal at the kitchen table when a car door thumped outside.

Mom was here, in her bedroom with the door shut, lying down, and Dad was at work, so I was curious who it was.

When I peeked through the front window, I saw Mr. Henderson on the porch, tie off, sport coat over one arm, and a folder in his hand.

I opened the door. "Hey, Coach."

On our last call, I'd called him that and gotten enough of a reaction that I did it for fun this time. He gave me a grimace, which really only guaranteed that I was going to do it more.

"Morning, Blake. You got a minute to talk business?"

"Yeah. Come on in."

He stepped inside, looking around the entry.

"Your mom home?" he asked.

"Yeah, but she's asleep. We can talk in the kitchen."

"Kitchen's fine," he said.

We sat at the table, and he put the folder down between us and smoothed it with his palm.

"So," he said, "I'm guessing you've already got some idea how that little hunch of yours about the Windows launch panned out."

"I saw some stuff on the news about it, lines out the door, midnight releases. Looked crazy, but I don't know numbers or anything."

In reality, I hadn't even been paying attention, but I knew what the reaction was from the dream since the news played it up for weeks afterward.

I'd watched more TV in the dream version of my life, since it all happened before everything fell apart.

He nodded like that was what he expected. "Exactly. So I wanted to break down how this all worked, since it's our first go. You told me that it was going to be a huge release, and I think your words were, 'people are going to go nuts.' I took that and asked myself, 'Okay, who makes money if that happens?'"

He flipped open the folder. There were a few printed sheets, neat columns of numbers I pretended I could read.

"I spread the money across a basket. Microsoft got the biggest chunk, obviously. Dell. A couple of chip manufacturers. Some retail names that were going to move a lot of boxes. You were right about the demand. Once the launch hit, the volume was unreal. The whole sector ran."

I looked at the paper like it might translate itself. "So ... how good is 'unreal'?"

He pulled a check from the folder and slid it toward me.

"Good enough that this is your first distribution from HB Capital LLC," he said. "This is your twenty percent cut after we closed out the Windows trade and reset the books. Normally, I would have let those investments ride a little bit longer, because I think the wave will carry until Christmas, but we got the big bump already, and we need all the capital for our next play."

I picked up the check. The number was a lot more than I was expecting. Had this been before the gambling, I would have probably been floored by it.

Was I starting to get jaded?

"You're serious."

"Dead serious," he said. "That's after we've rolled the principal and profits forward. We started with about two hundred grand for this play. Between the move up and where I chose to take profits, we did very well."

I stared at the check again and set it down before I crumpled it. "HB Capital?"

"That's the name we decided on when I was talking to your dad. I know, it's presumptuous that I get first billing, but I thought it would be hard for someone to look at us from the outside and accept the fifteen-year-old got the top spot. Besides, I thought your ego could handle it."

"Barely," I said, which got a laugh.

"Seriously though, if people look into it, they'll see your part is the money and mine is the legwork, and we want this to look as much like that's all there is to it, to keep people from asking too many questions."

I wasn't really even considering all of that. I was just looking at the name on the check, knowing what the B stood for, and felt my head reel a little bit.

"I'm not complaining. HB Capital. Man, that's cool. So now we move on to Sony, right?"

"That's the next thing I came to talk about." He tapped the papers. "I've already lined up our next trade. Sony."

I frowned. "Sony, like PlayStation Sony?"

"Correct. I dug into the filings, the product roadmap, the competition, and I like the setup. I don't think it's going to be the same kind of rocket as that Windows trade, but strong enough that I'm comfortable putting real money behind it."

"How much is 'real money'?"

"We're going to take the profit we just made and add back in all of the principal from the Windows basket," he said. "Call it around two hundred and sixty thousand, give or take. Roughly half our total equity at this point."

"So just big swing after big swing."

"For now, yes. We're too small for it to be any other way, but, and I want you to hear this part, it won't always be this big. The more we grow, the smaller the percentage we'll put into any one idea. These early swings look dramatic because the base is small. We will not make a habit of putting half of everything we own into a single trade."

"That's probably good thinking."

He smiled. "That's why I'm your partner. Your job is to give me your hunches on where the world's about to change, and my job is figuring out how to bet on it without going broke."

He flipped to another sheet. "Couple more updates. We technically have our first employee now."

I blinked. "We do?"

"Her name's Nicole Yeates. She's been with me for years, keeps the trains running at my current business, but there's been less for her to do the last few years. She still works for me, but I've brought her on with us part-time for now, although that could change as the workload increases. I have her handling paperwork, statements, making sure the filings are clean, and some accounting. She'll be the one sending you monthly summaries once we get things a little more formal and will be someone you can call if you need financial information."

I was still stuck on the first sentence and had barely taken in everything else.

"So ... she works for us?" I asked.

"She works for me, and some of her time is now allocated to our operation. But for all practical purposes, yes, you've got somebody on payroll helping to manage your money."

I felt a quick, stupid flare of pride at that.

"Where's all this happening?" I asked. "The, uh, 'operation.'"

"Out of my office in Dallas for now. No need to rent space or do anything flashy. We're using my existing setup, licenses, infrastructure. It keeps your costs down and lets us move fast. That will, of course, change once we start bringing on traders and the like to give us more cover for your trades. And maybe make a little money the old-fashioned way."

"That's fine with me. I'm not picky about addresses."

"Good, because we're going to keep it boring on the surface as long as we can. No attention, no headlines. Just steady work."

He closed the folder and rested his hands on it.

"Bottom line, your first hunch hit. We both made a little money, we put some more profit into the business, and we're set to roll that into Sony."

"Just ... Wow. I knew you were the right guy to go to. I'm just shocked we're seeing money so soon."

He stood, tucking the folder under his arm again.

"I am too, honestly. You keep coming with the hunches, and this will be far from the last of these you see," he said, pointing to the check.

"I will," I said.

The student lot was already jammed when Dad pulled up to the stadium. Lights from the field spilled over the fence and washed across the gravel, and I could hear the band working through the fight song while people climbed the bleachers.

It hit me harder than I expected when I stepped out of his patrol car. This was my first varsity game.

Every row on our side was packed. Kids painted in blue and white at the front, dads in work shirts with school caps, moms with blankets and seat cushions, little kids running along the rail. Even the far side had a good crowd, Irvin's maroon and white scattered through the visitors' section and along the fence.

This was not freshman ball at a half-empty field anymore, or even JV.

We came out of the field house together in two lines, helmets under our arms. The turf felt a little springier under my cleats than it did during practice, or maybe that was just my legs. The drumline started a cadence when we got close to the field.

Our cheerleaders formed a run-through in front of a big paper sign with *Mustangs Road to State* across it.

I bumped fists with Andre as we lined up behind the banner.

The band hit the fight song again, the cheerleaders started shouting, and we sprinted through the paper and onto the field, blue jerseys flaring out behind me. The bleachers shook when the crowd jumped, and for a second, the whole place felt like it leaned toward us.

It was the season opener, my first varsity start, and it was time to see if all the work I put in meant anything.

We lost the coin toss and Irvin deferred, so it was our ball to start. Coach Holloway met us as we came off the sideline.

"First call is 22 Zone, check to slant if they load the box," he said. "You know what you're doing. Go run the offense."

I took the play, jogged out with the offense, and the noise swelled again. Irvin's sideline was as loud as ours, and it was clear they wanted this, too. They had made the long drive and did not intend to roll over.

We lined up at our own thirty after a short return. I skipped the huddle and called the formation, checking the defense. They kept both safeties back but had the linebackers creeping, although not enough to check out of it.

I stepped under center, felt Andre's hand on the ball, and watched the safety on the wide side. On the snap, I opened to Noah and shoved the ball into his stomach. Our left side caved their front in, and Noah hit the crease between Albert and Bryce, bending his run off Andre's hip and dragging a linebacker for seven.

It was second and three, and the nerves were finally settling down as things got moving. It was the same stadium, the same field, the same ball, just with more people watching.

We huddled for the first time.

"Trips right, 64 Stick," I said. "Mickey, you've got the option. Read that backer."

We moved fast. They stayed two high, nickel look, backer shaded toward Mickey. On the snap, I caught, planted, and fired to Henry in the flat when the backer widened with Mickey's stem. Six more yards, first down near the forty-five.

On the next play, their linebackers were already biting on Noah. On the snap, I sold the fake, feeling Noah squeeze past. The strong safety stepped downhill. Henry crossed from right to left behind the linebackers. I set my back foot at about seven yards and let it rip into the hole that opened between the safeties. The ball hit him on the numbers, and he tucked it and turned upfield, getting dragged down at their thirty-five.

The crowd roared.

They gave us a single-high look this time, corner ten yards off Austin, inside leverage. On the snap, I dropped straight back, keeping my eyes in the middle as Noah cleared on his checkdown. Austin pushed vertical to twelve, broke out toward the sideline. The corner tried to drive on it, but I had already let the ball go for the far hash. It left my fingers in a straight line and found Austin right at the boundary for about thirteen yards.

Now we were at the twenty-five. First drive, and everything was clicking.

Coach sent in the next play, Trips right, 62 seam choice, and I knew what he wanted. We needed to put pressure down the middle.

I looked over the defense and saw the middle safety cheating toward Mickey's side, suspicious of the three-receiver set. Noah shifted to my left, giving us a little extra protection if they brought pressure. On the snap, I took a quick three-step drop, eyes left on Brian's move to hold the corner.

Mickey pushed up the seam from the slot as the weak-side backer tried to collision him, got one hand on him, and lost him. The safety was half a step late. I drove the throw into the window right down the hash. The safety recovered just enough to get a hand in and tip it.

The ball ricocheted off Mickey's forearms into the end zone and caromed away as the home side groaned at the same time I did. That had been six if I got a little more air under it or if he squeezed just a hair harder.

That's football, however. That left us with second and ten.

We rotated. This time, Austin had the corner route. I took the snap at the gun to give us a little more time, and Irvin came with a four-man rush. I slid into the pocket as Keith rode their end past my right shoulder, and Noah cut a blitzer that tried to shoot the A-gap. I pumped at Henry in the flat to hold the corner and let Austin work.

He cleared the underneath defender at about ten yards, then bent his route toward the back pylon. The safety who had just broken up the last pass, overcommitted inside, expecting another seam. There was a slice of daylight over Austin's helmet and in front of the sideline.

I put it there.

Austin caught it and got his toes down just before his momentum carried him into the paint behind the end zone and the line judge threw both arms up.

The stadium blew open. Andre hit me in the helmet with both hands while we jogged off, but nobody lingered. Mickey grabbed the ball and flipped it to the ref as special teams sprinted on the field. Gerald knocked the extra point through, and the scoreboard clicked over to 7–0.

Defense went out and handled their business. Irvin tried a little of everything on their first drive, some inside zone, a quick screen, a hitch, but our front four ate most of it. Calvin broke up a third-and-six out route, and their kicker ended up trying a long one after a holding call pushed them back. The snap and hold were solid as the ball sailed just over the bar. 7–3.

The rest of the first quarter turned into field position. We traded punts, both sides feeling out what the other wanted to do, and we finished the period with that four-point lead and the sense that nobody was backing down.

Early in the second, we took over on our own thirty, and Coach sent in a simple script, inside zone, quick out, then a shot if we got the look. Noah bounced the first carry off Elton's hip for eight before Brian worked a speed out from the far side on second down, catching it and dragging his feet for another ten.

On the next play, we went play-action again out of a heavy set. I sold the fake to Joe at fullback and wheeled back around. The linebackers sucked in, eyes on Joe's shoulders. Henry released from the line and dragged across, but the safety jumped him. Austin had a post route backside against single coverage, and the corner tried to sit on his break, but Austin stemmed him upfield, then cut at fifteen. I threw before he came out of it, trusting the space.

The ball hit him right when he cleared the corner's outside shoulder, and he rolled through the tackle and landed with his back on their forty-five.

Everything was working. We went no-huddle from there, forcing them to keep their bigger personnel on the field so we could wear them out. A couple more quick throws spread them out and had us in the red zone again.

Third-and-goal from the eight, Coach dialed up a sprint-out to the right with a play designed to give me a run-pass option.

I took the snap, rolled toward the field side, and my eyes checked the routes in order. Henry sat at the goal line, bracketed, and Austin pushed to the back corner, hand up, but the safety had already broken that way. I pumped, reset my feet, and tried to drop the ball over the safety.

Too much juice. Austin leaped and got a fingertip on it, but the ball sailed just out the back. Another close call and a miss. The entire home side groaned in one long sound that seemed to ride my shoulders.

On the next try, we went for a short, controlled pass, and they rushed four. The middle of the field was open, and Mickey released from the slot, stemmed inside, then snapped his route off right at the goal line, turning his body toward me and giving me his numbers. The backer who was supposed to be there hesitated, caught between Noah in the flat and Mickey. That was all I needed.

I hit Mickey in the chest, and he turned, took one step, and crossed the line before anyone hit him.

Touchdown, and after the extra point, it was 14–3.

Irvin didn't go away, though. On the kickoff, they got a good return out past their thirty and then settled into an old-school drive. They used misdirection, a counter step with the tailback, a naked boot where their quarterback rolled and hit a receiver leaking out late, and steady runs that chewed yards. A fumbled exchange that bounced right back to their back on third down kept things alive for them.

They finally stalled inside our ten. Third-and-goal from about the four, they pulled their guard and tried to run power off tackle. Julius guessed right and shot his gap, meeting the back in the hole. The collision was so hard I felt it in my knees. The back staggered, then went down at the one when Lucas crashed in to finish it.

It was fourth down, and their coach thought about it, then sent the kicking team out again. The short field goal cut it to 14–6.

We still had time before the half.

On the next kickoff, Noah brought it out to the thirty and we went into a two-minute drill, lots of quick game, the clock our second opponent. We played fast and moved the chain and with under a minute left, we were at their thirty-two, one timeout.

Coach gave us a shot play with a check to a curl if they bailed. At the line, I saw both corners dropping, safeties at twelve yards. We did not have the right leverage for the deep look, so I killed it, tapped my helmet, and called the curl.

Austin pressed up to twelve and snapped back to the ball near their sideline. I got it out on time, and he kept both feet in as he caught the ball right by the white. From where I stood, I thought he had it.

The side judge came in and ruled him out. There is no replay in high school ball, so we had to live with the call. The home crowd hated that. Coach did too, but he swallowed it and sent Gerald on.

Gerald split the uprights from forty-nine. 17–6.

We kicked off with maybe thirty seconds left, and I figured we were jogging into the locker room up by eleven.

Their quarterback had other ideas.

On second down, we went into a basic Cover Three, corners bailing, safeties deep, linebackers dropping into their zones, and Irvin lined up in trips. Our communication was a half-beat late with the inside receiver running a deep post, the outside receiver on our side pushed vertical and bent toward the sideline.

Calvin and Luke both reacted to the inside route, their eyes on the quarterback, and the outside receiver slipped past in the confusion by a yard or two. The quarterback planted, hit his back foot, and launched.

From my spot on the sideline, I watched the receiver track the ball over his shoulder and haul it in stride around our twenty. Luke tried to chase him down, but the receiver had angle and momentum and scored standing up.

Their crowd exploded, and our side went quiet for the first time all night. The extra point was good and we went into halftime up 17–13 instead of rolling over them.

"Fourteen to three in the middle of the second and we let them back in," Coach Holloway said as we gathered up in the locker room. "That is the difference between good teams and great ones. You want that road to state? You shut that door. Now you go back out there and do it."

We nodded, taped up what needed taping, and went back out.

Second half, they got the ball first and our defense made sure they stayed with them.

Irvin tried to ride the momentum, coming out with tempo. They ran a quick-screen to the wide side that Wilbur cut down, then tried a deep comeback that Calvin broke up. On third down, they set up a draw, hoping we were in a passing front. Brandon knifed through their line, grabbed the back by the waist, and spun him down for a two-yard loss.

We got the ball back, but the third quarter started like a fistfight with both defensive lines controlling things. On our first drive, I took a sack on a long-developing play-action when their defensive end beat our tackle across his face.

It wasn't the worst hit I'd had, but we needed to do better at holding the pocket.

On the next series, I tried to squeeze a dig route into Henry and a linebacker got a hand on it. The ball floated just long enough for their safety to dive and intercept it, but the back judge waved it off when the ball scraped the ground. The visitors still fed off that, talking more, chesting up a little.

They answered with pressure of their own. On the next Irvin drive, on second down, Julius shot through on a twist with Tyler, met the quarterback at seven yards, and buried him. Two plays later, Tyler came off the edge untouched on a long-developing screen and dragged the quarterback down again.

The clock ticked down and the score stayed 17–13.

Late in the quarter, something finally loosened for us.

We got the ball around midfield after a shanked punt and Coach signaled in a shot concept off zone action. On first down, Noah picked up five behind a strong push from the right side. On the next play, I sold the fake to Joe, then turned and rolled left. Their defensive end bit hard on the run and disappeared inside. Space opened in front of me, but their outside linebacker stayed with me. Henry's crosser pulled one safety and Austin streaked across the field on a deep over route, dragging the other.

The linebacker took one step toward Henry when I pumped. That half-step was all I needed to turn upfield off his shoulder. I'd been doing well at not scrambling during practice and hadn't made a go of it all game, but I saw the open field and said screw it.

I tucked the ball and ran.

Cliff Daniels had said to keep it in my bag and pull it out when I knew the moment was there, and this was the moment. I cut once at the hash to avoid an arm tackle, then squared toward the pylon. A safety came downhill, chopping his steps at the goal line. I lowered my shoulder and jumped at the last second.

We collided in midair. His helmet smacked into my ribs, and my body jolted, but I extended the ball inside the line before we crashed into the end zone. The side judge ran in, arms up. Touchdown.

When I stood up, my chest ached and my lungs burned, but the noise from our side of the field poured over me, washing that away. Andre shoved me from behind, laughing, and Noah slapped my helmet as we jogged back.

God, I loved football.

Gerald drilled the extra point. 24–13.

Irvin responded by driving again. They moved the ball with underneath stuff, taking advantage of the softer zones we drifted into after stretching the lead. A slant here, a fullback dive there. They reached our thirty, then our twenty, feeding their bruiser of a back on inside runs.

On second down, their quarterback decided to test us deep again. They ran a double move outside, hitch-and-go, hoping we'd gotten lazy. Calvin had not. He stayed patient, let the receiver sell it, and when the quarterback lofted the ball, Calvin turned and beat him to the spot. He rose, extended both hands, and caught it at our four-yard line, rolling through the receiver as they went to the ground.

The ref signaled our ball. Our sideline went crazy, but we did not have much time to enjoy it. We were still backed up on our own goal line. The third quarter wound down with us grinding out two first downs and then punting, content to flip the field and make Irvin work again.

We opened the fourth still up 24–13, and both defenses were tired.

Irvin put together their best drive of the night to start the quarter. They leaned on quick passes and ran their tailback off tackle behind a pulling guard. A swing pass converted a third-and-four when our linebacker slipped and they reached our red zone again, and for a second, it felt like that halftime bomb was about to turn into a pattern.

They had first-and-goal at our seven. On first down, they ran inside, and Julius stacked the guard and stopped the back at the four. Second down, they spread us out and tried a quick slant. Calvin broke on it and almost had another pick.

They had fourth-and-goal at the four and brought in heavy personnel, two tight ends and a fullback. Everyone in the stadium knew what was coming. On the snap, their line fired out low as the back lowered his shoulders, and everyone met in a mess of bodies right in the middle. When the ref finally peeled guys off the pile, the ball was inches inside the two.

Their coach kept the offense out there. Fourth-and-goal.

This time, they flared the tailback toward the flat and sent the fullback into the line alone, hoping to catch us crashing. Our linebackers did not bite. Julius met the fullback at the hole one-on-one, wrapped his legs, and spun him backwards with the kind of hit you feel in your bones. He stopped him short.

It was a turnover on downs at our two.

The student section was pounding on the rail so hard the metal rumbled. You could feel it under your feet.

The first thing we needed to do was to get off our own goal line. Two inside gives to Noah got us some breathing room, one to the five, one to the nine. It was third-and-three, and the safe call would have been another run and a punt. Instead, Coach sent in a play-action.

Irvin loaded the box, showing blitz. Their corners walked up, safeties flat-footed at eight yards. They wanted a safety or a tackle for loss in our end zone.

On the snap, I turned and flashed the ball at Noah. The linebackers stepped forward, eyes on him as Austin released outside off the line, gave a little jab, then sliced back in. The corner tried to jam him, missed with his hands, and Austin slid across his face.

I planted at three steps and drove the ball into his chest. He caught it at about the sixteen, shrugged off a weak arm from the corner, and surged out to the thirty before a safety dragged him down from behind.

We'd managed to get out of the bad positioning, and the field was now opened up.

We went to work from there and crossed midfield with around five minutes left in the game. Irvin needed a stop, and their safeties crept closer, linebackers showing pressure from both gaps.

This time, Mickey was in the slot to the right, Austin wide, Brian backside alone. The look was perfect. Press outside, one high safety shaded to the trips.

I took the snap from under center, turned, and sold the fake to Joe. The linebackers crashed hard, and the safety froze with his eyes on the backfield, then took a step toward the run.

That was all Mickey needed. He pushed vertically from the slot, then cut hard inside, shoulders low, presenting a clean target. The backer responsible for that zone was a step late through traffic.

I ripped the throw on rhythm, right past the ear of that backer, waist-high. Mickey secured it at about the eighteen, turned upfield, and split the angle between the safety and corner. They hit him at the five, but his legs kept moving as he fell forward into the end zone.

It was my third passing touchdown and fourth score of the night.

Gerald's extra point stretched it to 31–13.

Irvin still had some pride, and even though the game was out of reach, they didn't give up. Against our softer coverages, they put together a late drive. Short outs to the boundary, a draw play that caught us with only six in the box. We were trading yards for seconds now.

They reached our twenty, then our ten. On second-and-goal from the eight, they caught us with a fade to the corner against our backup corner, making it 31–19 after the touchdown. Down by twelve with little time left, they went for two.

They emptied the backfield and spread us out. Our defense stayed in man, with a linebacker eying up the quarterback. On the snap, the quarterback tried to roll right and hit a quick out.

Tyler and Julius had other plans. Tyler beat his tackle inside, Julius looped around, and they met at the quarterback just as he planted, dragging him down near the twelve.

The ref waved off the try. They came away with no points.

Nothing came of the last drive, putting the final at 31–19. My first varsity game and my first varsity win.

As soon as the handshake line was finished, I started toward the field house when one of the coaches grabbed my arm and pointed toward the track.

"Reporter-Telegram wants you," he said.

A short woman with a notebook and a camera bag waited by the numbers, just off the field. A laminated Midland Reporter-Telegram pass hung from her collar.

"Blake, you got a second?" she called.

I jogged over, helmet in my hand, sweat still running down my neck. My pads felt twice as heavy now that the game was over.

"Sure," I said.

"Lori Crane, Midland Reporter-Telegram," she said, clicking on a small tape recorder and held it up. "Sophomore starter, first varsity game, four touchdowns. How did it feel out there?"

For a second, I flashed on the media session. Talk about the team, not ourselves.

"It felt great to finally get out there with these guys," I said. "Our line did an amazing job, gave me the time I needed most of the night, and our receivers made big-time plays. My job was just to get the ball to them and run what Coach called."

She nodded and scribbled a few words. "You guys jumped out to a big lead, then they hit that long one before half. What did the coaches say in the locker room to settle things?"

"Coach Holloway reminded us that good teams finish. We let up for a series, and they made us pay for it. At halftime, the message was pretty simple: do your job, trust your teammates, and close it out."

"You ran for a big touchdown in the third, and word from the All-American Camp this summer is that you love to scramble. Did the coaches prepare you for that, or did you just see the chance and go for it?"

I was surprised she'd talked to people from the camp. It wasn't until that moment that it occurred to me she might have done some homework on us before coming to cover the game.

"We knew coming in that if they took away some of our outside plays, there'd be open lanes. Our coaches have put in some plays to let me move around, but most of that was just reading what their ends were doing. The real credit is to our receivers for running off the coverage and to Joe and Noah for forcing them to respect the run."

She smiled and shook her head, like she was realizing I wasn't going to showboat. "One more, and I'll let you go. There's been a lot of talk around town about this team and the word 'state' getting thrown around. How do you keep from looking ahead after a win like this?"

"By not listening to the talk. Irvin's a good team, and we're happy to start out right, but it's one game. We've got film to watch tomorrow, and I'm sure the coaches will point out all the screw-ups we made. This wasn't a perfect game, and we have a long way to go to get to state. If we focus on the next practice and the next opponent instead of December, we'll be in a lot better shape."

"Good," Lori said. "That'll play. Thanks, Blake."

"Thank you," I said.

By the time I reached the field house, most of the guys were already inside, and the energy was high.

Mickey grabbed my shoulders and shook me. "Four touchdowns, man!"

Austin threw a rolled-up towel at my head. "Would have been more if you hadn't overthrown me."

I laughed it off, batting the towel away. I knew he was messing with me.

I tried to push through toward my locker, but they hemmed me in, shouting, clapping my helmet, retelling plays I had just lived through like they were already stories. My ribs still hurt from that goal-line dive, and my legs felt heavy, but it was the best kind of tired.

The door at the front of the locker room banged open, and Coach Holloway gave a single, short whistle blast. Everyone froze like someone had flipped a switch.

"Take a seat," he said.

We all turned toward him, still half standing, then sat on benches or in front of our lockers. He looked around the room slowly, taking in every face.

"That was a good win," he said. "Not a perfect one. We jumped on them early, then let our foot off the gas, and a good team will always take advantage of that, but we cleaned it up in the second half. Defense, you stood up in the red zone when it counted. Offense, you answered when they got close."

He paused, letting that hang for a second.

"This was one step. One. If any of you walk out of here tonight thinking it means anything more than that, you're already behind. Irvin isn't going to be watching film of us next week. Our next opponent is. You want that road to state everyone keeps talking about? You show up Monday ready to work harder than you did last week. Every snap, every rep, every study hall. You understand me?"

"Yes, sir," the room answered.

He nodded once.

"Now ... there were a lot of guys who could get a game ball tonight. Julius, that fourth-down stop was as big as anything we did. Andre, line, you kept our quarterback on his feet. Receivers, you made catches when we needed them. But there's one kid who spent all summer getting himself ready for this," Coach Holloway said. "Morning runs, extra film, dragging half of you up to the school at sunrise and on the field all summer, almost every day, practicing. He's young, and he's going to make mistakes, plenty of which we saw tonight, but he also stood in the pocket, took hits, kept this offense moving, and did it with his mouth shut and his eyes up. That is what a quarterback at Wheaton High is supposed to look like."

His gaze went right through the front row and locked on me.

"Game ball tonight goes to Blake Sims."

The room exploded as helmets hit the lockers, and someone grabbed my shoulders, shoving me forward into the open space.

Coach Holloway picked the ball up from the stool beside him, tucked it under his arm, and waited for the noise to die down.

"This doesn't mean you've arrived," he said. "It means this is the standard now. Understand?"

"Yes, sir," I said.

"Good man," he said, putting the game ball in my hands.

Chapter 22

Sunday, it was time to head to Li's for more training with Yesica, and not even having to walk in the heat was going to take away from my good mood. Two days after the game, I was still flying high.

The streets around downtown were quiet. Most of the after-church crowd had finished lunch and gone home. Arriving at the store, I could see Li through the glass at the front counter with poster board spread out in front of her, a cup full of markers next to her elbow.

She must have been really focused because she jumped a little when I pushed the door open and the bell dinged.

"You're late," she said, annoyed.

"For what?" I said as I dropped my gym bag by the counter.

"Existing. You're supposed to appear anytime something needs to be carried or someone needs to be annoyed."

I walked closer and leaned on the counter. "You've got both of those covered without me."

There were three poster boards laid out. One said *Li for Sophomore Rep* in block letters. Another had *Vote Zhu, Make Wheaton True* across the top, half-finished. The third had only her name drawn in outline.

"They're letting you run again?" I asked. "I thought once you'd seized power, you were term-limited."

She rolled her eyes. "No, you didn't, 'cause you're not an idiot. Student council does not have term limits, and it is 'serve,' not 'seize.' I am running for sophomore rep and secretary."

"Both?" I raised my eyebrows. "Going for the whole shebang this time."

"Secretary is a good steppingstone to vice-president and then president, although it usually goes to a junior or senior." She uncapped a marker. "But there is no rule that says that, and I should be able to make up for it by having you backing me."

"I should have seen that coming. So what am I doing this time?"

"Same as last year. Talk to everyone you can and get them to support me, convince the other guys to do the same. Melanie is running against me openly, and she may have burned some bridges with the whole Tammy thing last year, but she still has friends."

"I guess I can do that to support Li Zhu, woman of the people," I said. "Although I'm still not sure how much my help counted towards your win last time."

"It helped, but this year I think you can carry it for me, now that you're ... the thing."

"The thing?" I asked.

She flicked the corner of my Wheaton football T-shirt. I hadn't realized I grabbed the one with MUSTANGS in big letters across the chest.

"You know what I mean. Varsity quarterback leading the school to its first real shot at state," she said. "It was already a big deal last week, but this next week people are going to be nuts. You should've heard how everyone talked about you in the crowd on Friday night."

"Oh, it was good, was it?" I asked, grinning again.

"Stop fishing for compliments."

"Says the girl wanting to exploit my fame," I said.

"Well, you gotta be good for something."

I laughed.

"Okay, okay. I'll do what I can; tell me what else you need and when."

"Good." She nodded, like she expected that answer. "Now go on to the back. Yesica has been here ten minutes already."

"Work, work, work," I said, picking up my bag and heading past the aisles of furniture toward the back.

The back-room door was open, and Yesica was standing by the heavy bag.

"You finally decided to show up," she said. "I thought maybe the big star forgot about us little people."

"You heard."

"Li couldn't stop bragging about you when I got here."

"She did, did she?"

"Stop fishing for compliments and get ready," she said with a snort.

I slid my hands into the wraps, pulling them snug around my wrists and knuckles. She picked up the focus mitts and slipped them over her hands.

"Warm up," she said. "Shadow, feet, get your shoulders ready. Then we'll start putting things together."

I took my spot in the middle of the room, bouncing in place and rolling my shoulders before switching to light jabs in the air, adding a cross, focusing on how my hips turned, and my back foot came with me.

"Feet first," she corrected.

I worked the basic step forward and back, left and right. Jab, step, cross, bring it back.

"Okay," she said. "Enough dancing. Mitts."

I stepped up. She raised the mitts in front of her chest.

"No more baby punches. Today we do chains. Jab, cross, hook, one-two-three. You hit where I tell you, and we'll see if we can make your brain and hands talk to each other."

"Sounds dangerous," I said.

"It is if you do it right."

She held out her left mitt.

I snapped a jab into it, making a popping sound in the leather.

"Again," she said.

Jab.

"Add the cross."

Jab, cross.

She moved the right mitt slightly higher and to the side.

"Now the hook. Same leg you jab with, turn on it and bring your elbow with you. Don't slap it, hit through."

Jab, cross, hook.

The hook drove into the mitt, and my left shoulder protested. I'd thrown a lot on Friday, and it sometimes stayed tender for a few days.

"Better. Again, thirty times. Don't count, just live there."

We fell into a rhythm as she called out small corrections between sets. "Hands back to your face. Turn your hip, not just your arm. You're getting your front foot out of line, and it's messing up your balance."

We went at it for twenty more minutes, sweat sliding down my back while my shoulders burned. If nothing else, this was a hell of a workout.

"Good," she said finally. "Go drink some water."

I dropped my hands and walked over to my bag where I kept a water bottle, and drank hard. Yesica leaned against the wall, tugging one mitt loose so she could wipe her forehead with her wrist.

"Okay," she said. "So talk to me about what happened at the college at the start of summer."

"What?"

"Sun told me about it when she first asked me to teach you, but she didn't go into a lot of details. Before we really get going, I want to know what is in your head when you think about fighting. Why you're here?"

"Because Li's mom told me to, and it's not smart to argue with her," I said.

Yesica clearly didn't find that funny, because she just stood there, waiting.

"There was this guy, Elijah," I said after a beat. "We grew up together playing pee-wee ball and were tight in middle school. He, Jake, Mason, and I used to be close, but last year I stopped putting up with their crap, and they didn't like it."

"What kind of crap?" she asked.

"Just basic bully stuff, you know, picking on kids, going out of their way to hurt people to make themselves feel big. Half the time it was just talk, but half the time it wasn't, and they wanted someone to back them up and laugh at their bullshit. I got tired of it."

"So they got tired of you," she said.

"Pretty much. We had it out, and I told him to get lost, and then I started working hard getting recognition on the team while he got benched for trying to sabotage the team to make me look bad. He was never a thinker. Late in the year, he jumped me in the bathroom to show me who's boss, and that didn't go great for him, although honestly, it didn't go well for me either; we were just kind of swinging at each other."

"It's easy to get hurt fighting when you don't know how, even if the other person doesn't know how either. What happened at the college?"

"We were at this seven-on-seven tournament, and I thought we'd moved on, although they were both still kind of pissed at me 'cause they weren't getting the playing time that they thought they should get. And it got worse after I convinced Hunter, who was one of their bunch, to ditch them before he ruined his chance to get real playing time. Elijah blamed me for that, too. In between games, I was headed to the dorm, and they were waiting for me. They didn't say anything; they just came in swinging. I fought them off as best I could, but there were two of them, so I was kind of screwed. I went down trying to cover up, but mostly I just saw shoes and grass. They got in some shots before someone came, and they ran off. Li's mom saw me after. My face looked like I ran into a truck, and my hand was kind of messed up."

"Did the school do anything?" she asked.

"Yeah, they got kicked off the team. Elijah ended up moving, I guess so he could find a team to play on since he's banned from playing here. He's gone, so that part's over."

"There will be others like him, though," she said.

"There are. I almost had it out with this guy, Trevor, at the camp this summer. Different jerk, but same idea. So yeah, when Li's mom said I need to learn how to defend myself, she was right. 'Cause you're right, there will always be others like them, so I need to know how to protect myself."

She watched me, then pushed off the wall.

"Good," she said.

"Good?" I asked.

"Good that you know what you want," she said. "The reason matters. You shouldn't learn to fight because you think it's cool or you want to hurt people. You should learn because you need to know how to defend yourself."

I nodded.

"Okay," she said. "Drink time is over. Back to it."

I walked back to the center of the room while she tugged her mitt back on and cracked her neck.

"This time, we add the body. Jab, cross, hook to the body, then finish upstairs. One-two-three-four. When you change levels, bend your knees rather than folding at the waist like a lawn chair. You aren't ninety years old."

"Got it," I said.

She held the mitts at different heights to show the targets. When she called 'Jab,' the first punch snapped out, followed by the cross lining up down the middle.

"Hook to the body," she ordered, so I dipped my level, turned on my front foot, and drove the hook into the lower mitt, feeling the shift in angle pull at my lower back.

"Now bring it back up. Same side, hook to the head. Your weight comes with you, but your feet stay under you."

I pivoted, dragging the strike up until my forearm met the mitt with a dull smack.

"That is the chain. Again, and make it flow. Remember, feet ... feet ... feet, punches come from the ground."

We went through it over and over until she started moving, as she called it, sliding to her right so I had to step with her while keeping my stance. Jab, cross, body hook, head hook, and then she shifted the other way, forcing me to adjust without crossing my feet.

"That back hand keeps coming home. If you drop it, you're going to get hit. Every time."

She smacked my shoulder with one mitt after I let my right hand drift.

"Home," she said. "Do it again."

We went until my arms felt heavy and my breath came in short pants. Finally, she clapped the mitts together.

"Footwork now," she said. "Take your gloves off."

I shook out my hands and set the gloves on the crate while she walked over to the corner to pick up a roll of tape. In quick moves, she laid out strips of tape in a cross on the floor with lines running front to back and side to side.

"You stand in the middle. Each line is a lane. You step into one, then back to center, forward, back, side, center. We can add punches later, but for now, we teach your feet not to get stuck in cement."

I stepped onto the center point.

"Okay," she said. "Front line, step, step back. Okay, left line, step, step back. Right, back. Don't hop or slide. Heel, toe, and keep your hands up."

She circled me as I worked the pattern, and when I overstepped and crossed my feet, she kicked out, smacking against my foot or shin.

"Too far, keep your steps small. If you cross, you're going to lose balance and fall."

We added a punch each way. Step forward, jab, back. Step left, hook, back. Step right, cross, back.

"Okay," she said. "Break."

I sagged from my stance and reached for my water again.

"You know why I'm teaching you this, right?" she said.

"Self-defense."

"And do you know how that is different than just learning to box?"

"No, but I assume you're going to tell me."

Instead of explaining directly, she started a story.

"When I was starting out in Medellín, I trained at this gym where half the guys were fighters and half were just trying to stay off the streets. There was this one kid, maybe seventeen. He was really talented. He had fast hands, good footwork, and won every sparring session because he knew how to score points. One night, he's walking home and three guys try to rob him. He squares up like he's in the ring, bouncing on his toes, hands up proper, waiting for an opening."

"I assume it didn't go well."

"It didn't. They broke his jaw and took everything he had. Do you know why?"

"No."

"Because he was trying to box them. He was thinking about technique and looking good and landing clean shots and not about ending it fast and getting out."

"What should he have done differently?" I asked.

"Given them his wallet and avoided the fight altogether. Losing the money he had on him would have been cheaper than losing the money plus having to go to the hospital. Short of that, he could have hit the first guy as hard as he could and run for it. There are no points for style when you're getting jumped, and it doesn't matter how right or wrong it is. There's just winning or losing, and winning means you walk away without getting hurt."

She picked up the mitts again but didn't put them on.

"That's what you need to understand about guys like these bullies of yours. They're not looking for a fair fight. They're looking to hurt you when you're not ready, when you can't defend yourself, and to get what they want from you. The best thing I can teach you about fighting is to not fight, to see it coming and avoid it. Only worry about fighting if you can't avoid it, if they corner you and you have no choice. If that happens, don't try to box them. Hit them hard enough and fast enough that they stop being a problem."

"That's what you're teaching me," I said.

"That's what I'm teaching you. If you got into a ring with what you know, you'd lose on points. But we aren't worried about that. We're worried about how to end a fight, not how to look good in one. First shot to the throat, the nose, the ribs, wherever it hurts most, no dancing around, no waiting for your moment. You hit, you make sure it counts, and you're done, because every second that fight goes on is another chance for you to get hurt worse."

I thought about the bathroom fight with Elijah last year, how we'd just swung at each other until someone pulled us apart. How at A&M, I'd tried to cover up while he and Jake kicked me. Neither time had I been thinking about ending it.

"So yeah, we're working on combinations and footwork and all that technical stuff, and all of it has a point, but we're reaching the point where it's important to know how to make decisions. When to walk away, when to get help, and when you absolutely have to fight, how to finish it before it finishes you."

"Got it," I said.

"Good. Now let's see if you can remember that body hook when you're tired. Same combination, but I'm moving this time. You follow, you adjust, you stay balanced."

We got ready and went at it again. She circled, changed angles, made me work to line up my shots, and every time I hesitated or tried to make it look clean, she'd stop and correct me.

"Faster. You're not trying to be pretty, you're trying to connect ... Again, if that was a real hook, he'd still be standing. Put your hip into it ... Move after you throw, don't stand there admiring your work."

By the time she called the last break, I was wiped out.

"Good work," she said. "You're starting to understand the difference between training and fighting. Still got a long way to go, but you're doing better."

"Thanks," I managed.

"Don't thank me yet. This is going to hurt you a lot more before you're ready."

I laughed. "Sounds fun."

"It's not. But it's necessary." She walked over to her bag and pulled out a towel, wiping her face. "Alright, I'm starving. There's a taco truck I saw on the way here. You buying?"

"Yeah, I can do that," I said.

"Good. Go get Li. She's probably done with whatever she was working on."

The locker room was loud, everyone talking over each other while changing out of practice gear. I still had my extra practice with Coach Holloway to work on notes Coach Moreno sent over, but Coach had made a comment last week that if I was always breaking off and doing my own thing, it would make it harder to lead, and that I should spend time with the guys.

Plus, I enjoyed this small break. Everyone was so focused when we were on the field. This was when we all got to goof off and act like kids.

"Yo, Blake," Andre called from across the row. "Are you coming to Jimmy's after?"

"Can't. I've still got extra practice with Coach Holloway."

"Course you do," Mickey said, pulling his shirt over his head. "You're always doing something. You're going to burn out, you know?"

"I'm fine, but before I have to head out, I need you guys to do something for me."

"Jesus, what now?" Mickey asked. "Isn't it enough that you have us doing extra runs and conditioning already?"

He was in my morning group and, admittedly, I had held them after practice a few times last week to get those who wanted it more time.

Was I doing too much?

Not what I needed to address today, but something to think about.

"Relax, it's not about football. Student council elections are happening next week, and I need all the sophomores to vote for Li for sophomore rep and for secretary."

Tyrell, who was at the next locker over, snorted. "What does a secretary even do? Is she going to answer phones in the office or something?"

Jerry stuck his head around the corner. "Yeah, man. She's going to bring the president coffee and take notes while he makes executive decisions."

A few guys laughed.

"It's not that kind of secretary," I said.

"Then what kind is it?"

I shrugged. "I have no idea, something with meetings and keeping stuff organized, I think. All I know is Li wants it, so we should back her."

Mickey raised his eyebrows. "So are you and Li together now or what?"

"No. We're friends. That's it."

"Uh-huh. You spend every free minute at her mom's shop, you vanish with her at lunch, she sits with your folks at games. But suuuure, she's not your girlfriend."

"She's just my friend," I said. "I'm allowed to have friends who are girls without it turning into a soap opera."

"Yeah, but you like her," Tyrell said.

The row across from us buzzed with a few "oooohs."

"Man, I've never worked this hard for my own family," Hunter said. "You better send her flowers or something."

"Y'all are idiots," I said, throwing Mickey's towel at him. "I'm asking y'all for a tiny favor that takes five seconds in homeroom instead of discussing my love life."

"Wait, isn't Melanie running for it too?" Jamal asked. "I heard someone talking about her at lunch."

"Yeah," Austin called from the next row. "She's all over it, man. She's got the cheer squad working the band kids."

"She does?" I asked.

I honestly hadn't been paying attention to her at all this year.

Austin stepped around the end of the row, towel over his shoulder. "Yeah, there was a group of them gathered around the band table at lunch, leaning in, doing the hair thing, laughing at their jokes. You could see those guys' brains melting."

"For a band guy, a cheerleader walking up and using his name is basically a religious experience," Mickey said. "You know they're voting for whoever she says just so she might talk to them again."

The row broke up laughing.

"Well then, we've got to counter that. She's going heavy at the guys in those groups; we should hit the girls. Band girls, drama girls, whoever. You guys are supposed to be the hot shit in the school. Time to step it up."

"So we help your new crush beat your old one," Jerry said. "That's what I'm hearing."

"It has nothing to do with Melanie," I said. "Okay, that's a lie. I would like to see her lose, but I want to see Li win more."

"I don't know," Hunter said. "I might vote for Melanie just to see what you do. It might be the only fun part of student council."

He might have ditched Elijah and gotten on board with the team to protect his future in football, but Hunter was still kind of a dick.

"Do whatever you want, but for those of you who want to do me a favor, you put Li's name down. For the juniors or seniors, talk to the sophomores you know, push them to vote for her too."

"What are we supposed to say? 'Vote for Li because Blake said so'?" Andre asked.

“Tell them whatever, say she’s smart and actually gives a shit. She was freshman rep last year, she did the work, and she won’t treat it like a joke or a popularity contest.”

“Unlike certain people,” Miguel said under his breath.

“Exactly,” I said.

“So this is what fame feels like,” Jerry said. “Already using your power for political corruption.”

“Yeah, that’s me, political fixer.”

The guys laughed.

“Alright, Kingmaker,” Hunter said. “What else are you going to make us do? Raise taxes? Get a weight room named after you?”

“Blake Sims Memorial Urinal,” Mickey said. “For services to democracy.”

“Y’all are stupid,” Andre said.

“Are you going to run too, Blake?” Gabriel asked. “President Sims, quarterback slash student council overlord?”

“Hell no. I’ve got enough going on; I just want Li to win.”

Hunter grinned. “I’m still voting for Melanie. Somebody’s got to keep you on your toes, Blake.”

“Do whatever makes you happy,” I said.

Jerry pointed at him. “Please. Hunter just wants an excuse to go tell Melanie he voted for her. ‘Hey, I supported you; maybe we should go to Napoli’s and talk about your campaign.’”

A ripple of laughter went through the row. I guess I wasn’t giving the reaction they wanted, because the guys turned on Hunter as if they smelled blood in the water.

“Shut up,” Hunter said. “I don’t need an excuse to talk to her.”

“Sure you don’t,” Mickey said.

“I’m not scared of her,” Hunter said.

“You’ve got something for her,” Tyrell said.

Hunter flipped him off.

“Alright, I did my job. Do what you guys can, please,” I said, picking up my helmet and heading back toward the field.

That earned me a few more jeers and comments, but I ignored them as I made my way outside, still thinking through their comments. I didn’t realize Melanie was running against Li, but it made sense. She’d tried to tank her run last year, and I knew Melanie held a grudge like no one else.

I was probably going to have to deal with that sooner or later.

Chapter 23

I left school at two thirty with a pass from Mr. Brennan. He did have questions, even though I'd already told him my mother had cancer and I was helping to get her to and from appointments, but he'd eventually signed off. Coach Holloway was easier. He just wished me luck and said to push harder tomorrow.

Mom was waiting by the car when I got home, already wearing her blue scarf. She'd been in her room when I left for school this morning, still in bed, too nauseous from the chemo to move. Now she stood by the passenger door, one hand on the roof for balance.

"You didn't have to come home to get me," she said. "I could have driven myself."

"No, you couldn't."

It was almost pro forma, but she dropped it after that. We both knew the chemo had hit her hard, and even though she'd finished the treatment, she still felt sick all the time.

And the headaches really hadn't gotten better.

I unlocked the car and helped her into the passenger seat. She moved carefully, like everything hurt, which it probably did. The chemo had stripped away more than just her hair.

She should be on the upswing from it now that the chemo was actually done, though. The doctor had said that it would be the worst after the last round.

The drive to Midland took about forty minutes. She kept her eyes closed, cheek against the glass like the coolness made the nausea easier. I left the radio off, hoping she might sleep a little.

"What if it didn't work?" she asked about halfway there.

"It worked."

"You don't know that."

"The last scan looked good. Dr. Mitchell said so."

She didn't respond, just pulled the scarf tighter around her head.

We arrived at the hospital, and I helped her out of the car and across the parking lot. She leaned on me more than she wanted to admit, her breathing labored by the time we reached the entrance.

On top of still feeling nauseous, her headache was pretty bad today, too.

The waiting room was half full, and she sank into a chair as soon as we got there, closing her eyes while I checked us in. The receptionist smiled sympathetically and told us it would be about fifteen minutes.

It was closer to twenty when the nurse finally called us back. Mom had started to doze off, and she wavered a little bit as she stood, forcing me to catch her elbow so she wouldn't bang herself up.

"I'm fine," she said.

"Okay."

We followed the nurse to an exam room. The nurse took her vitals and frowned at the blood pressure reading but didn't say anything, just wrote it down and left.

Dr. Mitchell came in a few minutes later with a folder of films tucked under his arm. His face was that practiced doctor neutral that just made me feel more concerned.

"Mrs. Sims, Blake," he said, shaking our hands before sitting on the little rolling stool. "I have some good news. The chemo's done what we hoped, and the tumor's shrunk from five centimeters down to just under three."

"That's great. So that means you can go in and operate now, right?" I asked.

"It does, and I'd like to schedule surgery for October fifteenth. That gives us another few weeks for the swelling to go down completely and to rebuild some of your strength."

She didn't say anything.

"The surgery will take six to eight hours," Dr. Mitchell went on. "We'll go in through the skull, remove the tumor, and close. You'll spend at least a day in post-surgical where we can keep a close eye on you, and then you'll be moved to a regular room. Most patients go home after about a week."

"What are the risks?" My mother's voice came out quietly.

Dr. Mitchell's expression became more careful. "With brain surgery, any surgery, there are risks. Usually, those include things like infection, bleeding, and seizures. There's also a small chance of stroke or permanent neurological damage which might cause changes in cognition, personality, and motor function. In rare cases, death."

Her face went white.

"I want to make it clear, those are rare circumstances, and we have made excellent progress with surgeries like this. We've done this procedure many times, and the overall survival rate is over ninety-five percent, with serious complications occurring in less than five percent of cases. The fact that your tumor has responded to chemo and has shrunk makes it even more likely to be successful, as it gives us a little room to make sure we get it all out without harming any of the surrounding tissues."

The color drained out of her face.

"Five percent." She was staring at her hands. "One in twenty."

"Mom ..."

"What if I'm the one?" she asked. "What if I'm the one in twenty?"

"Mrs. Sims," the doctor said. "I understand you're scared. This is a very scary situation, but without the surgery, the tumor will continue to grow. Your symptoms will get worse."

"So either way, I might die."

"I would say with the surgery, your chance of surviving is ninety-five percent. Without it, your chances drop closer to ten percent. The risks from not operating are so much higher than the risk of surgery."

My mother turned her head toward me, her eyes were shiny, the eyeliner she still insisted on wearing smudged at the corners.

"I don't think I can do this."

"You have to."

"What if I wake up different? What if I don't wake up at all?"

"If you don't do this, then you're guaranteeing you won't. You heard the doctor."

Dr. Mitchell cleared his throat. "Mrs. Sims, I can't promise that nothing will go wrong; no one can. But you're relatively young, otherwise healthy, and the tumor's benign and accessible. You have every advantage."

My mother wiped her eyes with the back of her hand.

"When do I have to decide?"

"The surgery's scheduled for October fifteenth, but if you need more time ..."

"No." She took a shaky breath. "If I think about it too long, I'll talk myself out of it. October fifteenth."

Dr. Mitchell nodded. "I'll have my office send you the pre-op information. You'll come in on October eleventh for scans and blood work. Any other questions?"

After she indicated she didn't have any, he shook our hands again and left. She sat on the exam table for a long moment, then slid off carefully, wobbling until I grabbed her arm.

"Let's go home," she said.

We walked back through the hospital in silence. In the elevator, she leaned against the corner and closed her eyes. I didn't try to make conversation.

"Blake, if something happens during surgery ..." she said after we got into the car.

"Mom, don't."

"I'm serious. If I don't wake up, or if I wake up wrong ..."

"You're going to be fine."

"Stop saying that!" Her voice cracked. "You keep saying that like you know, like you can control it, and you can't. Nobody can."

I started the engine, letting the AC blow hot air until the air cooled down.

She was staring out the windshield, hands twisted in her lap. "I didn't want this. Any of it. You know that, right? I didn't ask for a tumor in my head, I didn't ask to lose my hair. I didn't ask to have my fifteen-year-old son dragging me to appointments because I can't be trusted to make my own decisions."

"That's not ..."

"It is. You pushed me into this. You and your father, both of you, backing me into a corner until I had no choice."

"You had a choice. You were choosing to die."

"Maybe that was my choice to make."

We sat there in the parking lot, the engine running, neither of us looking at each other.

"I'm terrified," she said finally, quieter. "I'm so scared I can barely breathe. I hate all of this."

I didn't know what to say to that.

"Just ... if something goes wrong, tell your father I tried. That's all I want. Tell him I tried."

I put the car in reverse and backed out of the parking spot without answering.

The next day, I was distracted all day and had trouble focusing. I couldn't stop thinking about what Mom had said after her appointment. I knew she was scared of the surgery and everything, but it almost sounded like she was ready to give up.

I'd basically been going through the motions all day: classes, drills, and homework. I just needed a break from everything that was going on, a way to get my mind off of all of this and feel a little normal for a while.

I was going through CDs, looking to put some music on so I could zone out, when I saw the CD from Charlie. I'd meant to call her, but it had been one thing after another, and now it was halfway through September. I found the slip of paper where she'd written her phone number and dialed it.

It rang three times, and I heard her voice. God, how I missed her voice.

"Hello?"

"Hey, it's Blake."

"Blake! Oh my God, I was starting to think you'd forgotten about me."

"No, I just ... things got kind of crazy here. I'm sorry I didn't call sooner."

"It's okay, I'm just glad you called now. How are you? How's everything going?"

I sat down on my bed, the phone cord stretching across the room. "It's been okay. No, that's a lie; it's been a lot. We got the results back on my mom's tests; she's got a brain tumor."

"Oh my God, Blake. I'm so sorry. Is she okay?"

"They're doing surgery in October. It's benign, which is good, but it's big, and it's started causing her a lot of problems. She's been really sick, and that was before she started chemo. She's absolutely terrified, and Dad's busy at work, which we need because his job provides the insurance, so I've been trying to help out."

"That's so scary. How are you handling it?"

"I don't know. I just keep trying to make sure she goes to her appointments, that she doesn't back out. She almost didn't do the chemo at all. I had to threaten to quit football and drop out of school just to get her to see a doctor."

"You threatened to quit football?"

"It was the only thing that worked. She wouldn't listen otherwise."

There was a pause, and I could hear her breathing on the other end of the line.

"That must be so hard. Watching someone you love go through that and not being able to fix it."

"Yeah. It is. I'm terrified too, but I can't say anything to her, because she needs support, not to deal with my issues."

"I imagine. It's amazing you're able to hold up with all of that. Are you doing okay? Like, are you taking care of yourself?"

"I'm trying. I've been keeping busy with football and school, just trying to keep myself distracted, mostly. Actually, I started taking boxing lessons."

"Boxing? Seriously?"

"Yeah. Li's mom set it up after that fight I told you about at the seven-on-seven tournament. There's this woman named Yesica who drives down from Lubbock once a week to teach me. She used to fight professionally."

"That's kind of badass."

"It really is. It's hard, but I'm learning a lot."

"Is it helping? I mean, do you feel like you could actually defend yourself now?"

"Not yet, but I think I will. We haven't been doing it long, and it's only once a week, so I'm still just learning the basics. Yesica's tough, though. She doesn't go easy on me, and she's teaching me the practical stuff. It's a lot harder than I thought it would be."

"I bet. I've seen some boxing matches on TV; those guys are insane."

“She actually fought men,” I said. “In exhibition matches. She’s like five foot nothing. I can’t even imagine.”

Charlie laughed. “I kind of want to meet her now.”

“You’d like her. She’s funny, and she eats more than any person I’ve ever met.”

“How’s football going? You’ve had your first game, right?”

“Yeah, last Friday. We won, thirty-one to nineteen. I threw three touchdowns and ran one in.”

“That’s amazing! How did it feel?”

“Honestly? It felt good. Really good. I was nervous going in because it’s varsity, and everyone is expecting me to take us to state, but once we got on the field, everything just clicked. The line gave me time, everyone was doing their jobs, and I could see the defense clearly.”

“What do you mean, see the defense clearly?”

“Like, I could read what they were doing. Where the gaps were, which linebacker was going to blitz, whether the safety was cheating up or playing deep. Coach Moreno has been really pushing that, and it’s starting to pay off.”

“That sounds really complicated.”

“It is, but it’s also kind of like a puzzle. You’re trying to figure out what they’re going to do before they do it, and then you exploit it.”

“Do you think you’ll keep winning?”

“I hope so. Our next game is this Friday against Riverside. They’re not as good as Irvin, so we should be okay, but Coach Holloway keeps saying we can’t get complacent.”

“Ray says the same thing. His coach is always on them about staying focused.”

“How is Ray? And how’s his team doing?”

“They’re undefeated so far. Two wins. Ray’s throwing the ball really well, and they’ve got this running back who’s just destroying everyone.”

“That’s awesome. Ray deserves it.”

“He does; he works so hard. Sometimes I think he works too hard, actually. He’s always watching film or doing extra workouts. Mom has to make him take breaks.”

“Sounds familiar.”

She laughed. "Yeah, you two are kind of similar that way. Obsessed with football and terrible at relaxing."

"Hey, I relax."

"When? When you're doing homework or taking boxing lessons or going for extra practices?"

"I listened to that CD you made me. That counts as relaxing."

"Oh, you did? Did you like it?"

"I loved it. Especially No Doubt. Her voice is funky, but ... good, you know."

"I know, right? That's one of my favorites on there. I've listened to it like a hundred times."

"Thanks for making it for me. I've been playing it a lot."

"Good. I'm glad you like it. I wasn't sure if you'd think it was too weird that I made you a CD."

"It wasn't weird. If I get to see you again, you should burn one for me with whatever new stuff you've started listening to."

Maybe that was the wrong thing to say, because there was another pause, and I could hear her shifting on the other end.

"So how's volleyball going?" I asked.

"It's good. We're three and one so far. I'm playing middle blocker, which is fun because I get to hit a lot. Coach says I need to work on my blocking, though; I keep getting caught out of position."

"What does that mean?"

"Like, I commit to blocking one hitter, and then the setter dumps it over to the other side, and I'm too far away to get there in time. It's frustrating because I know I should read it better, but I keep getting faked out."

"That sounds like reading a defense. You just have to watch the setter's hands and body language."

"That's what Coach says, too. I'm getting better, but it's hard when everything happens so fast."

"I get that, football's the same way. You think you have time, and then suddenly you don't."

"Exactly, but it's fun, and I like playing. It's one of the only times I don't have to think about school or anything else. I just get to play."

"How are your friends doing?"

"Oh my God, it's been so dramatic. Okay, so you know how I mentioned my friend Amy before?"

"I don't think so."

"Well, she's one of my teammates. So Amy broke up with her boyfriend Derek back in June, right after school ended. They'd been dating for like eight months, and she said she just wasn't feeling it anymore. Fair enough."

"Okay."

"So my other friend Brittany asked Amy if it would be weird if she went out with Derek, and Amy said no, that she was totally fine with it. She even encouraged it, said Derek was a great guy, and Brittany should go for it."

"Let me guess."

"Right? So Brittany and Derek start dating in July, and at first everything seems fine, but then Amy starts acting weird whenever they're around. Like making comments about how fast Brittany moved on her ex or talking about all these inside jokes she and Derek used to have. Really passive-aggressive stuff."

"That's rough."

"I know, right? And now Brittany feels terrible because Amy said it was okay, but clearly it's not okay, and Amy won't admit that she's upset; she just keeps saying she's happy for them while making everyone uncomfortable. So now our whole friend group is walking on eggshells because we don't know if we're allowed to hang out with Brittany and Derek together, or if that's going to set Amy off."

"Which side are you on?"

"I'm trying not to be on a side. I think Amy should've been honest about her feelings from the start, but I also get that it's hard to see your ex with your friend. And Brittany asked permission, so I don't think she did anything wrong, but none of that helps because everyone's still miserable."

"That's a good way to look at it."

"It's just hard because Amy keeps asking me if I think she's being unreasonable, and Brittany keeps asking me if I think she should break up with Derek. I don't want to lose either of them as friends, but I also can't fix this for them."

"Maybe they'll work it out eventually."

"I hope so. I'm tired of being caught in the middle."

"That sounds really stressful."

"It is, but what can I do?" she said, laughing.

We fell into a comfortable silence for a moment, and my brain short-circuited.

"I miss you," I said before I could stop myself.

The line went quiet for a moment.

"I miss you too."

"I know we said long distance wouldn't work, and I still think that's true, but ... I don't know. I think about you a lot."

"Blake ..."

"I know. I'm sorry. I shouldn't have said that."

"No, it's not that. I think about you too, all the time actually, but we were right. We live in different states, and we're both busy, and trying to make it work would just make us miserable."

"I know."

"That doesn't mean I don't wish things were different."

"Me too."

Another pause, longer this time.

"We can still talk, though," she said. "Like this. Just checking in and catching up. That's okay, right?"

"Yeah. I'd like that."

"Good. So call me again next month. Don't make me wait so long. Same time, same number. And if something big happens, call me sooner. I want to know how your mom's doing and how your season's going."

"I will. And you can call me too, if you want. I'm usually home after practice."

"I'll remember that. Good luck with your next game and everything else. I'm rooting for you."

"Thanks, Charlie. Good luck with volleyball."

"Thanks. Talk to you soon."

"Yeah. Soon."

I hung up the phone and sat there for a minute, staring at the wall. The conversation had gone better than I expected, but it still hurt, like a dull ache that wouldn't quite go away.

Chapter 24

I came out of the field house, backpack slung over one shoulder, ready to start hustling. Morning practice had run a little long, and now I had maybe fifteen minutes before first period.

I practically jumped when I came through the door and almost ran into Li, who was standing near the field house door, her backpack at her feet, arms crossed. When she saw me, she picked up her bag and walked over.

"Stalker much," I said, laughing.

"We need to talk."

"Okay?"

She was in serious mode.

I kept walking toward the main building, and she fell into step beside me.

"I'm going to lose. I've been running the numbers all week, polling all the kids I could, trying to get an idea of who's voting for whom, and it's not good."

I glanced at her. "How bad?"

"Bad. Melanie's at about forty-two percent, I'm at thirty-one, and if I don't get sophomore rep, then secretary is out the window too."

"How much of the class have you checked?"

"Most, maybe seventy percent."

We reached the main building and headed inside, the hallway already crowded with students swapping books from lockers and talking in clusters. Li kept her voice low enough that no one nearby could hear.

"Voting's Monday," she said. "Basically, we have today and the weekend to fix this, and I don't know how."

I stopped at my locker and worked the combination. "How is Melanie so far ahead of you?"

"She's hitting every group she and the other cheerleaders can reach. Band kids, drama students, stoners, art kids, choir, and basically anyone who doesn't care about student council. She's making promises, telling everyone what they want to hear, and it's working. Meanwhile, I have Honors students, the AV club, the football team, girls' basketball, and that's it."

We stopped where the hallway split, since once the bell rang, she'd have to go one way and I'd have to go the other, and I leaned back against the glass of the trophy case near the main office.

"It's a popularity contest, Li. We knew that going in."

"I know it's a popularity contest," she snapped, then immediately took a breath and lowered her voice. "I know, but I thought if I had a better platform, if I had you get the football team and actually showed everyone that I have a plan to fix the open campus lunch schedule, it would matter. But nobody cares about the lunch schedule. They care that Melanie gave out candy attached to her flyers this morning and that her friends are flirting with them."

I was pretty sure it was the flirting and not the candy that was doing it. I'd seen it happening all week, cheerleaders stopping guys in the hallway, chatting them up, casually dropping Melanie's name and buddying up to the guys, and making it seem like they wanted to be friends.

Kids didn't care about student council, but they sure as hell cared about being popular.

"So what can I do to help?" I asked.

"I don't know, that's the problem. She's making it about personality and pretty girls, and I can't compete with that. I'm not charming. I can't fake it."

"Are you giving up?"

The warning bell rang, and students started moving faster through the hallways.

"Of course not," she said. "But I'm being realistic. Most of the time left before the election is the weekend. So whatever I do has to happen today or before homeroom on Monday."

"Tell me which groups you haven't reached yet and where they sit," I said. "I'll start there."

She looked at me. "You think you can convince them?"

"I can try, and I'll see what I can do about the other cheerleaders."

"What do you mean?"

"I don't know, but I'll figure it out. Give me the list before lunch and I'll do what I can today."

She looked at me for a moment, then nodded. "Okay."

The final bell rang, and Li headed into her classroom. We'd already put a lot of pressure on kids we knew, so I wasn't sure what we could do to fix this. I was honestly surprised Melanie had gotten so many of the cheerleaders to back her after she'd been all but ostracized last year.

I'd heard she'd been working hard all summer to get back into everyone's good graces, but I hadn't imagined she'd be able to pull it off.

My first step was to figure out how the hell she'd managed it.

After third period I hurried from my class to where I knew Brandy would be. Spotting her heading toward the cafeteria entrance with two other cheerleaders, I cut across the hallway, catching her arm and pulling her toward an empty classroom.

"Hey, I need to talk to you."

She jerked her arm back and spun around. "What the hell, Blake?"

The two girls with her stopped and stared, along with half the kids in the hallway.

"Just for a minute," I nodded toward an empty classroom across the hall.

"Like hell. If Mason sees you grabbing me, he's going to stomp your ass."

"I didn't grab you, and I don't care about Mason." I took a step back toward the classroom. "One minute, that's it. Please."

She looked at her friends, then back at me, trying to decide if this was worth the drama. "This better be good."

She nodded for her friends to go ahead without her and then followed me into the classroom. I pushed the door almost shut, leaving it cracked, and turned to face her.

"What?" She crossed her arms. "If you think I'm going to get back with you or something ..."

"I need information on Melanie."

"Why would I tell you anything?"

"Because you hate her as much as I do."

"I don't hate anybody."

"Get off it. I know you two butted heads since last year, and you were practically dancing with joy when she was on the outs."

She didn't say anything, just stared at me, and I knew I'd hit a nerve.

"Fine." She dropped her arms. "I don't like her, so what?"

"So how the hell did she get everyone back on her side? Last year, she was basically done after the Kenneth thing and trying to burn Tammy. Now she's on varsity, co-captain of all things, and running for student council with most of the squad backing her."

Brandy gave a harsh laugh. "Because she's a manipulative bitch, that's how."

"Yeah, that much I did know, but how did she actually do it?"

"She went on a sympathy tour all summer, going from girl to girl, crying about her big secret."

I'm an idiot. I should have seen that as her go-to move. Hell, she'd used it on me enough times.

"About her sister?"

"Yep. She told everyone how she just found out in the spring that her sister was really her mother and 'her whole life was a lie,'" Brandy said, putting a mocking tone on for that last part, rolling her eyes. "She said how it totally destroyed her and she didn't know what to do. She made it into this huge tragedy."

"What else?"

"Just how you dumped her when you found out, saying she was disgusting and you couldn't be with someone like her. How she got all messed up and went to that party and told Kenneth, and he, well, she didn't say he assaulted her, but she sure as hell implied that when she got drunk at the party he took advantage of her and forced her to sleep with him. She didn't use the R-word or anything, but she wasn't subtle in implying it."

"She didn't?"

"She sure as hell did, and everyone's buying it. Like, were they even here last year? Because that is not how I remember things with her and Tammy going down. I remember her parading around like she was so damn pleased because she replaced Tammy and got the quarterback, until both of them turned on her, putting her on the outs. But a few tears and a sob story about how scared she was, and everyone gets fucking amnesia. Of course, it's no coincidence the story about the assault didn't start until *after* Kenneth and Tammy left for school."

"That's such bullshit."

"I know. Kenneth would never."

"Not that, well, that too, but all of it. She didn't learn about her sister in the spring. She found out almost a year ago, maybe a little more. Every time we got into a fight after we started dating, she'd use it as an excuse. And she was chasing Kenneth for months before that party, throwing herself at him every chance she got. I didn't dump her until after I found out she cheated on me, because she kept making me feel bad for her, because of her home life, blah, blah, blah. I guess if it works, why change? I definitely didn't break up with her because I found out. I knew about it for months before we broke up. She's lying to make herself look like a victim, so everyone forgets what she actually did. That would explain why all the cheerleaders have kept their distance from me so far this year, looking at me like I'm an asshole."

"They've been talking about you, talking about how just because you got starting quarterback, you think you can treat people like that."

"And you all bought it?"

"I mean, do you remember you back in middle school? You were kind of an asshole. You didn't get on this 'better than everyone' routine until last year."

"I don't think I'm better than everyone."

"Keep telling yourself that. So what are you going to do about Melanie?"

"Blow up her lies."

She smiled. "How?"

"I have no idea," I said, pulling open the classroom door. "Thanks for the info."

"Whatever. Maybe remember it and stop treating me like a bitch."

"I'll try, although it would be easier if you stopped acting like one."

"Asshole," she said at my back as I turned into the hallway.

I made my way into the cafeteria, making a beeline straight for Mason, dropping into an open seat next to him.

"Blake." He looked up from his tray. "You eating?"

"Not yet. You still got Tammy and Kenneth's numbers at school?"

I slid back into my spot at the lunch table and picked at the tray in front of me, not really tasting anything. The calls had gone better than I expected, and I thought it might work, but now I had to wait and see how they reacted.

That was the hard part.

Mickey was in the middle of some story about his summer job at the feed store, something about Mr. Plummer catching a shoplifter trying to walk out with a fifty-pound bag of dog food under his shirt. The guys were laughing, and normally I would have been too, but I couldn't focus on it.

My eyes kept drifting down the table to where the cheerleaders sat in their usual cluster, about eight seats away on the same long bench that ran the length of the cafeteria wall. Melanie was right in the middle of them, animated, gesturing with her hands while she talked. The other girls leaned in, nodding, a few of them glancing in my direction and then away.

Brandy was on the far other side of their group, picking at her food and not really participating. She'd catch my eye every so often, then look away fast.

"So Mr. Plummer just stands there," Mickey was saying, "and goes, 'Son, that's not a maternity shirt.' And the guy tries to run, but the bag splits open and kibble goes everywhere ..."

Miguel laughed so hard he nearly knocked over his soda. "No way."

"I'm telling you, man, it was the funniest thing I've ever seen. The guy slipped on the kibble like he was on ice, arms windmilling like he was in a cartoon."

Eduardo nudged my shoulder. "Are you even listening?"

"Yeah," I said, not taking my eyes off the cheerleaders.

"What did Mickey just say?"

I blinked and looked at him. "Dog food."

"Close enough." Eduardo followed my gaze down the table. "What's going on?"

"Nothing."

"Doesn't look like nothing."

Before I could answer, Mickey, squinting past me toward the cheerleaders, said, "Dude, why are you staring at them?"

I looked back at him. "What?"

"You've been watching them for like five minutes straight." He glanced down the table, then back at me, grinning a little. "That's weird, man, even for you."

"I'm just thinking," I said.

Miguel said, "Thinking about what? You and Brandy are ancient history. You're not trying to get back with her, are you?"

"Not about Brandy."

"Then what?" Mickey asked.

I didn't answer. Down at the cheerleader end, Melanie stood up from the bench, her tray still half full, and headed toward the bathroom. The other girls kept talking, not even watching her go, meaning she was almost certainly coming back.

I waited until she'd disappeared around the corner, then pushed my tray aside and stood up.

"Where are you going?" Eduardo asked.

"Be right back."

"Blake ..."

But I was already moving, walking down the length of the table. They didn't notice me approaching until I was right behind Melanie's empty chair. I pulled it out and sat down, settling in like I belonged there.

Katie was the first to react. "What do you want?"

She didn't even try to hide the contempt, like she'd found something unpleasant on the bottom of her shoe.

"I want to set the record straight." I looked around the group, meeting each girl's eyes in turn. "Because you've all been told some lies, and it's starting to affect me."

"What lies?" Alexis asked.

"Lies like why Melanie and I broke up, what actually happened between her and Kenneth, and how long she's known about her mother. You're all getting played."

"Right," Hanna said in that dismissive confidence she'd perfected. "And we're just supposed to believe you?"

"I normally couldn't care less what you believe, but this is affecting me now, and it's affecting people I care about. So yeah, it stops now."

"You can say whatever you want." Katie crossed her arms. "Just because you're the quarterback doesn't mean you can do whatever you want to people."

"You're going to get some phone calls from Tammy and Kenneth," I said, ignoring her. "Although you should feel free to call them first if you want."

A few of the girls exchanged glances.

"Who's Tammy?" one of the freshmen asked. I thought her name was Amber.

"Last year's head cheerleader," Courtney said. "She graduated."

"Why would she call us?" Alexis demanded. "What does any of this have to do with her?"

"Because she and her ex are part of Melanie's lies. After those calls, maybe you should think about what Melanie told you about what happened with me and them, and what other lies she might have told." I let it sink in for a moment. "I'm going to be the starting quarterback here for a while, and the team is behind me. So ask yourselves ... is believing Melanie's lies worth making enemies with everyone else?"

"That sounds like a threat," Emily said.

"It's not a threat, it's a question. Are you really okay being played for fools, so Melanie can be varsity, be queen bee, and win student council? Which, by the way, she doesn't even actually care about. She just wants it because she hates Li for being my friend. Melanie has to make herself the victim in every situation because she doesn't want to admit the real reason we broke up is that she slept with Kenneth, and that's nobody's fault but hers."

"That's not what happened," Katie said immediately. "Melanie told us what you did."

"I'm sure she did."

"She said you dumped her because she wouldn't ..." Katie started to say, but I cut her off.

"Wouldn't what? Sleep with me? Is that the story she told you?"

"She said you were pressuring her," Hanna said. "You got angry when she said no, and that's why you broke up with her."

I almost laughed. That was so perfectly Melanie, flipping the entire situation to make herself innocent.

"Hanna, you were here last year when that all went down. How do you, of all people, believe that?"

Alexis said, "You're a guy. Guys do that."

"Some guys do, but I didn't, and I'm not going to sit here and argue about it, because that's exactly what Melanie wants. She wants you to get defensive so you'll dig in and refuse to believe anything contrary to what she's told you."

"Then why are you even here?" Katie demanded.

"To tell you the calls are coming from people who were actually there and who don't have a reason to lie to you. Hopefully, that is enough for those of you who were around last year to stop and think if what she said makes sense compared to what you know."

"What's Tammy going to say?" Courtney asked. Her voice was less hostile than the others, more curious.

"Ask her yourself."

"Just tell us," Hanna said. "If you're so sure we're being lied to, then tell us what actually happened."

I shook my head. "You need to hear it from them. Otherwise, you'll just think I'm making things up to cover my own ass."

"Maybe you are," Katie said.

"Maybe. But Tammy doesn't have any reason to lie for me, and Kenneth definitely doesn't owe me any favors."

"So you're saying you didn't do anything wrong?" Katie's voice was sharp with sarcasm.

"I'm saying talk to Brandy about it."

"Don't bring me into this," Brandy said immediately.

“See, here’s the thing,” I said, standing up. “You can choose to keep believing Melanie’s version of events. You can keep giving Li dirty looks and telling people not to vote for her and making my life harder because you think I’m some kind of villain, but when those calls come, when you hear what Tammy and Kenneth have to say, you’re going to have to make a choice.”

“What choice?” Emily asked.

“Whether you want to keep being Melanie’s puppets.” I looked at each of them one more time. “The freshmen weren’t here for the drama last year, so you don’t know, but the rest of you? I’m honestly shocked you let her do this to you. Also, Melanie’s known about her sister/mother for years. This was not new information for her. I can’t prove this point because only Melanie knows the truth, but you should really start considering if what she’s said makes sense.”

I turned to find Melanie frozen three feet away, her face cycling through shock, anger, and calculation. Her eyes moved from me to the circle of cheerleaders, all of whom were now staring at her.

“What?”

I just shook my head and walked away from them.

Chapter 25

The football spiraled toward Mickey, who adjusted his route to meet it, pulling it in before turning upfield. Andre had given him a free release off the line, working on his footwork for pass protection, only doing light contact against Randy Killam, our nose tackle, and the timing looked better than it had during Saturday's game.

"Better," I called out. "Again."

We'd been at it since six, running through passing concepts and blocking drills with whoever had shown up willing to put in some extra work before school. The field was still damp from the sprinklers, the grass slick enough that footing required attention, but it was a hell of a lot cooler, even in September, than it would be at our afternoon practice.

There were thirteen of us today. Me, Mickey, Miguel, Andre, Jerry, and Noah, plus two JV guys, Clarke Reeves and Connor, were on the offense side. Helpfully, we also had Tyler Atkins, Brandon Porter, Randy Killam, Ernest Druthers, and Lucas Verner, all from varsity, on the defense side. Having defensive guys meant we could really practice some of the things we needed to work on, like breaking coverage and line work, and also give our defense a chance to improve. Not that they were bad, but there had been some areas for improvement in Friday's game, in spite of our second victory.

Still, it was a good-sized turnout, which was getting more consistent since we'd started the morning practice sessions.

We did the next progression with Miguel running a curl route, trying to keep ahead of Ernest, our strong safety. He managed to get a step on Ernest and pulled it in, which was good for Miguel, but mostly because Ernest had made a mistake.

"You can't slow up when you see the ball coming in. I know you're trying to figure out the contact point, but that's when you need to put on speed," I offered. "Okay, run next. Jerry, you're in; Noah, take a break."

Jerry jogged into the backfield while Noah headed toward the sideline for water. The next drill had Jerry running a swing route out of the backfield while Andre worked against Brandon, who was simulating a pass rush.

I took the snap from Andre, dropped back three steps, and delivered the short lob to Jerry, who caught it and turned upfield. Brandon pushed Andre back a step at the point of contact, the kind of thing that happened all the time and could lead to someone breaking through if Andre had been more off balance. Not bad, but he needed to push back and use his weight to keep from breaking contact.

"Andre," Tyler said. "You're getting beat on that."

"It's fine."

"Looked like you were getting walked back to me."

"It's a drill," Andre said. "I'm not going full speed."

"Right," Tyler said, but in that way that it was clear he wasn't buying it.

We rotated through a few more concepts, working on timing, spacing, and fundamentals, just getting in extra reps everyone needed. Tyler made a few more comments, but honestly, Andre's technique looked solid to me, although I'd never claim to be an expert on what was good or only mediocre line work.

"Water break," I announced after we'd cycled through the full progression twice.

The group scattered toward the sidelines where we'd left bottles and towels. I grabbed mine and took a long drink. Mickey was off to one side working with Miguel on some stuff, which was great to see. I didn't want this to be all about me working with them, but everyone working with each other. If it were all on me, then we'd never be the team we needed to be to get to state.

Unfortunately, not everyone was working as they should.

Tyler walked directly toward Andre, who was standing alone near the bench, and said, "You need to tighten up your footwork. You're being sloppy."

Andre finished his drink before responding, "What?"

"You heard me. Get it together."

Everyone kind of froze in place, stopping to watch them. Andre was usually a pretty easygoing kind of guy, but the way he was looking at Tyler wasn't even a little bit easygoing.

"Maybe you should worry more about how you play on Friday nights and less about how I practice."

"What's that supposed to mean?" Tyler said, taking a step toward Andre, getting into his personal space a little.

"It means you guys go soft when we get you a lead. You gave up that touchdown in the fourth quarter. They were playing like shit and you just let them through."

"We didn't let anyone through," Randy said, coming up to join Tyler. "You don't hear us talking shit when you guys fall apart and Blake has to scramble, 'cause shit happens. We were up by like thirty-eight. Did you see them scoring the other three quarters?"

"What I saw is you going limp. Kind of like how everyone does when they see your sister," Andre said, going for the low blow as he got pissed that he was getting teamed up on.

"What the fuck did you say?"

Connor moved closer to one side of Andre and Mickey the other, while Brandon came up and joined Tyler and Randy.

"You heard me," Andre said, taking a step toward him, and he was big enough that he forced Tyler to back up an inch or take the bump. "You guys are always out here, waiting on us to take the team to state, riding on our fucking coattails. Hell, Blake had to twist your arms to get you to come to these extra practices, 'cause you all think you're too good for the work."

The confrontation was about to turn physical. They were all squaring up, and no one was backing down.

I set down my water bottle and walked straight in between them, forcing everybody to take a step back.

"All of you need to stop. **Right now**!"

"Stay out of it, Blake." Tyler didn't back down. "This is between us."

"What the fuck is wrong with you? Of course it's not just between you; it's between all of us, which means it's my business, too."

"He needs to watch his mouth about how we played on Friday," Randy said.

"Why? You think you were perfect? I know ***I*** wasn't. I got corrections a bunch of times when I walked off the field. I gave a bunch of corrections today; are you going to square me up, too?"

"Offense, always sticking together," Tyler said.

"This isn't about offense or defense. We have plenty of stuff to work on, and none of us is perfect. Was he a little out of line? Yeah. You were," I said when Andre gave me a look. "You were pissed when he called you out and reacted. I get it, but we're all on the same team. We're all trying for the same thing, to get to state. Does that mean sometimes we will get on each other's nerves? Of course it does, but beating the shit out of your teammate isn't going to make us better and it isn't going to get us to state. So yeah, Andre was going a little light today, but he also got a correction from the coaches on Friday after the game that his footwork was a little sloppy and he needs to work on it. And yeah, the defense could have locked down a little more on Friday, but they only got one touchdown and one field goal all game, so I don't think we can complain too much. You want to beat someone into the turf? Wait until Friday and use that energy against Amarillo. Now, both of you shake hands and let's try to run a couple more plays before we have to get going."

All of them just glared at each other, no one wanting to make the first move.

"I'm dead serious. Someone better shake some hands, or I'm going to tell Coach we need more people riding the benches so the backups can get some field time. Don't push me."

Tyler and Andre both glared at me for a second, but reached across and shook for the briefest of seconds. The other guys followed suit right after.

"Good. Now let's get some reps in, 'cause you all suck and nobody can touch me when I run it."

"Ohhh, it's on now, golden boy," Tyler said, but he was smiling.

The worst of it had at least been defused. I was actually surprised this hadn't happened more often. The coaches work hard to make sure everyone is aggressive and highly competitive. Sometimes that boils over and has to be redirected.

It's just how the game is done.

The hallway outside the science wing was a crush of noise and bodies, a solid wall of students desperate to escape the building now that the final bell had rung. I dodged a couple of kids and headed for the rear door and out to the field. While I needed to get changed and ready for practice, I also wanted to check on Andre, Tyler, and the other guys involved in the drama that morning.

I was almost at the door when someone yelled my name from behind me.

"Blake!"

I stopped and turned to find Li hurrying toward me, pushing through the students that were starting to thin out as they made their way to the other side of the school.

It wasn't hard to pick her out, since she towered over most of the other kids.

She was practically vibrating. That was the only word for it.

"I got the results," she blurted out.

"And?"

"I won." She gave a breathless laugh. "I won both, representative and secretary."

"Seriously? That's awesome, Li. Congratulations."

"It wasn't even close," she said, her words tumbling out faster. "Mr. Brennan posted the counts outside the office five minutes ago. I won the Rep with sixty percent of the vote. Sixty. Melanie didn't even break thirty."

"I told you you'd win. People know you're the one who actually does the work."

"I don't think that's it. You said yourself it was a popularity contest. I think something happened. This morning, a lot of the cheerleaders who pal around with Melanie suddenly started going to those groups they'd been pressing hard, like band and theater kids, and telling them to vote for me instead. One of the band kids said that they said Melanie was a snake and they shouldn't listen to her."

"I guess they saw through her little game."

There must have been something in the way I said that, 'cause Li's head snapped up and her eyes narrowed as she stared at me.

"What did you do?"

"Huh?"

"Don't play dumb with me; what did you do?"

I sighed and said, "I might have talked to a few of her friends and pointed out that she was selling them a load of crap. She's apparently been going around telling everyone about her mother, although saying she found out just this spring instead of years ago, and that it made her do crazy stuff like trying to steal Kenneth from Tammy. She also said I dumped her when I found out about her mother. She did a full sympathy tour over the summer. She also made suggestions that Kenneth forced himself on her. I guess someone might have pointed out the lies and then had Tammy call them to tell them the stuff she knew about, especially that Kenneth forcing himself on her was bullshit."

"Someone, huh?"

"Hey, people hate being lied to. Once they checked the facts, I guess they decided they were done being her puppets."

"I guess that explains it. I saw her in the hallway before the last period and she was looking crushed. She was all by herself. Nobody was even looking at her. It was kind of sad, actually."

"She made her bed, Li."

"I know." She paused. "It's just ... pretty brutal. To go from running the school to being a ghost in two days. Even if she deserved it."

"Well, this is the second time that has happened, so she should be getting used to it. She's gotta learn she can't just use people, lie to them, and expect them to stick around when the truth comes out. And the truth always comes out. But that's not why you won. I'm serious; you won because you're the best person for the job. The cheerleaders flipping just stopped her from stealing it."

That did the trick. The sympathetic expression slid away, replaced by that spark of genuine excitement again.

"Well, my mom's going to be happy. Another step in our thirty-year plan."

"Yeah," I said, not nearly as enthusiastic about that step as she was.

Not that I was one to talk. I had my long-term plan for college and beyond, too. The difference was that it was my plan, not someone else's.

But, if Li was happy, I wasn't going to judge.

"Anyway, it's all because of you, so thanks. I know I asked you to make all this happen, but I didn't expect ... all of this."

"You're welcome," I said, and then looked out the glass door, seeing several of the other guys making their way across to the field house. "I need to get to practice. Coach'll have my ass if I'm late."

"Right, sorry."

"Don't worry about it; just make sure you fix the vending machines like you promised on your posters. The one in the field house stole my quarter twice last week."

"I'll put it on the agenda for the first meeting," she said. "I gotta go anyway; I want to catch Eduardo before he walks home so I can tell him. He's going to lose his mind. Go on; go be the quarterback."

The Silver Spoon was packed wall-to-wall with students when we got there after the game. Even though this one was at home, we still had to get changed and showered before we headed out, so a lot of the students who didn't play beat us there.

Like we were conquering heroes, a cheer went up from several booths when we walked in, and Jerry threw his arms up like he'd won the whole thing personally.

We commandeered the entire back section, dragging three tables together until the waitress, a frazzled woman named Darlene who had been serving Wheaton football players since the seventies, waved a towel at us and told us to settle down.

It took a minute of shuffling to get everyone seated. We took up a massive block of real estate with me, Li, Eduardo, Andre, Mickey, Miguel, Jerry, Joe, Miles, Tyrell, Tyler, Julius, and Gabriel, plus the girlfriends.

Mickey slid into the booth side, pulling Emily Gold in next to him. They looked comfortable, like the breakup last spring hadn't happened, or at least like they'd decided to forget about it. Across from them, Jerry settled in, Hanna leaning against his shoulder. They'd gotten together the first week of school and, apparently, everything was going well.

Then there was Miguel.

He sat near the middle, and Sarah Marti slid in right beside him. She was practically glowing, her face still flushed from the game, and she was laughing at something Miguel said, her hand finding his arm and squeezing it. It was the kind of casual, instinctive affection that screamed new couple; the "we just started dating this week and I can't believe it" phase.

I couldn't help but turn and look toward the end of the table where Eduardo sat. Normally, he'd be right with Li and me, but he'd taken the seat furthest from us with a menu open in front of him, staring at the plastic-covered list of burgers and was very specifically *not* looking up when Sarah laughed again.

"I'm getting the Double Spoon," Jerry announced, tossing his menu onto the table. "I earned it. Did you see the safety's face when I lowered my shoulder on the goal line? It was sweet."

"If you mean did we see you trip and fall into the guy," Joe said. "Then yes, we saw that."

"It's called leverage, Joe. It's a tactic. You wouldn't understand anything about that. Besides, I scored, didn't I? Amarillo was supposed to be one of the powerhouses and we dropped thirty-one points on them. We're unstoppable, baby."

"They thought they were a powerhouse, that's for sure," Julius said. "They talked so much trash. The tackle, number fifty-five, kept telling me he was going to bury me on the fifth. I put him on his ass in the fourth."

The table erupted in laughter, but it was always easy to laugh after a victory, especially when it was by ten points. Not the drubbing we'd given the other team the last two times, but a clear win all the same.

Darlene came by with her notepad and I ordered a cheeseburger and fries. I was starved.

"They were soft," Gabriel said. "I watched them in warm-ups. They looked impressive, but once we popped them a few times, they folded. They didn't want to hit."

Although I didn't say anything, since there was no reason to tear anyone down, I couldn't help but think that was big talk for someone who played two minutes at the end of the game.

"They wanted to hit," Tyler said from the other end. "They didn't have the discipline to stay in their lanes."

"Same difference," Gabriel said. "We're three-and-oh. We blew out Irvin and Riverside, and now we handled Amarillo. I'm just saying, looking at the schedule ... who beats us? L.D. Bell lost last week, Wyatt is terrible. If we play like this, we run the table."

"State," Andre said. "Imagine it, bringing a trophy back to Wheaton. The first one in, what, twenty years?"

"Ever," Miles corrected him. "Wheaton has never won state in 5A. Last time we went, we were 3A."

"We're definitely going to state," Jerry said, grabbing a handful of crackers from the basket and ripping the package open with his teeth. "With this offense? We're unstoppable."

"Once we blow out Midland at Homecoming, it's all downhill," Julius added.

It was easy to get caught up in it, in the dream of it. I honestly felt the pull of it myself, but it was also dangerous to think that we were destined to make it. Like it was already written and nothing could change it.

That kind of thinking was how you got upset.

"We're not there yet," I said.

I hadn't meant for it to be so loud or direct, but I'd happened to say it just at one of those quiet beats in large groups where no one is talking, and all eyes turned toward me.

"Dude, don't be a buzzkill, we won by ten," Mickey said.

"I know, and I'm not trying to kill the mood, but let's not count our chickens just yet. For one, we have an easy schedule for now, with all the harder teams coming later. Riverside has lost every game they've played, including us. Yeah, Amarillo was good, but they're also not at the top either. Midland is supposed to have a killer team, as are Cooper and Eastwood. I'm just saying; don't start counting those eggs just yet."

"We won. Enjoy it," Miles said.

"I am enjoying it, trust me. I love winning, but you guys are talking about State and we weren't perfect tonight. We had lots of little errors. If we play against Midland like we played tonight, assuming we're better just because we're Wheaton, we ... will ... lose. We're good, and I think we have a solid chance to make it, but we aren't there yet. We can't walk around thinking we're unstoppable just because we beat Amarillo. We have to be better on Monday than we were today."

While I hadn't meant to be a buzzkill, what I said did have the effect of shutting down the conversation a bit, but it needed to be done. The worst thing we could be right now was overconfident.

Thankfully, the food came and conversation picked back up, not just about football, but about stuff in general. Classes and who was dating who and whatever the drama of the week was. I ate like a ravenous wolf, to the point Li gave me a look like I shouldn't be allowed indoors.

Of course, the switch from football did come with a downside. Instead of everyone focused on the team, conversations broke down into smaller groups around the table and couples started doing more coupley things. Sarah was feeding Miguel a fry, laughing as he tried to catch it in his mouth. It was sickeningly cute.

I looked over at Eduardo. He'd really screwed the pooch when he'd broken up with her just because he thought there might be something better for him. He was picking at his fries, eating them one by one. He caught me looking and gave a tiny, almost imperceptible shrug.

Darlene dropped off the checks, and the usual chaos of counting wadded-up dollar bills ensued. We shuffled out of the diner and everyone split up, going in their own directions, ready to call it a night now that their bellies were full and the adrenaline from the game was gone.

"See you guys Monday," Miguel said, his arm draped over Sarah's shoulders.

"Bye, guys!" Sarah waved. "Great game!"

I stood next to Eduardo as they walked away toward Sarah's house. His face was unreadable in the light of the streetlamp, and he didn't say anything, just shoved his hands into his pockets.

"Walk you home?" I asked Li.

"It's one block, Blake. I think I can manage."

"We're walking you," Eduardo said, turning away from the retreating couple, toward Li's mom's shop. "Come on."

Li gave me a look behind his back and said, "Okay. Let's go."

We started walking down the sidewalk, the noise of the diner fading behind us. My teammates were scattering, heading off to parties or home to sleep. Saturday and Sunday were the days we all had off, well, they had off from practice, and they were set to enjoy it.

"You okay?" I asked Eduardo as we walked.

"Yeah," he said, kicking a loose rock into the gutter. "I'm good."

I didn't believe him, not even a little bit.

Chapter 26

Saturday morning, I was out in the garage working on getting it cleaned out. On his way out to work, Dad had told me to get on it, saying it was getting too full of junk. Mom had been wanting to tackle it for almost a year, but had been putting it off until she felt better.

Of course, that 'until' had never happened.

I figured he was trying to do something, anything, to feel useful. Mom's surgery was still several weeks away, and there wasn't a damn thing he could do about it except try to be with her and comfort her as much as he could.

Which wasn't much.

So he was pushing for garage organization like that would somehow make a difference, like clearing out old magazines and broken tools would fix the fact that she had a brain tumor.

And honestly, I didn't think he was wrong. I kind of wished I'd thought of doing this already. I knew seeing it done would make her happy, and we were getting very little of that.

The first few hours weren't bad. I dragged out boxes of old National Geographic magazines from the eighties, sorted through Dad's collection of random home improvement supplies that spent more time collecting dust than being put to use, and hauled three bags of actual trash to the curb. The work was mindless enough that I could zone out and just keep moving.

The last corner of the garage was packed with the most stuff. So much stuff, most of it would be added to the garbage bags. The hardest part of it was the old Igloo ice chest shoved against the wall. I vaguely remembered this thing from BBQs in the park when I was younger, something we hadn't done in years.

I knew Dad would kill me if I tried to throw it out, so I decided to just move it with the other stuff we were holding onto and fill it up with smaller, non-toxic things like nails and whatnot. If we weren't going to put cold drinks in it, at least it could help me get all this crap sorted.

I grabbed the handle and dragged it out, the heavy metal and plastic bottom scraping across the concrete with a grating sound that made my teeth hurt.

As soon as I popped the latch, the smell hit me.

I knew that smell. I'd smelled it a month and a half ago when I'd found the cat that had crawled into the garage and died.

I didn't want to open it. Every part of me wanted to shove the ice chest back into the corner, finish cleaning around it, and pretend I'd never pulled it out. I could tell Dad that I'd gotten through everything, that the garage was done, and he'd never know the difference.

Of course, I couldn't do that. I already knew what was inside the chest.

I flipped the other latch and lifted the lid.

A cat lay curled on its side, fur matted and dark. This one was bigger than the first one, maybe somebody's pet that had wandered too far from home. It had twine wrapped around its neck in tight coils, the kind of rough brown stuff Dad kept in the toolbox for tying down tarps. More twine bound its front paws together, then its back paws, the knots neat and deliberate.

This wasn't like that first cat, that just looked like it had died where it stopped. This was done on purpose, and if I had to guess, the cat was alive when it happened.

You wouldn't need to tie up a dead cat.

I set the lid back down and stepped away from the ice chest. My hands were shaking. I shoved them in my pockets and stared at the closed lid, trying to make my brain work past the smell and the image burned in my brain.

This wasn't the first time Joshua had done something like this, beyond even that first cat, which was certainly his doing. In the dream-life, there had been stories, rumors that only made sense after the trial, after they'd found the bodies and the evidence and pieced together how long he'd been escalating. But those stories never had details about the beginning, about when it started, or what the first signs had been.

Maybe it had been like this then, too. Maybe I just hadn't known because I'd been too focused on football and girls and getting out of Wheaton to pay attention to what my little brother was doing in the garage, and then too focused on Dad's death and how to make up for him not being there and Mom not being able to walk.

Or maybe this was different.

Maybe the changes I'd made, saving Dad, forcing Mom into treatment, being home more instead of spiraling into drugs and failure, had pushed Joshua into a different pattern. Maybe instead of slowing him down, I'd sped him up.

I looked at the ice chest again. The twine around the cat's neck had been tied with the same knots we'd learned in scouts, even though neither of us made it out of Cub Scouts. I don't think I could remember how to do those, but Josh certainly did. He'd taken his time with this, planned it, executed it, hidden it where he thought no one would look.

I didn't even want to think about why he'd held onto it.

The real question was, what was I going to do about it? I had to do something; that much I knew.

I'd fixed Dad, I'd fixed Mom, or at least I was in the process of getting her help, but Josh? I'd left him alone. I couldn't directly fix him and I couldn't threaten him with anything, since he didn't care what drastic measures I took. He only cared about himself. I didn't know how to stop him short of getting him locked up, which I was worried might cause Mom to backslide. Maybe I was hoping that if I fixed Mom and Dad, they would manage to get him in check.

Looking at the ice chest, I knew I'd been fooling myself.

I closed the lid and carried it to the workbench where Dad would see it as soon as he came through the door.

This was going to make everything harder. Showing this to Dad meant another fight with Mom, and if she got too upset, it could cause her to back off on her treatment, but I couldn't let this keep going.

He'd stalked that girl in the spring, and if he was killing animals, how close was he to doing it to a person?

It would be hard on Dad, too, because it meant he'd have to choose between admitting what Joshua was becoming and pretending not to see it.

But I just didn't see what other choices I had.

I washed my hands in the garage sink, scrubbing until the smell was mostly gone, then headed inside to wait.

Mom was asleep in her room, knocked out by her afternoon medication, and Josh had left an hour ago with the family down the street for youth group at First Baptist. Mom hadn't told anyone she had cancer yet, but she'd started asking them to take him from time to time when she "wasn't feeling well."

Part of me had wanted to keep him here, but I also knew it would be easier to have this conversation with him gone, so I'd kept my mouth shut.

I just sat there in Dad's chair and kept running through what I was going to say, how I was going to make him listen this time. I'd tried this before, twice, actually, and still had no luck in getting him to listen. Once after Joshua got caught tormenting that girl in the spring, and also when I'd found him outside Li's mom's shop, stalking her. Both times, Mom had shut it down before Dad could really press her to do anything, and he'd backed down, not wanting to upset her.

We hadn't known what was wrong with her at the time, but he knew she was sick and dealing with something, and he hadn't wanted to make whatever it was worse.

I got that, but it also meant we kept not dealing with the problem.

But we couldn't keep kicking the can down the road. We needed to deal with this, and we needed to deal with it now.

Finally, after about a dozen false calls with a neighbor coming home or leaving, or just getting something from their car, I heard Dad pull his cruiser into the driveway and get out.

He came through the front door looking tired, the way he always looked these days, and then stopped short when he saw me sitting in his chair.

He must have read something was wrong on my face, because he asked, "What happened? Is it your mother? Did she ..."

"Mom's fine," I said, standing up. "She's sleeping."

"Then what?"

"I need to show you something in the garage."

Dad's eyes narrowed. He glanced toward their bedroom and then back at me. "Blake, what's going on?"

"Just come with me."

I led him through the kitchen and out the side door. The garage was still a mess, half-organized, boxes stacked against one wall, the old ice chest on the workbench where I'd put it.

Dad looked at it, then at me. "What is this?"

"Open it."

He set his keys on the workbench and lifted one of the lid. The smell hit him immediately, and he jerked, taking a couple of steps back.

"Jesus."

"I know it smells bad, but look. Look at its neck and around its paws," I said.

Dad looked at me like I must be out of my mind, but he did what I asked, going back to the ice chest, although keeping it at arm's length, and peeked in as best he could without getting his face too close to it.

For a second, he had a puzzled look on his face, and then the cop brain took over. He saw the ropes, the knots, and came to the same conclusion I had.

Or at least a similar one.

"Where did you find this?"

"In the old ice chest, pushed up in the back corner, under some tarps and other boxes. The latches were secured and closed, and other stuff was pushed in front of it. He didn't want us to find it."

"You don't know ... it could've been another animal. Coyote, maybe, or a feral dog."

"Don't do that, Dad. You know exactly what that is, and no amount of talking yourself out of it will change anything. A coyote or a feral dog can't tie square knots. And before you start suggesting one of the neighbors is hiding his trophies in our garage, look at the twine. It's the same stuff you have in your toolbox, the brown one you use with tarps. You know who put this in there."

Dad's shoulders dropped. He stared at the cat's body, his hands hanging loose at his sides.

"This isn't the first time either," I said. "You know that. I told you about the other cat I found in here, the one we all convinced ourselves had just crawled in here and died. You have to know he did that, too, right? It would be a wild coincidence otherwise. That's not all. Remember that girl at the birthday party in the park last spring? The one Mom said was just a crush?"

"Blake ..."

"He watches people, Dad. No, not watches, stalks. He went to Li's mom's shop and was trying to climb up and look in their window. And he went to the gym after school during basketball season to watch her play. He watches them and he figures out what scares them and then he uses it. I've seen him do it. You've seen him do it."

Dad rubbed his face with both hands. "Your mother ..."

"Mom isn't here right now." My voice came out harder than I meant it to. "And Mom has a brain tumor that's affecting her judgment, so even if she was, I don't think she'd be the right person to make any decisions. You've seen how she protects him. You've seen how she refuses to admit there's anything wrong."

"She's his mother."

"And you're his father and a cop," I said, closing the distance and grabbing his arm, making him look at me. "If someone brought you this evidence about a kid you didn't know, a kid from across town, a kid whose parents you'd never met, what would you think? What conclusion would you draw?"

Dad didn't answer. He didn't have to.

"He's sick. I don't know what's wrong with him, but something is. He doesn't feel things the way other people do. He doesn't care about hurting things; in fact, I think he likes it. Right now it's just cats, but I don't think that's where it will stop. In fact, from everything I've been able to read, that's where it *starts*. He will only get worse from here, and what happens when it's some kid down the street? Some girl who doesn't run fast enough?"

"That's not ..." Dad stopped. Swallowed. "You don't know that's going to happen."

"And you don't know it won't. You've seen everything I've seen. The cruelty to animals, the stalking, the manipulation, the way he lies without even blinking. You've seen all of it, and you've let

Mom convince you it wasn't that bad." I stepped back. "If he hurts someone, really hurts them, how are you going to live with that? How will either of us live with knowing we saw this coming and didn't do anything?"

Dad sagged against the workbench. In the harsh garage light, he looked older than I'd ever seen him … old, and tired, and completely beaten down.

"You're right. I know you're right."

"So what are you going to do about it?"

He let out a long breath. "I'll handle it."

"That's not good enough, Dad. That's what you said last time, which ended up meaning watching and waiting. It meant letting Mom smooth things over and hoping he'd grow out of it." I pointed at the box. "This is where watching and waiting got us. We can't wait anymore. We have to do something. *Now!*"

Dad closed his eyes for a second. When he opened them, they were wet. I felt bad for him. I may hate Josh for how he was to me and everything I knew from the dream, but he was still Dad's kid.

I couldn't imagine what it must be like to realize your child was evil.

"I don't know what I'm going to do," he admitted, his voice shaking and sounding smaller than I'd ever heard it before. He paused and took a few deep breaths, trying to get his emotions under control. When he started speaking again, he sounded more like himself. "There aren't a lot of people in this town who'd know how to deal with something like this. I could talk to the school counselor, or our doctor, or Pastor Green, but I don't think any of them would know what to do either."

"There has to be someone."

"Midland has more resources, mental health professionals, people who specialize in …" He couldn't finish the sentence. "I'll call my lieutenant tomorrow and see if he can put me in contact with someone who might have answers."

"And until then?"

"Until then, Josh doesn't leave this house except for school and church if your mother wants to go. No youth group, and he doesn't go anywhere without adult supervision. Not the yard, not the street, nowhere."

That was more like what we needed. "What about Mom?"

Dad looked at the ice chest one more time. "I'll deal with her. You're right; we can't let this keep going on. I should have listened to you sooner."

I wanted to say something, that it wasn't his fault, that Mom made it hard, that I understood why he'd wanted to believe everything was fine. But it was his fault, at least this time, and nothing was ever going to be fine again.

"Okay," I said instead. "I'll be inside."

I walked out of the garage and left him standing there ... alone, staring at the evidence of what his youngest son had become.

Chapter 27

The ball sailed three feet over Andre's head.

It wobbled through the air, a dying duck, before clanging off the chain-link fence behind the end zone.

"My bad." I waved a hand.

Andre jogged back and snagged the ball on the bounce, but he didn't throw it back. He just stood there, holding it, staring at me with his brow furrowed.

I wiped sweat from my forehead with the back of my wrist. The morning wasn't hot, not even quite to the seventies, but I was burning up and my skin felt stretched tight. Itchy.

I was so tired.

"Let's run it again," I said. "Post corner on one."

"Blake." Mickey stepped up from where the line would be, resting his hands on his hips. "That's the fourth one you've sailed. Do you want to take five?"

"I don't need five; I need to hit the receiver." I snapped and clapped my hands, trying to manufacture energy I didn't have. "Line up. Let's go."

I know he was trying to be helpful, and they kept at it because I asked, but I could see how they were all looking at me.

Just like the last several plays, everything was sluggish. My drop-back felt like I was moving through waist-deep water. I planted my back foot and tried to torque my hips as I fired the ball.

Another shit throw landed in the dirt, five yards short.

"Damnit!" I squeezed the bridge of my nose, trying to push the headache back.

The silence on the field was deafening. Usually, these morning walk-throughs had chatter, teasing and mocking, pushing each other to do better, but today twelve guys just stood there watching me fall apart.

"That's it," I said. "We're done. Go hit the showers."

"We've got twenty minutes left." Mickey said, jogging over, I guess so he could say it more privately. "We haven't even run the red zone package. We could just walk it through."

I didn't want to argue.

"I said we're done."

I turned my back on them and started toward the field house, not bothering to see if they followed.

I just didn't have the patience for any of it. Every time I closed my eyes, I relived yesterday. Finding the cat, laying down the law, and then the shit show that followed.

I kicked the metal door open and walked to my locker, slamming my fist against the door. The hollow *boom* vibrated up my arm, but it didn't make me feel any better.

I sat on the bench and dug the heels of my hands into my eyes.

I knew Dad coming down on Josh was going to be bad, but it was so much worse than I'd imagined.

To his credit, Dad had tried to remain calm. He'd sat Josh down at the kitchen table to talk. He'd tried to do it without Mom there, but she heard the commotion and, seeing mine and Dad's faces, guessed something was going on. To his credit, Dad hadn't let that stop him, though. He laid down the new rules. No going out, no unsupervised time in the yard or anywhere outside the house, and he would start therapy in Midland on Tuesday.

Josh had played it perfectly at first, the confused, hurt child, asking what he'd done wrong, why he was being punished.

That's when Dad brought up the cat, how it couldn't have been anyone else, how it connected with his other behavior. Dad didn't yell at him or anything, just said he was sick and he needed help. That he had impulses that were making him do things, and it wasn't his fault, but we had to deal with it.

Josh had just stared at him the whole time, his mask slipping. He glared with those dead, shark eyes and denied everything flat out. No hesitation, no guilt.

That was when Mom snapped, jumping to Josh's aid, defending him, and saying if Josh said he didn't do it, then he didn't do it, and how dare Dad punish Josh without talking to her about it first.

Never mind she'd punished me, unfairly, without talking to anyone. Josh had his own set of rules.

The screaming had gone on for an hour. Dad trying to explain everything, how it all pointed to Josh, how it was the only explanation, but Mom refused to hear any of it. She went so far as to say Dad preferred me because I was a jock like he was, and that he never treated Josh fairly.

Which was insane, considering the source.

The fight only ended when Mom, gripping her head, screaming that the stress was killing her, that her head was splitting open, retreated upstairs to the guest room where she locked herself in.

Neither of them slept in their room that night. Dad stayed on the couch, although I didn't know if it was because he couldn't stay in there without her or to make sure Josh didn't slip out.

Speaking of Josh, as soon as they were out of earshot, he came to my room and said he knew I was behind it all and he was going to get me.

God, the look on his face was terrifying.

I squeezed my eyes shut until I saw jagged bursts of light.

"Yo, Blake."

I jumped, my head snapping up.

Andre stood at the end of the row of lockers, a towel draped over his shoulder. Miguel and Mickey were behind him. They all looked worried.

"Are you okay, man?" Andre asked. "You look like hell."

"Yeah," I said, scrubbing my face with my hands. "I just didn't sleep much."

"Is everything okay?" Miguel asked.

"Just a rough night." I stood up and peeled off my sweat-soaked t-shirt, crumpling it into a ball and tossing it into my gym bag.

I didn't want to talk about it. If I talked about it, I might actually lose it.

"Sorry to hear that, man," Mickey said. "Don't worry about practice, everybody's got off days. We'll get it back this afternoon."

"Yeah." I grabbed my towel. "I'm going to shower before first period. Catch you guys later."

They lingered for a second, sensing the dismissal, then nodded and headed toward the showers.

I waited until they were gone, then leaned my forehead against the cool metal of my locker.

I was so tired. My bones felt heavy.

The shower didn't help.

I let the hot water beat against the back of my neck, trying to loosen the tension that had taken up permanent residence there. It didn't work. I dressed in jeans and a fresh shirt, slung my backpack over one shoulder, and headed into the main building.

The halls were already filling up. School was always noisy, but today it was unbearably so. It hit me like a wall, lockers slamming, people shouting, and just general chaos everywhere. I kept my head down and navigated the current, just trying to get to my locker before the bell.

I needed to talk to Dad when I got home. We hadn't talked much after the fight. I think everyone was just too drained, but he'd said something about therapy on Tuesday in Midland.

I know it was out of my hands now, but I wanted to know exactly what he had planned.

"Blake!" The voice was loud enough to break through the mental walls I'd put up, but I didn't stop.

I knew whose voice it was, and I just didn't have the energy for her today.

"Blake Sims! Don't you walk away from me!"

A hand grabbed my bicep, manicured nails digging in.

I stopped and turned.

Melanie looked perfect as always, hair sprayed into an immovable golden helmet, makeup flawless, outfit coordinated down to the socks. And she looked terrible. Her eyes were red-rimmed with dark bags under them that Visine hadn't quite managed to hide, her lips were cracked, and she had a small breakout that she'd tried very hard to cover up.

"Let go," I said, jerking my arm free.

She dropped her hand but stepped into my space, blocking the flow of traffic. People were starting to stare.

"You think you're real smart, don't you?" she hissed.

"I have no idea what you're talking about, and I honestly don't care. I have to get to class."

"Don't give me that, I know it was you. You went to Coach Newman and told her to put me on JV."

I blinked. With everything happening with Josh and Mom, I'd completely forgotten about Melanie and all her drama last week.

"What?"

"Don't lie!" She stabbed a finger toward my chest. "Coach Newman called me into her classroom this morning and said my 'attitude' wasn't reflecting well on the varsity squad. She said I was being moved down to JV for a 'probationary period' to work on my team spirit. *JV*, Blake! I was on varsity! I don't do JV!"

"Sounds like a you problem," I said, trying to step around her.

She scrambled in front of me again. "It's a *you* problem! You did this! You're poisoning everyone against me, first the election, now this, all because I tried to take your girlfriend's spot."

A little part of me felt bad for her. In her mind, it was the whole world against her, and she was constantly fighting an uphill battle. She couldn't see that she was fighting herself, and every time she had a setback, it was directly because of her own poorly chosen actions.

"I didn't talk to Coach Newman. I didn't have to."

"Bullshit. Then why won't any of the girls talk to me? Why did Katie and Sarah cancel my weekend plans? You told them something."

"I only told them the truth."

"You mean you lied to them."

"Stop." I held up a hand. "Just stop. I'm done, Melanie. I am so done with this."

"You ruined everything!" The shriek was loud enough that the hallway actually quieted. People stopped at their lockers, watching. "I was going to be someone! I had a plan! And you just came in and wrecked it because you're a jealous, petty little ..."

"Jealous?" I laughed. It wasn't a nice sound. "You think I did this because I'm jealous? You think I care enough about your little social ladder climbing to plot against you?"

I took a step toward her. For the first time, she flinched.

"You did this to yourself," I said. "All of it."

"I didn't! I was ..."

"Caught lying. You lied about Kenneth assaulting you, you lied about me being cold to you because I found out about your sister, and you lied about me and Li. Hell, you even lied about how long you knew about your sister."

"Shut up!" She looked around wildly, panic flaring in her eyes. "Shut up, Blake!"

"No. You wanted to have this conversation in the middle of the hallway. Fine, let's have it. You think the world is out to get you. You think you're the victim in some grand tragedy. You're not. You're just a bully who got caught."

"I did what I had to do!" Her voice trembled, tears spilling over. It was a good performance, the quivering lip, the wide innocent eyes. And one I'd seen a dozen times. "You don't understand what it's like. I have to fight for everything I have!"

"We all have problems, Melanie. My mom has a brain tumor. My brother is ..." I stopped myself. "We all have stuff, but we don't go around trying to destroy other people just to make ourselves feel bigger."

"I hate you. I hate you so much," she said, wiping her eyes, smearing mascara.

"Honestly? I don't care. I warned you. I told you that if you kept pushing, if you kept lying, it was going to blow up in your face. People don't like being manipulated, don't you get that? They don't like being used as pawns. The other girls didn't turn on you because of me; they turned on you because they finally realized you don't actually give a damn about them, or anyone else."

She opened her mouth, but I kept going.

"You want to fix this?" I asked. "Want to get back on varsity? Then stop lying and take some God-damned accountability for once in your life. Admit you screwed up, apologize, and actually mean it."

Of course, I knew she wouldn't do that. I could see it in her eyes, the calculation, the refusal to accept defeat. She was already trying to find a way to make this my fault, find a new angle.

"But you won't, because that's too hard. It's easier to just blame someone else. Always play the victim."

"You're going to regret this." It was supposed to be a threat, but it sounded empty.

"Maybe, but not today."

I walked past her. She didn't grab my arm this time, just stood there, frozen in the middle of the hallway.

I didn't look back.

I didn't feel triumphant. I didn't feel happy. I just felt tired.

The house was quiet when I got home, and not the peaceful kind of quiet. After the blowup last night that had everyone locking themselves in different rooms for the night, I'd half expected to come home to more drama.

I wasn't sure if that wouldn't have been better.

I dropped my gym bag by the door and walked into the kitchen to see if anything had been done about dinner.

Dad was sitting at the kitchen table.

I knew he was home because his cruiser was in the driveway, but I'd thought he'd worked earlier. Normally, he wouldn't have changed his clothes yet, but he wasn't in his uniform. In fact, he was in the same clothes he'd been wearing last night, and they looked slept in.

Had he called in sick to work?

A bunch of papers were spread out in front of him, along with brochures, a calculator, and a notepad covered in writing.

He looked up when I walked in, and I could see he had deep bags under his eyes.

"Hey," I said. "You didn't go to work?"

"No, I called off. I had some stuff I had to figure out. Practice go okay?"

"Fine," I said. "What's all this?"

Dad sighed, picking up one of the brochures and slid it across the table.

Whitmore Military Academy: Building Tomorrow's Leaders Today.

Below the bold letters was a picture of a brick building and an impressive-looking campus.

"It's a boarding school for troubled kids in Montana. Strict structure, regular counseling and psychiatric evaluation, highly supervised, and with zero tolerance. I spoke to the admissions director this afternoon, and based on some of Joshua's behavior and actions, they think he's a candidate for their program. They said they have had luck with similarly troubled kids in the past. It isn't an immediate fix. They won't have any beds for a couple of weeks, and I want to give your mother and brother one more shot at doing some kind of therapy here at home, but ... I need an option if that doesn't happen, and this sounds like it might work. It would be drastic, but it also might be our best option."

"A few weeks isn't a lot of time to get them to agree to therapy and find someone."

"I know, but we don't have time to go slow. You saw him yesterday, the way he looked at us. Well of course you saw it, you've been warning me about his behavior for a while. It's the first time I've seen his mask slip, though, and you're right, we can't keep him here. Not with Mom sick."

I pulled out a chair and sat. "You won't get an argument from me."

"I didn't think so, but that's the other problem. It's not cheap."

"How much?"

"Twenty-five hundred a month, plus a three-thousand-dollar enrollment fee for uniforms, initial setup, and whatever else, but that covers full room and board while he's there. So we're talking about a lot of money. Like thirty thousand a year, and insurance won't touch it. But it's also the best option I can find for your brother. I went to talk to the credit union today about pulling equity out of the house, but they said no."

"You didn't have to do that. You know I have the money to cover this, and I've been pushing for it. You just have to let me know what you need."

"You've already agreed to help with your mother's treatment, and yes, I know you made a lot of money with the gambling, but that's dried up now, and that money has to go to the private coaching you want for at least three more years, more camps, and you were talking about nutritionists and whatever else. I don't want you giving up your dreams to cover things we should be covering."

"I'm not. I've just moved it all over to investing."

"I know, and I think that was a smart move, but investing isn't like gambling on sports. It's not as easy as just picking what's going to work."

"Which is why I brought on Mr. Henderson. I know you've had a lot of things going on, so you might not have had a chance to see the stuff I left for you, but I've already made twenty thousand, and Mr. Henderson said he'll have another update for me this week or next. I wouldn't have put so much money into it if I didn't know what I was doing."

"I know it seems that way ..."

"Dad, I've proven to you, over and over, that I am not messing around. I was right about all the bets, and so far the moves I've provided the investing company are paying out. Look at the stuff Mr. Henderson sent over. I don't know what else I can do to prove myself to you."

He sighed and dropped his head into his hands. "You don't have to do anything to prove yourself. I know you're doing well, and I have no doubt you're going to make this thing between you and Mr. Henderson work, but you shouldn't have to. I should be able to provide for my wife and son. Joshua is my problem, as is your mom's cancer treatment. I know you're very capable; you've been showing that for more than a year now. I will never stop being impressed by how you're growing up and the man you're becoming, but what kind of a man would I be if I let my son step in every time we have a financial issue?"

"The kind of man who would do anything, even swallow his pride if that's what it takes. More importantly, I want to help. I want Mom to have the best chance possible of getting better, and I want to be able to do something to fix Josh. I'm in this family too, and it hurts me seeing them having trouble just as much as it hurts you. I might not be able to cure Mom or straighten Josh out, but I can at least take the worry about money off the table. You did the hard part, talking to people who know how to deal with him and finding this place. Spending money I've already made is easy. So let me do my part."

Dad was quiet for a long time, and I could see he was wrestling with it.

Finally, he said, "Your mother will never forgive me."

"She's sick. When she's better and the tumor's no longer pressing on her brain, she'll understand."

"I don't know."

"No one does, but what I do know is that keeping Josh here is dangerous for everyone, including him."

He made a sound, but he didn't argue. "I guess. I'll call tomorrow."

He stood, came around the table, and pulled me into a hug. It lasted longer than usual.

"Go to bed, Blake. You've got school in the morning, and you get up so early for your practices."

"Do you want me to be there when you tell her? I can back you up."

"No. This is between me and your mother. You stay out of it," he said, starting to walk away from me before stopping and squeezing my shoulder. "Thank you, son."

"Night, Dad."

He disappeared into his room, closing the door, which probably meant Mom was asleep up in the guest room again.

I stood alone in the kitchen.

I washed my glass at the sink.

I turned off the light and headed upstairs. I needed sleep and still had homework to do.

Chapter 28

A few days passed, and I didn't hear anything more about the military academy.

Either Mom took the news well, which I seriously doubted, or Dad was waiting for her to have one of her good days to bring it up. Given how things had been going around the house lately, I figured it was the second one. I guess there wasn't a huge hurry since we were in a holding pattern until a slot opened up for Josh, but the tension between my parents hadn't eased up. If anything, it had gotten worse, and they were still sleeping in different rooms.

While I really just wanted to put my head down and ignore it all, keeping focused on what I needed to do, it was getting harder.

Football was still going well, at least. We'd won our third game last Friday, and Coach Holloway seemed pleased with how everyone was playing.

That was about the only thing that was going well, though.

My classes were starting to suck. With everything going on, I was having trouble concentrating, and several times I'd caught myself staring out the window in the middle of a lecture, only snapping back when the teacher called on someone.

The real problem was that I wasn't getting any sleep.

I was exhausted. Straight bone tired. I was still getting up at five-thirty every morning for early practice, still staying up until eleven or twelve every night doing homework, but when I did finish my work, I'd get in bed and just lie there, worrying.

It was starting to show.

A couple of quizzes had come back with grades far below where they needed to be, and I'd had a disaster of an English test that I was still trying not to think about.

So when the office runner showed up during fourth-period Biology with a slip calling me to the guidance office, I had a pretty good idea what was coming.

Mr. Brennan's door was open when I got there, and he waved me in without looking up from whatever he was working on. I sat in the chair across from his desk and waited.

He finished making notes on a form, then set his pen down and looked up at me.

"Blake." He pulled a folder from his desk drawer. "I told you I'd be watching."

"Yes, sir."

"And I have been." He tapped the folder. "Do you know what's in here?"

"My grades, I'm guessing."

"You'd be right, plus notes from your teachers, who I'd asked to keep an eye on your work in particular." He opened the folder again and ran his finger down a page. "Two missed homework assignments in English and a thirty-seven on your last test. A failed quiz and lab assignment in Biology. And Mr. Mossley tells me you've been, and I quote, 'noticeably disengaged' during class discussions."

While I'd felt he'd had it out for me since our first meeting a few weeks ago, he wasn't wrong.

"When we met at the beginning of the year, I expressed concerns about your academic load, and you assured me you could handle it. You signed an agreement committing to maintain your grades while participating in varsity athletics."

"I remember."

"Then you also remember that I told you this arrangement would be closely monitored. Blake, you're not living up to your end of the agreement."

"I know things have slipped ..."

"Slipped is generous. It's barely a month into the school year, and if you're already missing assignments and failing tests, what happens in October? November? When the playoff games start and the academic demands increase?"

"I can handle that, I've just been dealing with some stuff at home," I said.

"I know about your mother's health, but my understanding was that it has been going on since the summer and last year, so you were aware of that when you signed the pledge."

"Yes, sir."

"Blake, in my twenty years as an educator, I've had this conversation more times than I can count. Student athletes who take on too much, who believe they can handle the pressure, who assure everyone they're different. The exception. And they never are. When grades start to slip, it's always the same thing: family problems, personal issues, circumstances beyond their control. Never any true accountability for their own actions and decisions."

"I'm not making excuses; I'm telling you what's happening."

"I'm sure you believe that, but here's what I've learned. 'Family issues' are often cited right before a student falls into ineligibility. It's a pattern I've seen repeat itself over and over. The explanations are always sympathetic, always understandable, but the outcome is always the same."

"So you think I'm lying?"

"I think you're a fifteen-year-old with a lot of pressure on you, and I think it would be very convenient if academic requirements could be set aside because of that pressure. I'm not saying your problems aren't real, I'm saying that effort and structure, not exceptions, are what will protect your future."

"I'm not asking for exceptions."

"Then what are you asking for?"

I didn't have a good answer for that since I hadn't come here asking for anything. He'd called me in and demanded answers.

Unfortunately, Mr. Brennan took my silence as confirmation of something. He pulled another paper from the folder and slid it across the desk toward me.

"I warned you that you were stretching yourself too thin. Regular classes, varsity football, and I'm hearing about some kind of early morning practice you've arranged. Now that the school year has started, it's not as simple as dropping you back down to remedial classes. The schedules are set, and the coursework has diverged. If your grades slip now, you face real consequences."

I looked at the paper. It was some kind of progress report, my grades listed out in neat columns.

"What kind of consequences?"

"If you fall below a 2.0 GPA or fail any core class, policy requires academic probation, and academic probation means potential loss of extracurricular eligibility."

"You'd make me ineligible?"

"I wouldn't make you anything. You would with your choices and actions. I want to be very clear about something, Blake. I will not manipulate paperwork to protect your playing time. I've seen other counselors do it, and I've seen administrators look the other way because a student was valuable to the team, and it never works out well for the student. That's not something I'm willing to do."

"I'm not asking you to."

"Good. Because I wouldn't, regardless. What I'm telling you is that your trajectory right now leads somewhere you don't want to go. You have perhaps three weeks to turn this around before the first grading period ends. If these trends continue, we'll be having a very different conversation."

I stared at him, trying to read something in his face. Sympathy, maybe. Understanding. Something that suggested he saw me as more than just another dumb jock destined to flame out.

I didn't find it.

"Is there anything else?" I asked.

"That depends on you." He stood up and walked to his filing cabinet, pulling open a drawer. "We are already having study sessions on Wednesdays, but I'm also going to require you to submit all your assignments to me for review before you turn them in to your teachers. I want to see that you're doing the work, not just skating by. I want you here, in my office, thirty minutes before school each day to show them to me and talk about what you have going on that day. Every day. If you still manage to fail and lose eligibility, I want you to know the system did everything it could to make sure you succeeded. If it happens, then I hope you understand I was right in the beginning, and next semester we'll get you back to a more appropriate level."

"Fine."

He looked frustrated, or maybe disappointed that I wasn't more grateful.

"You can go."

I grabbed my backpack and walked out of his office and down the hallway.

The probation threat and the extra requirements weren't what got to me; I wasn't happy to be losing morning practice mostly, which was more for the rest of the guys than it was for me. I'd probably be able to come in and get them started, and then take off early and let Mickey or Andre run the last little bit.

It was a massive pain in the ass and just another problem to deal with.

The hits didn't stop coming, either. I'd been waiting for the other shoe to drop ever since Dad decided on the military academy. He'd sounded pretty confident that he could handle Mom, but I knew how she was going to take it, and it wasn't going to be good.

I got my answer the next evening when I got home from practice. I could hear the shouting before I even got through the front door. I could hear Mom shouting clear out in the yard, not quite enough to make out the words, but she was definitely screaming.

Inside, I found them in the living room. Mom had a fist full of papers clutched in her hand, and was screaming while Dad was trying to calm her down, and Josh was just sitting on the couch, watching the two of them.

"You went behind my back! Plotting to send my son away like he's some kind of criminal."

"Heather, please ..."

"Don't 'Heather please' me, Thomas." She never used his full name unless things were bad. "I found these on your desk. Military academy? In Montana? What were you planning to do, just put him on a bus one day and hope I didn't notice?"

"I was going to discuss it with you when the time was right."

"When the time was right. You mean when you'd already enrolled him and driven him away so I couldn't do anything about it."

I dropped my bag by the door. Both of them looked at me, and for a moment, nobody moved.

"You were in on this too, I just know it," she screamed.

"I was," I said. No use lying about it or leaving Dad out on his own.

"Of course, you were. What are you going to do now? More threats to get your way? The two of you, always conspiring against the rest of your family, always treating Joshua and me like the enemy."

"Nobody's treating you like the enemy," Dad said. "We're trying to get both of you help. That's all we've ever wanted."

"Help him?" Mom stepped closer, jabbing a finger at Dad's chest. "You want to ship him off to some godforsaken military prison in the middle of nowhere. How is that helping him?"

"It's a school, not a prison. They have counselors, structure ..."

"He doesn't need counselors; he needs his family. He needs his mother."

Josh made a small sound from the couch. When I looked over, his lower lip was trembling, and he was trying as hard as he could to look scared and pathetic.

I wasn't buying it for a second.

"Mom." His voice came out in a small voice that sounded completely fake to me. "I don't want to go away. Please don't let them send me away. I'm sorry, I'll be better. I swear."

Mom, however, bought it completely, crossing over and sitting on the couch next to him, pulling him close. Josh buried his face against her shoulder, his body shaking with what looked like sobs.

Dad gave me a look, and for once, I knew he saw right through it too. It was a performance. Every bit of it.

"See?" Mom looked up at Dad. "See what you've done? You've terrified him."

"Heather." Dad reached into the folder he'd been holding and pulled out several photographs. "I need you to look at these."

"I don't want to look at anything."

"Please." He crossed the room and held them out to her. "Just look."

She snatched them from his hand. I didn't know what those were and edged close enough I could see a small part of them. That's all I needed. It was the cat, dead and bound like I'd found it inside the cooler.

"What is this supposed to prove?"

"That's a dead cat, and your son killed it and hid it in the cooler for ... I don't even know what he was planning on."

"You don't know Joshua did this. Anyone could have tied this up and put it in our garage."

"Heather ..."

"No." She stood up, keeping one arm around Josh's shoulders. "I'm not listening to this anymore. You are just looking to accuse him of everything you find, no matter what he says. No matter what actually happened."

"Heather, it's not just this. You heard what that other parent said, about him following their daughter around. You heard what the counselor said about his behavior at school. Do you think everyone is lying? This is a pattern of behavior. I've seen it at work, and it will lead to something so much worse than a dead cat. Joshua needs help. He's not normal."

"Don't you tell me what's normal. I've raised two boys. I know what's normal and what isn't. You want to talk about a problem, what about your precious firstborn? Do you remember what he was like in middle school, getting into fights and failing classes? We had plenty of calls about him from counselors, too, but I don't ever remember you talking about sending him off to military school."

"That's not the same thing."

"It's exactly the same thing. Boys act out and they push boundaries, but it doesn't mean we throw them away."

Josh lifted his head from Mom's shoulder. Tears streaked his cheeks, but when Mom wasn't looking, his eyes found mine. The corners of his mouth twitched. Just slightly. Just enough for me to see.

I had to look away.

"Nobody's throwing anyone away. The academy has a program specifically for kids who need structure and guidance. Professional counseling. A contained environment where he can't—"

"Where he can't what? Be a child? Make mistakes? He's twelve years old, Tom. Twelve. I'm not going to let you ruin his life," she said, letting go of Josh and storming to the end table, grabbing her purse. "I'm done listening to this."

"Where are you going?" Dad asked, edging, I think, to block her from the door.

"Away from here. If you want him gone so badly, then fine, we'll both go."

"Heather, stop. Let's talk about this."

"I'm done talking." She was already halfway up the stairs, pulling Josh behind her. "Joshua, go pack a bag. We're staying with Aunt Carol for a few days."

Aunt Carol wasn't actually our aunt. She was a friend of Mom's from college who lived in Lubbock. She disappeared down the hallway, but Josh paused, lingered on the stairs, and looked back at us before he disappeared out of sight, too.

We just stood there in silence as the sounds continued upstairs. When they came down, Mom had changed clothes and fixed her makeup, looking a little more put-together and calm. Josh trailed behind her, dragging a duffel bag. He'd washed his face.

Part of me wanted Dad to chase her, scream at her that he wasn't going to let her go, steal her keys, but it wasn't like he'd be able to keep her on lockdown forever. Short of handcuffing her and locking her in a room, which I was pretty sure was kidnapping, she was going, one way or another.

Mom stopped at the bottom of the stairs.

"I'll call when we get to Carol's."

"Heather, please. Don't do this."

"I'm going to protect my son, even if it's from his own father. I never thought we'd come to this, Tom. I really didn't."

"Neither did I."

She stared at him for a long moment before tugging on Josh's arm, pulling him toward the door.

"Let's go, Joshua."

"Yes, Mom."

Then they were gone, out through the front door.

Dad and I followed them out. She loaded Josh's bag in the back, then opened the passenger door for him. He climbed in, buckling his seatbelt like a good boy. Still playing up the act. Mom walked around to the driver's side.

"This isn't over," Dad said.

Mom paused with her hand on the door. "No. It isn't."

She got in, started the engine, and backed out of the driveway. I watched the station wagon turn onto the street, watched it accelerate away, watched until the taillights disappeared around the corner.

Neither of us spoke.

What could we say? Mom had played right into Josh's hands, moving him away from the increased supervision and the restrictions Dad had put in place.

I didn't know what he was going to do now that he was going to be allowed out again, but I was pretty sure it wasn't going to be good.

The next night we had a football game, and my head was not in the right place. Dad and I had stayed standing in the driveway for a long time, I guess hoping she'd come back. When we finally went inside, he locked himself in his room, not saying a word to me.

I didn't think he blamed me or anything, but his wife and youngest son had just left, and all of the plans he'd made to try and fix things went up in smoke in an instant.

To say it was a disaster was an understatement.

And I still had to play football. It was an away game, so at least I got out of afternoon classes and had half the afternoon to just stare out the window and think while everyone else was goofing off around me.

The good news was, we'd spent time watching L.D. Bell's film, and they were having a rough season. They were zero and three going into tonight's game while we were three and zero. Their defense was weak, and their QB had serious accuracy problems and tended to get jumpy whenever pressure was put on him.

No one was worried about winning.

I honestly wasn't even thinking about it. I was still thinking about what was going to happen with Mom and Josh as we went out for the coin toss.

We won, and Coach Holloway sent us out to receive.

After the kickoff, we lined up for our first drive. It was a simple concept: Mickey would run a shallow cross underneath while Brian went deep. If the safety cheated toward Brian, Henry would be open on a dig route across the middle, giving me lots of options.

The defense was showing a two-high safety look, corners playing off coverage about seven yards deep, all pretty standard prevent-the-big-play alignment that gave me a lot of ground for short runs.

"Red fourteen, red fourteen, set, hut!"

Andre snapped the ball, and I took my drop. Mickey broke across the formation on his shallow route as the linebacker dropped into zone coverage, cutting off that option. Brian was still working downfield; I needed another second for him to get separation.

But even as I was watching him, my mind started to wander. I was seeing Josh with his little smirk at me as he went up the stairs, and Mom bringing down their bags.

When I snapped to, the pocket had started collapsing. I stepped up, but my eyes were still tracking Brian instead of feeling the pressure. By the time I realized their defensive end had beaten Keith on the edge, it was too late.

I tried to slide left, but the defender wrapped me up from behind, and the ball popped loose as I hit the ground.

Thankfully, one of our guys got the ball back, but we'd lost eight yards.

"You good?" Andre asked, helping me up.

"Yeah."

But I wasn't.

I got my act together, and we moved the ball steadily after the fumble, working ourselves out of the hole we'd ended up in and getting a drive together, mostly made of short completions and a few runs.

By the time we were at midfield, Coach wanted us to take a shot at a big play, since the defense had started to cheat up, seeing how many short passes we were making.

"Trips right, four verts," came through my helmet.

I called trips right, four verts, which was four vertical routes to flood the deep zone and see if someone got in single coverage and got open.

When I got to the line, I saw their free safety was shading toward the trips side, leaving Miguel in single coverage on the backside.

Which was exactly what I was hoping for.

"Green eighteen, green eighteen, hut, hut!"

I kept my eyes locked on Miguel. He was flying down the sideline, the cornerback running stride for stride with him. I let it loose, putting some air under it and getting it right into his hands forty yards downfield. He caught it without breaking stride and picked up another fifteen before getting pushed out of bounds.

Fifty-five-yard gain.

"That's what I'm talking about!" Jerry shouted, slamming into my shoulder pads.

My focus didn't last. We did manage to score on that drive when Joe punched it in from the two-yard line, and our defense forced a three-and-out, which put us 7-0 at the start of the second quarter.

"I-right, thirty-four dive on one," I called in the huddle.

It was a simple run play. We just had to get Joe going downhill, set up play-action later.

We lined up. I started my cadence, but I was timing it wrong. Andre had been a little too fast on the snap, and I was going on pure autopilot and almost dropped the damn ball. I got it back together and managed a handoff to Joe for four yards, but it could have gone really bad.

Thankfully, no one saw that one. We ran it to Joe again on the next play and made another first down. Three plays later, we were in the red zone, first and ten from their eighteen.

On this play, Mickey would run a corner route from the slot, then break it back toward the post. If the safety bit on the corner, he'd be wide open.

I took the snap, started my drop. Mickey sold the corner route, and the safety jumped it, rotating toward the sideline, which let Mickey cut back inside toward the post, and I had a clean throwing lane.

But I hesitated.

Just for a moment, I second-guessed the read. Normally, I was more decisive than that, but for some reason, I wasn't sure. I was feeling off-balance and double-checked myself.

By the time I convinced myself to throw it, the window had closed. The safety recovered, getting a hand on the ball as it arrived. Mickey tried to adjust, but the deflection sent it straight to their cornerback.

Interception.

I stood there, hands on my hips, watching their corner jog back toward his sideline with the ball tucked under his arm. The L.D. Bell crowd went crazy.

Mickey slammed his helmet with both hands.

"My bad," I said. "Should've pulled the trigger."

Nobody responded. They just jogged off the field.

We did manage to recover, and by the third quarter, we were up 14-7. Still, I knew we should be dominating, but it really didn't feel like that. It felt like every field goal was a struggle to get, which was a problem against a middle-of-the-road team at best. We were letting them hang in it instead of closing this thing out.

Third and seven from our own forty-two, and we needed to convert, keep the drive alive, put this game away.

The play was for Mickey and Miguel to cross underneath, creating a natural pick if the defenders got tangled up while Austin ran a comeback on the outside as the safety valve.

We lined up, and I read the defense, which was showing blitz, six guys crowding the line of scrimmage.

"Blue eighty, blue eighty, set, hut!"

The line adjusted to counter the blitz, but their defense still brought it when the ball was snapped with all six rushers coming in hard. I had maybe two seconds before the pocket collapsed.

Mickey broke free on the mesh route, and I fired it to him, but I didn't set my feet, and the ball came out wobbly, floating instead of driving through the zone.

Their linebacker read it perfectly and jumped the route; he nearly picked it off for what would have been my second interception. Mickey managed to bat it down at the last second, keeping it out of their hands, but the play still ended incomplete.

It was fourth down, and we had to punt. No reason to give the other guys an easier chance to close on us when we didn't need to.

Coach Holloway gave me a long look when I came to the sidelines. I grabbed a cup of water and splashed it into my face, trying to clear my head.

Focus. I needed to focus.

By the fourth quarter, we'd traded field goals and were only up 21-19 with six minutes left. It was a one-score game, which was our closest game all season, and it really shouldn't have been.

We had the ball on our own thirty-five and needed to put together a drive that would eat clock and put points on the board.

On first down, Joe got five yards on a dive play, and we set up a fake handoff for the follow-up, where Joe would fake taking the ball while Brian would run a dig route across the middle. The hope was the linebacker would bite on the fake and zero in on Joe, leaving Brian open.

I took the snap under center, pretended to hand it off to Joe, and then rolled to my right. Brian was running his route, but their linebacker didn't bite. He dropped into coverage, sitting right in the throwing lane.

I bailed on the play and went on to my next read. Mickey was breaking open on a comeback route near the sideline. I could get it to him, but it'd be tight. Doable, but tight.

I planted my foot to throw, but their defensive end was closing fast from the backside. I saw him coming, tried to step up into the pocket to avoid him, but there was no pocket anymore. Keith and Elton had both been pushed back, and suddenly, I had defenders collapsing from three directions.

I tucked the ball and tried to run for it, even though I really didn't see my lane. I should have just thrown it away, but I thought if I could just get to the line of scrimmage, we'd have third and manageable.

I cut back toward the middle, saw a seam, and accelerated.

That's when their linebacker hit me.

He came in low, helmet driving into my thighs. My legs went out from under me, and I went down hard, the ball jarring loose as I hit the turf.

For a second, I thought I'd fumbled again, but the whistle had already blown. I was down before the ball came out.

Loss of three, putting us third and eight. It could have been worse, but not by a lot.

I pushed myself up slowly. My hip hurt where I'd landed, and my throwing hand was throbbing from where it had smacked the ground.

"You all right?" Joe asked, offering me a hand.

"Yeah."

Coach saw how I was holding my hand, though, and pulled me. The game was almost over anyway, and we were up, so he had room to do it. Gilbert did good for himself, converting the third down with a quick slant to Mickey, then moved the ball down the field with short gains, but we didn't get close enough. With two minutes left, we ended up settling for a field goal, putting us up 24-19.

Our defense held, and we won, but it sure didn't feel like it.

After the game, Coach Holloway found me near the locker room entrance. The rest of the team was filing inside, loud and celebrating, but I was dragging pretty far behind everyone. He grabbed my shoulder and pulled me aside.

"Walk with me."

We went around the corner of the stadium, away from the noise, to as private a place as you could find in a stadium full of people.

Coach Holloway stopped and turned to face me. His expression wasn't hard to read. He wasn't angry exactly, but he definitely wasn't happy.

"You want to tell me what's going on?"

"I just had an off night."

"Off night? Blake, you had a fumble, an interception, you missed a wide-open touchdown, and you took a sack on a play where you should've thrown it away. It was the worst I've seen you play since you've been at Wheaton. Your head wasn't in the game."

I didn't say anything. Just stared at the concrete under my feet.

"I'm not asking you to tell me what's going on. I know you've got problems with your mother and her being sick, but I need to know if you're going to be able to get your head on straight."

"I will. I'll get it together."

"I hope so." He crossed his arms. "Because tonight we were playing a team we should've beaten by three touchdowns. Instead, we barely scraped by with a five-point win. This is our last easy game before playoffs. We have Whyatt next week, then Lamar, and Midland homecoming week. Every single one of those teams is better than L.D. Bell. If you play against them the way you played tonight, we are going to lose. You understand that?"

"Yes, sir."

"Good. When you step onto that field, you need to leave all the other stuff at the door and focus on the game. All of those guys are counting on you to take us to state, but more importantly, you owe it to yourself to do the best job you can to make all the extra work you're doing worth it."

"I know. I won't let anyone down. I'll get my head on straight."

He studied me, then nodded slowly.

"I believe in you, Blake. I wouldn't have made you my starting quarterback if I didn't, but belief only goes so far. You need to show me I made the right decision putting so much on such a young QB."

"I know."

"Good." He turned back toward the locker room. "Now get cleaned up. We've got a long bus ride home."

I watched him walk away, then stood there for another minute, alone in the shadow of the stadium.

He was right. I knew he was right.

I just had to figure out how to actually do it.

Chapter 29

The walk to Li's mom's took forever, mostly because I was in my own head. As bad as Thursday night and then Friday's game had been, yesterday was even worse. Dad had called out again and spent a lot of it drinking, which wasn't like him.

And when he'd finally gotten Mom on the phone last night, things hadn't gone well. He'd made the call from his room and shut the door, but I got as close as I could to listen anyway.

This all affected me, too, after all.

"You can't just ... no, that's not how it works ... after so many days, truancy will ... should give a damn, Heather, what if he ..."

And on and on the argument went.

What was painfully clear was that Mom wasn't coming home this week, even though Josh had school. How she was going to get around his classes without making things worse, I had no idea, but she'd made up her mind, and she clearly wasn't listening to Dad.

I stopped in the lot behind the antique shop, steeling myself to deal with someone else. I half wanted to cancel on Yesica, except she'd made the drive all the way here and was doing me a huge favor by training me. I couldn't let my terrible week screw over someone else.

The back door into the storeroom was propped open again, and the sounds of gloves hitting pads were drifting through it, so I wasn't surprised to see Yesica was working the heavy bag when I got inside. She was ferocious, beating the crap out of it like it owed her money.

Considering how she was either in teacher mode or just being goofy and demanding food, it was rare that I got to see her like this, the athlete. She was amazingly fast, her hands flying in patterns I kind of recognized from her description that I was nowhere near able to replicate, even at half speed. And for her size, she was making the whole bag jump around like it weighed nothing.

It was truly impressive.

She must have sensed I was behind her because after a moment she stopped, steadying the bag with one glove, and turned.

"You look terrible," she said when she saw me.

"Thanks."

"Not like that, you just look like you're weighed down by something, not yourself."

I tried to shrug it off. "Just some family stuff."

I expected the usual adult interrogation, since she knew Mom had been sick and there were problems with my brother, although I'd never gone into specifics.

Instead, Yesica wrapped her arms around me and squeezed hard. Damn, she was strong. For a second, the wall I'd been holding up since Thursday night cracked and I let my forehead rest against her shoulder.

I was about to crumble and break down when she shoved me back hard enough for me to have to catch myself.

"Okay," she said, clapping her hands together. "Sadness is for after training. Right now, we work. Get your wraps on."

I blinked, the sudden shift giving me a kind of whiplash. "Just like that?"

"Just like that," she said, tossing a roll of yellow wraps at me. "The world does not stop because you are sad, which means we don't stop."

Now she was sounding like Coach Holloway. I sat down and started wrapping my hands. Honestly, the ritual helped.

"We're not doing mitts today, we're doing walls."

"Walls?"

"Stand up," she said, pointing to the brick wall on the far side of the room, between a stack of old paintings and a dusty armoire. "Put your back against it."

I did as I was told.

"In the ring, the ropes are bad and the corner is worse. If you get backed into them, you lose all of your options. The same is true in a real fight. You don't want to let them pin you. It makes it harder to defend yourself and gives them leverage to really wail on you. Understand?"

"Yeah."

"Do you?" she asked as she threw a very slow right hand at my head.

I reacted instinctively as she'd taught me, slipping my head to let the fist go by. I made it about a quarter of an inch before my head bounced off the brick wall.

"Oww," I said, surprised.

"See? Dead! You can't lean back, you can't slip, you can't dodge. But you need to know what to do in this situation, because it will happen sometimes. This time, when I punch, you do not move your feet yet. Instead, turn your shoulders and waist. Slip what you can, left to right, but use stronger parts of yourself to absorb the blow. Again."

She threw it again and I twisted my torso as she instructed. Going left to right, I was able to get out of the way just enough that her hand went past my ear.

Although this was choreographed and slow motion, it wasn't exactly inspiring that I'd be able to do it for real.

"Better. Again."

She threw a left and I twisted the other way.

"Elbows in! If you open your ribs, I can break them. Keep your elbows glued to your sides."

We did that for twenty minutes. Slip. Twist left. Twist right. My lower back stayed pinned to the wall, but my upper body moved constantly.

"Good," she said as she finally called a stop to that section. "Now, we add the escape. When you slip, you take a small step to the side. Not a big step, slide. You turn the corner."

She threw a right hook. I ducked under it, sliding my left foot out and pivoting my body away from the wall.

"No!" She caught my shoulder. "Too big. Just take a small step, create space where there isn't any."

We reset and went again. I dipped, slid my foot six inches, and pivoted. I was off the wall, facing her side.

"Good. Again."

For the next thirty minutes, she bullied me, trapping me against the brick and throwing punches, slow at first, then faster. I had to read her shoulders, dip, slide, and pivot.

"Don't look at my hands!" she yelled when I flinched. "Look at my eyes. Do I have to keep reminding you, my hands lie, my eyes tell the truth."

My legs burned from staying in a crouch.

"I'm ... tired," I gasped, missing a slip and taking a light slap to the ear.

"You do all this conditioning and training, and still you're tired," she said. "What's the point of all of it if you're still tired? Back to the wall."

"Can I get just a second?"

"No," she said, grabbing a medicine ball from the corner. "You want to rest, you rest while you work. Arms up. Brace."

"What are you ..."

Wham.

She slammed the medicine ball into my stomach. The air left my lungs in a rush. I doubled over, coughing.

"Stand up!"

I straightened up, wheezing. "Jesus."

She pulled the ball back, holding it in both hands again.

"No, Yesica. Tighten your core. Brace!"

Wham.

This time, I was ready. I flexed my abs, exhaling hard as the ball hit. It still jarred me, rattling my teeth, but I stayed upright.

"Better. Again."

Wham.

"Turn the hip into it."

Wham.

"Breathe out! *Shhh!* Like that."

If I knew getting the shit beat out of me was part of training, I might have passed.

"Ten more!" she said.

By the time she tossed the ball aside, my shirt clung to my chest and my abs felt like they'd been worked over with a hammer.

"Now you can get water," she said, pointing to the cooler.

I grabbed a bottle and downed it in one gulp. She sat on a bench pulled over to the side and patted the spot next to her. We just sat like that for a minute, although honestly, I was more focused on my soreness and breathing than anything else bothering me.

The endorphins were doing their job.

"You're angry."

"Yeah."

"Good. Anger is fuel, but it burns dirty if you don't filter it. Did I ever tell you my mother died when I was twenty?"

"Yeah, you mentioned it."

"It was the worst thing. My dad was gone by then, so she was the only person I had left other than some cousins and an aunt I didn't know. I was struggling, trying to get a place in amateur boxing, which really doesn't have a place for women. I was in a new country, I didn't know the language well yet, and my mom was back home all alone. I felt like the sky had fallen down and crushed me."

She turned to look at me.

"I had to give it all up and go back when she got really sick and I didn't know if I would be able to start again. I stopped training completely. For two months, I basically sat in a room and stared at the wall. I thought, *what is the point?*"

That hit close to home. "What happened?"

"Yeng came for me. I met her when my mother was here getting treatment, before we went back for the final days. She flew all the way to Colombia and dragged me out of bed. She told me I smelled bad and made me get in the shower. She put me in a car and drove me to the gym; day after day she did this. Then she got me to come back to the US and helped me get my life started again." She tapped my chest with a gloved fist. "You feel it here, right? It feels like everything's coming to an end, like it's going to kill you."

"Yeah. It feels like everything is falling apart."

"Things do fall apart. You can't stop that any more than I could stop my mother from dying. But just because things around you fall apart, doesn't mean *you* do. You're not a house, you're a fighter. You get knocked down on the football field, do you just lie there or do you get up and go again? You get hit, you bleed, and you punch back. They can hit you until you're hamburger, but the only one that can beat you, is you. Real fighters never give up and they never break."

"Yeah," I said, but I wasn't sure any of that was true.

She must have heard it in my voice, because she took my hand and said, "Listen to me. This is what I am teaching you. Not the punches, not the wall, none of that. It's all technique, but it's not real fighting. Real fighting is when you want to quit, when you want to go home and hide in your bed, that's when the work starts. Because if you can push through this, you can make it through anything. Fighting is here."

She tapped my chest again.

"Yeah," I said.

"Good," she said, letting go of my wrist. "Now get up. Rest time's done. Now you need to learn to slip the jab until you can do it in your sleep."

And just like that, we got back to it.

I had settled down a little bit after training with Yesica, but I still wasn't doing as well as I needed to.

When the final bell rang on Thursday, I sat there for a second, staring at the assignment sheet on my desk until Mrs. Gonzales, my Spanish teacher, said, "Blake?"

I looked up to see that I was the last person in the class.

"You planning on spending the night here?"

"Wha... oh, no. Sorry, I spaced out."

"For most of the class. You should get going. I know you have practice or something."

"I do. Thank you, Señora Gonzales."

"De nada," she said, smiling.

She was actually a pretty good teacher and really nice. I just couldn't pull it together today.

I kept my head down as I went into the hall, pushing through the sea of kids trying to get home. At least it was time for football.

I'd figured out that just losing myself in physical activity helped, like the boxing with Yesica.

If I made myself tired enough, I stopped worrying about things.

I turned the corner near the math wing, aiming for the double doors that led to the student parking lot and the path to the field house.

"Blake."

I slowed down. Ms. White stood in the doorway of her classroom, and she wasn't smiling.

"Hey, Ms. White," I said, turning toward the exit. "I'm actually running late for practice. Coach Holloway is on a warpath this week and ..."

"I know practice doesn't start for fifteen minutes," she said. "Come inside. We need to talk."

"Ms. White, really, if I'm late ..."

"Blake. Please."

It was the "please" that got me. She wasn't currently my teacher, but she'd been a big reason I got out of remedial classes at all, so I kind of owed her.

Plus, she'd always been nice to me. I checked the clock on the wall, which showed three thirty-five, and nodded.

"Okay. Five minutes."

I followed her into the empty classroom and she shut the door behind us, cutting off a lot of the noise from out in the hallway. I hadn't been in her room since last year, but that felt like a lifetime ago.

She leaned against her desk.

"I was in the teachers' lounge today and I overheard Mr. Brennan talking to Mr. Mossley."

"Okay."

"They were talking about you, specifically about your progress, or lack of it."

"He's already pulled me aside and talked to me. I know he's worried I'm not supposed to be on level and thinks football players should stay in remedial classes where they belong, but I told him I'll get it together, and I will."

"That's not exactly fair, Blake. He doesn't think you should be in remedial classes because you're a football player. He's worried because you're struggling and your grades are slipping. Badly."

"I'm not struggling. I got a B on the history test last week, and ..."

"I'm not just going off of what I overheard, Blake. After I heard them talking, I asked around to some of your other teachers, and what I'm hearing isn't good. Assignments not turned in, D's and C's on tests, failing some quizzes, even leaving some of them half blank."

"I ran out of time on that one."

"Mr. Mossley said you stared at the wall for most of the period and didn't start writing until about fifteen minutes were left."

"I've had a lot on my mind."

"I know you have football, and I know they have put a lot of pressure on you this year, but you can't play if you're academically ineligible, and we're only five weeks in. Midterms are coming up and your grades are already dipping. If you slip any further, what will your team do then? I know they're counting on you, which means they need you to be eligible."

"I know how the rules work."

"Then why act like they don't apply to you? This isn't the Blake Sims I taught last year. You were in multiple sports and working harder than anyone in this school. You'd stay late to ask questions and cared about the details. What's going on?"

I snapped. "Look, I'm sorry. It's been a rough week, okay?"

"You look exhausted. You have circles under your eyes."

"I'm fine."

"Are you? Because Mr. Brennan thinks you're overwhelmed. He thinks you moved up too fast, that the pressure of varsity and higher-level classes is breaking you. He wants to move you back to remedial math and regular science."

"He can't do that."

"He can if he thinks it's in your best interest, and from what I'm hearing, you aren't giving him a lot of reason not to."

"I am not going back to remedial classes. I belong in these classes."

"Then show us. Do the work."

"I will. Besides, you're not my teacher anymore, so maybe you should mind your own business," I muttered.

"Excuse me?"

"You think this is about laziness? You think I'm slacking off because I made varsity? I have real problems, Ms. White. Whether I solve for X doesn't make the top ten list of things I have to worry about."

"Blake, if there's something going on at home ..."

"It's none of your business."

"It is if you're in trouble. We all care about you and want to make sure you have the best chance to succeed."

"I'm not in trouble! I'm handling it! I handle everything! I fix the team, I fix the family, I fix the money. I'm handling it!"

She stepped back. "Blake ..."

"You want me to pass? Fine. I'll get an A on the next test. I'll show you I know the material and I can do it. I'm sorry if I haven't been doing everything everyone wants all the time, but there's only so much a single person can do. And don't tell me I'm failing because I don't care if I fail or not. You have no idea what I care about."

"I'm trying to help you."

"I don't need any help," I said, my voice shaking. "I need everyone to back off and let me breathe. I need to go play football because that's the only place where things actually make sense. And honestly, a football scholarship is going to get me a lot further than an English grade right now."

She looked disappointed. Disappointed and worried.

"Blake, if something is going on, we're here to help."

"If I want it, I'll ask for it. So back off!"

"Fine," she said with a sigh, moving to sit at her desk and waving at the door. "Go ahead. But I will tell you this. You are making a mistake. You're pushing away the people who are in your corner, and one day, you're going to turn around looking for help, and you're going to find out you're the only one left standing there."

I honestly felt like shit. She was concerned and I'd just ripped her head off. I just couldn't take one more coach, one more teacher, one more teammate asking me if I was 'okay' because I didn't do exactly what they wanted me to.

I'd had enough of it.

Deep down, I knew she meant well, and she really wanted to help. I just couldn't take it anymore. And the last thing I wanted to do was air out all the problems at home to everyone who asked why I wasn't performing as well as I should.

I knew she'd listen if I told her, but what could she do about it? Mom was an adult and could do what she wanted. Besides, it was three forty-two and I needed to get to practice. The last thing I needed was Coach Holloway jumping down my shit, too.

"I'll get the grades up," I said.

"I hope so."

I turned and walked out.

The hallway had already emptied out. I hurried outside and across the parking lot to the field house in the distance.

You're pushing away the people who are in your corner.

"Damn it," I said to myself.

She wasn't wrong.

Chapter 30

School might not be going well, but at least football was back on track. Yesica had been right. If I just let my body work and pushed everything else out, the game made sense again.

That was very evident on Friday night when we beat Whyatt thirty-eight to fourteen. All the screw-ups from the last game were gone, and I played like myself again. No more fumbles, no more interceptions, three touchdown passes, and I'd made a good scramble in the second quarter for a first down on third-and-long that extended a drive that we turned into points.

I was headed to the field house after the end of the game when Coach Holloway called out to me, "Blake, hold up a second."

I thought maybe I'd done something again and was about to get another talk, but I jogged over to him anyway.

It wasn't like I could ignore the coach.

"Good game, tonight. It's good to see you back to looking like yourself."

"Yeah, it felt good."

"Before you head to the field house to change, Channel Two from Midland sent a TV crew down tonight. They've asked if they could have a sit-down with you."

I had noticed a camera on the sidelines and had wondered what that was about, but just like everything else, I'd ignored it and focused on the game.

"Really?"

"Yep, let's go and get this over with."

The TV crew had set up two folding chairs facing each other with a camera on a tripod and some lighting equipment near the far end of the bleachers. A guy in a sports coat and khakis, holding a microphone, stood talking to a cameraman.

"Carter Riggs, KMID Channel Two Sports," he said, extending his hand as we walked up.

I shook his hand. "Nice to meet you."

"Hell of a game tonight," he said, and gestured to the chairs. "Have a seat. This won't take long, just a few questions about the season, and then we'll let you go change. Sound good?"

"Sure."

"I'll be right over there if you need me," Coach Holloway said.

I sat down, and a guy in a black T-shirt clipped a small microphone to my jersey.

"So, five and oh, that has to feel good?"

"It does, not that Whyatt was easy to beat. They really made us work for it," I said.

"That was very smooth," he said with a chuckle as he checked his watch, then looked at the cameraman. "We rolling, Dave?"

"Rolling," Dave said.

Carter stepped into the frame, turning his body slightly so he was facing me but still open to the lens. It was like he knew exactly where to stand.

"We're here at Wilfred Field in Wheaton with their star quarterback, Blake Sims, fresh off a thirty-eight to fourteen victory over Whyatt. Blake, that's five straight wins to open the season, putting the Mustangs in the hunt for state. How does it feel to keep that streak alive?"

"It feels great, Carter," I said, using his name like the media training person at camp suggested. "But honestly, the credit goes to the guys up front. The offensive line gave me all day to throw, and the defense really stepped up in the second half. All I had to do was put the ball where it needed to go."

"They certainly did a good job, but it was a little more than that. Three touchdowns and no turnovers. That big scramble in the second, word is that has become something of your calling card."

"I just try to take the plays as they come. Coach Holloway stresses discipline, and that's what we maintained tonight, and why we won."

"Speaking of discipline, you, Humble, and Midland Lee are the only teams to make it through pre-season undefeated, assuming those teams win their games tonight. People are starting to talk about the 'Race to State,' with your three names in contention. If you make it, it would be the first trip to state playoffs in Wheaton's history. Does the team talk about that? Is there a sense that you guys are chasing something historic?"

"We try not to look ahead and just take it one week at a time. If we start thinking about state, in November, we're going to get beat in October."

"That's a very veteran answer, which brings me to my next question. You're a sophomore while your two opponents are both seniors. They've been here before, and you haven't. Does the pressure get to you? A lot of people would say that's too much of a load for someone so young."

"I think my record speaks for itself," I snapped.

I don't know where that came from. At media training, they'd stressed how important it was to keep calm and cool, and that wasn't even a hardball question. I was the youngest QB leading a varsity team this year, and I knew people liked to ask about it.

He just managed to hit a nerve that had been sensitive all week. It was dumb of me to react to it.

"I didn't mean to imply you weren't," he said, faltering a bit, not having expected my reaction either. "But it is a unique situation."

"It is," I said, trying to rein it in. "And yes, the pressure is there, but I think it's there for everyone. Seniors, sophomores, it doesn't matter, we all want to win. My teammates trust me, and I trust them. That's what handles the pressure."

"Fair enough. You certainly played like a veteran tonight. Looking at the schedule, you face Midland Lee in two weeks. The Rebels are the heavy favorites to win the district, maybe even the state title."

"They're a great team," I said, back on script. "Midland always has a powerhouse program."

"I was actually over in Midland yesterday talking to some of their guys, and they're feeling very confident."

He paused, letting the silence hang for a beat. I got the feeling he was baiting me.

"I'm sure they were. Competitiveness is the name of the game, and we all think we're going to be the ones to walk home with the trophy."

"True, but it went a little beyond confidence. One of the players, their new receiver who is putting up some serious numbers, had some specific things to say about Wheaton and you in particular."

I frowned. "Me?"

I couldn't think of anyone at Midland I really knew. Maybe one of the guys I had a run-in with at the seven-on-seven tournament, but I couldn't even pick those guys out of a lineup, so I'm not sure why they'd be coming at me specifically.

"He seemed to think the Mustangs haven't had real competition yet, calling your schedule 'soft.' And he suggested that when you face a real defense, you're going to, and I quote, 'fold like a cheap lawn chair.' "

"Fold like a lawn chair? That's original."

"Probably not, but do you have a response to that?"

"Just that I wish them good luck, and I look forward to facing them on the field, seeing who's really ready for this or not."

Carter shook his head like he knew I wasn't going to take the bait and said, "I guess you're not taking the bait."

"I learned a long time ago that talking doesn't win games."

"Well said," Carter said. He turned to the camera. "That was Blake Sims, quarterback of the undefeated Wheaton Mustangs. They face Midland Lee on October twentieth in what is shaping up to be the game of the year. For KMID Sports, I'm Carter Riggs."

"And cut," the cameraman said.

Carter's posture relaxed instantly. "Good luck against Lamar. And Lee."

"Appreciate it," I said as Dave unhooked the mic. "Out of curiosity, who's their new guy who gave the quote? I've met some of the guys at Midland, and I don't think I know him."

"He certainly knew you, said he went to school here last year, in fact. Elijah Garner. Kid's got a mouth on him."

Elijah. Of course, it was him. Elijah's dad had business interests in Midland, and I knew he transferred to play somewhere else, but I didn't put two and two together until right now.

"Oh, yeah. I know him."

"Maybe a quote to add into the piece, then?"

"No, I'll leave it at what I said. We'll see what we see in two weeks."

"Fair enough. Good luck, you're going to need it. Midland is ... well, they're big."

He turned back to his equipment, barking orders at Dave about the lighting for the intro, leaving me to walk down the sideline toward the field house.

Elijah. Damn, I'd thought I'd put all his nonsense behind me, and now I was going to have to deal with him at the Midland game.

I should've known. I should've figured he'd end up somewhere close, still trying to make my life miserable.

Elijah, however, was a problem for the future.

Right then, I had to deal with what was happening at home *and* not let it crush me to the point that I couldn't get the stuff I needed done.

Thankfully, the rest of the weekend went better. Mom and Josh were still gone, but Dad had come out of his isolation a little bit and seemed more like himself.

Even if he was a worried version of himself.

I did get some good news Saturday morning when Mr. Henderson called with the September numbers.

Considering how the last few weeks had gone, I'd been half expecting bad news, but at least on that front everything was going well. The PlayStation launch had gone as expected, which I hadn't been worried about. He was still a little in shock that I kept making correct predictions. Between the Sony ADRs and some call spreads, neither of which I yet really understood what they meant, we'd made about eighty-five grand for the month. Not break-the-bank numbers, but a nice increase over the previous earnings.

Which was the goal for probably this first year. Kind of like in gambling, we just had to keep pumping the earnings back so we could increase our investments to larger and larger stakes.

Still, it was good money for me, and he was sending over a wire for twenty-one thousand more dollars and change. Considering some of the numbers I was doing before the gambling played out, it wasn't drop-everything kind of money, but if I could keep making twenty grand a month, I would be doing okay.

Well, if I didn't have to find a way to front Mom's medical bills, a military school if we ever got there, and private coaching. With all that, I needed the number to go higher.

Henderson had a plan based on everything else I'd told him, through the end of the year. I would just let him at it, and would keep cashing his checks.

Then it was Sunday and time for boxing. Yesica went hard at me again today, which I was finding was exactly what I needed. Just like I'd been able to focus on the football game on Friday when I let myself really get into the game, really getting into training pushed everything else out.

I guess it worked out in her favor, because I was starving and that meant taking Yesica to feed her as part of my payment for her training, which I think she liked over actual money, honestly.

She'd gone upstairs a few minutes before to talk to Li's mom, and I could hear them chatting in rapid-fire Spanish, which I only just realized she could speak, and thought how amazing it was she spoke three languages basically fluently.

Here I was, barely able to speak English, let alone Chinese or Spanish.

While they talked, I decided to see if Li wanted to go with us. Well, that, and I'd had something else on my mind I wanted to talk to her about.

I found her in the small living room, sitting cross-legged on the floor with textbooks spread around her because, of course, that's where she'd be.

"Hey," I said, leaning against the door frame. "Yesica's trying to convince your mom to go eat with us. Do you want to come along?"

Li looked up, blinking like she was coming out of a trance.

"What time is it?"

"Almost one."

"Already?" She glanced at the clock on the wall and frowned. "I've been at this for three hours."

"The first step is admitting you have a problem, Li."

"No, the first step is being prepared for my history test on Tuesday."

“Come on. You and I both know you’re ready and have been since last week. This is just you being a perfectionist. Come eat.”

She rolled her eyes but started gathering her books into a neat pile. “Fine. I could eat. Let me just tell my mom I’m going.”

“She’s in the kitchen with Yesica.”

Li stood up, stretching her arms over her head. At six-four, she nearly brushed the ceiling fan. I followed her toward the kitchen, but I knew once we got going, or left to get food with Yesica and her mom in tow, I wouldn’t feel brave enough to do the other thing I wanted to do, and if I didn’t do it now, I’d probably talk myself out of it.

“Hey, hold up a second.”

“What?”

“So you know homecoming’s coming up.”

“You know I’m on student council, right? Who do you think plans all that stuff?”

“Yeah, right. Of course. I was just wondering if you wanted to go. With me.”

The words came out easier than I expected, maybe because there was nothing complicated about it. Li was my best friend, I wanted to go to the dance, and I knew she probably needed to go because of student council, and also that she didn’t have a date. Going together made sense.

I think I might have said it a little too fast, ‘cause it seemed to catch her off guard.

“As friends?”

“Yeah, of course. What else would it be?”

“I don’t know, you’re the one asking.”

“I’m asking because I don’t want to go alone, and I don’t want to go with some random girl who’s going to expect me to be ‘on’ all night.” I made air quotes around the word. “You know how exhausting that is? Having to be charming and attentive and whatever else for four hours straight?”

“The horror,” Li said dryly. “I’m glad you feel you can be boring and inattentive with me.”

“That’s not what I meant. It’s just, after the whole Melanie thing, I’m not looking to deal with any of that any time soon. The drama, the games, trying to figure out what someone actually wants from you. I just want to go and have fun. And I figured you and me, we could actually do that."

Li was quiet for a moment, studying me with those dark eyes that always seemed to see more than I wanted them to.

"What about that girl from camp?" she asked. "Charlie?"

"What about her?"

"She won't get jealous?"

I shrugged. "No, I told you nothing could happen there. Charlie's cool, no doubt, but we both agreed it could never be a real thing. She lives in Georgia, I live here, and neither of us wants to do long-distance. So no, she won't care. She mentioned she's got a date for her homecoming."

"That's surprisingly self-aware of you."

"I have my moments."

Li leaned against the wall, arms crossed. "So you want to go to homecoming with me because I'm ... convenient?"

"Come on, don't be like that. I'm not saying you're a consolation, I'm saying I thought we both might want to go, and it would be cool to hang out with my best friend."

She almost smiled. Almost. "And what do I get out of this arrangement?"

"The pleasure of my company? Free food at whatever restaurant we go to before? A guaranteed dance partner who won't try anything weird?"

"You can't dance."

"I can dance."

"I've seen you dance, Blake. No, you can't."

"Okay, I can't, but I'll try. And I promise not to step on your feet more than twice."

I could practically see the gears turning in her head. She analyzed everything, weighed every option before committing. It was one of the things that made her such a good student and also drove me crazy sometimes.

"Fine," she said finally. "I'll go."

"Yeah?"

"On one condition."

"Name it."

She pointed a finger at me. "You don't abandon me the second your football friends show up. I'm not going to stand in a corner by myself while you do your whole 'team bonding' thing with Mickey and Andre."

"That's fair."

"I mean it. If you ditch me to go hang out with the guys, I will find you and I will make your life miserable."

"Noted. No ditching Li. Got it."

"And you have to actually dance with me. Not just stand around joking with your friends."

"I can do both."

"Blake."

"Fine, fine. Actual dancing. I promise."

She nodded, satisfied, and something like a real smile finally broke through. "Okay then. It's a deal."

"Great. Now, can we please go get tacos?"

"This is going to be a disaster," she said, but she was still smiling.

"Probably. But at least it'll be entertaining."

Chapter 31

I don't know why I thought asking Li to go to homecoming as friends would be no big deal, but I was wrong.

I don't know how everyone knew, but I started getting comments the moment I got to first period, and it was still going at lunch. I knew word spread fast. Small towns were like that. This really was no big deal, but apparently, everyone had missed the "as friends" part and jumped straight to "are dating."

By lunch, I was ready to tape a sign to my chest that said, "It's not like that," just to save myself the trouble.

The second I sat down at lunch, Mickey started in on me.

"Well, well, well," he said with that shit-eating grin he got when he thought he was being clever. "If it isn't the man of the hour."

"Don't start."

"What? I'm just saying congratulations on finally making moves."

"I asked her to homecoming. That's it."

"That's how it always starts," Jerry said. "First it's homecoming, then it's holding hands, then it's ..."

"Finish that sentence, and I'll shove your tray down your throat."

Jerry held up his hands in mock surrender, but he was laughing, as was everyone else. Well, everyone but Li, who kept her eyes fixed on her food and hadn't said a word since I sat down.

"Seriously, though," Gabriel said. "Why not? You're always together anyway."

"Because we're friends."

"Friends who are going to homecoming together," Connor added. "Which is, you know, a date."

"It's not a date. I needed someone to go with and very specifically didn't want to get a date, so we're going ***as friends***. End of story."

"I'm just saying, that's what a date is," Mickey mumbled just loud enough to be heard.

"No, a date is when there's romantic intent, and there's no romantic intent here. Right, Li?"

"Can we please talk about something else?" Li asked quietly.

"See?" Joe said. "She's not denying it."

"She's not denying it because there's nothing to deny. We're *friends*. How many times do I have to say it?"

"Until it stops being funny," Jerry said.

"So never," Mickey added.

The table erupted in laughter again. My patience was wearing thin. Under normal circumstances, I probably would have laughed it off, but the fuse on my temper had been short and was getting shorter, and I could see their comments were making Li very uncomfortable.

None of the rest of them seemed to see it.

Li must have had enough, though, because she pushed back from the table and said, "I'm going to the library. I have studying to do."

"Li, wait ..." I said, trying to stop her, but she was already walking away, her tray still half-full.

The table went quiet.

"I think she's mad," Mickey said.

"No shit, she's mad. You think maybe, just maybe, she didn't want the entire school talking about her? And you guys, sitting here talking about her like she's not even here. How would you feel?"

"Whoa, relax. We were just joking around."

"Yeah, well, your jokes just made her leave. Happy now?"

"Blake, chill," Jerry said. "It's not like we said anything that bad."

"You didn't have to. The whole point of us going together was that it wasn't supposed to be a big deal, just friends going to a dance. But no, you guys had to turn it into this whole *thing*, and now she's embarrassed, and I'm sitting here looking like an idiot."

"You had to know people would talk," Joe said.

"People, yes. Our friends, I'd hoped not. I guess I was wrong about you all, though."

"You were wrong about something," Eduardo muttered.

"What?"

"Nothing," he said, but he didn't look up like it was nothing.

He was leaning over his food, not making eye contact, hunched over.

"No. What did you mean by that?"

"I said it's nothing, Blake," he snapped.

Okay, so maybe Li and I weren't the only ones bothered by this. I didn't know what his deal was, although I had some guesses. He'd asked Li out and gotten shot down, and I'd told him it was a bad idea and not to do it. Now I was going to homecoming with Li, and everyone was saying I was dating her.

He was smart enough to know it wasn't like that, and we were just going together, not *together*, but he was letting all the teasing everyone else was doing build up and get to him.

I understood, but I didn't have the energy to deal with his being passive-aggressive toward me.

"If you've got something to say," I said slowly, "say it."

"I don't have anything to say."

"Bullshit."

"Blake," Andre said. "Maybe cool it, man."

"No, I want to hear it. Eduardo clearly thinks I've done something wrong, so he's going to make a big deal about it and make little comments under his breath ..."

"I said it's nothing. I'm not going to make a big deal out of it."

"Look, whatever you're thinking ..."

"I'm not thinking anything."

"You're clearly thinking *something*."

"Drop it, Blake."

I was done with everyone taking shots at me.

"Fine," I said, standing up. "Whatever. I'm done with this."

"Where are you going?" Mickey asked.

"Anywhere but here."

I grabbed my tray, dumped the contents in the trash, and walked out of the cafeteria.

I will admit, I felt a little bad going in so hard on everyone. They'd acted like that with everyone else, and I'd always joined in on the joking, but I guess I couldn't take it right now.

Well, Eduardo was going too far. If he wanted to blame me for doing something because he couldn't take being turned down, then I couldn't do anything about that.

He'd have to deal with his own shit.

I turned down the main hallway toward the library to find Li and see if I couldn't smooth this over. I knew she didn't like to be the center of attention, and I'd kind of dropped it all on her anyway.

"Running away?"

Melanie was coming up behind me looking as smug as I'd ever seen her. Which was saying something.

"Not now."

"Trouble in paradise already? You haven't even made it to the dance yet."

I wasn't going to deal with her and just walked away, but she wasn't done and fell into step beside me.

"I have to say, I'm impressed," she continued. "You really had everyone else fooled."

I didn't say anything to her.

"You denied, denied, denied the whole time, just saying you were friends, and now we see the truth, don't we?"

"You don't know what you're talking about. We're friends, that's it, and we're just going to homecoming as friends. We are ***not*** dating."

"No one believes that. You're such a hypocrite, complaining to everyone that I cheated on you and how I was a liar, going so far as to get me kicked off JV, when you were the one really telling lies and cheating."

"That's bullshit. We aren't dating. We weren't then, and we aren't now."

"That's not what everyone else is saying. For all your big talk about honesty and integrity, you're just as much of a fraud as you accused me of being."

She picked the wrong day to mess with me. I snapped.

"I don't give a shit what you think, but I know you don't actually believe any of that. You know I'm not dating her, but you're just so desperate to be a victim that you'll convince yourself that something happened even when it didn't. You think I don't see you? You think I don't know exactly what you are? You're a manipulator, a user who doesn't care about anyone except yourself. People are just props for the Melanie Show, and the second they stop being useful, you throw them away. You're a narcissist, plain and simple."

I don't think she expected me to go on the attack, and she took a physical step back in response.

"You don't know anything about me."

"I know everything about you. I know you're terrified that people will find out who you really are and what you really have to offer. I know you lie awake at night, worried that someone will see through the act and realize there's *nothing* underneath. That you're an empty shell that, if you disappear tomorrow, no one would notice. I know that the reason you're so desperate to tear other people down is because deep down, you think you're worthless, and if you can just make everyone else feel small enough, maybe you'll finally feel big."

Melanie's face had gone pale, and her lower lip trembled.

"That's not true," she said.

Part of me felt bad for her for just a second. She sounded so small as she heard the truths about herself that she always feared someone would see.

But then I remembered it was all true, and she'd picked this fight. She saw I was struggling and decided that was the moment to twist the knife. She brought everything down on herself.

"It's all true. You just haven't had anybody tell you to your face." I was breathing hard now, my hands shaking at my sides. "You want to compare yourself to me? Fine, let's compare. What did I do? I asked a friend to homecoming. What did you do? You accused a guy of assault because he didn't want to leave his girlfriend for you. I called out your lies to people you were manipulating. You tried to destroy people's reputations for fun. We are *nothing* alike, Melanie. Nothing."

She was shaking now, her eyes filled with tears. I'd seen her fake cry, how she'd give dry, heaving sobs, and this wasn't that. She was fighting hard to keep the tears in.

Part of me wanted to feel victorious, that I'd made her feel even a little bit of responsibility for what she'd done over the last year and a half, but honestly, I just felt hollow.

"You're a monster," she said, her voice cracking.

"Maybe, but at least I'm an honest one."

I turned and walked away. Behind me, I heard her choke back a sob. She fled in the opposite direction.

I didn't look back.

I was just so tired. Tired and angry. Everything was falling apart at the seams, and everyone, from the coaches to Mr. Brennan to my father, all expected me to keep going. To push through.

They needed me to make sure the school got its first state win. They needed me to make sure someone could pay for Josh's school. They needed me to do ten times more work than anyone else to prove I wasn't just a dumb jock. They needed me to make sure my mother got treatment.

Everyone needed me, but when I needed someone it was 'just keep pushing, Blake,' 'keep your head down and focus, Blake,' 'we're all counting on you, Blake.'

I was done with it.

But I couldn't just crawl into a corner and fall apart. I had to go find Li and make sure she was okay because I was responsible for making her feel bad, just because I asked her to homecoming as a friend.

It was bullshit. All of it.

I found Li where she said she'd be, in the library, sitting at one of the tables near the back with a textbook open in front of her. She wasn't reading it, though. I'd seen her study, and it was an intense thing, like she was trying to drink the book in with her eyes. Now, her eyes were glazed over and she wasn't really looking at anything.

I slid into the chair across from her. "Hey."

She didn't look up. "Hey."

"I'm sorry."

She looked up at me, a confused expression on her face. "For what?"

"For putting you in this situation. I should have thought about how people would react before I asked you. I just figured ..." I shrugged. "I don't know what I figured."

"That people would believe you when you said we were just friends?"

"Or not even care."

Li closed her textbook. "Well, that was stupid. You're the star quarterback and the school's golden boy. Of course, they'd care."

"Well, I know that now," I said, trying to make a little joke.

It didn't land.

"It's not that I don't want to go. I do. I just wasn't expecting everyone to treat it like we announced our engagement."

"I know, and I totally get it. If you want to back out, I will understand one hundred percent. No hard feelings."

"I don't want to back out. I want to go to homecoming, and I'm glad it's with you because it's low pressure. We can just have fun with our friends instead of all the drama that comes with an actual date. The problem is everyone else."

"Yeah. The guys didn't mean anything by it, you know. They were just giving me a hard time like they always do."

Li shook her head. "No, they weren't."

"What do you mean?"

"I mean, they weren't just teasing, they were serious. They actually think we're dating, or that we should be, or whatever, and it's not just them, it's everyone. People I barely know have been asking me about it all day."

"People like gossip. They like thinking they know something everyone else doesn't."

"I know that. It's just ..." She trailed off, looking down at her hands. "I'm not used to being the thing people gossip about. For most of my life no one ever noticed me, and now suddenly everyone's watching to see what happens next."

I hadn't thought about it that way. I'd had the one good football season in my dream life, and then spring last year where people were starting to talk about me. It wasn't quite to the level it was this year, but people definitely had opinions about me and were vocal about it. But when I'd first talked to Li, mostly out of guilt for what I'd done to her in the dream, she'd been the person who ate lunch all by herself every day, walked home by herself, and didn't really have a social life.

Some of that had turned around since she started playing basketball, but not to this level.

"I'm sorry," I said again. "I'll do what I can to get it to die down. I can at least make sure my teammates know to knock it off."

"I doubt it'll help."

"Probably not," I admitted.

"That's okay." She gave me a small smile, the first one since she'd left the cafeteria. "I'll live. It's just homecoming. In a month, nobody will even remember. What is it you said last year, they'll have some new drama to worry about."

"Exactly. Maybe you can start dating Andre. That'll really get them talking."

She rolled her eyes, but her smile widened a little. "Shut up."

We sat there for a minute in what felt like our normal comfortable silence, then Li said, "I still need a dress."

"Oh, yeah. I guess that's a thing, and I probably need a suit. I don't think I even own one that fits anymore. We should go shopping together."

"I don't think I can find a good dress here. I'll probably have to go to Midland for it."

"So let's go to Midland."

"Okay."

"How about tonight? I can skip practice for one day, and I don't really feel like spending time with those jerks after what they did. I need a day to be mad at them. Besides," I added, "I owe you for all of this, so let me make it up to you."

Li considered it. "Yeah, that sounds great."

"You'll have to drive, though. My permit only works with an adult."

"My mom doesn't exactly love me driving long distances. Or short distances. Or at all."

"I'll talk her into it. Your mom loves me."

Li gave me a skeptical look, and I grinned like an idiot at her to make my point.

"I don't know why. You're a dork."

"Yes. Yes, I am," I said, grinning even bigger.

It actually wasn't as hard as Li thought to convince her mom. She really did like me.

It took about twenty minutes of me explaining that Li was an excellent driver and this was a big moment of getting to adulthood, and it's better her first long drive be out here in West Texas, where there were fewer people and she was a phone call away, than at Harvard where Li would certainly end up and have to make trips to D.C. on her path to becoming president.

Okay, I may have laid it on a little thick with the last section of my argument, and both women rolled their eyes at me, but my charm worked, and we got the okay.

Well, it did come with a list of conditions and rules longer than my arm, but I'd take it if we got the yes.

By the time we pulled into the shopping center in Midland, the sun was getting low, and my stomach was reminding me I'd skipped lunch after the cafeteria disaster.

"This one?" Li asked, pointing at a dress shop with a window display full of homecoming-appropriate options.

"Works for me."

The store was one of those places that smelled like perfume and had way too many mirrors.

"What color are you thinking?" I asked.

"I don't know. Not pink."

"No, not pink."

I couldn't even imagine Li wearing a pink dress. She pulled out a dress that was aggressively purple. Like, the kind of purple that would be visible from space.

"Try it on," I said.

"You're kidding."

"I'm not. You'll never know until you see it on."

She gave me a look but took the dress into the fitting room. Two minutes later, she came out looking like a very tall grape.

I tried to keep a straight face. I really did.

"Don't say anything," she warned.

"I wasn't going to."

"You're laughing."

"I'm not laughing."

"Your face is laughing."

“My face doesn’t know what it’s talking about.”

She retreated back into the fitting room while I choked down my laughter.

The next dress was dark blue and actually looked pretty good, but Li shook her head at her reflection. “Too plain.”

“I don’t know, I think it’s classic.”

“That’s another way of saying it’s plain, Blake.”

“I’m not sure that’s right, but okay.”

She tried on a green one that made her look like she was going to a Renaissance faire, a silver one that she actually paused in front of the mirror for, and a black one that made me forget how to form words for a second.

“That one,” I said when she came out.

“Really?” She turned to look at herself in the three-way mirror.

It was simple, black, fitted, with an open back that showed skin, but not so much skin her mother would be mad.

“Yes. It shows off your muscles, which you hide under big clothes most of the time. It’s elegant and classy, and sexy without being so sexy your mom will get mad.”

“Sexy?”

“Sexy.”

She stared at her reflection for a long moment, tilting her head like she was trying to see herself the way I was seeing her.

“Okay. This one.”

On the way to the register, we grabbed a suit for me that would match her dress. It was dark gray, nothing fancy, but it fit without needing alterations.

When the woman behind the counter started ringing everything up, I said, “I’ve got it.”

Li put her hand on my arm. “Blake, no. I can’t let you do that. This is expensive.”

“Why not?”

“Because I help out at my mom’s store and I get paid for it. You don’t even have a job.”

“Excuse us a second,” I said to the cashier and pulled her aside.

I’d been putting off this conversation because I didn’t know how to explain it, but I guess now was as good a time as any. “Actually, here's the thing. I have money. A pretty good amount, actually. I've been investing since last year."

She raised an eyebrow. "Investing?"

"Yeah, and I've gotten pretty good at it."

"That's great, but I can't let you sell off your investments or whatever to pay for this. Besides, I've read up on the market and I know how slow it can be, especially with how much you must have had to start. I'd be afraid this would wipe out everything you've made."

"Not even close. I've done really well."

"What's really well?" she asked, still sounding very skeptical of the whole thing.

"I made twenty-eight thousand last month," I said, holding eye contact so she could see I was serious.

Her mouth dropped open. "What?"

"Like I said, I've done really well. I'm working with a friend of Coach Plummer's who owns an investment company, and we've just formed our own investment company. I have a knack for guessing what's going to be big. At this point, I make more than both my parents, every month."

"Holy shit. You make more than my mom does in a month."

"Yeah, I know. It's why I haven't said anything, not just to you, but to anyone. The only person who knows is my dad and Coach Plummer. I haven't told anyone else because I don't want things to be weird. And because most of the money is going to pay for my mom's chemo, and hopefully her surgery if she goes through with it."

Her expression shifted from shock to something softer. "Oh."

"But I'm doing well enough that I can afford this without a problem. So please, let me do this."

She looked at me for a long moment, and I could see her wrestling with it. Li wasn't the type to let people do things for her. She didn't like owing anyone anything.

"Please," I said again.

Finally, she nodded. "Okay."

We went back to the register, I handed my card to the woman behind the counter, and she rang everything up without comment. When she handed me the bag with Li's dress, I passed it to her.

“There. Now we’re ready for homecoming.”

Li held the bag like it was something precious. “Thank you, Blake.”

“Don’t mention it.”

“If that’s how much you make in a month, how much are you worth?” she said as we got in the car.

“Don’t make it weird.”

“I’m not; I’m just interested is all.”

I sighed and looked at my hands, trying to decide if I was going to tell her or not.

“You don’t have to tell ...”

“Almost a million,” I blurted out, interrupting her.

“***WHAT!!***”

“You can’t tell anyone. Literally no one knows. Most of that is wrapped up in investments so I can’t just get to it, so it’s not like I have that kind of money sitting around. And besides my mom’s chemo, I’m going to, I think, pay to send my brother to a special school where he can get ... help. Plus, it’s how I’m paying for the camps, and the special coaching, and all the other stuff I’m going to need coming up.”

“Oh.”

“I’m telling you this so you know how much I trust you, Li. You’re my best friend, and I’ve been planning to tell you for a while, but ... I honestly had no idea how to just drop that into conversation.”

“I imagine.”

“You can’t tell anyone.”

“I won’t, but ... maybe you can talk to me about what you’re doing sometimes. I find finance really interesting.”

“Uh, yeah, I can do that.”

“Good,” she said, starting the car.

“A millionaire. Jesus,” she said as she pulled out of the lot.

“Shut up,” I said, but we were both smiling.

Chapter 32

The rest of the week went a lot better than it started.

We beat Lamar on Friday, our sixth win in a row, and while they were a much better team than some of the others we'd faced, we managed to keep a lead through most of the game and stayed a touchdown ahead of them the whole time.

It wasn't exactly the prettiest game I'd played, and in the third quarter, I thought we were cooked when their defense started reading us well, but Coach saw it too and switched to a run game, with hardly any passes the rest of the quarter.

By the fourth, I'd been able to start throwing again, and they couldn't just hammer our receivers since we'd shown them our running game worked, too. Still, it got a little too close a few times, and I knew Coach was going to tear us apart after that.

He'd already promised practice was going to kick into high gear, and I told the guys who normally came to my morning practices the same thing. We had Midland Lee next Friday, and it was going to be a big game. Not only were they our biggest rivals, but it was also our homecoming game, which meant all the extra nonsense that came with that: pep rallies, the dance, the parade, the whole production.

The last thing any of us wanted to do was walk into the gym for the dance after getting our first loss of the year.

I was doing my best to compartmentalize. The gossip mill had found something new to chew on. Apparently, Kati Johnson, one of the seniors on varsity cheer, got caught sneaking out late on a school night with this twenty-year-old who went to the junior college in Odessa, and everyone zeroed in on that, hard.

I kind of felt bad for her, but I was also glad I'd moved off the front page.

With us no longer the talk of the school, things with Li had started to settle down. Melanie was also keeping her head down, which helped. I'd see her in the halls sometimes, usually alone or with one or two people who hadn't completely abandoned her, and she'd look away before we made eye contact. I didn't feel good about what had happened with her, exactly, but I didn't feel bad either. She'd made her choices.

So, yeah. Things at school, at least, were looking up. Things at home still sucked, but it was the same level of suck, so that at least hadn't changed. Mom was still in Lubbock with her friend, refusing to come home, and had basically stopped her treatment. She'd been mostly in a holding pattern before her surgery, so that wasn't the end of the world, but her surgery was coming up on Monday, and if she missed it, there would be a long gap until they could reschedule.

I was still holding out hope, but each day that hope got a little weaker.

It was just after dinner, and I was up in my room desperately trying to get back on top of my homework, which, as much as I snapped at Ms. White, I really was falling pretty far behind.

"What?!" I heard yelled from downstairs.

That got my attention since Dad and I were the only ones home, so I had no idea who he was talking to, let alone in such a panicked tone of voice. I went to the top of the stairs and realized he was on the phone in the kitchen.

"When did he leave?" A pause. "And Heather's not—" Another pause, longer this time. "Carol, I need you to slow down. Tell me exactly what happened."

That was enough to get me down the stairs. I found him standing by the phone, with one hand pressed against his forehead, eyes closed.

"I understand. I'm leaving now. No, I'm calling some people I know in the department," he said and hung up, just standing there for a second, leaning his head against the wall.

"Dad?"

He opened his eyes. For a second, he looked like he'd aged ten years since dinner.

"Joshua ran away."

"What?" I said, repeating him from earlier.

"I'm not clear on what happened, yet. They set some kind of rules for him and he freaked out. There was a big fight, and when Carol went up to check on him an hour later, the window was open, and he was nowhere to be seen."

"What about Mom?"

Not that Mom would ever try to keep him from doing whatever he wanted.

"Carol says she won't get off the couch and is barely responsive."

"I'm coming with you," I said.

"Blake ..."

"You're going to need help looking for him. Lubbock's a big city, and he's sneaky as hell. I've caught him hiding in odd places twice this year. Two sets of eyes are better than one."

He hesitated. I could see him weighing the options, the part of him that wanted to protect me from whatever we might find versus the part that knew I was right.

"Fine," he said. "Get your jacket. We're leaving now."

The drive to Lubbock took about one hour and nine minutes, which was almost twenty minutes faster than that drive would normally take. My dad pushed the speed limit the whole way, his knuckles white on the steering wheel, weaving in and out of traffic. Neither of us talked much for the first thirty minutes.

"When we find him ..." I started, breaking the silence.

"We'll deal with it."

"I mean, what if he's not just running away? What if he's ..."

I didn't finish the sentence. He knew what I meant.

After several more beats of silence, he said, "I've been thinking the same thing."

At least he realized the real problem. Josh running away was bad. Josh running away for another reason was way worse.

We went back to driving in silence.

When we got to Lubbock, we went straight to the police station. Dad knew a guy there from some joint training thing a few years back named Bowen. I didn't go in with him, though. Dad was trying to figure things out and honestly was flustered enough that I don't think he wanted to deal with me at the same time.

I cut him some slack and waited in the car while he went inside. Twenty minutes later, he came back out with a stocky guy with a thick mustache.

"Blake, this is Sergeant Bowen. He's going to help coordinate the search."

Bowen nodded at me. "Your dad says you might know some places to check?"

I didn't, not specifically, but I knew how Joshua thought, or at least, I thought I did.

"We should check Aunt Carol's neighborhood first," I said. "He doesn't know this area, so if he's locked in on someone, it would probably be someone he saw near the house. After that, our best bet is places like parks, playgrounds, that kind of thing. Places where kids might be."

Bowen's expression didn't have a big reaction, but I could see in his eyes that he picked up what I was saying right away. He glanced over at my dad, worried.

"I'll put out a description to patrol units," he said. "White male, twelve years old, five-six, light brown hair. What was he wearing when he left?"

"Let me run inside and call Carol," my dad said.

While he made the call, Bowen pulled me aside. "Your dad told me a little about the situation. The behavioral stuff."

"Yeah."

"We're treating this as a runaway for now, keeping it low-key." He paused. "But if you think there's a chance he might be a danger to others, I need to know."

I didn't think about lying, not even once. Hell, I'd been trying to get someone to listen to me about Josh for more than a year.

"I think there's a strong chance. I'm not positive, but he's ... done things to animals, so if he hasn't hurt anyone yet, he will. I think he's better somewhere others can see him. But yeah, to someone smaller than him, he's definitely a danger."

"Okay. Okay," Bowen said, repeating himself as I dropped that bomb.

My dad came back. "Carol says he was wearing jeans and a black hoodie. She thinks he might have taken some money from her purse, but she's not sure how much."

“Enough to get somewhere?” Bowen said. “Bus station, maybe. Or just food and supplies to hole up for a while.”

“He’s not trying to get somewhere. I’m positive he’s not running to or from anything. He just wants to be somewhere he can do what he wants, and no one will tell him no.”

“Then we check the neighborhoods,” Dad said, “Then the parks.”

Bowen nodded. “I’ll dispatch units to MacKenzie Park, Clapp Park, and the Civic Center area. Those are the biggest spots where kids hang out after dark. You two want to take your own vehicle, cover some of the smaller areas?”

“Yes,” my dad said. “Give us a radio so we can stay in contact.”

Bowen went back inside and returned a minute later with a handheld radio, and then we were back in the car, heading toward Aunt Carol’s neighborhood.

We stopped at her house first. Carol was waiting on the porch, arms wrapped around herself.

“Tom, I’m so sorry. I tried to stop him, but he just, he looked right through me. Like I wasn’t even there.”

“It’s not your fault, Carol.” My dad put a hand on her shoulder. “Which way did he go?”

“The backyard. I think he cut through the Sloanes’ property. Their dog was barking like crazy around eight o’clock.”

My dad looked at me. “That’s south. Toward the park on Forty-eighth.”

I nodded. Dad knew Lubbock better than I did.

We spent the next hour driving through neighborhoods, stopping every few blocks to get out and look. We checked every inch of any park or playground we could find, in drainage ditches, under bridges. Nothing.

Occasionally, we’d get updates from Bowen over the radio, but there was no sign of him. Not at MacKenzie Park, not at the Civic Center. One unit thought they saw someone matching the description near a convenience store on Nineteenth, but it turned out to be a different kid.

Around eleven, we pulled into the parking lot of a small park in one of the nearby neighborhoods. I didn’t know the name of it— It was just a few swings, a slide, a cluster of benches around a dead fountain.

We walked the perimeter first, checking the tree line and the bushes along the edges. When we found nothing, we moved inward, toward the playground equipment.

I tried to put myself in Joshua's head. If I were him, where would I go? Not the playground itself, not enough kids, although maybe he'd seen people driving around and he was hiding, waiting for people to stop looking for him.

"Dad," I said. "Back there."

I pointed toward a dense cluster of oaks on the far side of the park. The kind of spot where you could wait for someone to come by alone at night.

As we got closer, I heard voices. Not Joshua, other people. Then I saw flashlight beams cutting through the darkness ahead of us.

"Lubbock PD," someone called out. "Anyone in the area, identify yourself."

We emerged from the tree line to find three officers sweeping the area, their lights crisscrossing through the shadows. One of them recognized my dad and jogged over.

"Deputy Sims? Bowen sent us to help. Nothing so far, but we're doing a full sweep."

"Thanks," my dad said. "We've done a good check of this area. Maybe expand the search to the residential streets north of here. Check backyards, anywhere a kid could hide."

"Will do."

I wasn't confident we were going to find him. There were so many places a kid could hide, and only so many of us.

Around one-thirty in the morning, the radio crackled.

"Tom, it's Bowen. You need to come back to the station."

My dad grabbed the radio before it finished crackling. "Did you find him?"

"Yeah." There was a pause. "He's been here the whole time."

I looked at my dad, confused. "What does that mean?"

He didn't answer. He just got back in the car, and we were at the station in under ten minutes. Bowen was waiting for us outside, and the look on his face told me this wasn't going to be a simple "we found your kid, here he is" situation.

“What’s going on?” my dad asked as we got out of the car.

“Let me explain. Patrol got a call around eight reporting an incident at a park where this family event thing happened tonight. There were some complaints of an older boy hanging around the little kids, talking to them, asking questions. When the dad confronted him, the boy wouldn’t even talk to him, just stayed focused on the kids. They tried to get the kids away, but he just followed them until they got in their car and drove away. They called from their home to report it. We got two more reports similar to that within a few minutes of the first one. He didn’t do anything, but ... it scared a lot of people.”

“That’s Joshua,” I said.

“When my guys rolled up, he changed his story three times about why he was there. First, he said he was waiting for his aunt, then he said he was meeting a friend, then he said he liked the swings.”

“The swings,” I repeated, because that was the dumbest part, and my brain latched onto it like a dog.

Bowen looked at me. “That’s what he said.”

Dad asked, “So you took him in for loitering?”

“No, they didn’t book him or anything,” Bowen said. “They just couldn’t figure out whose kid he was, and they didn’t want him walking away and doing it again somewhere else. He wouldn’t give a name, and they said he kept trying to turn it into a game. He gave one of my officers a fake last name, then tried another one until my guys gave up and treated it like a juvenile John Doe situation. We’ve got a social worker in the building. I only just found out he was here. It just never occurred to me to check holding to see if we had a kid matching the description. I put him in an interview room.”

Dad blinked hard once, like he was forcing himself to stay calm.

“Take us to him,” Dad said.

Bowen didn’t argue. He just turned and led us inside.

Bowen stopped at an empty desk where a woman who looked maybe thirty was sitting.

“Tom,” Bowen said to her. “This is Ms. Carver. She’s with the county.”

Ms. Carver stood up and shook Dad’s hand first, then mine.

"Mr. Sims," she said. "Blake."

I didn't like how calm her voice was.

Dad said, "Where's my son?"

"In Interview Two," Ms. Carver said. "Before we go in, I need to talk to you a minute."

Dad didn't say yes. He didn't say no. He just waited.

Ms. Carver glanced at Bowen, then back to Dad. "Joshua has been ... concerning. I'm not saying that to insult him. He didn't show appropriate concern about why he was being brought in. He wasn't scared or confused, and he didn't ask to call family. The only thing he asked for was a soda. When I asked him basic questions, he tried to steer the conversation away, and when I wouldn't let him do that, he gave multiple stories. When I asked him why he was talking to younger children he didn't know, he said he was 'just curious' and asked me if I had kids. He also refused to give us his real name the entire time."

"And you were going to send him to detention," Dad said, his voice shaky.

"Not tonight, but ... it depends on what happens next."

Dad looked back at Ms. Carver.

"What happens next?"

"If you pick him up tonight and you say you'll cooperate with a safety plan, he leaves with you. If you refuse to take him, or if you tell us you can't keep him supervised or meet the safety plan, then we involve juvenile intake, and he can end up in detention until the court decides what to do with him. Nobody here wants that as the first option. Either way, this incident is going into our system tonight. I'm documenting the officers' observations, what Joshua said, what he refused to say, and what you tell me about supervision at home. Then I'm sending that documentation to the CPS office in your area so they can follow up where you live."

When Dad didn't say anything, I asked, "Follow up how?"

"A home visit. They'll contact you. They'll want to speak to all of you, including his mother, and they may speak to the people at his school. They'll look at what support you have in place and what risks exist in the home. If they think you can keep everyone safe with a plan, that's where it stays. If they think you can't, it escalates."

Dad said, "My wife has surgery Monday."

"I'm sorry," she said. "Tell the local office that as soon as they call. It will change things a little, but it doesn't undo tonight."

"So what do you need from me right now?" he asked.

"I need you to be honest," she said. "About his behavior, about supervision, about whether you can keep him from leaving again. And I need you to understand this isn't punishment. This is a response to risk."

Dad swallowed hard. "Can I see him?"

Ms. Carver nodded. "Yes. And when you do, how you handle it matters, too. If he walks out of here and the adults around him act like this is nothing, that tells my local office everything they need to know."

"This way," Bowen said.

He took us down a hallway to a door with a small window, knocked once, opened it, and motioned us in.

Josh sat at a table with his hands folded, like he was waiting for dinner. His hoodie was off, folded on the chair next to him, and he smiled when he saw us.

"Hey," Josh said.

That was it. Not, "I'm sorry" or "I was scared." Just, "hey."

Dad stopped two steps inside the room.

"Joshua," Dad said.

Josh looked from Dad to me, and his smile got bigger, like this was funny now because we were all together.

"You guys were looking for me," he said.

I stared at him, and I swear it took real effort not to step forward and grab him by the shoulders and shake him until whatever was broken in his brain fell out.

Dad said, "Why didn't you tell them your name?"

Joshua shrugged. "I don't know, didn't feel like it, I guess."

Dad asked, "Why were you at the park?"

"I don't know, I was just there."

"With little kids," Dad said.

Joshua shrugged again. "So? I just wanted to hang out with some kids and have fun. It's so boring at Carol's house."

"Do you understand what you've done tonight?"

"What's the big deal?" he said, flopping back in his chair.

I could feel a fit coming on.

Ms. Carver spoke from the doorway. "Joshua, do you understand why the parents at the park were uncomfortable?"

"They were overreacting."

"Why?" she asked.

"Because people are stupid."

Dad said, "Stand up."

Joshua didn't move.

Dad said it again. "Stand up."

Joshua finally stood, slowly, like he was giving Dad the courtesy of compliance.

Dad pointed to the door. "We're leaving."

Joshua glanced at me as he walked past, like he was checking if I was impressed. In the hallway, Dad stopped and faced her.

"We're taking him home," Dad said.

Ms. Carver nodded. "That's the better option right now if you want to avoid juvenile detention, but my report stands, and CPS will follow up."

Dad nodded once. "I understand."

"Can we stop for food? I'm hungry," Josh asked.

The drive to Aunt Carol's was silent. Joshua sat in the back seat, staring out the window like we were on a road trip instead of the aftermath of a manhunt. My dad's grip on the steering wheel was white-knuckled.

When we got there, the lights were all on, and Carol was waiting on the porch again, but this time Mom was standing next to her, wrapped in a blanket. She looked pale and fragile.

We got out of the car, and Mom's eyes went straight to Joshua. "Baby, are you okay?"

"I'm fine, Mom." He walked right past her into the house without even slowing down.

She turned to my dad. "Tom, what's going on? Carol said something about the police, and social workers, and ..."

"Inside," my dad said. "We need to talk."

We all went into Carol's living room. Joshua had already gone to sit on the couch and had flipped on the TV like nothing had happened. Mom sat down across from him, still watching him like he might disappear again.

"Heather. CPS is involved."

That got her attention. "What? What did you do?"

"I didn't do anything. Joshua was picked up by police earlier tonight. He was found acting strangely around a group of younger children at a park, and a social worker evaluated him and recommended a formal referral."

"That's ridiculous. He's twelve years old and was probably just playing."

"He wasn't playing. The social worker was very concerned about his behavior. They were thinking about putting him straight into juvenile detention."

Mom's face went through about three different expressions in two seconds. Confusion, denial, and finally, fear.

"They can't ... they can't take him, can they?"

"They're not going to take him tonight, but someone from CPS in Midland is going to arrange a home visit. They're going to want to talk to both of us, Heather, about his behavior and what you've been doing to address it."

"I haven't ... he doesn't have behavior problems!"

"Heather." My dad's voice cracked. "Stop. Just ... stop. I can't do this anymore. I can't keep pretending everything is fine when it's not. Our son was just described as 'manipulative' and 'concerning' by police officers who spent an hour with him. These are cops with years on the street dealing with murderers and gang members, and they said our son creeped them out. A veteran social worker was 'shaken' after talking to him. *This isn't normal.*"

Mom didn't say anything. She just sat there, staring at Joshua, who just zoned out, watching TV.

"We have to go home," my dad continued. "Tonight. Joshua needs to be back in Wheaton before anyone can claim we're hiding him or running. You can stay here if you want, or you can come home. It's your call. But if you stay here, you need to understand what that looks like to CPS."

"You have surgery on Monday," I reminded her.

"I know."

For a minute, I wasn't sure what she was going to do, then she finally said, "Okay. I'll come."

Carol helped her pack while my dad and I loaded Josh into the car. He went without a fight, which was somehow worse than if he'd thrown a tantrum. He just climbed into the back seat, buckled his seatbelt, and waited.

Mom came out a few minutes later, still wrapped in her blanket. She hugged Carol, said something I couldn't hear, and got into the front seat. She didn't look at any of us.

The drive home took forever. Nobody talked, not even a peep. Except for Josh. He hummed some tune I didn't recognize the whole way back.

The only time he stopped was when he caught me looking at him. He gave me this smile like we were best friends.

Then he went back to humming.

Chapter 33

I didn't sleep much that night. Every time I started to drift off, I'd hear Joshua humming in my head, that same tuneless noise from the car ride home, and my eyes would snap open again.

By the time the sun came up, I'd maybe gotten three hours total, and none of them were good.

I dragged myself out of bed around eight and found Dad already in the kitchen, nursing a cup of coffee that looked like it had been sitting there for a while.

"Where is everyone?" I asked, pulling out a chair.

"Joshua is still asleep," he said. "Your mother is in the living room. She's been up for a while."

"Did you sleep at all?"

He shook his head. "I spent the night thinking about everything, and I'm done waiting."

"She's going to fight you. Especially with the surgery tomorrow, she's going to say it's too much stress."

"I know. Get your brother up and tell him to come to the living room."

I nodded and headed upstairs.

Josh's door was closed, but I didn't even pause, just pushed it open without knocking. He was sprawled on his bed, mouth open, sleeping like he hadn't terrified a park full of families twelve hours ago.

"Get up," I said.

He groaned and rolled over, pulling the sheet up. "Go away."

I grabbed the bottom of the sheet and ripped it off him. "Dad wants you in the living room. Now!"

Joshua sat up, blinking. He looked so normal. That was the thing about him that always messed with my head; if you didn't know how psychotic he was, you'd just see a twelve-year-old boy with messy hair.

"What's his problem?" Joshua muttered, rubbing his eyes.

"Move, Josh."

He rolled his eyes but swung his legs out of bed. "Can I put pants on?"

"Hurry up."

When we got downstairs, Mom was on the couch wrapped in her quilt. She looked worse than Dad. When we walked in, she looked up, and her face softened immediately when she saw Josh.

"Hi, baby."

"Hey, Mom," Joshua said.

He went to sit next to her until Dad intercepted him.

"On the chair, Joshua," Dad said.

He froze and looked at Mom, then back to Dad.

"Why can't I sit with Mom?"

"Because I said so. Sit on the chair."

Joshua huffed and dropped into the recliner. I took the spot on the other end of the couch. Dad stood in the middle of the room holding the folder from Whitmore Military Academy.

"We need to make a decision," Dad said. "And we need to make it right now."

Mom pulled the quilt close. "Tom, please. Can't this wait? I have to be at the hospital at four tomorrow afternoon, and my head hurts. I can't handle a fight right now."

"We don't have time to wait, because on Monday, while you're getting ready for surgery, CPS is going to be opening a file. They're going to be calling the school and our neighbors, and if we don't have a plan in place, a real plan, not just promises, they are going to make one for us."

"They aren't going to do that," Mom said, waving a trembling hand. "You're overreacting. The woman last night was just trying to scare us. Joshua didn't break any laws."

"He doesn't have to break a law for CPS to get involved. He just has to do something that makes the state concerned for his safety or the safety of other children. He refused to identify himself to a police officer, he stalked a group of children, and he lied repeatedly. That's enough."

"He was playing!" Mom snapped. "He's a child, Tom. He has an active imagination. He was pretending to be someone else. Kids do that."

"He's twelve, Heather, not five. Twelve-year-olds don't go to parks alone to watch toddlers. They don't give police fake names for an hour just to see what happens."

"He was scared!"

"He wasn't scared," I said.

Mom turned on me. "Stay out of this, Blake. You've hated him for years. I know you love seeing him in trouble because it makes you look like the perfect son."

"I don't love this," I said. "I hate this. I hate that we had to drive to Lubbock in the middle of the night. I hate that I found a dead cat in our garage last month."

"He didn't kill that cat!" Mom shouted. "It was sick! He told me he found it like that!"

"He tied it up, Mom, with knots all around it. Did he tell you that part?"

"Stop it!" She put her hands over her ears. "I don't want to hear it! I can't take this stress, Tom. Do you want me to die? Is that it?"

In the past, that would have stopped him, but this time he didn't even flinch. Too much had happened.

"I want our son to stay out of prison, because that is exactly where he is heading."

He threw the folder onto the coffee table. It landed with a slap that made Josh jump.

"That is the application for Whitmore Academy," Dad said. "I spoke to the admissions director on Friday, and they have a spot open for immediate intake. It's a therapeutic program. They have counselors, psychologists, and structure that can help him."

"It's a prison for bad kids. You want to send him away to Montana? He's a baby, Tom, he needs his mother."

"He needs help that we can't give him," Dad said. "We have tried it your way for years. We've made excuses, we've covered for him, and look where that got him."

"I can handle him," she insisted. "Once the surgery is over ... once the tumor is out, I'll be myself again. I'll be able to watch him. I've just been sick, that's all, that's why things have gotten out of hand. It's my fault, not his. Don't punish him because I've been sick."

"This started way before the tumor."

"That's not true!"

"It is true," Dad said. "And you know it."

Josh spoke up. "Mom? I don't want to go."

He was doing that thing where he was trying to sound like a small child instead of a pre-teen again.

Mom reached out for him, but he was too far away. "I know, baby. You're not going. I won't let him take you."

"I promise I'll be good," Josh said, tears in his eyes. It was a good performance. "Dad, I'm sorry, I was just bored. I won't do it again, please don't send me away."

Dad looked at Joshua for a long time. He loved him; that was the killer. He wanted to believe him. He wanted to hug him and say it was okay. I could see it in his eyes.

"I know you don't want to go," Dad said gently. "But this isn't a negotiation, son. You need to learn things that we can't teach you here. You need to learn responsibility and empathy, and you're not learning them in this house."

"I hate you!" Joshua screamed, turning on a dime. "You're trying to get rid of me!"

"See?" Mom said. "He's terrified! You're traumatizing him!"

"He's manipulating you, Heather!" Dad yelled back. His patience finally cracked. "Look at him! One second he's crying, the next he's screaming. He is playing you!"

"He is not!"

"Goddamnit, Heather, wake up!" Dad slammed his hand on the wall, making us all jump. "Wake up! The social worker told me that if we don't take severe action, she is going to recommend removal. Do you know what that means? It means foster care, it means a group home, it means strangers raising him."

"They wouldn't," Mom whispered.

"They would. And it's not just Joshua."

Mom blinked. "What?"

"If CPS decides that we are unfit, if they decide that we are enabling a dangerous child and refusing to protect the other people in this house, they don't just take the problem child. They take ***all*** the children."

I was pretty sure Dad was bluffing here. If I were younger, closer to Josh's age, maybe, but at almost sixteen, there would have to be active danger for me in the house.

What actually hurt was that this didn't really seem to bother Mom. No screaming about not losing me.

"I doubt they'd take Blake, but you can't do this without my consent."

"Watch me," Dad said. "I'll go to a judge tomorrow morning before your surgery, lay out every single thing Joshua has done for the last three years, the police report from Lubbock, and photos of the cat. I'll ask the state to order his removal to the school if I have to, but odds are that would still put him in the system."

"Mom," Joshua said. "Don't let him."

The spell was breaking. I could see it in her eyes. The fear of losing control, the fear of the surgery, the fear of the state coming into her house, it was all piling up.

Mom looked at the folder on the table. She reached out a shaking hand and touched the cover.

"How long?" she asked.

"The term is a year," Dad said. "But it depends on his progress. He stays until he's ready to come back. After his first month, he'll get to come home during holidays, so it won't even be that long till he comes home for Christmas."

"A year?"

"We can visit," Dad said. "Once he reaches the first level of privileges. We can write. We can call."

"It's so far away."

"It has to be. He needs a reset."

Mom looked at Josh again. "Josh ... maybe ... maybe it's for the best, just for a little while."

Josh's face twisted. "No! You promised! You said you'd never let him send me away!"

"If they take you to a foster home, you'll be gone forever. I couldn't bear that. This is a school, your dad says it's nice."

“It’s a jail!” Joshua screamed. He jumped out of the chair. “I’m not going! I’ll run away! I swear to God, I’ll run away, and you’ll never see me again!”

Dad moved fast. He stepped in front of Joshua, blocking the door.

“You are not going anywhere,” Dad said. “Go to your room. Pack a bag. We leave in two hours.”

“Mom!” Josh shrieked. It was a primal, desperate sound.

Mom covered her face with her hands and sobbed. “Do what your father says, Joshua. Please. Just do what he says.”

Josh stood there for a second, looking from Mom to Dad. He realized, finally, that he was out of options. His manipulations weren’t working anymore.

He turned his head and looked at me. His eyes were pure venom.

“You did this.”

I just stared back.

“Go pack,” Dad said.

Josh spun around and stomped upstairs, slamming his door so hard the pictures on the wall rattled.

The silence that followed was absolute. Dad walked over and sat on the coffee table in front of her, reaching out to take her hands.

“Heather,” he said softly.

She pulled her hands away. “Don’t,” she sobbed. “Just don’t. You won, alright. You got what you wanted.”

“I am saving him. We are saving him.”

“He’s going to hate me. My baby is going to hate me.”

“He’s going to grow up. He’s going to be safe, and so are we.”

“I’ll go make sure he’s actually packing,” I said, wanting to give them some privacy.

Dad nodded without looking at me. “Thanks, Blake.”

I could hear Josh throwing things around in his room as I climbed the stairs. I stopped at his door and listened. He was muttering to himself, a low, angry stream of words I couldn’t catch.

For the first time, it felt like we might be able to avoid him becoming what he had become in the dream. Although I couldn’t be sure.

But then I remembered the look he gave me. The pure hate.

I opened the door. "Need help?"

Joshua threw a sneaker at my head. I caught it easily.

"Get out."

"Make sure you pack warm clothes," I said, tossing the shoe onto his bed. "Montana gets cold."

I closed the door and went to my room. Two hours later, the car was loaded. Dad had borrowed a friend's sedan, since he couldn't leave his patrol cruiser at the airport, and we needed Mom's station wagon to get her to her surgery.

Mom had retreated to her bedroom and didn't come out to say goodbye. She said it was because her head hurt, but I think she just couldn't face him.

Josh came out of the house and walked past me without a word, getting into the back seat of the car.

Dad came out last, carrying a small duffel bag for himself. He stopped on the porch where I was standing.

"I'll be back late tomorrow night," he said. "Or Tuesday morning. I'll call you after I get him settled and I get checked into a hotel. Are you sure you can get your mom to her surgery?"

"Yeah, I'll take care of it," I said.

"Carol is a phone call away if something happens. Hopefully, I'm back before she's released from the hospital."

"Okay."

"Call me if she gets ... if she needs anything."

"I will."

He hesitated, like he wanted to say more, but there were no words for this. He just nodded and walked to the car.

I watched them pull out of the driveway, stood there until the car disappeared around the corner.

The rest of the weekend was brutal in its silence.

Mom stayed in her room pretty much the whole time, and when she did come out to use the bathroom or get water from the kitchen, she wouldn't even look at me. I tried to talk to her twice, and both times she just walked past me like I wasn't there.

By Sunday night, I was actually looking forward to Monday, anything to get out of that house. The tension was suffocating.

I'd already talked to Coach Holloway about missing afternoon practice. He wasn't thrilled since I'd just missed it to go shopping with Li the week before, but when I explained my mom had surgery scheduled, he understood. Family came first, and I could make it up Tuesday.

The plan was simple: go to school, come home around three, and drive Mom to the hospital for her four o'clock check-in. Dad would meet us there as soon as he got back from dropping Josh off. The surgery was scheduled for six, so he probably wouldn't be back before the surgery happened, but he should be there while she recovered.

So Monday afternoon, I walked back to the house and started working through how the evening was going to go in my head. The first thing I noticed was that Mom's station wagon wasn't in the driveway. While she could have gone out running errands, she hadn't been doing much of that lately, and I doubted she'd do it right before her surgery.

The other weird thing was that the front door was unlocked.

"Mom?" I called out as I stepped inside. Nothing. "Mom, we need to leave in like thirty minutes!"

Still nothing.

I dropped my backpack and went looking. The kitchen and the living room were empty. Sometimes when she went somewhere, she'd leave a message on the answering machine, but the light wasn't blinking.

Her bedroom door was open. Inside, her nightstand was cleared off, the various pills for her headaches, both actual ones and the nonsense herbal stuff the quack had been giving her were missing.

I don't know why I checked, but I looked in her closet and found it half empty. The hangers were still there, but maybe a third of her clothes were gone. Dresses and the nicer stuff she'd stopped wearing when she got sick were there, but everything else was gone. The same was true in the dresser drawers.

All of her everyday clothes were gone.

Worse, her jewelry box was also missing.

"No," I said out loud. "No, no, no."

I ran to the hall closet where we kept the luggage. Two of the suitcases were missing, the big blue one and the smaller rolling one.

She left. She'd decided to skip her surgery and leave us.

I went to the kitchen on autopilot, checked the answering machine again, even though I knew there were no messages, and then looked for a note anywhere she might have possibly left one.

I found nothing.

Dad had called the night before and left his flight information, saying that Josh was at the academy and they were already working with him, which was great and all, but I needed him here to help deal with this.

Instead, he was somewhere over Colorado or Kansas, thirty thousand feet up with no idea what he was coming home to.

There was nothing I could do but wait.

I tried calling Carol once, thinking Mom might have gone there again, but she said she hadn't talked to Mom since we left Lubbock. I asked her to call if she talked to her and that I'd have Dad call her once he got home.

I didn't know what to do with myself.

I paced the living room, sat on the couch, got up, checked the driveway, sat back down, over and over until I started to drive myself crazy. I made myself a sandwich but realized I wasn't hungry at all as soon as I'd made it, turned on the TV, and couldn't even focus on that.

Every time I heard a car on our street, I jumped up and looked out the window. But it was never her or Dad, just someone else on the street.

Around eleven-thirty, headlights finally swept across the front window, and a car pulled into the driveway. I was out the door before he even had it in park.

He climbed out looking exhausted. The trip must have been bad since Josh was fighting it so hard, plus the stress of having to put your kid in a place like that.

And I was about to make it a lot worse.

"She's gone," I said before he could even get to the porch.

He stopped mid-stride. "What?"

"Mom, she's gone. She wasn't here when I got home from school. Her car was gone, along with two of the suitcases and a bunch of her clothes."

He stood there for a second, keys still in his hand. "That doesn't ... maybe she went to the hospital early. Maybe she ..."

"The hospital called when she missed her appointment and said they'd have to give the slot to someone else. She's gone."

He didn't say anything. He just walked past me into the house, looking around like he expected to find something I'd missed.

"Tell me exactly what you found," he said.

"I got home around three. Her car wasn't in the driveway, and the front door was unlocked. There were a few things out, like a coffee cup on the kitchen counter that was empty and dry, and she'd clearly packed bags. Her drawers were empty, but there were a few socks and things she'd dropped while she was packing and left behind. I looked everywhere for a note, but there isn't one, and she didn't leave a message on the machine."

He stood there in the middle of the kitchen, his hands hanging at his sides. For a second, he looked lost, like a kid who'd wandered away from his parents at a fair.

"Where would she go?" he asked.

He wasn't asking me, just saying it out loud.

"I called Carol. She hasn't seen or heard from her, but I told her you'd call later."

Dad pulled out a chair and sat down.

"This is my fault," he said.

"No, it's not."

"I pushed too hard with Joshua. I should have waited until after her surgery, should have ..."

"We had to deal with him. He was only getting worse. And that may not have stopped her either. She's been fighting this surgery since day one. I had to threaten her to get her this far. Josh was just an excuse."

He covered his face with both hands. "I don't understand her, Blake. I've been married to her for twenty years, and I don't understand her. She has something growing in her brain that is going to kill her, and she runs away from the only thing that can save her."

"She's scared."

"We're all scared! That doesn't mean you abandon your family!"

His voice broke on the last word. I knew he was really worried because normally he wouldn't talk to me about this kind of thing. This was 'private' stuff and not for kids.

"What do we do?" I asked.

"I don't know. I need time to think. I can file a missing persons report and put out a description of her car, but if she's gone of her own volition, there's nothing we can do. She's an adult."

"That's it?"

"For now. I need to think, and I need to sleep to clear my head. You need to sleep too; you've got school tomorrow."

"I'm not going to school while Mom's missing."

"Blake ..."

"I'm not." I met his eyes. "Don't even try to argue with me on this."

He stared at me for a moment, then nodded.

"Fine. One day. But if she's not back by Wednesday, you're going. Life doesn't stop because ..."

He couldn't finish the sentence.

"I know."

We sat there in the kitchen, neither of us moving.

"She's going to die," I said. "If she doesn't get that surgery, the tumor's going to keep growing, and it will kill her."

"I know what the doctor said."

"So she's either going to come back and get the surgery, or she's going to die alone somewhere. Those are the only two options."

Dad reached across the table and put his hand on my arm. "We're going to find her."

I wanted to believe him, I really did, but sitting there in that empty house, it was hard to believe in anything. All the knowledge I had of the future, and not a bit of it did any good.

"I'm sorry," Dad said. "For all of this. You shouldn't have to deal with this at your age. You should be worrying about football and girls and grades, not ... this."

"Yeah, well, that's not the hand we've been dealt."

He gripped my arm for a second, then let go. "Get some rest. I'm going to make some calls, see if anyone's heard from her."

I kind of half nodded and went upstairs, but I couldn't fall asleep. I lay in my bed, staring at the ceiling, listening to Dad's muffled voice as he worked the phone downstairs.

At some point, the calls stopped, and the house went quiet.

Chapter 34

The week crawled by with no answers.

Dad heard through a law enforcement buddy he'd asked to do some discreet drive-bys that someone matching Mom's description might be staying with Yogi Theodor, the quack healer she'd been seeing, but they weren't able to confirm anything, and her car wasn't there.

It was possible she'd moved on from there, knowing Dad would be looking for her.

Dad filed the missing person report after seventy-two hours, like he said he would, giving descriptions of Mom and her car to every department in the region, and then we just waited. There was nothing else to do. She was an adult who'd left on her own, and unless she committed a crime or turned up in a hospital, we were stuck.

With Dad being a cop, we would probably get notified if they found her, but if she didn't want to come home, they'd close the missing persons report, and that would be that.

I went to school Tuesday, like Dad insisted, but I might as well have been a ghost. I sat through classes without hearing a word, sucked at football practice, and just barely made any effort at all.

I knew inside I was making a mistake. I'd already gotten pulled aside because of my grades, and I'd already seen how bad games went when my head wasn't in it, but I just couldn't get it together. Things were falling apart, and I just didn't know what to do.

I remembered Yesica's advice, and I tried putting my head down and just playing, to at least fix the football part, but I couldn't. At least with the cancer diagnosis, we had a plan. Yeah, it was scary, but there were steps being taken.

Now, there was nothing. No plan, no options, nothing.

People noticed, of course. Li, Eduardo, Coach Holloway, they all asked me what was going on, but every time I even started to try to talk about it, I almost lost my shit. I just needed some time for Dad and I to figure out what the hell we were going to do if she didn't come back, if we got a call next year that she'd been found dead in a motel, the untreated tumor finally catching up with her.

Every time I thought about the next step, I just shut down a little more.

By Friday, homecoming night, the pressure felt physical.

The parking lot at Wilfred Field was already packed when Dad dropped me off. Homecoming was always the biggest game of the regular season, and with us undefeated and facing Midland Lee, pretty much the whole town had turned out.

"I know you're not okay," he said. "But try to focus on the game. Your teammates are counting on you."

I just nodded and grabbed my bag, making my way to the field house, trying to clear my head. Coach Holloway gave his pre-game speech about pride and tradition and representing Wheaton, but the words bounced off me.

With everything going on, I'd completely forgotten Elijah would be here, playing for Midland. It wasn't until I got on the field and saw him that I remembered.

I tried to ignore him and focus on loosening up, but I could feel him watching me from across the field. After ten minutes, he started drifting closer, talking to a Lee teammate but angling toward our side.

"Hey, Sims!"

I turned. Elijah stood about fifteen yards away, grinning like we were old friends.

"Ready to get your ass beat tonight?"

Normally, that kind of thing would have just rolled off me, but not this week.

"Walk away," Mickey said.

I didn't move.

Elijah took a few steps closer. "What's the matter? Upset that you're not so special when you're facing real competition?"

I still didn't say anything.

"Or what? You gonna cry about it? Maybe call your mommy?" he said, laughing.

That was enough. At the mention of my mother, I was ready to put all the pain and hurt I felt all week straight into his face. Maybe beating the shit out of him would make me feel better.

I charged at him, but Mickey and Andre, who'd both been watching and getting closer to me, I guess predicting this was coming, grabbed me, practically lifting me off the ground as I fought to get past them.

"Let it go," Mickey said. "We have a game to play. He's not worth it."

"Tonight's gonna be fun," Elijah said, still grinning, thinking he'd just gotten my goat and not knowing how close he'd come to me killing him. "I'm gonna make you look like the fraud you are."

More of our guys crowded around, forming a wall between me and Elijah. Across the field, a couple of Lee's coaches noticed the confrontation and started heading our way.

"Gardner," one of them yelled.

"Just being friendly," Elijah called back to them, holding up his hands. "See you out there, Sims."

He jogged back toward his team. I'd stopped struggling, but I could feel how red my face was. I was seeing murder.

"Don't let him get in your head," Andre said.

Too late for that.

The game started physical.

Lee's defense came out aggressively, blitzing on the first play and nearly taking my head off before I could get the ball away, and I heard Elijah talking trash from the sideline even during the play.

I missed Joe on an out route that should have been routine. The ball sailed high, and Joe had to leap for it, but he couldn't bring it down. Second down, I forced a throw into coverage, trying to hit Brian deep, and their safety nearly picked it off.

Third and long. The pocket collapsed, and I tried to scramble, but one of their linebackers caught me from behind, driving me into the turf. The hit wasn't late, but it was hard, and I stayed down for a second trying to get air back in my lungs.

Andre offered me a hand up. "You good?"

"Yeah."

We punted, and Lee took over. Their quarterback was decent, nothing special, but Elijah had definitely made progress and was playing really well, making two momentum catches on that first drive, including a third-down conversion where he beat Calvin on a slant and picked up eighteen yards.

Our defense held them to a field goal, but we were down three-zero.

The rest of the first half was ugly. I kept missing throws, forcing reads, trying to make something happen instead of taking what the defense gave me. Twice, I held the ball too long and took hits I could have avoided. Once, I scrambled for a first down when I should have thrown it away, and the safety lit me up right as I got to the marker.

We managed one touchdown on a drive where I finally settled down and hit Austin on a post route, but Lee answered with a touchdown of their own, Elijah catching a fade in the end zone that he celebrated like he'd won the Super Bowl.

At halftime, it was ten-seven, Lee.

In the locker room, Coach Holloway tore into us. "I don't know what the fuck that was, but it wasn't Wheaton football. That was the most uncontrolled, undisciplined football I've seen in my entire career. If we don't get it together, they're going to take us apart. Blake, I need you to settle down. You're pressing. Take the easy completions, move the chains, and let the game come to you."

Everyone looked at me, and I knew they all knew when he said undisciplined, he meant me. I was the weak link tonight.

I knew I needed to get it together, but between Mom and Elijah and hell, even Josh, I couldn't get my head in the game.

And all of Elijah's shit talking wasn't helping either.

The third quarter started a little better. I hit Mickey on a screen pass that he took for twenty yards, then found Miguel over the middle for another eighteen. We were moving, and the rhythm started to come back.

We were nine and goal line when things fell apart. They were pressing hard, and the pocket was collapsing on our second down after I'd already blown a pass, with two of their defensive linemen beating our tackles.

I don't know where my head was at. I saw them coming, had nowhere to go, but instead of throwing it away, or even scrambling, I froze. I just stood there as they smashed into me, one low and one high.

The impact folded me at the waist, twisting me and flipping me end over end twice before the ground came up and smashed into me.

I tried to push myself up, but my lower back screamed, and my legs didn't want to work right. For a second, I thought I might pass out.

"Blake!" Andre was there, down on one knee. "Don't move, man. Don't move."

Guys crowded around, and someone shouted for the trainers.

The pain was a constant fire centered in my lower back and radiating down my legs. I wanted to get up, wanted to walk it off, but when I tried to move, everything hurt worse.

"Stay still," Mickey said.

Mr. Lassiter, our head trainer, sprinted onto the field with his medical bag, with Mr. Romero right behind him with more equipment. The crowd had gone silent.

"Alright, everyone back up," Lassiter said, kneeling next to me. "Blake, can you hear me?"

"Yeah."

"Good. Can you feel your legs?"

"Yes."

"Can you move your toes?"

I tried. They moved. "Yes."

"Good. Where's the pain?"

"Lower back," I groaned.

"Stabbing or dull?"

"Stabbing."

"Any tingling? Numbness?"

"No. Just pain."

"Alright. Let's get him on a backboard. Blake, we're going to lay you flat and get a board under you. Tell me immediately if anything feels worse."

Mr. Romero put a neck brace on me.

I could see faces sliding past me out of my peripheral vision as they carried me off the field, looking up at the sky.

Dad was already pushing through to the sideline as they brought me off, his face pale.

"How bad is it?" he demanded.

"Possible compression injury," Mr. Lassiter said, not breaking stride. "He has sensation and movement, but with this kind of impact, we don't take chances. Ambulance is on the way."

They got me into the training room and Mr. Lassiter had me lying flat on the table while Mr. Romero gathered supplies. Mr. Lassiter kept asking questions: could I feel this, could I move that, did the pain change when he pressed here or there. Everything worked, which we all took as a good sign, but everything hurt.

"We're leaving you in a collar and on a board for transport," Mr. Lassiter said. "Until we get imaging, I don't want to risk anything with your back."

"I don't need ..."

"Blake," Dad said, cutting me off. "Let them do their job."

The ambulance arrived within ten minutes and the paramedics consulted with Mr. Lassiter, checked my vitals again, and loaded me into the back. Dad climbed in after me.

"Sir, you can follow in your vehicle," one of the paramedics said.

"I'm coming with him."

I stared at the ceiling of the ambulance as we pulled out, the siren mercifully silent. I guess I wasn't in big enough trouble to need them to run the sirens; we only had the lights going. Mr. Lassiter had me sent to Midland Memorial, which was a good drive, but it apparently also had the imaging equipment I'd need.

"I really sucked tonight," I said.

"I don't care about the game right now, Blake."

I cared, because it might be my last game ever.

The hospital ceiling had a crack in it.

I'd been staring at it for what felt like an hour, lying flat on a gurney in some examination room while machines beeped and people came and went. They'd taken me for X-rays, done some kind of scan, poked and prodded my back, and now I was just waiting.

Dad sat in a plastic chair next to me. It had been a bad week for him, with Mom leaving, having to take Josh to the school, and now me getting hurt. He hadn't said much since we got here, but he hadn't left either.

"You don't have to stay," I said.

"I'm staying."

The door opened and a doctor walked in, a thin guy with glasses and a clipboard.

"Alright, Blake. Good news first," he said, pulling up a stool. "Nothing's broken. No fractures, no structural damage to the spine. Your vertebrae look fine."

"So I'm good?"

"Not exactly. You've got significant swelling in the muscles around your lower spine, and there's pressure on the surrounding tissue. The impact compressed everything pretty hard. Right now, your body's trying to protect itself, which is why you're in so much pain."

"But it'll heal, right?"

"I think so, but a lot depends on how quickly the swelling goes down and the pressure comes off. This will all take some time; we're talking at least three weeks minimum before you should even think about contact sports. Could be longer depending on how your back responds to rest and treatment."

Three weeks put us at the playoffs.

"I can't be out three weeks."

"Blake ..." Dad started.

"We're in the middle of the season. We're undefeated. I can't just ..."

"You can, and you will," Dad said.

The doctor changed the subject, saying, "I'm also concerned about the concussion you sustained. Combined with the spinal trauma, we're keeping you overnight for observation."

"Overnight? No. No way. I feel fine."

"You feel fine because you were given pain medication in the ambulance. Once that wears off, you're going to feel very different." He looked at my dad. "Mr. Sims, I need to be clear about this. If Blake tries to return too soon, he risks extending his recovery significantly. We're talking months instead of weeks. And if he takes another hit to that area before it heals properly, there's potential for permanent damage."

"He'll sit out."

"Dad ..."

"Blake." His voice left no room for argument. "You're going to do what the doctor tells you to do."

I wanted to fight it, but the look on his face shut me down. The door opened again and Coach Holloway walked in with Mr. Lassiter right behind him.

"How bad?" Coach asked.

The doctor ran through it again: the swelling, the pressure, three weeks minimum, possible longer recovery, overnight observation.

"Three weeks puts us at the first round of playoffs," Coach said. "Assuming we make it."

"We'd make it if I played," I said.

"I've seen this before, Blake. Kids think they're invincible, rush back too soon, and end up done for the season, or worse, done for good."

"We can set up a rehab schedule," Mr. Lassiter said. "Physical therapy, controlled exercises, gradual return to mobility, but I agree, Blake stays off the field completely until we get medical clearance. No practice, no drills, nothing. He can observe games, and that's it."

"Observe?" I asked. "Coach, the team needs ..."

"The team needs you healthy for the playoffs," Coach said. "What they don't need is their starting quarterback making a minor injury into a major one because he couldn't sit still for three weeks. Gabriel can handle the games."

"Gabriel's not me."

"No, he's not," Coach said. "But he's what we've got right now, because you decided to stand in the pocket like a statue instead of throwing the ball away. That's not on Gabriel. That's on you."

I physically felt the words. I wanted to defend myself, to explain that my head wasn't in the game because of Mom, because of everything, but what was the point? He was right. I'd played like crap, and now I was paying for it.

"I'm telling you once, Blake," Coach continued. "You try to force your way back early, you're going to make this worse. Do you want to end up paralyzed, living in a wheelchair?"

"No, sir."

"Then you rest and do what the doctors tell you. You come to practice, you watch film, you stay mentally engaged, but you do not touch a football until you're cleared. Are we clear?"

"Yes, sir."

"Good." He looked at Dad. "Tom, I'll make sure the school knows he's excused for as long as he needs and gets help going to class and whatnot."

"Appreciate that," Dad said.

"I'm going to get you some muscle relaxers which should help take some of the pressure off for a bit," the doctor said. "They'll make you drowsy, which is fine, you need rest. We'll do the additional tests first thing in the morning, and if everything looks good, you can go home tomorrow afternoon."

"Is there any chance it'll take less than three weeks?"

"There's always a chance, but I wouldn't count on it. Your body's going to tell you when it's ready, not your calendar," he said, and left.

"I'll put together a detailed schedule and drop it by tomorrow," Mr. Lassiter said. "We'll start with gentle stretching once the swelling goes down, then build from there. The key is gradual progression, no shortcuts."

"Right."

"Get some rest, Blake," Coach Holloway said. "I mean it. The team's going to be fine. Your job right now is to heal."

He and Mr. Lassiter stepped out into the hallway, and I could hear them talking to Dad in low voices. Something about the game—we'd won, apparently—and about managing the team's expectations.

I wanted to listen and was happy we'd won, but all I felt was the fear that I was losing something I'd worked so hard to build.

A nurse came in a few minutes later, a middle-aged woman with kind eyes. She checked my vitals, hung a new IV bag, and injected something into the line.

"This will help with the muscle spasms," she said. "You're going to feel sleepy pretty quickly."

She wasn't wrong. Within minutes, things started to blur, and a warmth spread through my limbs.

"Alright, let's get you to your room," she said, unlocking the wheels on the bed. "You've got a private one down the hall. Your father can stay as long as he likes."

Dad walked beside the bed as she wheeled me out, one hand on the railing like he was afraid I might roll away. Through the doorway, I could see Coach Holloway and Mr. Lassiter still talking to the doctor.

They were probably discussing me. My injury, my timeline, my future.

And I couldn't do a damn thing about any of it except lie here.

Chapter 35

Dad left around nine to handle insurance paperwork and make phone calls. I told him I'd be fine, I wasn't going anywhere. He didn't laugh.

My back hurt. The medication helped, but every time I moved even a little, there was a dull ache that spread from my lower spine up through my ribs.

I tried not to move, just stared at the ceiling. At least the crack was different to the one in the exam room. That was progress.

A soft knock came at the door. I expected a nurse, maybe someone checking vitals again.

"Yeah?"

The door opened and Li stepped in.

She was still wearing what she'd had on at the game, jeans and one of those blue and white Wheaton pep shirts and she looked tired. Or worried. Maybe both.

"Hey," she said, closing the door behind her.

"Hey." I tried to push myself up a little and immediately regretted it. Pain shot through my lower back, and I dropped back against the pillow. "Damn."

Li crossed the room and pulled the visitor's chair closer to the bed. "Don't try to move. I heard they brought you here and came as soon as I could. What did the doctors say?"

"Bruised ribs, a concussion, and some kind of compression issue in my lower back. Three weeks minimum before I can even think about playing again."

"Are you in pain?"

"The medication's helping, but yeah, every time I try to move my back, it reminds me it's there. How'd we do?"

"We won."

"What was the final?"

"Fourteen to thirteen."

"We should have done better. My fault."

"Blake ..."

"It is. I wasn't in the right headspace."

"Yea, I saw you talking to Elijah."

"He came up to me before the game and made a crack about my mom. It wasn't even a good crack, but with everything going on, I just snapped. I let him get under my skin and was distracted the whole first half, and then I took that hit because I held the ball too long instead of throwing it away. Stupid."

Li didn't argue. She knew me well enough to know that would make it worse.

"You should have gone to the dance," I said.

"What?"

"Homecoming. You spent all that time picking out that dress and convincing your mom to let you go. Now you're sitting in a hospital room."

Li shrugged. "The dance would have been like every other school event, me standing near a wall while other people talked around me. I wanted to see you, see how you were doing."

I moved, trying to find a position that didn't hurt, and Li reached out to slip a hand behind my back, adjusting the pillow for more support.

"Better?"

"Yeah." It actually was. "Thanks."

She sat back in the chair, hands folded in her lap. "What's been going on? I gave you your space this week because it seemed like you needed it, but you've been really distant. Did something happen with your mom's surgery?"

I'd been avoiding this conversation with everyone, Eduardo, the guys on the team, but Li was here asking, and I was too tired to keep pretending everything was fine.

"The surgery didn't happen."

"What do you mean?"

"She left a few days before she was supposed to have it." I looked at Li. "There's more. We found out Josh was killing cats, deliberately. Tying them up and ..." I couldn't finish the sentence.

"My dad and I tried to get him into this military academy that helps kids with problems like that, but Mom didn't want to do that. She and Dad fought about it to the point she went to stay with a friend in Lubbock, then Joshua ran away while they were up there, and the police and Child Protective Services got involved ..."

"CPS?"

"Yeah. They threatened to take both of us if my parents didn't do something, so Dad finally got Josh into the school. They flew out last weekend. While he was gone, Mom packed her stuff and left without a note. Just disappeared."

Li went pale. "I'm so sorry. I had no idea."

"How could you? I didn't tell anyone." I laughed without humor. "I've been worried all week; it's really messed with my head. So when Elijah said something about her, I let it get to me. I can't stop thinking, what happens if she never comes back?" What if the tumor keeps growing and she dies somewhere alone because I pushed too hard on the Josh thing and made everything fall apart?"

"You can't control what she does, only what you do. You had to do something about Josh. If he was really ... that's not normal or safe. If you hadn't pushed, he would have gotten worse or hurt someone."

"Yeah, I know. Logically, I know that."

"But it still feels like your fault."

"Yeah."

She nodded. "I think that's only natural, to want to take the blame on yourself cause it's the only thing you can control. It doesn't mean you did the wrong thing."

I wanted to believe her, but I wasn't sure how. Neither of us said anything for a while. Somewhere down the hall, a phone rang.

Li looked at her hands. "I didn't know any of this was happening. I should have asked, done something."

"There wasn't anything to do."

"Maybe. When I heard you were in the hospital, I thought ... I didn't know what to think."

"I'm okay."

"You're lying in a hospital bed with a back injury and a concussion."

"Okay, I'm mostly okay."

She almost smiled.

"I'm scared," I blurted out.

The word felt strange coming out of my mouth since I didn't admit to being scared out loud to anyone.

"Scared of what?" Li asked.

"That the injury might be worse than the doctors are saying, that something could be permanently wrong. That I might never play the same way again."

"Did the doctors give any indication of permanent damage?"

"No. They talked about recovery, rest, and physical therapy. They said if I follow the program, I should be fine but I keep thinking about how the hit felt, those two linebackers folding me in half, and there was a moment when my legs wouldn't respond. What if that happens again? What if something's broken that they can't see?"

"The doctors know what they're doing. If they said you'll recover, then you will, you just need to let that happen."

"I don't know how to do that. To just ... wait. Everything I've done the last two years has been about pushing harder, working more, and outrunning whatever's coming next." I laughed. "And now I'm stuck in a bed and I can't do anything."

"Maybe this is different. Maybe this is the one situation where pushing makes things worse. Sometimes the only move is to wait and let other people help."

I took her hand.

She didn't pull away. Her fingers were warm, her grip light but present. We stayed like that for a moment, neither of us saying anything.

"I'm glad you're here," I said.

"I'll stay as long as you need."

We talked for a while after that about nothing heavy. Li told me about stuff she was dealing with on student council and how Mrs. Gonzales had assigned some brutal homework over the weekend. I told her about the weird food they'd brought me earlier, some kind of Jell-O thing that tasted terrible. She laughed at that, and for a few minutes, I forgot about my back, about Mom, and about everything except that Li was sitting next to me and we were talking like normal people.

But the medication was doing its job, making my eyelids heavy, and the conversation slowed as I fought to keep track of what she was saying.

"You need to sleep," Li said.

"Yeah." I didn't argue because I didn't have the energy. "Will you stay until I fall asleep?"

"Yes."

"Good."

I let my eyes close. The sounds of the hospital faded, and the pain in my back dulled to something distant, almost manageable. Li's hand was still in mine as I drifted off.

They released me Saturday morning, and I spent the rest of the day in bed, trying hard to find a position that didn't hurt, while Dad fussed over me. Sunday afternoon, I needed to get out of the house and away from his constant attention, even for just a little bit. I also had to see Yesica.

I didn't want to lose boxing, and I'd promised Yesica I'd never miss a practice, so even as bad as I felt, I needed to explain what had happened to her.

The first thing I'd learned was that I hated crutches.

Normally, I would have walked there, but not today. Even without the crutches bothering me, everything was still a little sore, so Dad had dropped me off on his way to the store so he could get some stuff to make for dinner. He'd told me I had thirty minutes total and to do no training at all.

That was a warning I didn't need. In the state I was in, there was no way I could do training.

"Blake." She stopped wrapping and set the tape aside. "Yen told me what happened. How are you doing?"

"About as well as you'd expect. I wanted to come by and let you know I can't train for a while, at least three weeks, maybe longer depending on how the physical therapy goes."

"What did the doctors say was wrong?"

"I have some kind of compression issue in my lower spine, plus bruised ribs. They told me if I follow the recovery program, I should be fine, but I don't know. Part of me keeps waiting for them to find something else."

"I'm glad it's nothing permanent. I will still come down next week. Since nothing is broken, they will probably clear you for physical therapy soon and I can help with that. I have training in rehabilitation work to build strength back the right way so you don't hurt yourself again."

"Oh, yeah. That'd be great. I appreciate it."

While I did appreciate it, I was having trouble being excited about anything, and I think it showed.

She noticed. Yesica noticed everything.

"Hey, it's going to be okay. I've seen fighters come back from worse than this. You're young and strong and your body wants to heal."

"Sure."

"I mean it, Blake."

"I know you do, but I'm having trouble believing much of anything right now."

"I know. It's why it's important to stay active. Injuries like this can get in your head. Go, spend a few days relaxing, and then come back next weekend ready to work on getting better."

I nodded and left. I knew she meant well, but I wasn't feeling much like a pep talk. I also wanted to go see Li. Getting up the stairs was a production; my arms were tired and my back was reminding me why I was on crutches by the time I reached the top.

Li's door was open and she was at her desk with books spread out in front of her.

I knocked on the doorframe.

She turned. "Blake, they let you out."

"I wanted to talk to Yesica and let her know I can't train for a while." I sat on the edge of her bed, grateful to finally be off the crutches. "And I wanted to thank you for coming to the hospital the other night."

"You don't need to thank me for that."

"Yeah, I do."

"No. I wanted to be there. I came because I needed to see for myself that you were okay."

I didn't know what to say to that.

"What's wrong?" Li asked.

"Nothing and everything, I guess." I tried to laugh, but it came out wrong. "People keep asking me that and I don't really know how to answer anymore."

"Then just talk to me and don't worry about having an answer."

The problem was I'd been holding it together since it happened. In the hospital with Dad, with the coaches who came to check on me, with everyone who asked how I was doing, I'd said the right things and acted like I had it under control, but I didn't.

And it felt like Li was the only one I could tell that to.

"I'm scared," I said.

"Of what?"

"Everything. I'm scared about my back, about whether the doctors are telling me everything or just saying what they think I need to hear. I keep wondering if there's something wrong they can't see on the scans, something that won't show up until it's too late to fix."

"Blake ..."

"Football is the only thing I've been able to control this whole year. Everything else, Mom, Josh ... I couldn't do anything about any of that. So I put my head down and just played football. It was the place where I could just be me and not have to worry about anyone else. And I put everything into it and now that's slipping away and I don't know how to handle losing the one thing that actually made sense."

My voice broke on the last part, my eyes getting wet. I looked away, embarrassed to be sitting here crying in front of her.

"Everything's falling apart at once. My mom is gone, all the stuff with Josh, my back might never be the same."

The tears were falling now and I couldn't stop them. I wiped at my face with the back of my hand, feeling stupid and exposed.

Li sat next to me on the bed and put her hand on my arm.

"You're not alone in this. I'm here, Eddie's here, and you have more people in your corner than you realize. You don't have to carry all of this by yourself."

I looked at her.

I don't know if it was the exhaustion or the fear or the desperate need to feel something other than broken, but before I could think about what I was doing, I leaned forward and kissed her.

It wasn't smooth or planned. My lips found hers and for a second, I just forgot about all of those problems. For one moment there was only this, her, and the warmth of her mouth against mine.

Li froze for a second before pulling away, her eyes wide and confused.

"Blake. What are you doing?"

I didn't have an answer. I don't think I even knew.

"I don't ..." I started, but I didn't know how to finish the sentence.

There was a sound and we both looked up to see Li's mom in the doorway.

Her expression was impossible to read, not angry exactly, but definitely upset.

"Mom. It's not what it looks like, we were talking and ..." Li said, standing up.

Li's mom raised one hand and Li went silent.

The quiet stretched out. Li's mom's eyes moved from her daughter to me.

"Blake. You should go now."

"Mrs. Sun, I can explain ..."

"Now."

I pulled myself up from the bed, my back protesting the movement, but I ignored it. Li stood by her desk with her arms wrapped around herself, refusing to look at me.

"Li," I said.

"Go," Li's mom repeated, stepping aside to only barely clear the doorway.

I looked at Li one more time, hoping she'd say something, but she kept her eyes fixed on the floor.

I went.

The stairs were worse going down than they'd been coming up, each step jarring my spine. Behind me, I heard Li's mom close the door to Li's room and her voice as she started to say something to Li, but I couldn't make out the words.

Yesica was still in the back room when I reached the bottom. She looked up, saw my face, and got concerned.

"Everything okay up there?"

"Fine. I need to go."

She didn't push or ask what had happened. She nodded and watched me make my way toward the front door.

I didn't wait for Dad to pick me up. I couldn't be there any longer. I just wanted to go home, lie in bed, and pull a blanket over my head and make the world go away.

Chapter 36

Monday morning was worse than I expected.

My first two classes were filled with people who either kept staring at me or wanted to offer what I'm sure they thought was sympathy, which only pissed me off each time.

It was worse in between classes when I could feel everyone staring at me. And then there were the crutches. The halls were never what I'd call roomy, but trying to maneuver around the crowds of people was a nightmare, and my back screamed every time someone bumped into me.

I kept my head down and focused on not falling.

I went around a corner and looked up just to make sure I wasn't going to walk into a large group. Li was standing near the library entrance talking to a girl I didn't recognize. She must have felt me looking because her head swung around and she made eye contact with me.

I changed direction immediately, heading back the way I came, even though I couldn't get to my next class that way.

"Blake."

I didn't stop walking.

"Blake, stop."

With me on crutches, it wasn't hard for her to catch up, and she stepped in front of me, blocking my path before I could get more than a few feet down the hall.

"I need to get to class," I said, trying to go around her.

"You can wait a few minutes," she said, cutting off my path again. "I called you yesterday. Three times."

"I was sleeping."

I hadn't been sleeping, just staring at the ceiling, listening to the phone ring, and feeling like the biggest idiot in the world.

"You weren't sleeping at six in the evening. We need to talk."

"I really don't think we do. I think you and your mom made everything pretty clear yesterday. Message received."

"Blake, please." She looked around. "Not here. Come on."

She turned, grabbed my sleeve, and pulled me into a nearby empty art room.

"What?" I said, pulling my arm free.

"Sunday was a mess. The way it ended, with my mother walking in ... I just didn't want things to be left like that."

"Seemed like that was exactly how you wanted things to be left. She told me to get out, you didn't say a word, and I got out."

"I was in shock, Blake."

"Fine, you were in shock. So, what do you want now? You want to make sure I know my place? Don't worry, I got it. Friends, strictly platonic, no touching the merchandise."

"Stop it. Stop trying to push me away with the sarcasm because it doesn't work on me."

"I'm not pushing you away. I'm refusing to stand here and pretend Sunday didn't happen. You made your choice, so let me go."

"I stopped you because I knew you were hurt and embarrassed by what happened, and I wanted to try to fix it."

"There is nothing to fix. I made a mistake and misread the signals. I thought ... I don't know what I thought, but it doesn't matter. I was wrong, and it won't happen again."

"Are you done?"

"I don't know, are you?"

Li looked at me. I could tell I was getting under her skin, and a part of me felt bad about that, but the rest of me didn't care.

"I care about you, Blake, more than almost anyone else in this school. You're my best friend."

"But. There's always a 'but,' isn't there?"

"But what happened on Sunday ... it can't happen again."

"Yeah, I gathered that," I said. "You don't have to keep hammering it in. I get it. I'm not your type or what your mother thinks should be your type. I don't know, maybe I'm just too much drama. Whatever it is, we're not going to happen."

"This isn't about types or drama, and it's not about my mother either."

"Bullshit, it's entirely about your mother. She walked in, gave me the death glare, and you froze. If she hadn't walked in ..."

"If she hadn't walked in, I would have stopped it anyway."

"Yeah, I remember you pulling away."

"Fine, but do you remember *why* you did it?"

"Because I like you, Li. We spend every day together. You're the only person who actually treats me like me and not like I owe them something. Is it really that crazy that I might have feelings for you?"

"It's not crazy, but I am not convinced you're actually feeling those things. Look at the timing, look at what's happening in your life."

"I was finally being honest with you."

"You were crying. You were shaking, terrified about your back. You were talking about your mom disappearing and being afraid you were never going to play again. You were falling apart."

"So that makes it fake? Because I was having a bad day, nothing I felt was real?"

"You didn't kiss me because you've been secretly pining for me for months," Li said. "You kissed me because you were drowning and I was the closest thing that looked like a life raft."

"That's not true," I said, although even I didn't believe how I said it.

"Isn't it? Think about it. Before the injury and before your mom left ... did you ever try anything with me? Did you ever look at me like that? You were focused on football and fixing everything around you. The first time you looked at me was when you ran out of other options."

"That is such a load of psychobabble crap. I realized how important you were to me. Sometimes it takes a crisis to see what's right in front of you."

"That's not how things actually work, Blake. You hit rock bottom and were looking for anything to pull yourself back up. You're using me as an escape. You're scared, Blake. You are terrified."

"So I'm not allowed to be scared?"

“You are allowed to be scared, and I want to be there for you while you’re scared. I want to listen when you need to vent, and I want to be your friend, but I don’t want to be your nurse or your therapist.”

“You think you know everything.”

“I know that if we cross that line while you’re in crisis, we will destroy our friendship. I value you too much to let that happen, and I’m not willing to be a casualty of your bad year.”

I hated that I knew she was right. It just made me feel worse. I already worried I’d done it for the wrong reason, and I knew my feelings were all jumbled up. But what I felt now was embarrassment, which was stacked on top of fear and loss.

I wanted it to stop. I was so angry; I just wanted to hurt everyone around me.

“You know what I think?” I said. “I think this is all just an excuse. I think you’re scared.”

“I am scared. I don’t want to lose my best friend.”

“No. You’re scared of *her*. You’re scared of your mom and what she thinks.”

“This isn’t about her.”

“It’s always about her. You talk about me drowning? Look at yourself, Li. You couldn’t play basketball because it would mess up her plan for you. You could barely have friends because you have to be this perfect little daughter and live up to what she wants you to be.”

“Blake, stop.”

“You’re a puppet.” I knew I was going too far, but I couldn’t stop. “You stand there talking about self-respect and boundaries, but the truth is you’re just doing exactly what you’re told. You’re never going to have your own life because you’re too busy having hers instead.”

The silence was absolute.

I saw the hit land, and I knew it had hurt her. Not because it was completely true, but because it was what she was afraid of. I knew her biggest fear was tied between disappointing her mother and disappointing herself by only doing what her mother wanted, and I went right in for the kill.

I waited for her to yell or slap me.

Instead, she said, "I made this decision. Me. I decided that I deserve to be with someone who wants me for *me*, not because their life is falling apart."

I opened my mouth, but she held up a hand, stopping me.

"I understand you wanted to hurt me because I said no and you feel small right now, so you wanted to bring me down there with you, which just proves to me that I made the right decision. That isn't the kind of thing you do to someone you have feelings for. It's not even the kind of thing you do to someone you are just friends with."

Part of me wanted to apologize. Somewhere in the back of my head, I knew I was messing this up. I wanted to say, *I'm sorry, I didn't mean it, I'm just messed up right now.*

But I didn't. I was hurt all over again, and I didn't know how to make it stop. I felt completely hopeless.

"I have to go," I muttered.

I turned, awkwardly pivoting on the rubber tips of the crutches.

"Blake," Li called out.

I didn't stop because I couldn't look at her again. If I did, I would break down completely. I had to get through the rest of the day, get to class, and keep moving.

After leaving Li, I didn't go back to class.

I just wanted to be somewhere nobody would bother me. Instead, I headed down toward the gym and out the side door that led to the football field and the field house.

Of course, it didn't occur to me that, with no classes happening and one period before lunch, the field house would be locked.

Nothing was going my way today.

I looked across the empty practice field toward the bleachers. At the far end, the section nobody used because it faced away from the parking lot and the main building, which made it about as isolated a place as you could get during the day.

I knew some of the stoners and burnouts liked to hang out there, skipping class and smoking. I'd always thought of them as losers with nothing better to do, but right now, that actually sounded perfect.

I hobbled my way in that direction and, sure enough, there was already a group of five of them gathered under the bleachers, huddled in a small circle.

They all looked up, I guess afraid they were about to get busted or something, when I walked up, stopping just at the edge.

Two of the guys, one big guy in a faded Metallica shirt and a skinnier one with patchy facial hair, I'd seen in the halls and knew they were seniors, although I'd never talked to them. Two of the others, a girl with black hair that looked just off enough that I was pretty sure it was dyed, was smoking a cigarette, and a guy leaning against a support beam, I'd never seen before and had no idea what grade they were in.

The fifth, a girl wearing an oversized army jacket with wavy brown hair, looked vaguely familiar, although I couldn't place where I knew her from except that I'd seen her face before.

"Did you get lost?" the girl in the army jacket asked.

"Got a beer?"

Several of them were holding paper-wrapped containers that I was certain had beers in them, although they were at least smart enough to keep them nominally covered.

I don't think any of them expected me to ask for one, because for a moment, nobody moved. They all just kind of glanced at each other like this was maybe some kind of trick.

"For real?" the skinny guy asked.

"For real."

"Whatever, man," the big guy said with a shrug, reaching behind him to grab a brown paper bag that he then held out toward me.

I tucked one crutch under my arm, took the bag, and drank from the half-empty, warm can inside. The beer was cheap and tasted like aluminum, but it was alcohol and that was all that mattered.

"What'd you do to your leg?" the dyed-hair girl asked.

"He hurt it at the homecoming game," the skinny guy said to her before turning to me. "I work concessions at the stadium. You got absolutely blasted by those two linebackers. Swear to God, I thought they killed you."

I didn't really have anything to say to that. It was about as good a description of the hit as I'd heard yet.

“Jesus, Todd, shut up,” the girl in the army jacket said, and then patted the ground next to her. “You should sit down before you tip over.”

It seemed like a good idea. Besides, the crutch was digging into my armpit. I passed the can to her and lowered myself to the ground next to her, ignoring the protest in my back, and set my crutches down. She took a sip out of the can, watching me as I eased myself onto the ground, and handed it back to the big guy.

“So, really, what’s with you being over here with us? Hiding out? Shouldn’t you be off with your friends?” she asked.

“I just ... can’t be around them right now.”

She looked at me for a second and then shrugged.

The skinny guy, Todd, pulled out a pack of cigarettes, shook one loose, and held it toward me. “You want one?”

I looked at it. I’d never smoked before. I did remember smoking once or twice in the dream life, but it was one of the vices I’d never picked up.

I don’t know why, but I took one anyway.

Todd tossed me a lighter. It took me a few tries but I got it to catch and lit it, sucking in smoke as I did.

I instantly remembered why I never picked up smoking. It tasted like shit and felt like sandpaper ripping down my throat. I coughed immediately, hard enough that my back spasmed and the cigarette nearly fell out of my mouth.

That gave all of them a good chuckle, but I didn’t get the idea that they were being mean about it, more like they’d seen this before.

“Easy there, cowboy. Don’t try to inhale the whole thing on the first go. Little puffs until you get the hang of it,” the girl next to me said.

I tried again with a smaller inhale, holding it in my mouth rather than my lungs and letting it out slowly so it burned without making me cough.

“That’s better,” she said. “Although it’s not really smoking if you just hold it in your mouth.”

I took another drag, tried to inhale it and ended up coughing again, which made her laugh.

I decided to just hold onto it for a minute and take my time with it. Todd leaned over to look out from under the bleachers, but I guess he didn't see anything cause he leaned back and lit his own cigarette.

"Heard your mom bailed?" the girl said when the conversation lagged.

That caught me completely off-guard.

"What? How do you know that?"

"'Lexi here's practically your stalker. She's got a thing for the jocks and she's been eyeballing you for ..." the big guy started to say, grinning.

"Screw you, Denny," she said, hitting him pretty hard, but I could see her cheeks go a little pink. "Come on, you know what kind of a place this is. Little towns like this, news travels faster than a cold."

I just grunted in reply. I didn't want to get into it. The can came back around to me and I took another drink, longer this time, and passed it on.

"Anyway, that sucks," she said, I guess seeing that I didn't want to talk about it. The can came back around and I finished off the beer this time. Denny reached into the backpack next to him and tossed me another can without being asked. I caught it, cracked it open, and drank.

The alcohol was starting to do its job, softening the edges of my anger and making me feel loose. I still felt like garbage, but it was a duller, more manageable kind of garbage.

The girl with the black hair reached into her jacket and pulled out a joint, lighting it for a long hit before passing it to Todd. He took a hit and passed it to Denny, who took his turn and held it out toward me.

I looked at it.

In my dream life, alcohol had been my drug of choice. I had a memory of getting high a few times, and while it did mellow me out, I just never went looking for it.

I also remembered the speech Coach Heidemann gave last year and Coach Holloway gave to non-freshmen this year. Both had been very clear on the policy for drugs. *Any player caught using drugs will be immediately dismissed from the team, no exceptions, no second chances.*

We got random drug tests twice each year, and I'd only had one so far, so theoretically I could get another one any time. Which led me to think about everything I'd built over the past year and a half and what I was putting in jeopardy.

Of course, none of that might matter anymore. I know everyone kept saying it would be okay and I'd recover, but my back was still killing me and everyone was always sugarcoating everything.

"Coach has rules about drugs," I said. "We get drug tested, and players can get kicked off the team for that."

The girl in the army jacket, whom the big guy had called Lexi, leaned a little closer and said, "Look, you're your own guy; nobody here is gonna make you do a damn thing you don't want to, but nobody's gonna care either. You do you. We're not the cops. So, forget all that. What do *you* want, right now?"

She was right. Even if I did get better, I thought about Mom and Li and everything that was happening and wanted to just say screw it. I wanted to just do something reckless and throw it all away, so everyone stopped looking to me all the time to be so goddamn perfect constantly.

I reached out and took the joint from Denny, bringing it up to my lips and taking a long pull from it. It was kind of how I remembered it from the few times I'd smoked it in my dream life, different from the cigarette, heavier and warmer.

I held it for a moment and then started to exhale slowly, which then turned into another wracking cough.

"My man," Denny said, laughing and taking it back from me.

Chapter 37

If I thought classes were hard to deal with, practice was even worse.

Not from their perspective, I guess. Gabriel was running the offense fine, hitting his throws, and making decent reads. He seemed ready to start his first game, which is what really sucked. It wasn't that I wanted him to do badly; I wanted us to win and lock our spot in for the playoffs. It was because, for the first time, it seemed like they didn't need me as much as I wanted them to.

Selfish, but it's a hard lesson to learn, finding out you're replaceable.

I spent two hours on the bench with my back seizing up every time I moved, watching my teammates do what I was supposed to be doing. Coach Holloway was completely focused on Gabriel and the offense, getting them ready for Friday, and I was just ... forgotten.

The trainers checked on me twice to ask if I needed anything, and I shook my head both times, even though I probably could have used some work on my back after spending the day on crutches. But I didn't want the rest of the team to see me as any more useless than I already was.

I wanted them to know I'd be back soon and couldn't be replaced.

By the time practice ended, I was stiff, frustrated, and ready to be anywhere else.

I grabbed my crutches and skipped the locker room entirely, thankful I'd brought my backpack with me. A few guys asked how I was holding up, and I gave them the same answer I'd been giving everyone.

"Fine. Getting better."

I don't think anyone believed me.

The parking lot was mostly quiet since the players were changing and parents hadn't shown up yet, but one truck sat idling near the curb.

While that wasn't so surprising, Lexi, the girl from under the bleachers, leaned out the driver's window with one arm dangling over the door.

"You look like you could use a ride," she called out.

"How'd you know where to find me?"

"It's not exactly a mystery," she said, jerking her chin toward the field. "The whole town knows when football practice ends. So, do you want to get out of here or what?"

I looked back at the locker room door, then at her truck. The alternative was asking for a ride from one of the guys, going home to sit in that empty house, and waiting for my dad to get back from work so we could pretend everything was fine.

"Sure."

I went to the passenger side and opened the door. Getting in was awkward with the crutches since I had to angle them between my legs and slide onto the seat carefully to avoid jarring my back. Lexi watched but didn't offer to help, which I appreciated. She waited until I was settled and pulled out of the lot.

"I also wanted to see if you'd actually get in the truck or run back to your real friends."

"I got in, didn't I?"

"Yeah. You did."

We drove north through town and straight on out of it, with Lexi taking some of the back roads instead of the state road, heading past one of the smaller ranches toward where there were a bunch of oil derricks.

"Where are we going?"

"Nowhere in particular," she said. "Driving's just something I do when I need to think, or not think. I figured you could use more of what you came looking for this morning."

"What's that?"

"Escape."

I guess I was more obvious than I thought. I settled into the seat and watched the flat landscape roll past, the brown grass and pump jacks bobbing in the distance between clusters of mesquite trees. I was surprised that the silence felt comfortable. Lexi fiddled with the radio, landed on something grungy that I recognized from one of the CDs Charlie had made me, which in turn made me feel a little guilty for a moment.

I had just started thinking about that when the song ended and a commercial came on; she turned it down.

"How's the back holding up?"

"Stiff but manageable. The waiting is what drives me crazy."

"Waiting's the worst."

"I'm usually better at it, but I don't know, it's different this time."

She didn't ask what I meant or push.

"Did you go back to class after the bleachers?"

"Yeah, the new counselor has it in for me, so I kind of had to finish out the day."

"How was it?"

"Ehh, it was school. I'd rather have been somewhere else."

"Sounds like a shit day."

"It was."

We passed the ranch and hit open road.

"So why were you waiting for me?"

"I told you. Figured you could use a jailbreak."

"You don't even know me."

"I know enough." She kept her eyes on the road. "Denny's an idiot, by the way. I wasn't *stalking* you."

"Says the girl who was waiting in the parking lot for me to finish practice."

She laughed.

"Fine. I don't know, most of the athletes are such assholes, you know, and you weren't. You just sat there and hung out and didn't make it weird." She shrugged. "Plus Denny and Todd are like ... they're fine, whatever, but they're kind of ..."

She trailed off, gesturing vaguely.

"Kind of what?"

"Forget it."

"No, what?"

"Sometimes I like a guy who's a little more solid. Happy? Athletes have better bodies than guys who live on cigarettes and cheap beer."

"So you're saying you think I'm hot."

I couldn't help keep the shit-eating grin on my face.

"You're being annoying on purpose now."

"Little bit."

She shook her head but she was smiling.

"So you're here because you think I'm hot and not an asshole?"

"Exactly. Besides, you looked like you needed a break from all the people pushing you for something, and I was looking to have some fun, so I figured maybe we could help each other out."

Now it was my turn to be taken aback.

"What do you mean, help each other out?"

Instead of directly answering, Lexi pulled the truck onto a dirt track. We bumped along for a quarter mile until we reached an old, abandoned pump station surrounded by nothing but scrub brush and empty land, where she turned the truck around and parked, cutting the engine and turning to face me.

"I thought we could start with this," she said, pulling out a baggy with several joints in it.

She pulled one out and lit it, taking a long drag and holding it before handing the joint over to me. I didn't hem or haw this time. I'd already crossed this line once today, so what was one more hit?

I took it a little slower than I did earlier and only coughed a little.

"You're still bad at that."

"I'm a slow learner."

We passed the joint back and forth, each taking turns on it. The high settled into my limbs and, just like earlier in the day, it took away some of the pain in my back.

Finally, though, the silence got the best of me.

"As my stalker, you know everything about me, but I don't really know anything about you. Hell, I don't even know your last name."

"Cole. Alexis Cole, but nobody calls me Alexis except my mom when she's pissed."

"Alexis," I said, testing it out.

"Don't."

I held up my hands. "Lexi, it is."

"So what do you want to know?"

"I don't know, the basics I guess. Are you from Wheaton originally?"

"No, I was born in Lubbock. My dad got a job when I was ten and moved us here."

"So it's just you and your parents?"

"Just my mom. My dad died when I was twelve. We stayed because my mom was already working at the hospital."

Her tone made it very clear she did not want to discuss it anymore, so I changed the subject.

"Any hobbies? Aside from picking up football players and taking them into the middle of nowhere to get high."

"Well, that is my main one. I used to do some dance when I was younger, but I gave it up after ... after. I don't know, all that stuff kind of fell off. Now I just do whatever makes me happy, you know."

I couldn't help but laugh, "No, but I'm starting to get the idea of it. So that's the whole story of Lexi Cole?"

"That's the version you get for now."

"What about after you graduate?"

"I don't care as long as it's anywhere but here."

"What's so bad about Wheaton?"

"It's fine if you fit in but I never have. I figured out early that people in small towns need someone to talk about and my family always seemed to be the source of their gossip."

"Like what?"

"That I'm easy, possibly gay, probably on drugs," she said, laughing and holding up the joint. "And definitely trouble. Someone started a rumor my freshman year that I was a hooker because I got a ride home from an older guy once. He was actually dating my mom and she asked him to pick me up, but people like to start shit."

"That's messed up."

"Like I said, people in small towns get bored and gossip. And when there's not enough to gossip about, they make stuff up. It doesn't bother me anymore."

It sounded like it did, but I didn't push.

"Well, I think you're cool."

She laughed. "Considering you're only a few degrees off from all the geeks and try-hards, I'm not sure how good your judgment on what's cool or not is, but I appreciate it."

We fell into silence as we finished the joint, just kind of letting the high settle in and enjoying the late afternoon.

"I'm a lot more like you than you think," I said finally. "Everyone is always watching me and talking about me. Everyone has this idea of who they think I should be."

"What is that?"

"It depends on the person and what they want. And they all want something. They want a golden boy, a meal ticket, proof that they're great at their job by holding me up as an example. Whatever. I'm tired of always having to meet someone else's expectations. Sometimes I want to just say fuck it and let it all fall apart, just to spite them."

"I get that. Actually, it's kind of brave. Most people are too scared to admit when they want to watch it burn, so they just keep letting people ride them."

"That's been my method so far. I just don't know what to do now. Like, I've had this whole plan and ... now what?"

"How about this?" she said, leaning forward suddenly and kissing me.

Her lips were warm and tasted like smoke and something sweeter underneath. I had a feeling this was going to happen. Even without her talk about finding me attractive, I'd felt this chemistry between us. It wasn't like the thing I had with Charlie. That had been ... innocent, I guess.

This was more raw. I grabbed her and pulled her into me, kissing her back hard. I guess that was the right move, because she moaned a little, one hand bracing against my chest while the other gripped the front of my shirt.

Her hands moved down from my chest to my stomach, her fingers trailing across the fabric of my shirt, and then she suddenly stopped and pulled back.

For a second, I was wondering what I'd done when she grabbed the hem of my shirt and tugged it up.

"What ..."

"Just looking," she said, grinning as she stared at my abs. "Damn. I knew you were in shape, but this is something else."

That I had not expected.

"I, uhh, work hard for it," I said, still a little off balance.

"Good for me, then," she said and moved back into me, kissing me again.

Her hands didn't stop exploring, though. She ran her palms across my chest, my shoulders, and then back down my stomach, tracing the lines of muscle like she was memorizing them. Every touch sent heat spreading through me.

I felt a small twinge in my back, but at the moment I didn't care at all. Her weight pressed against me, one of her hands finding the back of my neck while the other stayed low on my stomach, fingers just barely brushing just inside the waistband of my jeans.

She didn't push further than that, and I didn't get the feeling we were going to go further than this, but she didn't need to. Just that much contact was enough to make my head spin.

Well, that and the weed, probably.

We kissed until my lips felt bruised. She couldn't seem to get enough of touching me, constantly running her hands all over my body. I did the same, my hands sliding down her back and then up inside her shirt, feeling her skin, although also staying away from anything too forward. I might have expected something, but I was still a little off balance by the whole thing, and the fact that we'd met like six hours ago, so I thought it best to let her take the lead for now.

And then, as suddenly as she started, she pulled away and slid back into the driver's seat.

"I've got some places to be," she said, almost matter-of-factly, like she was telling me she had to pick up groceries or forgot to set the clock on her VCR.

That didn't help with the feeling of being off balance. She was very hard to read.

"I can take you home."

"Uhh, sure."

I thought maybe that was it, a little smoking and making out was all she was looking for, but as she pulled back onto the asphalt road, she reached over and put her hand on my thigh, very high up on my thigh, and left it there.

"I'm taking you somewhere Saturday night," she said. "It'll be perfect. Nobody will know you there or care about who you are. You'll get to leave all your troubles behind for a night."

"Where?"

"It's a surprise. Just clear your schedule and wear something that isn't completely lame."

"It's a date."

Her smile widened. "Yeah. It is."

I was lying on my bed, flipping through an old *Sports Illustrated* without really reading it, half-thinking about Lexi.

We'd been hanging out under the bleachers every day at lunch since Monday, me, her, Denny, Todd, and the rest of the 'burnouts.' It beat sitting at the team table, pretending everything was normal. Eduardo had tried calling a couple of times this week, but I'd managed to dodge those. After how he'd acted when I'd asked Li to homecoming, and that *had* just been as friends, I was certain he was going to rip into me for 'going behind his back,' and I wasn't ready for that conversation yet.

I hadn't managed to dodge the guys on the team, but since I was only seeing them at afternoon practices and I'd called off the morning practices until I got better, they were too focused on getting ready for tomorrow's game to hound me too much.

The only thing I regretted about the week was that Lexi and I hadn't repeated what happened in her truck on Monday. We'd talk, smoke a little, and she'd give me these looks that made it clear she was interested, but she never made a move and I wasn't sure if I was supposed to. She was hard to read like that.

The phone rang, pulling me out of my thoughts.

My first instinct was to ignore it. It was probably either Eduardo or Li, both of whom wanted to guilt me into 'acting normal again.' I just didn't have the energy for it.

By the fourth ring, I reached over and at least checked the caller ID, and saw it was from a Georgia area code, which I knew for only one reason.

I may have been in "fuck it" mode, but I realized something I'd forgotten to do, and there was just enough guilt that I picked it up.

"Hello?"

"Blake? It's Charlie."

"Hey, what's up?" I asked, trying to sound normal.

"What's up? Blake, I've been worried about you. You haven't called or anything, and I heard you got hurt."

"I've just been busy ... wait, how did you know I was hurt?"

"Li called me."

I was shocked enough that I sat bolt upright, and then winced as my back protested.

"Li called you?"

"Yeah, she tracked down my number."

That honestly was completely out of left field. Li was smart enough to find someone's number if she wanted to, but I was surprised she'd go to that much effort.

"She told me about the injury. About what happened at homecoming, and your mom."

Damn, she was just out there spilling my entire life to people. She couldn't give me the time of day, but she had no problem telling my business to others like it was hers. Just more proof that I was right about how everyone was using me.

"Blake? Are you still there?"

"I'm here."

"Talk to me. What's going on with you?"

"Nothing, everything's fine, and Li's overreacting."

"We talked for a little while, and she doesn't seem like the type to overreact."

"Yeah, well, you don't know her."

"I know her well enough to know she wouldn't call a girl in Georgia she's never met if she wasn't seriously worried about you. She said you've completely bailed on all of your friends and aren't acting like yourself."

"She's just mad because we had some personal problems between the two of us, and she didn't like that I stood up for myself finally."

"Yeah, she told me about your trying to kiss her."

I could hear the hurt in her voice, which just stung all the more. We'd agreed we weren't seeing each other, so how was it she got to be mad I tried to move on?

"Oh, no, you don't get to be mad at me. We agreed we couldn't see each other."

"I'm not mad at you, Blake. If you two did get together and you were happy, then I'd be happy for you. I'm just worried about you. This isn't like you."

"How do you know what is or isn't like me? We spent like, two evenings together and had, what, a half-dozen other conversations. Yeah, we got along and had fun, but don't act like you know me, Charlie."

She didn't say anything for a moment. I was coming off a little mean, I knew that, and I was probably being unfair. But I'd had enough of people telling me how I should act or feel about things.

"You're right, we didn't get to spend a lot of time together, but I got to know you well enough that this isn't the Blake I knew and liked. I know you're under a lot of stress, so I get it, but ... you should talk to us. Let us help you."

"I'm doing fine on my own."

"You don't sound fine, you sound ... angry."

"What? I don't need a lecture from someone who isn't here and doesn't understand what's happening."

"What's that supposed to mean?"

"It means you're in Georgia living your life, and I'm in Texas dealing with real problems. A phone call doesn't fix anything, Charlie. It doesn't change anything. It's just words."

She went quiet again, this time letting the silence stretch out long enough that I wondered if the connection had dropped.

"I'm trying to be there for you even from far away because that's what friends do. That's what, whatever we are, does. If you don't want that, just say so."

I thought of a dozen things to say, from telling her no, I did want to talk, to just spilling my guts about everything that had happened, to every step in between.

Instead, I said, "I don't want to talk right now. I'll call you when things settle down."

"When will that be?"

"I don't know."

I could almost hear her thinking during the pause, trying to figure out what to say that would get through to me.

"Pushing away everyone who cares about you is only going to make things worse, Blake."

"Goodnight, Charlie."

I hung up before she could respond.

I felt bad as soon as I did it. I almost picked the phone up and called her right back to apologize. I knew I'd gone a step too far.

But I didn't.

Instead, I rolled over, grabbed my Walkman from the floor, and put the headphones on, trying to let the music drown out everything, including my own thoughts.

I knew she was right, that I was pushing people away. But every time I talked to someone, it reminded me that they all wanted something from me. They didn't want me to be happy; they wanted me to be exactly what they thought I should be.

And I just couldn't keep doing that.

Chapter 38

Friday night, we were in San Angelo to play Central High, and I almost wondered why I came. I felt like dead weight as I came down the tunnel from the San Angelo locker rooms with the rest of the team as the guys jogged past me toward the field. A few of them, Mickey, Joe, and Andre, clapped me on the shoulder as they went by, but nobody said much. Their game faces were already on.

I made my way across the track and settled onto the end of the bench closest to the offense. It felt weird, sitting on the bench in my jersey without pads on, not doing warm-ups or any of the normal stuff. It had been weird at practice all week, but this was ten times worse.

The guys were acting weird, too.

They were scattered in small groups during warm-ups, clustered together for conversations and not nearly as focused as they should be this close to kickoff. Mickey and Austin were off by themselves near the end zone, and Andre stretched alone, something I'd never seen him do.

Gabriel threw with one of the backup receivers, working through his arm-loosening routine. His motion looked fine, but he'd lost a lot of the zip I'd seen him have during practice as his confidence had started to build.

He was nervous as hell.

San Angelo won the coin toss and elected to receive, and they brought it out to the thirty-three-yard line before we stopped them. Our defense dug in on the first series. Central tried to pound the ball up the middle and got nothing, then their QB overthrew a receiver on third down. They had to punt it, and we were pinned down at our own twelve.

Gabriel jogged onto the field with the offense and got the guys set. The first play was a handoff to Noah that picked up four yards. Not tremendous, but not the worst ever either. On the second, Gabriel dropped back on a quick slant.

He was slow on his reads and telegraphing everything he was doing, and Central's linebacker saw it, drifting into the passing lane while Gabriel stared down Jerry. Gabriel never looked off the receiver or the safety covering him, and ended up throwing it right into the linebacker's chest.

The San Angelo sideline erupted. Their linebacker didn't even have to move his feet, just caught the ball and took off toward our end zone before we managed to drag him down at the thirty.

Gabriel came off the field with his helmet still on, head down. He walked right past Coach Holloway and dropped onto the bench about ten feet from me, staring at the ground. I tried to catch his eye, but he wouldn't look up.

Coach Holloway went over to him and crouched down. I couldn't hear what they were saying, but knowing Coach and from his body language, he was trying to pep-talk some of the nerves out of Gabriel.

Four plays later, Central punched it in to put the game at seven to zero.

Central kicked off, and we returned it to our twenty-five. Gabriel trotted back out, and for a minute it looked like he'd settled down. He completed a short out to Mickey for six yards, then hit Austin on a quick hitch for another five, which gave us a first down. The crowd behind me got a little louder.

Third and six from our own forty-two. Gabriel dropped back for another pass. Brian broke open on a crossing route, a good five yards of separation. In my head, I was screaming, "Throw it, throw it now!"

Instead, Gabriel hesitated, and the window closed when a trailing linebacker jammed Brian. Gabriel had been standing there a long time, and the pocket was starting to go, forcing him to scramble right, feet tangling as he tried to reset, and he threw off his back foot. The ball sailed high and behind the receiver into the hands of a San Angelo safety lurking in zone coverage.

His second interception. I slammed the bottom of my crutch against the ground.

The offensive line trudged back to the sideline as Mickey and Austin got into it. Mickey pointed at Austin's chest, saying something I couldn't hear. Austin shoved Mickey's hand away and fired back. They were in each other's faces before Andre stepped between them.

Central scored again, putting them up fourteen to zero up with three minutes left in the first quarter.

The second quarter started with Gabriel putting together a decent drive. He checked down when he needed to and didn't force anything stupid, getting us into field goal range. When the kick went through, the score moved to fourteen to three.

For a minute, I had some hope that we might be turning it around.

It didn't last.

On the next possession, on first down from our own thirty, Gabriel took the snap, pump-faked, and fired a bullet into coverage that had no business being thrown. The ball sailed incomplete, and Jerry, who'd been the target, threw his hands up in frustration.

Our defense had its first slip-up just before halftime, misreading some coverage and Central added another touchdown. Twenty-one to three.

In the locker room, Coach Holloway was in a state.

"That was some of the worst football I have seen in years! This is not the team that won six straight games. Where the hell did that team go?"

Nobody answered.

"The offense can't move the ball if Gabriel keeps throwing to the other team," Andre said.

"Man, shut up!" Gabriel shouted. "Receivers aren't getting open, and the line isn't giving me time to ..."

"Both of you, stop," Tyler said. "We're all making mistakes out there."

"Defense gave up thirty-five points in two games," Austin said. "Check your own house before you start talking about ours."

"What'd you just say to me?" Tyler asked.

More voices piled on, overlapping, everybody talking at once. I couldn't pick out individual words anymore, just the rising pitch of guys who were frustrated and scared and looking for someone to blame.

"Enough!" Coach Holloway's voice boomed.

The room went dead quiet.

"This right here, all the finger-pointing, this is exactly what losing teams do. This is what teams that don't make the playoffs do. Is that who you want to be?"

Silence.

"We're going to make adjustments. We're going to run the ball more to try to take some pressure off Gabriel, but every single one of you needs to execute your assignment on every play. Not some plays. Every play. Does anyone have a problem with that?"

Nobody spoke.

"Get your heads right. You've got twelve minutes."

The door opened, and players started filing past me. Gabriel looked at me, and then looked away almost as quickly. I think he was expecting me to yell at him, or do something.

I didn't have the energy for that.

The second half started better. Coach Holloway called runs on seven of the first eight plays, and the offensive line started moving people. Noah found holes, picked up chunks of yards, and the drive ate up almost six minutes of clock before Noah punched it in from the three, putting us down eleven.

Our defense forced a three-and-out, and the crowd got loud for the first time since the kickoff.

Things were looking up until two plays later. We had second down at midfield, and Coach Holloway called a play-action pass since they were starting to cheat up, expecting us to run. This should have been Gabriel's bread and butter. He faked the handoff, rolled right, and looked for Mickey on a deep out.

He threw it before Mickey finished his break.

The ball sailed behind Mickey, bouncing off his fingertips and right into the chest of a Central cornerback who took off up the sideline. Our guys chased him, but he had a hell of a head start. He didn't score, but he got to our forty before we finally shoved him out of bounds.

Gabriel dropped to one knee on the field, head down.

Two plays later, Central converted the turnover into another touchdown, putting us at twenty-eight to ten with half the fourth quarter left to play.

The fight went out of us completely.

Mickey caught a short pass over the middle and barely tried for extra yards, going down as soon as a defender touched him. I'd never seen him do that.

We managed one more score late when Gabriel finally connected with Brian on a slant that Brian took thirty-five yards to the end zone. That was great and all, but it put us down twenty-eight to fourteen with less than a minute to go.

The final whistle blew, and I stayed on the bench as the Central players rushed the field, hugging and jumping around at midfield. Our guys filed past me toward the tunnel, most of them avoiding eye contact.

Mickey stopped for a second. "We need you back out there, man."

"Yeah."

He nodded and kept walking.

Gabriel was the last offensive player off the field. He walked slowly, helmet in his hand, and when he got close, he glanced over. He didn't say anything. He just looked at me with empty eyes as he kept walking toward the locker room.

I pushed up off the bench with my crutches and looked at the scoreboard one more time.

San Angelo twenty-eight, Wheaton fourteen.

My back ached from sitting in the same position for three hours. Central fans streamed onto the field, celebrating like they'd just won state.

Maybe they felt they had. Until the last game, we'd been undefeated, and San Angelo was not one of the better teams in our district. They'd already lost two, so one more loss would have put them out of range of making it to the playoffs, since only two teams from each district got to go.

This win meant they still had a chance. It, however, meant the opposite for us. Most of our wins had been in the five preseason games that we played against teams in other districts in our region. The last five regular-season games were the ones that counted, where we played the teams in our district to see who would be the top two to make it to the playoffs.

We'd won our first one against Abilene High, but then we'd had that disaster against Midland. With this loss, we were one and two. I'd looked at the other teams in the district before the game, and going into this, Midland, Abilene Cooper, who we played next week, and Monterey were all undefeated in the games that counted.

Realistically, even if we won both our next games, we might still be out of it, since it was very possible that more than one team would end three and two, in which case they looked to score differential to determine who the runner-up after Midland was.And considering how we played tonight, I wasn't sure we were going to win our next two games.

Thankfully, the next night I had Lexi's plan to distract me from the terrible game and likely loss, not just at State, but making the playoffs at all.

Dad was at work, and even if he wasn't, we'd hardly talked since Mom left, which was another reason I was happy Lexi had a plan. She had a carefree way of dealing with things that I really needed right now.

"You're eager," Lexi said as I opened the passenger door.

"I need to get out of there," I said, tossing my crutches on the floor behind the seat and climbing in.

She pulled away from the curb before I'd even closed the door all the way. "Then I've got just the thing for you."

"Where are we going?"

"My friend's band is playing a gig at a bar in Midland."

I looked over at her. "I'm fifteen; I can't get into a bar."

Lexi smiled with her eyes on the road. "You worry too much."

I didn't push. She clearly had done this kind of thing before, so I figured, "What the hell?" Part of me knew I should care, should think about what I was getting into, but that part felt very far away tonight.

The drive to Midland took about forty-five minutes with the radio on some station playing grunge I didn't recognize, Lexi singing along at the top of her lungs.

When we got to Midland, she turned off the main drag into a strip mall on the edge of town where the parking lot was half-full with older cars and a few motorcycles clustered near the entrance to a really small-looking bar with a sign above the door that said, 'Live Music Tonight.'

Well, that's what I thought it was supposed to say, but enough of the letters were burned out that it said, "Li.. ..sic T.night."

Lexi cut the engine and looked over at me. "Stay close, don't talk to the door guy, and try not to look fifteen."

"Great advice."

"Just do it."

Lexi waited for me, surprisingly patiently, as I awkwardly got my crutches back out, then she led the way across the parking lot toward the entrance where a big guy in a black T-shirt sat on a stool by the door.

When he saw Lexi, he smiled and said, "Hey, girl. Henry's already inside."

"Thanks, Mick." She nodded toward me. "He's with me."

The guy looked me over, his eyes stopping on my crutches for a second, then he shrugged.

That was it. There was no ID check or any questions to be had.

Inside, the club was darker than I expected and loud as hell with music thumping from speakers mounted by the stage. The place was cloudy from all the cigarette smoke and smelled terrible.

A band was setting up equipment on the stage, cables snaking across the floor while a guy in a flannel shirt adjusted a microphone stand and another tuned a bass guitar. The space between the stage and the bar was packed with people, all of them older than me by at least five or six years. Some danced to whatever music was being piped through the speakers, while others stood in groups, talking and drinking, waiting for the band to set up.

Lexi grabbed my hand and pulled me through the crowd. People bumped against us as we moved, and I tried not to trip over my crutches or step on anyone's feet, but nobody looked twice at me. In the dim light, with the noise and the press of bodies, I could have been anyone.

We ended up near the bar where a group of people stood in a loose cluster. Lexi immediately started making introductions.

"This is Blake," she said to a guy with a goatee and a Nirvana shirt. "Blake, this is Mike."

Mike nodded at me. "Hey."

"And that's Michelle," she said, pointing to a girl with purple streaks in her hair. "And Frank, Liam, and Amy."

They all seemed to be in their early twenties and already pretty buzzed. A couple of them looked me over with mild curiosity, probably wondering what a kid on crutches was doing there, but nobody asked.

She seemed to know everyone, hugging some people, exchanging quick words with others.

Introductions made, she pulled me toward the stage where a shorter guy with dark, wavy hair tuned a guitar. He had his back to us, adjusting something on the amp, and when Lexi called his name, he turned around with a grin.

"Hey, babe," he said, setting the guitar in its stand and hopping down from the stage.

That's when he kissed her.

It wasn't a quick peck but a real kiss, his hand dropping down and groping her ass, which got her to lean into him.

I was completely confused.

When they broke apart, Lexi kept her arm around his waist.

"This is Blake," she said. "Blake, this is Henry."

Henry was maybe five-seven, soft around the middle, with a long face and light brown eyes that seemed friendly enough. He grinned and slapped my arm in a way that was probably meant to be welcoming.

"No shit? Finally bagged you one, huh?" he said to Lexi. "She has been dying to get her hands on someone like you. I tried out for baseball once in junior high and they not-so-subtly suggested I try something else. Lexi loves a guy with muscles."

Henry's physique suggested he hadn't tried out for much of anything in a while. He caught me looking and laughed.

"Yeah, yeah. The rock and roll lifestyle ain't exactly a fitness program."

I stood there, my brain trying to catch up with what I'd just seen.

"Your boyfriend," I said.

"Yeah." Lexi said it like it was the most obvious thing in the world. "Henry plays guitar."

"Hank!" someone shouted from the stage. "We're on in five!"

Henry kissed Lexi again, quickly this time. "Gotta go. Blake, stick around after, yeah? We'll hang."

He climbed back on stage and picked up his guitar.

Lexi tugged my arm and pulled me toward the bar.

"What do you want?" she asked.

"What?"

"To drink. What do you want?"

I looked at the bartender, a woman in her thirties who was already looking our way. My brain was still stuck on Henry, on the kiss, and on the casual way Lexi had introduced me to her boyfriend and how he'd seemed almost happy I was with her.

"Whatever you're having," I managed.

Lexi ordered two beers, and the bartender handed them over without even glancing at me. I took a long pull from the bottle, the beer cold and bitter, and tried to figure out what the hell was going on.

The band kicked into their first song, and the crowd pressed forward. They were playing something that sounded almost like Pearl Jam but rawer, less polished. The singer screamed more than sang, but it worked somehow.

Lexi pulled me into the middle of the crowd, close enough that I could feel the heat coming off the stage lights. People around us bounced around, some shouting along to lyrics I didn't know. A guy with a shaved head slammed into me from behind, then grabbed my shoulder and yelled an apology before throwing himself back into the crush of bodies.

I couldn't really dance with my crutches, so I just stood there and let the music wash over me. It was loud enough that I couldn't think, which was maybe the point. Lexi moved next to me, her eyes on Henry, her body swaying to the beat.

After three songs, the crowd loosened up a little and I made my way back to the bar. My back was starting to ache from standing, and I needed another drink. Lexi stayed near the front, and I watched her from across the room while the band played.

Henry was decent. Actually, he was better than decent, maybe. He had that thing some performers have where you couldn't look away from him, even when the singer was the one at the microphone. After one of the songs, he caught Lexi's eye and grinned down at her, and she blew him a kiss.

I made it back to the bar and the bartender put another beer in front of me without being asked. I didn't question it and assumed it was going on the band's tab.

The set went on for another twenty minutes while I drank my beer and then another one.

Between songs, Lexi came back to check on me. She'd touch my arm, lean close to say something about the music or the crowd, then drift away again. I guess that was nice, although it was weird how she kept going back to Henry. I watched her move between worlds, between him and me, and I couldn't figure out what I was supposed to be feeling.

I felt confused, mostly, and stupid. I shouldn't be jealous or anything. It's not like we were together. I just didn't really understand.

The first set ended, and the band took a break. Henry set his guitar in its stand and hopped off the stage, making a beeline for Lexi. He wrapped his arms around her from behind and kissed her neck, and she laughed and turned to kiss him properly.

Then they both walked over to where I was standing at the bar.

"Your boy looks lost," Henry said to Lexi, nodding at me.

"He's fine," Lexi said. "Just not used to places like this."

"First time in a bar?"

I nodded, which wasn't exactly true. I'd been to plenty in the dream life, but those had been narrower, holes-in-the-wall, with barely enough room to sit at the bar type places. Not places with a stage and a bunch of people dancing.

Henry laughed. "Well, enjoy it, man. Beer's cheap and we're all having a good time."

"That's true," I said.

"Good, good." He downed a shot and wiped his mouth with the back of his hand. "We got one more set, then we're done, so stick around, yeah? We're all going to Mike's place after."

He kissed Lexi one more time, then headed back toward the stage when the drummer waved him over.

Lexi leaned against the bar next to me. "You want another drink?"

"Lexi ..."

"Yes or no?"

I looked at her. She looked back, her expression giving away nothing.

"Yeah," I said. "I want another drink."

She flagged down the bartender and ordered two more beers.

"Stop," Lexi said.

"Stop what?"

"Thinking so loud. I can practically hear it." She finished her beer and set it on the bar. "Come on, let's get closer to the stage."

"You have a boyfriend."

"I have a beer that's empty and a band that's about to start. You coming or not?"

She didn't wait for an answer, just headed toward the front of the crowd. I grabbed my crutches and followed.

The second set started, and I let myself get lost in the noise again. This time, I stayed near the back, leaning against a pillar that took some of the weight off my back. Lexi drifted between me and the front of the crowd, sometimes dancing near the stage, sometimes appearing at my elbow to check on me or steal a drink from my beer.

The band played harder this set, faster, and Henry threw himself into it. At one point, he stepped up to the mic and dedicated a song to "my girl in the front row," and Lexi whooped and raised her hands. The song was loud and messy and kind of beautiful, and I watched Henry play it while Lexi watched him.

I was definitely getting drunk now. The room had that soft, tilted quality, and my thoughts moved slower than they should have.

When the second set ended, Lexi grabbed my arm.

"Come on. Want some air."

I followed her toward a side door, grateful to escape the noise, the heat, and the press of bodies. The night air hit me when we stepped outside, cooler than in the club, and I realized how sweaty I'd gotten in there.

We stood out there for a minute, Lexi finishing her drink, until one of the band guys came out and disappeared into the dark. A few minutes later, he returned, driving a beat-up old van that he pulled right up to the door.

As if on cue, the rest of the band popped out the door, pushing equipment, talking, and laughing.

I watched them for a second, then turned to Lexi.

"So what's the deal?"

"What do you mean?"

"You know what I mean. Your boyfriend is right there. We've been …" I didn't finish the sentence. "And he's acting like everything's normal."

"Because it's normal for us."

I stared at her, waiting for more.

"It's not that complicated. Henry and I have an arrangement. Sometimes he hooks up with girls from the shows and sometimes I spend time with other guys. It works for us because neither of us wants to own the other person."

"That's …" I didn't know what word I was looking for.

"That's what? Weird?" She tilted her head, studying me. "Wrong? Some people just don't work the same way everybody else does, Blake. We figured out what works for us. I thought you, of all people, would get that."

I guess I could get how she'd figure that, after the complaining I'd done, but I don't think that would ever be something I could do.

"He knows about us?" I asked.

"He knows I've been hanging out with a football player who needed to get away from his life for a while." Lexi pushed off the wall and stepped closer to me. "He doesn't care, and neither should you."

"I don't know if I can just …"

"Stop." She put her hand on my chest. "Stop asking about my boyfriend. Stop trying to figure out what this means or what box to put me in. That's the whole point, there's no box."

I didn't know what to say to that.

"Pay attention to me," she said and kissed me.

Her mouth tasted like beer and cigarettes, and my hands went to her waist without thinking about it.

"Come on," she said when she finally pulled back, and pulled me toward her truck.

The band was still loading gear, Henry among them, and I forced myself not to look in that direction. Lexi opened the passenger door, and I climbed in. She went around to the driver's side, but instead of starting the engine, she slid over next to me and kissed me again.

The kiss was harder this time and more urgent.

Her hands went under my shirt, fingers tracing along my sides until they found the edge of my back brace. She pulled back a little.

"You talk too much, Blake."

"I didn't say anything."

"You're thinking too much, I can hear it." She leaned down, her lips brushing my ear. "Shut up."

I shut up.

Her hands went down my stomach again, but this time they didn't stop, finding the button and popping it open. I barely had time to question what she was doing before she started pulling my pants off. It wasn't hard to get the hint, and I was drunk enough not to question it. It wasn't romantic, just need, raw and simple.

I lost track of time as the sounds outside faded. Ten minutes later, we fumbled in the dark pulling our clothes back on.

I leaned my head back against the seat, staring at the fabric roof of the cab while I rebuttoned my pants. I'd had sex in the dream life, but like everything from the dream, it was more like something I'd watched someone else doing. A memory, but one I'd never actually had.

This was nothing like that, though. It was enjoyable but also more meaningless than even the few one-night stands I'd had in the dream.

"I'll be right back," Lexi said, smoothing her hair down and kicking the door open.

Through the windshield, Lexi walked over to the white van. The guys were laughing about something where Henry stood by the open back doors. Lexi walked right up to him, said something I couldn't hear, leaned up on her tiptoes, and kissed him.

It wasn't the hungry way she'd kissed me against the wall but casual and familiar. Henry said something back, grinned, and slapped her on the ass before turning to slide a guitar case into the van.

And that was that, she said something else, waved, and then jogged back to the truck, hopped in, and slammed the door.

The drive back to Wheaton was quiet. I stared out the window at the dark landscape, my thoughts scattered. I'd just had sex with a girl whose boyfriend was loading band equipment while it happened.

I didn't know how to feel about any of it.

"Hey," Lexi said, breaking the silence.

I looked over at her.

"There's a Halloween party on Tuesday night that should be fun." She glanced at me. "You want to go?"

"Yeah," I said.

The word came out automatically.

Lexi smiled. "I'll pick you up at eight."

When she pulled up to my house, the porch light was on, but the windows were dark. I grabbed my crutches from behind the seat.

"Had fun tonight," Lexi said.

"Yeah. Me too," I lied.

Chapter 39

I at least got some good news at my doctor's visit Monday afternoon when he checked me over and said there was enough improvement to ditch the crutches. My back still ached when I moved wrong, and I was supposed to take it easy, but at least I could walk on my own again.

It was a small victory.

School itself had been strange. Eduardo had tried to follow me out to the bleachers at lunch, but I'd blown him off saying I just wanted some time to think, and yet when I got to the group, Lexi was almost distant the whole time I was there.

I was having trouble understanding her. We'd done what we'd done in her truck on Saturday night, but that seemed like it was nothing to her. Between that and her dating Henry, I was having trouble figuring her out.

After she basically ignored me all day at school the few times I saw her and tried to interact, I thought maybe she'd decided against taking me to the Halloween party she'd mentioned, but she showed up at eight just as promised.

Dad was at work again, so at least I wouldn't be asked where I was going.

Lexi's truck sat at the curb, engine running. I grabbed my jacket and headed out.

"No costume?" she asked as I climbed in.

"I didn't really feel like one. Besides, you're not wearing one either."

"Sure I am. I'm going as someone who doesn't give a shit about Halloween," she said with a laugh as she pulled away from the curb. "Works every year."

The drive to Lubbock took about an hour. She sang along to the songs she knew and made up words to the ones she didn't, same as before.

"So where's this party?" I asked during a commercial break.

"At a friend's house near Texas Tech. Actually, you met him, Frank, at the bar on Saturday."

"Oh, yeah," I said, vaguely remembering the name but not being able to put it to a face. "Is Henry going to be there?"

Lexi glanced at me with that half-smile she had when she thought I was being stupid. "Of course. He's already there helping set up."

The neighborhood near Texas Tech was mostly small duplexes and apartment complexes that looked like they were all being rented out by college students living off campus.

There was also more than one Halloween party going on on this block, from the looks of it. Thankfully, Lexi seemed to know which house we were going to, although finding a parking spot took some doing. The street was packed with cars.

"This is it," she said when she finally found a spot.

The house was two stories of peeling paint and dead lawn with people spilling out onto the porch and the front yard, most in costume.

I got out of the truck and stretched, feeling my back twinge in protest. The doctor had said to take it easy, but something told me this party wasn't what he had in mind.

"Try not to look so nervous," Lexi said.

"I'm not nervous."

That was a lie. I don't know why, but I felt more out of place here than I had at the bar. Maybe because I was a little closer in age to most of these people, but still far enough away that it would be obvious I shouldn't be there. Or maybe because it was less packed than the bar, so I was more likely to get noticed.

Whichever, I definitely had the 'high school kid trying to fit in at a college party' vibe.

"Sure you're not."

Inside, the house was packed. The living room had been cleared of furniture except for a couple of beat-up couches pushed against the walls, and people were dancing in the middle of the space where a coffee table probably used to be while loud industrial music played.

I looked over the room. If I had to guess, not everyone went to Tech, and there were some older people, meaning mid-twenties, mixed in with the twenty-year-olds.

We made our way toward the kitchen with Lexi leading and me trying not to bump into people.

Henry found us before we found him.

"There she is," he said, appearing out of the crowd with that big grin of his.

He wrapped his arms around Lexi and kissed her, his hand sliding down to rest on the small of her back.

I stood there and watched, again.

When they broke apart, Henry turned to me, grinning like I was an old friend.

"Blake! Glad you could make it, man," he said, slapping me on the shoulder.

"Wouldn't miss it."

"Here," he said, grabbing a red cup from a nearby table and pressing it into my hand. "The punch is a little funky, but two or three glasses and you won't care."

I took a drink and honestly, had he not told me it had alcohol in it, I wouldn't have known. Which was probably part of the point.

"Good, right?" Henry said, slapping my shoulder. "Enjoy yourself, man, this is gonna be a hell of a night."

He put his arm around Lexi's waist and steered her toward a group of people near the back of the house. And just like that, I was on my own.

I finished the cup in three more swallows and went to find another.

The kitchen was a disaster zone of empty bottles, half-filled cups, and a big cooler filled with ice and more of the mystery punch. I filled my cup from the cooler and took a long drink.

"What are you supposed to be?" a girl in a cat costume, black leotard, ears, whiskers drawn on her face with makeup, asked.

"A burnout."

"That's not a costume, that's a lifestyle," she said with a laugh.

"Fair point."

"What school do you go to?"

That was a question I was definitely not going to answer truthfully.

"Small place. Nobody's heard of it."

"Try me."

"You wouldn't know it."

Her interest faded fast. "Whatever. Cool jacket, though."

I'd grabbed my dad's faded brown leather jacket, mostly because I couldn't find mine when Lexi showed up, but also because I'd always liked it.

The girl drifted away, and I refilled my cup a third time.

Henry had been right; the punch was starting to hit me hard, although part of that might have been the fact that I hadn't eaten much today. Whatever the reason, I was starting to get that nice, fuzzy-headed feeling I'd been looking for.

Not quite the 'I don't have problems anymore' level of drunk, but I was getting there.

I moved through the party, letting the crowd carry me from room to room. Mostly, I just watched people, and when I did talk to someone, it usually only lasted for a minute or two. I don't know if everyone knew each other or not, but I definitely felt like the odd man out.

I wandered into some kind of back room that might have been made as an enclosed back porch thing, but had been turned into some kind of smoking area, with a ratty old couch, a coffee table, and a few chairs.

I found Lexi there, sitting on the couch between Henry and some other guy. Henry was on her left with his arm stretched along the back of the couch behind her, while the other guy was on her right, leaning in close like he was telling her a secret, and Lexi's hand rested on Henry's thigh.

I couldn't help but wonder if she was sleeping with this guy, too.

When she saw me in the doorway, she smiled and waved me over.

"Blake! Come sit down."

The other guy looked up at me, clearly annoyed at the interruption.

"Go get me a drink," Lexi told him.

He looked annoyed but did as she told him. I hesitated for a second, then sat down in the spot he'd left.

Before I could say anything, Lexi turned and kissed me hard, though her hand was still on Henry's leg.

From the corner of my eye, I saw Henry watching us, smiling.

I didn't know what to do with my hands, so one ended up on her waist while the other just sort of hung there, and I tried not to focus on how weird this was.

Lexi pulled back and grinned at me like she could read my thoughts. "Relax."

"This'll help," Henry said, leaning forward and holding out a small bag of white powder. He set a little mirror thing on the coffee table and started cutting lines with a credit card.

What the fuck.

Two other people materialized from somewhere, a girl with green hair and a guy in a cowboy hat, whom Henry waved over. They each took turns bending over the mirror before Henry went next, pressing one nostril shut and snorting a line.

Then he offered the mirror to Lexi.

She didn't hesitate, taking the line and sitting back, wiping her nose with the back of her hand.

"You want some?" Henry asked, turning to me.

"I'm good. I'll stick with the booze."

He shrugged and passed the mirror to someone else.

I could see the drugs working their way into Lexi's system.

Her eyes got kind of glassy and she got twitchy, telling this story about some club Henry was playing at and a guy who'd gotten up on stage. It was hard to follow since she kept doubling back on it, and when she'd retell a part, it wouldn't be the same as before.

The other three seemed to be into it, laughing as Henry added bits to the story, which only made it more confusing.

"I need a refill," I said.

They were too engrossed in their conversation to care.

Back in the main room, I decided to switch to something harder and found a bottle of vodka, adding a healthy amount to the punch in my half-filled cup.

A guy in a skeleton costume, I don't know if he was the same one I'd seen before or not, was looking at me as I dumped a bunch of vodka in the cup.

"Slow down there, bud. You're going to be on the floor before midnight."

"I got this," I said, taking a long pull straight from the bottle.

The party kept going on around me with people dancing, laughing, and disappearing into back rooms in pairs and groups. I leaned against a wall and watched it all happen, my brain kind of disconnected from the rest of me.

Lexi appeared in front of me at some point.

"You look miserable. Why aren't you having fun?"

"I'm having fun."

"You're a terrible liar," she said with a laugh, taking my cup and finishing what was left before kissing me again. "Damn, you made that strong."

She handed me the empty cup and disappeared back into the crowd.

I went back to the kitchen for more vodka and punch; the room definitely tilting now.

Wandering down a hallway, a door opened into a bedroom where two people were tangled up on a mattress, so I backed out fast. Another door led to another bedroom filled with smoke and about six people passing a bong around. I stood in the doorway for a minute, watching them, before deciding I didn't feel like getting high, and backing out.

The living room had gotten more chaotic while I was gone, with more people and less space, while the music seemed louder, or maybe I was just drunker. Through the press of bodies, I spotted Lexi dancing with Henry and another girl, the three of them pressed together and Henry's hands on both of them and the other girl's arms wrapped around Lexi from behind.

I decided I needed some air.

The front porch was cooler and quieter, so I sat down hard on the steps and my vision swam for a second before settling.

A girl in a witch costume sat down next to me and offered a cigarette. I took it, let her light it, inhaled, and coughed.

"You okay?"

"Great. I'm great."

"Sure you are, honey," she said with a laugh, patting my shoulder before going back inside.

I decided against finishing the cigarette and flicked it into the dead grass, watching the ember die out before pushing myself to my feet.

The world tilted for a second before righting itself.

Back inside, I made my way through the crowd toward the kitchen, bumping into people and muttering apologies. The vodka bottle was still there, mostly empty now, and I poured what was left into a fresh cup before adding some of the mystery punch on top.

Someone in a vampire cape said something to me, so I nodded like I understood and kept moving.

Things got a little hazy after that.

I remember being in the living room watching people dance, then sitting on the arm of a couch talking to someone about football, though I couldn't tell you what I said. Later, I was outside again, then back in.

The party kept going on around me, and I kept drinking.

At some point, I found myself leaning against the wall near the front door when Lexi appeared in front of me with red eyes.

"We're leaving," she said.

"What?"

"Henry's being an asshole. I'm so done with this shit. Let's go."

I blinked at her. "Okay."

She grabbed my arm and started pulling me toward the door. I stumbled after her, nearly tripping over someone's foot.

We made it outside, and she kept walking, hauling me down the sidewalk toward where she'd parked.

Lexi stopped at her truck and fumbled in her pocket, pulling out her keys. She stared at them for a second, then shoved them into my hand.

"Here, you drive."

"What?"

"I'm too messed up. You drive."

I looked down at the keys in my palm. Some distant part of my brain, the part that hadn't been drowned in vodka and punch, tried to send up a warning.

"Lexi, I don't ..."

"Just get in the damn truck, Blake! I want to go home."

She walked around to the passenger side and climbed in, slamming the door behind her.

I stood there with the keys in my hand, knowing this was a bad idea because I was too drunk to be behind the wheel and didn't even have a license.

But this was my era of "fuck it," so I got in.

The seat was too far forward. I spent a minute trying to figure out how to adjust it, my fingers clumsy on the lever, before finally getting it to slide back enough that I could fit my legs. Lexi slumped against the passenger window, her eyes closed.

I pulled away from the curb slowly, my hands gripping the wheel at ten and two like I was taking a driving test. The street was mostly empty now, the other party houses dark or the noise dying down.

Getting out of the neighborhood took longer than it should have because I made a wrong turn, had to double back, and almost ran a stop sign before catching myself at the last second.

Lexi didn't say anything. I wasn't even sure if she was awake.

Eventually, I found a main road and turned onto it, heading toward what I hoped was the way out of town.

I was going the speed limit, or maybe a little under, keeping both hands on the wheel and my eyes on the road while trying to focus and drive as soberly as I could.

I don't know exactly when I drifted over the center line. I didn't even realize I'd done it until I saw the headlights coming toward me and jerked the wheel back to the right.

I jerked the wheel too hard, causing the truck to swerve and overcorrect.

That's when red and blue lights flashed from the side of the road a little ways behind us, pulling out and coming up on us fast.

Shit!

"What's happening?" Lexi asked from the passenger seat as I pulled over to the side of the road and put it in park.

"Cops."

"Shit."

My thoughts exactly.

The deputy appeared at my window. He was maybe thirty, with a crew cut and a face that looked like it had never smiled in its life.

"License and registration."

I hesitated, trying to think what I should do. The guy just stared at me.

"I don't have a license."

The flashlight beam moved from my face to the interior of the truck, then back to my face.

"You don't have a license."

"No, sir."

"How old are you?"

"Fifteen."

He leaned closer to the window.

"Have you been drinking tonight?"

I should have lied, but my mouth went faster than my brain.

"I had a couple of drinks."

"Step out of the vehicle."

I fumbled with the door handle and managed to get it open. When I stepped out, my legs felt like they went wobbly, so I grabbed the truck door to keep my balance.

"Stand over here by my vehicle."

I walked to where he pointed, trying to keep my steps steady while my back brace dug into me.

"Do you have any physical problems or disabilities that affect your balance, walking, or standing?"

"I have an injury in my back from football," I said, lifting my shirt so he could see the back brace.

His flashlight flicked toward it. Another patrol car appeared, and a second deputy was walking toward the passenger side of Lexi's truck.

"I'm going to have you perform some field sobriety tests. Do you understand?"

"Yes, sir."

"Put your feet together and keep your hands at your sides."

I did that as best I could without swaying, but I knew I was weaving a little just standing in place.

"Keep your head still and look at this pen."

I looked at it, squinting a little because it was dark and hard to see.

"Follow the object with your eyes only. Do not move your head."

He moved the pen left and right, up and down slowly, and I thought I was doing pretty well, but after a moment, he put it back in his pocket and said, "Turn around and put your hands behind your back."

"What?" I said as I started to turn around.

"You're under arrest for driving under the influence and operating a vehicle without a license."

I felt cold metal against my wrists as the handcuffs clicked in place, biting into my skin a little bit and holding my arm at an uncomfortable angle. He leaned me against the car and started patting me down, going through my pockets and pulling stuff out, although I only had my house keys and wallet on me. Once he had those set on the roof of the car, he pulled me a step back from the car, which almost caused me to fall over, and opened the door.

"Watch your head."

I ducked and slid onto the plastic seat. The door closed behind me.

Through the window, I watched the second deputy talking to Lexi. She was out of the truck now, standing on the side of the road with her arms crossed.

Headlights appeared from the direction of town, and a car pulled up behind the patrol cars, and Henry got out, along with two other people I recognized from the party.

Lexi walked over to the first deputy and said something I couldn't hear through the glass. They talked for a moment as she pointed toward Henry. The deputy then waved her toward them, and she walked over to where Henry was standing. He said something that made her laugh and then left her by the car while he walked toward the pickup.

I waited for her to look at me or acknowledge that I was sitting in the back of a cop car because she'd shoved her keys into my hand and told me to drive.

She didn't.

Instead, she climbed into Henry's car with his friends, and a few seconds later they pulled away, the pickup following behind them. I watched her disappear down the road.

The deputy got into the front seat and started the engine.

Ten minutes later, the deputy walked me through the side doors of the police station. It was weird to think I'd been here just a few weeks ago, but in such a different way.

I was led into a holding area where he put me on a bench, connecting the handcuffs to some kind of chain thing on the bench, basically locking me in place, before going to a counter where another deputy sat behind a computer.

The two stood there for what seemed like forever, going through paperwork and talking. They were just far enough away that I couldn't hear them clearly.

Eventually, he got me up again and started to lead me over a spot near the counter where a camera was mounted on the desk when a man walked into the booking area.

Something about him seemed familiar. It took me a second to place the face before I realized it was the guy who helped us with the search for Josh, Detective Bowen.

"Hold up a sec," he said.

The booking deputy stopped, looking confused.

"Blake, I got a call you were in here. I've called your father, and he's on his way."

I was so confused, trying to figure out who could have called him. "You did?"

"One of the deputies who picked you up recognized you from the search for your brother."

"Oh."

"Hold up on processing him," he said to the deputy. "Just put him in the holding cell until I come back for him."

"Sure," the deputy said and led me down a hallway lined with cells.

The holding cell was about what I expected with a metal bench bolted to the wall, a toilet in the corner, concrete floors, and cinder block walls.

I sat on the bench and stared at the floor.

I knew I had lucked out big time.

I was being given a break that others wouldn't get, and part of me wished I wasn't. I was just so tired of everything. All the bullshit.

I leaned back against the cold wall and closed my eyes.

I sat there for over an hour listening to deputies moving through the station outside my cell and phones ringing at the front desk while my back ached from the metal bench.

I didn't really look up again until I heard footsteps just outside my cell.

"Your father's here," Bowen said.

I stood up and followed him down the hallway toward the front of the station. The alcohol had mostly faded now, and I was left with a massive headache pushing against the back of my head.

Dad was standing near the front desk in his uniform, the disappointment and anger on his face clear as day.

I stopped a few feet from him, unable to meet his eyes.

Bowen looked at me. "I hope you understand what kind of break you're getting here."

I just nodded.

"Thanks again," Dad said to him.

Bowen gave him a sad nod, almost like wishing him good luck, and headed back into the restricted area.

Dad walked toward the exit, and I followed him outside into the night where his patrol car was parked near the entrance.

He opened the driver's side door and paused, looking at me across the hood.

He didn't say anything.

I climbed into the passenger seat and closed the door. He started the engine and pulled out of the parking lot.

Chapter 40

We drove in silence for the first five minutes.

Dad kept both hands on the wheel, his jaw set and eyes fixed on the road ahead. I sat in the passenger seat with my arms crossed, still feeling the edges of the alcohol even though most of it had worn off. My head ached, but my back ached worse. The brace dug into my ribs every time I moved.

"I can't believe you did this," Dad finally said.

I didn't respond.

"Blake, you've always been more mature than this. Over the last two years, you've been so responsible. I don't understand where this came from. I expected better from you. Do you have any idea what could have happened tonight? You could have killed someone. You could have killed yourself. You could have gotten a DUI on your record that would follow you for the rest of your life. Everything you've worked for, football, the grades, all of it, could have been wiped out in one night from one stupid decision."

I just kept staring out the window.

"I know," I said.

"I don't think you do," he said, his voice harder. "I've seen what happens to kids who make choices like this. I've seen their futures disappear. I've had to tell parents their children aren't coming home because someone got behind the wheel when they shouldn't have."

"I said I know."

"Then why? Why would you do something so reckless, so irresponsible? This isn't you, Blake. This isn't the person you've been showing me."

I knew he was right, that I'd screwed up big, and I didn't have any excuses for it. I'd gotten some weird vibes from Lexi, but I still went. I knew I shouldn't have been driving, but still did it.

Him lecturing me, though, was bullshit. After everything that happened, he didn't get to be the one to tell me I'd made choices that ruined everything.

"You don't get to be disappointed," I said.

Dad turned toward me before snapping back to the road. "Excuse me?"

"You heard me; you don't get to be disappointed in me. Not after everything you let happen."

"What the hell are you talking about?"

The words came out before I could stop them or think about whether I should say them.

"I warned you about Josh for months. Even before the cats, I told you about him stalking that girl at the birthday party. I told you about him trying to spy on Li through her window. I brought you evidence and I begged you to do something, and every single time you told me you were handling it, that you were taking care of it. What exactly were you handling? Because from where I'm sitting, nothing changed until I forced the issue myself."

"Blake ..."

"No. You don't get to 'Blake' me right now." I turned toward him in my seat, ignoring the awkward pressure of the brace. "I watched Josh get worse and worse while you kept telling me to be patient and that I didn't understand. You kept saying you'd talk to Mom, but what you were really doing was pretending that if everyone just stayed calm, the problems would solve themselves."

"I know I made mistakes with Joshua."

"Mistakes is a hell of a word for what happened. You let him escalate for years while Mom protected him from every consequence. You watched our family fall apart and kept going to work and coming home and acting like everything was fine. You know what I shouldn't have had to do? I shouldn't have had to threaten my own mother to get her to see a doctor. A fifteen-year-old shouldn't have to issue ultimatums to force his mother to get treatment for a brain tumor. That was your job. You were supposed to be the adult; you were supposed to protect this family."

Dad pulled the cruiser to the side of the road and put it in park before clicking on the hazards.

He turned to face me. "What are you talking about?"

"I'm talking about why she finally agreed to see a real doctor and get diagnosed. How I convinced her to get chemo and the surgery."

"She said she realized it was time; that she'd been thinking about it."

"She was never going to think about it, and you know it. She was completely gone into her wellness thing and becoming more unstable. I told you about that, too, and you said you were handling it. It was clear she was never going to make that decision for herself, so I took the option away from her, which is something you should have done. I told her I'd drop out of school, quit football and get a job so I could monitor her full-time. I told her I'd file a complaint with CPS about Josh's behavior and her neglect of both of us so we'd get taken away. I was ready to throw everything away if she didn't change her mind. Thankfully, she did, but nobody had a problem with that because you all got what you wanted out of it. You got the problem solved without ever having to confront anyone or be the bad guy."

"Why didn't you tell me?" he asked.

"What would have been the point? I'd been pushing you to do something and talk some sense into her for a full year. I could see she was getting worse and someone had to do something, so I did something. I fixed it." I slammed my hand against the dashboard, sending a jolt through my injured back. "That's all anyone wants from me: fix everything. Handle it. Figure it out. But when I need someone, when I need an adult to step up and do the right thing, suddenly it's not possible."

Dad turned and slumped back in the seat, staring out at the road ahead, lit by the headlights and the hazards blinking off and on.

He didn't say anything for a long time.

"You're right," he finally said.

I'd been ready for an argument or for him to tell me I didn't understand how complicated things were.

"What?"

"You're right about all of it. I failed. I failed as a father and as a husband. I saw the warning signs with Josh, well, you pointed them out to me, and I kept hoping things would improve on their own. I watched your mother deteriorate and kept believing she'd come around if I just gave her space and time. I put too much on your shoulders, way too much, and I'm sorry."

He looked so sad, and part of me, a big part of me, wanted to let him off the hook. To say it was okay, that he was trying his best.

But he wasn't.

"Sorry doesn't fix anything. Sorry doesn't bring Mom back from wherever she ran to or help slow whatever Josh is becoming. Sorry doesn't change the fact that I've been carrying this family on my back while trying to be a student and an athlete and somehow keep my own life from falling apart."

"I know."

"Do you? Because I'm tired, Dad. I'm so damn tired of being the one who has to hold everything together."

"I know you are and I can't change what happened. I can't go back and do things differently, even though I wish I could." He wiped his face with the back of his hand. "But I can do better going forward. I need you, God knows I've needed you more than any father should need his teenage son, but I also need you to trust that I'm trying, even when I fail. Can you give me that much?"

I looked out the window at the dark highway as a truck passed going the other direction.

"I don't know," I said.

"Blake ..."

"I'm tired of being responsible for everyone else's problems. I'm tired of being the one who sees what's coming and has to figure out how to stop it. I just wanted one night where I didn't have to think about any of it, and look where that got me."

Dad put the cruiser back in gear and pulled onto the highway, silencing the hazard lights.

"I understand wanting to escape," he said after a while. "I've felt that way more times than you know. The difference is that escape never fixes the problems; it just delays them while creating new ones. You learned that tonight the hard way."

I didn't respond.

We drove the rest of the way in silence. Dad kept both hands on the wheel with his eyes on the road while I kept my head against the window, watching the mile markers pass in the darkness.

Dad turned onto our street and pulled into the driveway where the porch light was on, though the rest of the house was dark. He shut off the engine but didn't move to get out.

"We'll figure this out," he said. "You don't have to carry it alone anymore."

I didn't answer. Instead, I opened the passenger door and stepped out of the cruiser and walked into the house, leaving him sitting in the car alone.

I woke up with my head aching and my mouth tasting like something had crawled in there and died.

The light coming through the windows was way too bright, and I was still wearing yesterday's clothes. This was the first time I'd slept in the back brace, and I knew I was never going to do that again.

It hurt like hell.

I went downstairs and looked out the window. Dad's cruiser wasn't in the driveway, which meant he must have left for work without waking me, which was fine since I didn't want to talk to him anyway.

I made it to the kitchen, drank two glasses of water from the tap, and found some aspirin in the cabinet above the stove. The microwave clock said it was almost noon. School had started hours ago, and I wondered if Dad had called me in absent or if I was going to be suspended or expelled when I went in tomorrow.

A knock on the front door made me wince. I ignored it.

The knock came again, harder.

"Blake Sims, I know you are home. Open this door."

I froze at the unmistakable voice.

Li's mom knocked a third time. "I am not leaving until you open the door. I have nowhere else to be."

I opened the door. Li's mom stood on the porch and looked me over with the expression of someone looking at a mess they had to clean up.

"You look terrible," she said.

"Thanks."

"May I come in?"

I stepped aside, and she walked into the living room and sat down.

"Look," I said before she could start, "what you saw when you walked in with me and ... it wasn't what it looked like. Li didn't do anything wrong. I kissed her, she told me to stop, and I did."

"I know."

"She wasn't ... wait, what?"

"I know what happened since Li told me everything. I am not here about that."

"Then why are you here?"

"Your father came to see me this morning."

That caught me off guard. "My dad went to see you?"

"Yes. He asked if I would come speak with you. He said you had a difficult night and he was worried about you, but didn't think you would listen to him right now."

He was right about that part.

"I know about your going out to a party last night, the drinking, and getting arrested."

"Great, so everyone knows," I said, standing and throwing my hands up.

"Sit down, Blake."

"I don't need to ..."

"Sit."

I sat back down.

"Your father is worried about you. He sees you destroying yourself, and he does not know how to reach you, so he called me because he thought perhaps I could. I am not sure he was right, but I told him I would try."

"I'm fine."

"Do not lie to me, you are not fine and you know it. You were arrested last night for drunk driving, you have been skipping school, you've been making choices that could ruin your future, and from what I hear, you have been spending time with people who do not care about you. This is not fine. This is a boy who is drowning and too proud to ask for help."

"You don't know what's been going on."

"I know more than you think. I know about your mother's illness and your behavior. I know about the pressure you've been under. Your father told me about the threats you made to force your mother into treatment and that you've been carrying all of this for a very long time while feeling like no one else cared."

I just looked down at the floor. I was a little surprised my dad had told her so much.

"I know you feel like everyone else has failed you and left all of this for you to handle. That is why I came to talk to you, because I would like to know why you believe you had no choice but to handle everything alone."

"Because I didn't have a choice. I asked my dad for help over and over, and he didn't do anything."

"Yes, your father failed you, and he knows this. I have spoken to him at length about what he did wrong and how he let you down. But I have a question for you. Who else did you ask?"

I opened my mouth to answer and then shut it again.

"You have coaches who care about you, yes? You have business partners who are invested in your success. Yes, I know about that," she said when I looked surprised she knew I had a business partner. "You have teachers who have worked with you to improve your grades. You have Yesica who drives two hours every week to train you. And you have me. I know you didn't come to speak to me, so I ask again, who else did you ask for help?"

"I didn't want to bother other people with my private family business."

"And how did keeping them private work out for you?"

I had no response to that.

"So you told yourself you had no choice but to handle everything alone, but you have to know that that is not true. You have people who would have helped, and you chose not to ask them because you decided you knew better, that you could fix everything yourself. This is pride, Blake, and pride is not the same as strength."

"I didn't want to air my family's dirty laundry to everyone."

"So instead, you let it crush you until you made a series of terrible decisions that could destroy your future. You could have killed yourself last night, you understand this, yes?"

"I know," I said.

"Good. Then perhaps you can hear what else I have to say. A lot of things have gone wrong, I am not minimizing that, but you need to cut everyone, including yourself, some slack. You need to look honestly at some of the choices you have made."

"Like what?"

"Like with Li."

I flinched. "I thought you said you weren't here about that."

"I am not here only about that, but it is part of a larger pattern I need you to see. I want to address something first. I know you have told her that I hate you and am angry at you, and I wanted to make it clear that is not true."

"Could have fooled me," I said under my breath.

"Don't mumble. If you have the courage to say something, then say it, otherwise do not. And yes, I was scared. Li is in many ways a sheltered girl. I admit that is my fault; I have kept her too protected. She has not dated or spent much time with boys. I think you and Eduardo are the first real close friends she's ever had, so when I walk in and find her kissing a teenage boy whose hormones could override his judgment at any moment, I overreacted."

"I wasn't going to ..."

"I know, but in that moment, I did not think. I reacted as a mother who saw her daughter in a vulnerable position. I was not angry at you, I was afraid for her. I should have handled it better. I should have spoken to you then instead of sending you away; that was my mistake. I'm telling you this now because you need to understand that not everything that happened was about you failing or being rejected. Sometimes people react badly out of fear, which brings me to what I actually need you to hear. About what happened between you and Li."

"She told me she didn't want to be with me. I got the message."

"Did you? Because from what Li told me, that is not what she said at all. I am going to ask you something, and I want you to answer honestly, not just say what you think I want to hear or what makes you look better. Can you do that?"

I nodded, though I wasn't sure I could.

"When you kissed Li, was it because you have real feelings for her, or was it because you were scared and lonely and she was there?"

I didn't answer. I'd had a lot of time to think about it and what I said to Li about it, and I was ashamed to admit why I'd done it.

"Li is your friend. She has been your friend through everything. She came to the hospital when you were injured, she has kept your secrets, and she has supported you even when you pushed her away. And in your moment of fear, when everything was falling apart, you tried to turn that friendship into something else because you wanted to feel less alone. She saw it even when you could not. She recognized that you were acting out of desperation, not genuine feeling, and she cared about you enough not to let you use her that way."

The word "use" hit hard.

"I wasn't using her."

"Then what would you call it? You were hurting, afraid, and needed something to make the pain stop. Li was there, being kind to you as she always is, and you decided to take what you needed without considering what it would cost her. She was trying to protect you both, and that is not rejection. That is a friend who sees you more clearly than you see yourself and loves you enough to say no."

I rubbed my face. My hangover made everything worse.

"And what did you do when she tried to explain this to you? When she tried to tell you why she was pulling back?"

"I attacked her," I said.

"You did. You were hurt and angry, and instead of hearing what she was saying, you made her the enemy for not giving you what you wanted. This is what I need you to understand, Blake; this is exactly what your father did. Your father was not honest with himself about how bad things were. He acted out of fear and chose avoidance instead of facing hard truths, and when you tried to confront him with reality, he got defensive and shut down instead of listening. What did you do when Li tried to tell you the truth about yourself?"

"I did the same thing," I said, feeling like the smallest worm in the earth.

Thankfully, she didn't look triumphant or throw it in my face.

"You have been so focused on what everyone else did wrong that you cannot see your own reflection in their failures."

I sat there, unable to look at her. Everything I'd been telling myself for the past week and a half—that I was the only one who'd been trying, that everyone else had failed me, that I was justified in my anger—it was all falling apart.

"I am going to tell you something about myself. When my husband died, I was very angry. At him, for leaving me; at the world, for taking him; and at myself, for all the things I should have said and done while he was alive. I pushed everyone away. I told myself that no one could understand what I was going through, that I had to be strong for Li, that asking for help was weakness. It took me years to realize that I was not being strong, I was being weak. I was so scared of needing anyone that I almost destroyed the relationships that could have saved me. Grief and fear make people stupid and selfish; I know this from experience. It is easy to turn inward and convince yourself that you are the only one who truly sees, who truly understands, who truly tries, but that is a trap, and you fell into it. The question is whether you can climb out."

"What am I supposed to do?"

"Stop pretending you are the only one who is right. Stop holding onto your grievance like it is something precious. Your father made mistakes, and Li hurt you, but you made mistakes too, and you hurt people too. Cut everyone some slack, including yourself. Not because what happened does not matter, but because holding onto this idea that you alone were righteous and everyone else failed you is going to poison every relationship you have. When you are ready to stop carrying everything alone, there are people who will help. But you have to actually let them in."

I didn't know what to say. She got up and left me just sitting there, thinking about what she'd said.

I didn't move from the couch for a long time. I just sat there, finally seeing all the ways I'd deluded myself.

Chapter 41

I got to school early Thursday morning before most of the buses arrived. While it wasn't unusual for me to be at school this early, or even earlier, normally, I just stayed out on the field.

It was weird being inside the school itself.

The hallways were mostly empty, with a few teachers walking to their classrooms and a kid or two who'd shown up early for their own reasons. I found a spot near Li's locker to wait where I could see the main entrance.

I'd spent most of yesterday thinking about what Li's mom said and how I'd been so convinced I was the only one trying or seeing things clearly that I couldn't see my own reflection in the failures I was accusing everyone else of. I used Li because I was scared and lonely, then attacked her for not giving me what I wanted.

It wasn't a comfortable thing to sit with.

The hallway started filling up around seven-thirty as students came through the main doors in small groups, laughing and talking. Li came through the entrance at seven forty-five.

She carried her backpack over one shoulder, her dark hair pulled back in a practical ponytail, walking with her head down and focused on something in her hands. She didn't look up until she got to her locker and then stopped cold when she saw me standing there.

I could see her ready herself for another fight before she started walking toward me again.

"What do you want?" she asked.

"I wanted to apologize."

She looked at me skeptically, and I almost faltered, worried I'd burned this bridge too badly.

"When I kissed you in your room, I wasn't thinking about you. I wasn't thinking about what you wanted or what it would mean for our friendship. I was scared about my injury and because of all the stuff happening in my family, and I tried to use you to fill a hole that had nothing to do with you. That was wrong."

I couldn't take the silence when she didn't respond immediately, so I just kept rambling.

"What made it worse was how I acted afterward. When you tried to explain why you were pulling back, I attacked you instead of listening. I said things to hurt you because I was hurting. You didn't deserve any of that, Li, none of it."

"No," she said. "I didn't."

"Your mom came to see me yesterday."

Li's cool finally slipped. "My mother came to see you?"

"Yeah. I got into some trouble Tuesday, and Dad was worried about me and wasn't having a lot of luck getting me to listen, so he asked your mom to step in. Your mom helped me see some things I couldn't see on my own, like how I was making the same mistakes I accused my dad of making. How I was getting defensive and lashing out instead of hearing what anyone was trying to tell me."

"What do you want from this conversation, Blake?"

"Nothing, except to tell you I'm sorry for what I did to you. It wasn't fair, and you have every right to be angry at me and never be my friend. If you can forgive me, what I'd like, if you're willing, is to find a way back to being friends. We can rebuild it slowly and on your terms. Eduardo can be a buffer if that makes it easier, but I want our trio back. I miss it."

Li studied me for a long time, not putting me out of my misery.

"Your rejection hurt me," she finally said. "Not because you tried to kiss me; I knew why you were doing that, and I knew you were hurting. What really hurt was how mean you got afterward. I thought our friendship was stronger than what happened."

"I know."

"When you kissed me and then attacked me for saying no, it confirmed something I was afraid of. That I was never important to you except for what I could give you in that moment and that our friendship was just convenient until you needed something else. How am I supposed to trust that you won't do this again the next time things get hard?"

"Hopefully, I have learned from this and can be a better person next time. I can't promise I won't screw up; hell, I can almost guarantee I will, but I can promise to be honest with you about what I'm feeling and to talk to you when I'm struggling instead of acting out or expecting you to fix it. That's the best I can offer."

Li went quiet again. I stopped babbling or trying to fill the silence. I'd made my pitch, and if I kept trying to convince her, it would only do the opposite.

All I could do was wait.

"I miss my friend," Li said finally. "I'm glad to have him back, but this is going to take time, Blake."

"I know."

She moved past me to her locker and started working the combination. I stepped aside to give her space.

"Eduardo has been worried about both of us," she said as she pulled out her books for first period.

"I know. I'm going to talk to him too."

Li tucked the books against her chest and closed the locker. "The three of us should get lunch together today."

"I'd like that."

She looked at me for another moment, deciding whether to say what was on her mind. "Don't make me regret giving you another chance."

"I won't."

Li turned and started walking toward her first class, and I let myself relax. While it didn't go as well as I'd hoped it would have gone, it also went a lot better than I worried it could have.

She'd given me a second chance, and I could work with that.

The final bell rang, and I grabbed my bag from under my desk and headed for the door. It had been a hell of a day, my apology tour.

Li had, of course, been the hardest, since I'd done her the most wrong, but she was far from the only one. Eduardo I'd mostly just avoided, so his had been pretty easy. The guys from the team, I think I was carrying more guilt than anything for messing up our season.

They didn't hold any grudges and let me off the hook right away. The only other person I'd really let down at school, other than Li, was Ms. White, who'd gone out of her way to try and get me refocused on school, and I'd kind of thrown it back in her face.

I had dug a hole with her, and this semester was going to be a problem, no doubt about it. I did ***not*** go see Mr. Brennan. Yeah, I had basically proven his point, but he'd never been on my side. I'd been an object lesson for him and nothing more. Thankfully, I'd done well enough the first half of the semester that my apathy over the last several weeks or so wouldn't tank my grades, not put me in the failing range, so it was recoverable, especially since I still had a month and finals to turn things around.

All in all, I'd had to spend most of my day eating crow and apologizing for being a dick to everyone I talked to for the last two weeks.

There was one person left I knew I was going to end up talking to, though, that wasn't part of the apology tour. I'd mostly managed to avoid her all day until I cut across the parking lot toward the field house when she finally caught up with me.

Lexi.

She stood by the fence that separated the field and the parking lot with her arms crossed, looking annoyed.

"Where have you been?" she asked.

"What?" I asked, stopping a few feet away.

"I waited for you yesterday and today, but you never showed up."

I could only assume she meant she'd waited at the bleachers, because I'd kept to my actual schedule, so I wouldn't have been hard to find if she'd actually come looking for me.

"Why would I come by?"

"Are you avoiding me now?"

"I think it's easier to say I'm done with you."

The amusement drained away to something guarded.

"Okay. What's your problem?"

"My problem is you left me there."

"Left you where?"

"Don't play dumb with me, at the side of the road getting arrested by the cops. You gave me your keys and insisted that I drive, and when I got pulled over, you had Henry come pick you up and drove away without looking back, leaving me to deal with the consequences."

Lexi rolled her eyes.

"Oh my God, are you still upset about that?"

"I sat in a holding cell for over an hour, so yeah, I'm upset about that."

"It wasn't a big deal."

"Not a big deal?"

"Look, I already have a minor in possession on my record, and I couldn't afford another one. If I'd made a big scene, they would have arrested me too, and then we'd both be screwed. Besides, you're a cop's son. I knew they'd go easy on you since cops always look out for their own."

"That's your excuse?"

"It's not an excuse, it's the truth. And it worked out, didn't it? You're standing here instead of sitting in juvie somewhere. Did you go to jail? No. I bet you didn't even get booked."

She said it like she'd done me a favor.

"I can't believe you would do that to someone after everything that happened between us," I said.

Lexi actually laughed.

"Blake, come on, it's not that deep."

"What?"

"We hooked up one time, it's not like I'm your girlfriend. That's just how things work sometimes. People have to look out for themselves." She shrugged. "Don't take it personally."

She was right about one thing, because I'd known what I was getting into when I started hanging out with her. I'd gone to her because I was angry and scared and wanted to stop thinking about everything that was falling apart, and she'd offered an escape.

"You're right," I said. "I knew what I was getting into. I came to you because I wanted to stop thinking, and that was on me. I own that. The difference is that I can't be around someone who would abandon me like that and not even look back."

"This is exactly why I don't deal with guys like you," she said.

"Guys like me?"

"Yeah. You wanted to play at being wild and reckless, but the second things got real, you turned into a whiny kid who needs someone to hold his hand. You're just like every other loser who thinks hanging out with me makes him interesting and then blames me when his life falls apart."

What's crazy was, she probably believed that. She used people and abandoned them as soon as she didn't need them anymore, and then thought it was their fault that they turned against her.

"I'm done," I said. "Whatever this was, it's over."

"Whatever."

"Have a good life, Lexi."

I walked toward the athletic building.

"You'll be back," she called after me. "They always come back when they realize their normal friends are boring and nobody else wants to deal with their problems. Enjoy pretending you're better than everyone!"

I didn't turn around or respond. What would be the point?

I caught Coach Holloway outside the field house right after the final bell, before he could disappear into his office to start game prep.

"Coach, you got a minute?"

He stopped, keys in hand, and looked at me with that guarded expression I'd been seeing a lot lately. I couldn't blame him.

"What do you need?"

"I want to apologize for missing practice Wednesday, and for not being involved at the Central game the way I should've been. Gabriel was struggling out there, and I just sat on that bench feeling sorry for myself instead of helping him through it."

Coach Holloway didn't say anything, just waited.

"We're one and two in district, and if we lose tonight, there's no way we make playoffs. Everything we worked for all season will be gone. I still want to go to state. I know we can beat Cooper, and if you'll let me, I want to work with Gabriel between plays, during warm-ups, whenever I can. I think I can help him get through this game."

Coach Holloway studied me for a long moment before speaking. "I'd been hoping you'd step up sooner than this, Blake."

"I know. I haven't been the leader I promised you I'd be, not since before homecoming, honestly. I've had ..." I stopped and tried again. "Things have been difficult at home, and I let it affect everything else."

"I noticed."

"After the game tonight, I'd like to talk to you about it, not to make excuses, but because I need some help from adults who know more than I do about handling this stuff, but that can wait. Right now, we have a game to win."

Coach Holloway looked at me for a moment and nodded once.

"Good," he said. "Now do what you should've been doing all along."

A few hours later, I found Gabriel near the thirty-yard line warming up his arm with short passes to one of the backup receivers.

"Hey."

He caught the ball on its return and held it, not looking at me. "Hey."

"How are you feeling?"

"Fine," he said. "Ready to go."

I'd heard that tone before. From myself, usually, right before I was about to do something stupid, because I was too scared to admit I wasn't ready.

"Okay," I said. "Can I give you one thing to think about?"

Gabriel looked at me, and I could see in his face that he expected me to criticize him or remind him of the three interceptions last week.

"Last game, you were locking onto your primary receiver every play," I said. "You'd pick your guy pre-snap and stare him down the whole way, and when the throw wasn't there, you either forced it anyway or froze up."

His expression hardened. "Thanks for the ..."

"I'm not criticizing you; I'm trying to help you. Tonight, I need you to trust your progressions. It's the big thing Coach banged into my head over and over last year. If the primary's not there, you go to your second read, and if the second read's covered, you check down to your third. You know how to do this from practice; the problem is you're getting scared out there, stopping your thinking and just staring at one guy."

Gabriel didn't argue.

"Before every snap," I said, "tell yourself, 'primary, secondary, check-down,' say it in your head. And when the ball's in your hands, let your eyes move, don't lock on. Trust that you'll see the open man if you actually look for him."

He was quiet. "That's it?"

"That's it. Go through your reads and trust your eyes. The throws will be there if you let yourself see them. You can do this, Gabe. I promise. You are good enough to beat them, but you have to trust what you've learned in practice."

He stared at me for a long moment and nodded.

"Okay," he said. "Yeah. Okay."

Cooper won the toss and elected to receive. Their return man took it to the twenty-eight, decent field position, and their offense trotted out looking confident.

Cooper's quarterback was a senior, bigger than Gabriel, with a strong arm but questionable decision-making. Their game plan was obvious from the first play: pound the ball up the middle with their running back, a stocky kid who ran like he was angry at the ground.

They picked up four yards on first down and three more on second, converting the third with three on a quick slant.

Our defense looked shaky, not bad, but not as good as they normally could be. I chalked it up to nerves. The whole team had done the math on what this game meant for us and knew what was on the line. Cooper kept moving the ball until they were inside our twenty.

Then Justin read a screen pass perfectly, blowing up the running back in the backfield for a loss of four.

Cooper's quarterback got greedy on third and long and tried to force a ball into double coverage where Calvin picked it off at the eight-yard line.

Our sideline erupted. I grabbed Gabriel's arm as he headed onto the field.

"First drive, what's your mantra?"

"Primary, secondary, check-down."

"Say it before every snap, don't think about anything else, and just let your eyes do the work."

He nodded, pulling on his helmet.

The first play was a handoff to Joe for five yards. Gabriel took the snap on second down, looked left at Mickey, who was covered. For a moment, I thought he might stay on Mickey, but I saw his head turn and he found Jerry on the underneath route for seven and a first down.

We were moving.

On the next passing play, Gabriel again started with his primary, saw the coverage, moved to his second read, and hit the throw. It wasn't a spectacular play, just a simple completion for six yards, but it was exactly what he needed to be doing.

We drove from our own eight to midfield before Cooper's defense held and we had to punt.

Gabriel came off the field looking, if not confident, at least a little less terrified.

"That was good," I told him. "Really good. You went through your progressions on that third-and-four. I saw you check off Mickey and find Jerry."

"It felt slow, like I was taking too long," Gabriel admitted.

"You weren't, trust me. When you're actually going through your reads instead of panicking, it feels slower than it is because the clock in your head lies to you, so just keep doing what you're doing."

The first quarter ended scoreless, but Cooper struck first in the second with a long pass over the top that our safety bit on to make the score 7-0.

Gabriel looked rattled when he headed out for our next drive. I intercepted him before he reached the huddle.

"Hey. That touchdown wasn't on you; defense gave up that play. Your job hasn't changed. Just stick to your mantra."

"Got it."

"What are you not going to do?"

"Read the receiver."

"And if your first read isn't there?"

"Move to the second."

"That's it, nothing's changed. Go move the chains."

The drive started slow with a run for three and an incomplete pass where Gabriel stared down Mickey the whole way so the corner read it easily.

He looked at me, and I mimed moving his reads. He nodded and hit his helmet twice, as if to knock it into his head.

The next drive stalled, and we punted, but on the next possession, Gabriel started finding his rhythm again with a completion to Jerry on a second-read throw, a check-down to Austin that went for twelve after the catch, and a deep ball to Miguel that Gabriel only threw because he had looked off the safety first.

We kept grinding for eight plays and sixty-two yards. Gabriel connected with Jerry on a comeback route at the twelve, his third progression on the play and the exact read he was supposed to make, before Austin punched it in from the four on a draw play.

Tied game.

Gabriel jogged off the field, almost smiling.

"That touchdown drive," I said. "You went through all three reads on the throw to Jerry at the twelve."

"Primary was doubled," Gabriel said. "Secondary had a guy draped on him. Jerry was just ... there."

"That's what happens when you trust your progressions. The open guy shows up."

Halftime came with the score still tied at seven. Coach Holloway made adjustments, pointed out where Cooper's defense was vulnerable, and reminded everyone that we had thirty minutes to save our season.

I pulled Gabriel aside in the locker room.

"Second half, they're going to start jumping routes. They've seen you going through progressions now, so they're going to try to bait you. Show you one coverage, then rotate into something else after the snap."

"So, what do I do?"

"Same thing you've been doing. Don't guess, just read what's actually there when the ball's in your hands, not what you think you saw pre-snap. They want you to commit early and throw to where you think a guy's going to be, so make them wrong by seeing what's real."

Gabriel nodded slowly. "Primary, secondary, check-down. Read what's actually there."

"You've got it."

We received the kick in the third quarter and started on our own twenty-five.

Gabriel hit Mickey in the flat for eight yards on the first play, then handed off to Joe for another four on the second to keep us moving.

Then Cooper adjusted, and their corners started baiting, showing soft coverage then breaking hard on the routes. Gabriel's first throw sailed incomplete when he committed to his primary too early before the safety rotated over.

He looked at me from the field, frustrated.

"It's okay!" I shouted. "See it, then throw it! Not before!"

Coach Holloway walked by me as I did and swatted me in the arm with his clipboard, giving me the nod that told me I was doing a good job.

Third and ten.

I watched Gabriel take the snap. Cooper showed Cover Two then rotated into Cover Three, and Gabriel looked toward his primary, who was covered, before his eyes moved left to find Miguel on the deep crossing route and let it fly.

Forty-yard gain to the thirty-five.

I was on my feet. Gabriel came off the field after we scored three plays later, score now 14-7. I grabbed his shoulder.

"That third down. You saw them rotate, and you adjusted."

"Miguel was wide open once I got off Mickey."

"Because you trusted your eyes. That's exactly it."

Cooper answered with a drive of their own. Their running back was wearing down our defense, four and five yards at a time, and they tied it up early in the fourth quarter.

14-14 with six minutes left.

Gabriel looked at me before the offense took the field.

"What do you need?" I asked.

"I feel good. I'm seeing it now. Just ..."

"Then trust yourself. You've been making the right reads all second half. Keep letting your eyes work."

We started on our own thirty after a touchback where Jerry got us five yards and Mickey added seven more on Gabriel's second read of the play for a first down.

We kept moving as Gabriel found his rhythm, seeing the field and cycling through his progressions without hesitation. A completion here and a run there bled the clock as we drove.

Two minutes left. First and goal from the nine.

Jerry got four yards up the middle. Second and goal from the five. Coach Holloway called a timeout and gathered the offense.

"Power right," he said. "Jerry up the middle. We punch this in and run out the clock."

I was standing at the edge of the huddle, and something bothered me. I had been watching Cooper's defense all game, and on that last play, their linebacker had cheated inside before the snap. He had guessed run and we got lucky that Jerry still picked up four yards.

"Coach," I said.

He looked at me, annoyed at the interruption.

"Their linebacker is jumping inside before the snap, and he's going to be there again on power right."

"We can push through ..."

"We can't. We should do a play-action. Roll Gabriel right; hit Mickey on the corner route. They've been cheating run all quarter. The safety's going to bite hard on the fake, and Mickey's been beating his man one-on-one all game. It'll be there if Gabriel goes through his reads."

"You're sure about this?" Coach Holloway asked.

I looked at Gabriel, who had been making the right reads for two quarters now, stopped locking on or panicking, and was playing quarterback the way he was supposed to.

"Gabriel can make that throw," I said. "He's been seeing the field all game. If the corner route isn't there, he'll find what is."

Coach Holloway looked at Gabriel. "You confident you can go through your progressions on this?"

Gabriel glanced at me, then back at Coach.

"Yes, sir," he said. "I'll see what's there and make the throw."

Coach Holloway held the moment for a beat before nodding.

"Play-action right with the corner route to Mickey as your primary. If it's not there, find your check-down and don't force anything."

The team broke the huddle, and I grabbed Gabriel's arm one more time.

"Sell the fake. Primary, secondary, check-down. Let your eyes tell you where to throw."

He nodded once and jogged onto the field.

The crowd noise swelled. Cooper's defense dug in, expecting the run. Gabriel took the snap and faked the handoff to Austin. The linebacker bit hard, and the safety came rushing toward the line.

Gabriel rolled right with his eyes on Mickey in the corner of the end zone, one-on-one with the corner just like I had predicted.

He set his feet and threw.

The ball spiraled toward the corner of the end zone where Mickey had his man beat by two steps.

Catch, and touchdown.

The sideline exploded. I was running before I knew it, bad back and all, to where Gabriel was getting mobbed at the ten-yard line. The scoreboard flashed 20-14.

By the time I reached the pile, half the team was already there. Gabriel emerged from the mass of bodies, helmet askew, looking like someone had just told him he'd won the lottery.

"You did it," I said, grabbing his shoulder pads. "You saw it, and you threw it. That was all you."

"The safety bit so hard on the fake, Mickey was just standing there."

"Because you read it right. You went through your progression, and you trusted what you saw."

The rest of the team surged around us, everyone yelling, slapping helmets. We still had to kick the extra point and stop Cooper one more time, but none of that mattered in this moment.

Gabriel had done it.

I stepped back and let the team swallow him up. My back ached, and I was pretty sure I had aggravated something running onto the field, but I didn't care.

We were still in it.

Chapter 42

Saturday afternoon, I started catching up on yard work. My effort was still minimal because all I could do was sit on my butt in one spot and weed, but I managed to get most of Mom's flower garden cleaned up. I'd been mostly keeping up with it after she stopped work on it last year, but for the last month, I hadn't really done much of anything, and it had started to look ratty.

I was also putting off the last stop on my apology tour because I was kind of dreading it. After dinner and my shower, though, I couldn't ignore it anymore.

I was home alone, so I sat at the kitchen table and dialed the number.

After three rings, Charlie's mother answered. "Hello?"

"Hi, this is Blake Sims. Is Charlie available?"

"Oh, Blake! Yes, hold on one moment."

Muffled voices and footsteps drifted through the line, followed by a click as someone picked up another extension.

"I've got it, Mom."

A pause followed, and then the other line hung up.

"What," Charlie said.

It wasn't hostile, exactly, but not warm either.

"I'm calling to apologize."

Silence stretched on the line.

"For how I treated you the last time we talked. I was cruel and dismissive, and I hung up on you when you were only trying to help. You were being a good friend, and I punished you for it. That was wrong, and I'm sorry."

Silence stretched again.

"What changed?" she finally asked. "Why are you calling now?"

"Someone knocked some sense into me, and I realized how childish I was being, how I was pushing away everyone who cared about me. So I've been apologizing to the people I hurt along the way, and you're one of them."

"How are you doing now?"

"Better than I was a week ago. That's about all I can say."

"And physically? Your injury?"

"Still recovering. My back's getting better, but slowly."

"Will you be able to play? Ray's been keeping up with your school's stats and reading the local sports pages from out there. He said your team is borderline for playoffs."

"We're still in it because we won last night, but it all comes down to our last game and how everyone else did this week and next. Even then, I'm not sure if I'll get to play in that game or not. If we lose, I might be done until next year."

"That sucks."

"Yeah."

I knew what was coming next.

"What about your mom?"

"Still no word. My dad filed a missing person report, but since she packed her stuff and left on her own, the police are treating it as a domestic situation rather than an emergency. He's followed up on a few leads, but hasn't been able to confirm where she is."

"Blake, I'm so sorry. I've been thinking about you and your family ever since we talked. I just ... I wish you had let me be there for you instead of pushing me away."

"You're right. I should have."

"What happened? After we talked, I mean. You sounded so angry, and then you just disappeared."

"I became a major asshole, is what happened. I was scared and angry and drowning, and instead of letting anyone help, I shoved everyone away and attacked anyone who tried to get close. After our last call, I kept spiraling and made choices I'm ashamed of. I started hanging out with people I never would have associated with before, drinking and doing other things, putting myself in situations that could have destroyed everything I worked to build."

"Blake ..."

"I got picked up on a DUI."

Heavy silence filled the line.

"I got lucky. A detective who knows my dad recognized me and let me off, turned me over to my dad instead of processing me, but I was so close to throwing everything away. That's partly what knocked some sense into me. Realizing how close I came to losing everything."

"Have you talked to Li?" she asked.

"Yeah. I apologized to her, too, for what happened between us."

"What did happen? She wasn't very clear when she talked to me, just that you were in trouble."

"I was wrong about her and about us. When she tried to set a boundary, I attacked her instead of hearing what she was saying. She gave me another chance, and we're slowly rebuilding things. Eduardo, too. The three of us have been spending time together again."

"I'm glad you worked things out with her," Charlie said. "When Li called me before our last conversation, she sounded genuinely scared about what was happening with you. For her to track down my number and call a stranger in Georgia ... that showed how much she cared."

"I know that now. I'm grateful she didn't give up on me, even when I gave her every reason to. I'm grateful you haven't given up on me either. Or at least, I hope that's what you still being on the phone means."

"No," Charlie said. "I haven't given up hope on you."

I hadn't realized how much I needed to hear that.

"So," Charlie said. "Enough about your disasters. Want to hear about my life?"

"God, yes!"

"Ray's doing amazing! They're definitely going to the playoffs. He threw four touchdowns last week, and there's been some talk about him getting looked at by a few more schools. Dad's trying not to make a big deal about it, but I can tell he's excited."

"That's great. Ray deserves it."

"He does, although don't ever tell him I said that. What else ... volleyball season ended. We made it to regionals but lost in the second round. I cried for like an hour, which was embarrassing."

"That sucks. I'm so sorry."

"It's okay. I'll just have to do better next year. What about you? Besides the obvious stuff. What's been going on besides trying to piss off everyone in your life?"

We talked for another hour or two after that. Charlie told me about a fight she'd had with her best friend over something stupid and how they'd made up even though things still felt weird, and I told her about the guidance counselor who had it out for me, the mandatory study halls, and the progress reports. She told me about a book she was reading for English that she actually liked, some old novel about a guy who got shipwrecked.

We talked about music. She was into a new band I'd never heard of, and she promised to make me a tape.

I felt a lot better when I hung up the phone. I'd managed not to burn bridges with any of my friends. I'd be eating crow for a while, but considering how much of a dick I'd been, I was lucky.

Dad sat next to me, flipping through a Sports Illustrated as we sat in the waiting room at the orthopedic clinic in Midland. It was quiet. He wasn't nervous, but I sure as hell was. This was the check-up that would decide if I got to play this week, which could mean the rest of our season.

The final game in district play was Lubbock Monterey. They weren't the best team we'd played all year, but they were better than Cooper, and they would be hard to beat for sure.

Only the top team and the runner-up from each district got to go to playoffs, and Midland was still undefeated, giving them a lock on playoffs. Abilene and Cooper were both already out of it, each having won only one game so far this year. They were playing each other, so one would end at one and four, and the other two and three, which wasn't good enough to go to state.

Our real competition was San Angelo Central, who'd beaten us several weeks ago, and Lubbock Monterey, who we were playing tonight. The three of us were all tied up at two and two, but San

Angelo was playing Midland, which didn't look good for them. If Midland really wanted to screw us, then they would have let San Angelo win their game. Midland would still get to the playoffs, but even if we beat Lubbock, we'd be tied with San Angelo three and two, and since we lost to San Angelo, they'd get the runner-up spot.

But I didn't think Midland, even as much as they hated us, would do that.

Which meant it really came down to this game for the runner-up. Either us or Lubbock would be going to the playoffs.

I wanted it to be us.

"Blake Sims?" a nurse said, pulling me out of my thoughts.

We followed the nurse back to an exam room where she took my vitals and then led me to a machine where they could get new X-rays of my back. After that, she took us back to the exam room and told us the doctor would be in shortly.

Shortly turned out to be twenty minutes.

Dr. Russell was an older guy, maybe fifty, with gray at his temples and glasses that made his eyes look slightly too big.

"Blake. Mr. Sims." He opened the folder he was carrying. "I've taken a look at your imaging results from last week, these updated scans and the notes from your physical therapist. Before we talk about where we are, I'd like to check Blake's range of motion."

He had me bend forward, then backward, then twist side to side. Most of it felt okay, better than okay, actually. When I twisted to the right, though, something pulled, and I couldn't hide the wince.

"That hurt?"

"A little. Not as bad as before."

"Okay, good news first. The swelling around your lower spine has gone down significantly, and the bruising has healed faster than I expected given the severity of the initial injury. See this area here?" he asked, putting the X-rays up on the light board thing. I couldn't really tell what I was supposed to be seeing, but I nodded anyway. "Three weeks ago, this was a mess, but now it's looking much better. Honestly, your improvement has been fairly remarkable. But, you aren't fully healed yet."

I made a face, and Dad put his hand on my shoulder, basically telling me to just be patient and hear him out.

"Blake has made good progress. The compression injury and bruised ribs have healed enough for normal activity like walking and light exercise, but football is not normal activity. If he takes another significant hit to the same area, we could be looking at much more serious damage."

"What kind of damage?" Dad asked.

"Long-term back problems, chronic pain that could affect him for the rest of his life. If those same vertebrae get compressed again while they're still vulnerable, he might need surgery."

"So what are you saying? I can't play?"

"I'm saying that there is a real risk. Medically, you can play with precautions, but the risk is higher than it would be for a fully healed athlete. I can't make this decision for you. I can only give you the information."

"Blake, this is not worth it," Dad said. "You've got two more years of high school football and four years of college eligibility after that. I'm not willing to risk your long-term health for one regular-season game."

"Dad ..."

"No. I've watched you work too hard to throw it all away because you couldn't wait three more weeks."

"What precautions?" I asked Dr. Russell. "You said I could play with precautions. What would that look like?"

"There's an upgraded back brace that provides more support than the one you've been wearing," he said. "We can add padding inserts to your shoulder pads that would help absorb impact. Your coaches would need to limit your exposure, fewer plays with you running and fewer situations where you're likely to take a hit."

"What else?"

"If you take any significant contact to your back, you come out immediately, no playing through pain. If something feels wrong, you tell your trainers and you don't argue about sitting out."

I could see that Dad was still leaning toward having me sit out.

"This game determines whether we make playoffs. If we lose, the season is over, and everything the team worked for, everything I worked for, it's gone. I understand the risk, and I'm willing to accept it. The doctor just told us there are ways to reduce the danger, and I will follow every single precaution exactly. Please. Let me make this decision."

"Be straight with me," Dad asked Dr. Russell. "Do these precautions genuinely lower the risk, or are they just making everyone feel better about a bad idea?"

"The upgraded brace and padding provide real protection. Limiting mobility-based plays removes the highest-risk situations. The risk isn't zero, I won't pretend it is, but it's manageable if Blake and his coaches follow the guidelines strictly."

Dad looked at me the way he used to when I was a kid and he was trying to figure out if I was telling the truth about something.

"If you take one bad hit, you're coming out and staying out. No arguments, no 'just one more play,' you're done."

"Okay."

"You will wear the upgraded brace and the extra padding."

"I will."

"And you will not argue with trainers or coaches about your condition during the game. If they say you're out, you're out, even if you think you're fine."

"I promise."

Dad looked at Dr. Russell.

"Write it up."

"I'm writing clearance with specific restrictions," Dr. Russell said, pulling out a pad. "Limited plays where you're running, upgraded protective equipment, immediate removal from game upon any significant back contact."

He tore off the paper and handed it to Dad. "There's a medical supply store just off the highway that carries the brace he needs. Pick it up before Friday."

"What about practice?"

"Light participation only, no contact drills. If your condition changes between now and game time, the clearance is revoked." He looked at me over his glasses. "I mean it, Blake, this is conditional. If you wake up Friday morning and something feels wrong, you call me. Understood?"

"Understood."

"Good luck on Friday," Dr. Russell said, extending his hand. "I hope it's worth it."

"It will be," I said, shaking it.

The bus rolled to a stop outside Monterey's stadium, and I could feel the energy. Their home crowd was loud, even in the parking lot, and it was clear they understood the stakes of this game as well as we did.

Coach Holloway caught me as the team filed off the bus and pulled me aside while the others headed toward the visitor locker room.

"Are you sure you're up for this?"

"The team needs this game, Coach."

"That's not what I asked."

"Gabriel did great against Cooper and kept us alive, but Monterey isn't Cooper. They're faster, they hit harder, and if we lose tonight, there's no playoffs and no shot at state."

"Okay, but we're going to be watching you closely. The doctor's restrictions still apply. Any sign of pain, any hit to your back that looks wrong, and you're out, no arguments and no second chances. Do you understand?"

"I understand."

"Say it back to me."

"Any sign of pain, I'm out. No arguments."

He nodded. "Go warm up."

As rowdy as the home side was for this game, we weren't going into the lion's den on our own. The visitor side of the stadium was packed with what looked like half of Wheaton. We'd had a huge convoy following our buses, and there was blue and white everywhere. I found Dad was sitting near the fifty-yard line and that he was with Detective Bowen.

I was a little surprised the detective had come out to see the game, even if we were in his city.

I raised a hand and waved. Dad waved back and Bowen gave me a small nod.

Warm-ups went fine with my arm feeling good, my legs strong, and the brace doing its job keeping everything stable. The only thing that I was having trouble with was getting my full throwing motion. The larger brace and extra padding were making it hard to get a full range of motion.

I didn't say anything because I was worried Coach might pull me, but I would have to figure it out if I was going to make this work.

Coach played it very safe for most of the first quarter, going back to his old playbook of a run-heavy play rotation. I knew what he was doing, trying to keep me protected and safe while letting Miles and Jerry carry the load and control the clock.

The problem was, Monterey knew it too.

Miles took the handoff on the opening play and hit the line hard, but their defensive end shed his block and met Miles in the hole after maybe two yards.

Second down was the same story as Miles tried to bounce it outside, only to find their linebacker waiting for a one-yard gain.

On third and short, Coach called another run. I handed the ball to Jerry this time, only for their whole defensive front to collapse on him like they'd known he was coming.

We punted with no gain.

Not the best way to start the game.

Monterey took over at their thirty-one and went to work. Their quarterback, a senior who'd also started for them last year, picked apart our run defense with short passes and misdirection, moving the chains like he was running a clinic.

The first quarter was winding down when their quarterback dropped back from our twenty-three. Their receiver ran a crossing route, breaking wide open in the middle of the field. The QB hit him in stride for a touchdown.

Their home crowd exploded.

Seven to nothing.

"Coach," I said before the kickoff team even got on the field.

"I know what you're going to say."

"The running game isn't working. They've got eight in the box on every play. They're stacking it because they know we're trying to protect me."

Coach didn't respond.

"We need to open up the passing attack. That's the only way we're going to move the ball."

"Blake ..."

"I didn't come back to watch, I came back to play."

He turned to face me, clearly fighting with himself. He knew I was right, but he was also trying to think ahead to playoffs and needing to keep me healthy for that.

I hoped he'd see that if we lost this, then staying healthy for playoffs didn't matter.

"Find the open man," he said finally. "And do not take unnecessary hits. And no scrambling. If you try and run it, I will bench you for the night."

"Yes, sir."

The second quarter started with me under center for a passing play for the first time since homecoming, and the crowd noise dropped ... not silent, but quieter, like everyone was holding their breath.

I took the snap and dropped back.

The brace was still restricting my movement more than I'd like. My first read was covered, their corner sitting in the passing lane. I shifted to my second option where Mickey was breaking open on a slant about fifteen yards downfield.

I planted and threw.

My back protested, a dull ache radiating through my spine as I released the ball. I ignored it. The spiral wasn't perfect, but it was good enough.

Mickey caught it in stride for fourteen yards.

The Wheaton sideline erupted.

I found my rhythm after that. Austin ran an out route and I hit him for eight, then Brian caught on a short crossing pattern and turned it into fifteen through contact, breaking one tackle and nearly breaking another before they dragged him down.

We stalled at the Monterey eighteen, and our kicker put it through the uprights for a field goal to make it seven to three.

Monterey answered with another methodical drive. Their offense was built for this, grinding out yards, eating the clock, keeping our defense on the field. They moved into our territory, but this time our guys stiffened the defense in the red zone. Tyler and the defensive line stuffed two consecutive runs, and on third down, Tyler blew through a gap and hurried their quarterback into an incomplete pass.

They settled for a field goal, making it ten to three.

That was the score at halftime.

"The running game is not working against this front," Coach said once we were in the locker room. "They're selling out to stop it, and we're playing right into their hands. That stops now. Blake showed he still has it, so we're going to switch back to the passing game, but we need to be careful. If we win this and make playoffs, we're going to need him and we're going to need him healthy. That means the offensive line has a job to do. Blake cannot take hits, especially to his back. Your job is to give him a pocket and hold it on every snap. Every single one."

Andre stood up. "We're not letting anyone through. Period."

The rest of the line followed his lead until they were all making noise about how they were going to stop every attempt to get through to Blake.

It was heartening, to be sure.

"That's what I wanted to hear," Coach said. "Now go win this game."

We received the kickoff to start the third quarter, and we started a drive of short passes. Nothing flashy and no big plays, but it moved the chains and kept them honest. Mixed in with that was an occasional draw to Miles that actually worked now that they were expecting the throw. I did manage one big play with a pass that Mickey caught on a corner route for twenty-two yards that put us in their territory.

We moved all the way to the Monterey thirty-one-yard line and Coach called for another big pass play, since they were starting to adjust to the short game.

I dropped back to look downfield. The pocket held for three seconds as Mickey broke free in the end zone, shaking his defender at the goal line, and I started my throwing motion.

That's when Elton got beat.

A Monterey linebacker crashed through the gap on the outside and caught me just as I released the ball. The hit drove into my side and spun me to the turf.

The impact radiated through my back brace and into my spine, not the crippling agony from homecoming, but bad enough. I lay on the ground for several seconds, my vision swimming, the stadium lights blurring into white streaks above me.

Andre was the first one there, dropping to one knee beside me before whipping around toward Elton.

"What the hell, man? You let your guy through!"

"I didn't ..."

"You had one job! One job! Protect the quarterback!"

"Andre," I said, pushing myself up to one knee through gritted teeth. "Calm down, you can't stop everyone."

Andre looked at me, then back at Elton. "Watch us try."

I got to my feet slowly and waved off the trainers rushing onto the field. "I'm fine."

"Blake, we need to check ..."

"I'm fine."

Coach Holloway was on the sideline waving Gabriel over and pointing for me to come to the sideline.

I shook my head and pointed at myself, then at the line of scrimmage.

The trainers checked my mobility anyway, asking about pain levels. I lied and told them the brace absorbed most of the impact. I don't think they believed me, but they let me stay in.

The play I'd thrown before getting hit was incomplete. Mickey had been open, but my release had been off because of the impact. It didn't matter now.

I got back in the huddle. "Same play. Mickey, you had him beat. We're running it again."

I dropped back on the next play, but they'd seen our plan already and had Mickey covered, so I delivered a strike to Miguel on a crossing route for eighteen yards before finding Mickey on a fade in the corner of the end zone two plays later.

Touchdown.

We were tied at ten.

The Wheaton fans in the visitor section made themselves heard over the disappointed home crowd, going nuts in the stands, but I didn't have time to enjoy it.

Our defense forced a three-and-out on Monterey's next possession.

I led another drive where Brian caught back-to-back passes that moved us inside their thirty, and then Mickey ran an amazing post route for a thirty-four-yard gain and our second touchdown, putting us up seventeen to ten.

The fourth quarter was when we made our statement.

Coach kept us on the field for a drive that bled four minutes off the clock. Short passes, occasional runs to keep Monterey honest. When we were at the twelve, he called a screen pass to Hunter, who'd just come in to give Miguel a breather. It was Hunter's time to shine, and he did it, catching the pass and getting behind his blockers, carrying the ball into the end zone.

Twenty-four to ten.

But Monterey wasn't done. Their quarterback led a desperate drive that ate up most of the next three minutes before their running back punched it in from the two, putting us at twenty-four to seventeen with five minutes left to go.

We got the ball back, and I went right back to work. Three consecutive completions moved us into Monterey territory. On second and eight from their twenty-three, I faked a handoff to Miles and looked downfield.

Mickey was streaking across the middle of the field, a step ahead of his man. The window was tight, their safety was closing fast, but I'd made this throw a hundred times in practice.

I let it go.

The ball sailed straight into Mickey's hands, and he took it into the end zone untouched.

Thirty-one to seventeen.

Coach signaled from the sideline as the offense jogged off and caught my arm before I could sit down.

"Gabriel finishes this out."

"Coach ..."

"There's only two minutes left, we have this game secured. There's no reason to risk another hit."

"With all due respect, I'm finishing what I started," I said.

Coach paused. "Blake ..."

"They know how big this game is for them and if they push it, they could still sneak one out. We need to run down the clock and play smart. Let me win this."

He looked at me for a long moment, then muttered something to Coach Easley. I couldn't hear what it was, but he let me go and didn't argue further.

I was right about how much they wanted it. Even with us slowing things down and playing out the clock as much as possible, Monterey still managed a late touchdown with ninety seconds remaining. Their quarterback hit their tight end on a corner route that our safety bit on too hard, putting the score at thirty-one to twenty-four.

They tried an onside kick and Miles fell on it at our forty-three.

Coach Holloway looked at me, then at Gabriel, clearly thinking he was going to pull me. I didn't wait and jogged out onto the field before he could say anything. He didn't fight me. We managed to get a first down on two plays, at which point it was all over and I took a knee to let the last few seconds on the clock run down.

The final whistle sounded.

I pushed myself up from the turf, not sure if my legs would hold me as the pain in my back radiated down into my hips and up into my shoulders. But I didn't let it show.

Andre reached me first, wrapping me in a hug that was both crushing and careful, like he was trying to celebrate without breaking me.

"We did it, man. We did it."

Mickey was next, then Jerry. The rest of the offense swarmed me at midfield, helmets raised, everyone shouting over each other. Miles grabbed my facemask and screamed something I couldn't understand. Elton slapped my shoulder pads hard enough to make my back spasm.

We'd done it. We'd made the playoffs.

Chapter 43

I had a long time to think on the bus ride home. I'd made my apologies and refocused on what was important at school, but there were still things I needed to fix.

I'd let myself fall into a pit of despair and decided I couldn't do anything about my situation, which was exactly the opposite of what I'd decided after the dream.

When I'd had it, and realized what it meant, I hadn't just said, "Well, there's nothing I can do." I'd made sure the danger to my father was removed and started fixing the mistakes I'd made in that version of my life.

That's what I needed to do now. Well, it's what I was doing, getting back on that track, but I hadn't finished getting everything back. There was still one glaring problem that I'd let sit without being addressed.

And it was time to change that.

We were required to ride home on the bus, even when our family was at the away game, so Dad, along with the rest of the Wheaton caravan, followed the team buses back to school, where there was an impromptu party.

In Texas, when the local football team does well, the whole town celebrates. I celebrated with them. It was a great time, knowing that we were headed to the playoffs after being so close to not making it, and everyone deserved to party.

But I'd had something else on my mind the whole time, and as soon as things started slowing down a little bit, I signaled my dad that it was time to head home.

"You didn't want to stay?" he asked as we got in the car.

"No. We need to talk," I said.

"I don't like the sound of that," he said.

Dad glanced over at me as he pulled out of the parking lot. "You sound serious."

"I am."

"This about your mother?"

"Yeah."

He nodded slowly. "Okay. Let's wait until we get back home."

The house was dark when we pulled into the driveway. Dad unlocked the door and flipped on the kitchen light, then grabbed two glasses of water without asking if I wanted one. We sat across from each other at the table, and I could see him bracing himself.

"The police aren't looking for her," I said. "Not really."

"I know, she left on her own and without evidence that something illegal happened, it's a personal matter and there's not much they can do but put our report in the system."

"Your resources are limited, too. You can't take time off to drive around Texas hoping to spot her car, and there's only so much your coworkers are able to do to help."

"I'm aware of my limitations, Blake," he said, frustrated and a little annoyed that I was pointing out all the things he wasn't going to do.

"That's why I'm going to hire a private investigator to find her."

Dad's eyebrows went up. "Come again?"

"I know Mr. Henderson has worked with people like that before. Security consultants, investigators, that kind of thing. I'm going to call him, see if he has any recommendations. I've got a few other contacts I can reach out to as well."

"I thought about that," he said after a moment. "Hiring someone, even looked into a few names the week she left."

"Why didn't you?"

"Because I'm not sure she wants to be found. She packed her bags, took her car, and left without a word. Maybe we need to respect that."

"We don't have to respect that. She's sick. You heard what the doctors said about how the tumor affects thinking and judgment. The seizures, the mood swings, the paranoia, that wasn't Mom making those decisions, that was the golf ball-sized mass pressing on her brain."

"I know that ..."

“Do you? Because it sounds like you’re ready to write her off.”

His eyes flashed. “Watch it.”

“Then stop talking like giving up is an option.”

We stared at each other across the table. Dad didn’t back down.

“Dad, I’m not trying to hurt you or be mean. I’m trying to share that this is where I was those weeks I kind of lost it. I’d just given up. I know you haven’t, but I think you might be close. I know it seems like we don’t have a lot of options left, but we do. We just have to be prepared to go far enough to see them through. I know I’m willing to. Are you?”

Dad stared at me for another long moment, and then he looked away, down at his hands.

“What if we find her and she refuses to come back?” he asked.

“Is that why you haven’t tried to go further to find her? I know it’s scary to think she’d refuse to come back, but we have to figure out some way to address that, too. Get her declared medically incapable of making her own decisions, maybe. Something like that. There are options, if we’re willing to go that far.”

“If we do that, then we lose her anyway. She’ll never forgive us.”

“No, the her that’s being affected by the tumor would never forgive us, but once we have it dealt with, once the tumor is gone, the real her will be back and she’ll be happy to be alive.”

“How can you be so sure? I’ve looked into this. Even once the tumor is removed there can still be personality changes.”

“I know, and if she still doesn’t forgive us and leaves, at least we know she’ll survive. I’d rather her gone and alive than gone for good. I love her enough that if those are my two options, I’ll pick alive every time. Wouldn’t you?”

I don’t think Dad had thought about it from that angle before. He was quiet again, but I could see that he was thinking it through, and not just staring at his hands in despair.

I wasn’t going to give him a chance to decide against it, though. I wasn’t going to risk her on Dad being too afraid to pull the trigger.

“I’m doing this whether you approve or not,” I said. “I’m going to start making calls tomorrow.”

“Blake ...”

"But I'd rather have you with me on this, because once we find her, it's going to take both of us to bring her back. She's not going to listen to just me."

The silence stretched out. Finally, Dad nodded.

"Okay," he said. "Make your calls. Let me know what you find out."

I let out the breath I was holding. "I will."

We'd let despair take over for too long. It was time to start living again.

To Be Continued ...

About the author

Travis writes science fiction, fantasy, and thriller novels (and the occasional coming-of-age story), with the hope of transporting and enthralling readers. Publishing novels since 2015, Travis's passion is creating worlds and characters that live and breathe, and experiencing the joy of those stories with his readers.
When not writing, Travis enjoys connecting with readers and other writers, managing the popular Complete Marvel Reading Order website, where he works on his other passion for comics and graphic novels, and spending time with his family.
If you have enjoyed this book, please consider taking a moment to rate or review it wherever you found your copy, as it helps new readers find my works and ensures I can continue writing book into the future.

Find out more at:
amazon.com/TravisStarnes/e/B072YBDC3S/

Or visit
https://tstarnes.com

Signup to get free previews and notifications of upcoming books at
http://tstarnes.com/preview-notification-newsletter/

Also by

John Taylor Stories

Rebirth
False Signs
The Wrong Girl
Burying the Past
Family Ties
Election Day
Danger Close
Extraction
Designated Target
Border Crossed
Desperate Rendition
Broken Ground

Country Roads Series

Playing by Ear
Fanfare
Dissonance
Elegy
From the Top
Center Stage

Imperium Series

Volume 1
The Sword of Jupiter
The Trumpets of Mars
The Sands of Saturn
The Depths of Neptune
The Fires of Vulcan
The Triumph of Venus
Volume 2
The Wings of Mercury
The Plains of Pluto
The Clouds of Caelus
The Masks of Janus

Shattered Lands Series

In the Shadow of Lions
An Ending of Oaths
The Barons' War
Heavy Lies the Crown

False Start Series

Second Down
Scramble
Loss of Down

The Veilguard Saga

Threads of Destiny
The Blackstar Legacy

Stand Alone

Going Home
Before Later

www.ingramcontent.com/pod-product-compliance
Lightning Source LLC
LaVergne TN
LVHW010626110826
845149LV00014B/2786
* 9 7 8 1 9 6 0 7 4 7 3 9 6 *